# LOOPHOLE EX MACHINA

BOOK TWO OF THE INCARNATE ACCOUNTS

JUSTIN SCHUELKE

# COPYRIGHT

*For Mom and Dad.*

*Thank you for always nursing my dreams—and then providing the means to achieve them. I love you!*

# PROLOGUE

*Welcome back, class! For those of you who have forgotten, my name is Emery Luple, and I am an incarnate. I will be your tour guide through my life. Before we embark on today's epic journey, I am going to share with you a scene from my past. I know, it's a bit of a tease, and to be honest, I don't think I remembered it until later: I was only nineteen this time around and didn't have immediate access to all of my memories and experiences. What I always have, though, is a sense of drama—and sublime talent for telling a story. So close your eyes (but keep reading!), and let me transport you backward through time, where a stunning and clever lass is about to...* *oh, right, spoilers. I'll just show you, then.*
*Enjoy!*
*I'll be waiting for you back in chapter one, just a quick hundred and eighteen incarnations later!*

~

**Ancient Gaelic Ireland, 1647 years ago...**

*J* lifted the crude lantern before me, the beeswax candle nestled within the metal contraption burning dangerously low. Less than an hour of light remained, I gauged, before I would have to rely on the cheaper rushes in my pack. The lantern created a bubble of illumination around me but did little to pierce the darkness of the enormous chamber. High above, the ceiling was rough-hewn stone, thick stalactites curving down. Occasionally a large one stabbed into my pocket of light, like a giant beast's fang set to crush me in its maw. Condensation dripped from their tips, adding to the illusion of a salivating monstrosity.

I stumbled on the uneven stonework, and a chip of rock went skidding across the mosaic flooring. It kicked up dust—which I, *of course*, inhaled, resulting in a round of involuntary coughs, the sound echoing harshly in the crypt.

*"Oh, Emery, you always take me to the nicest places,"* Artie mused. As always, his rich and cultured voice sounded directly at my ear, regardless of where I'd stowed him.

I snorted in a very unladylike fashion but otherwise ignored the incarnate and returned to my scrutiny. The tomb was centuries old, possibly older, predating res publica and the Roman Republic. Ancient Egyptian, perhaps? If so, it lacked the mastabas of today's Egyptian tombs. I knew something about the architecture of Egyptian crypts, as my previous incarnation had been a first servant of Osiris... my remains were actually interred in one. And, if it were Egyptian, it would lend a lot of credence to Scota being an incarnate, as I had long suspected. There were too many legends throughout Éire Ghaelach about earlier Egyptian incursions to dismiss the possibility outright.

The thought made me pause. We'd lost so much knowledge recently in the clan wars, and it hurt to think about all the incarnates we'd likely lost, too. They would reincarnate, of course, but we might never know the deeds they'd achieved. Only those who lived to a venerable age would have ready access to their past lives' memories, and the outlook on life expectancy these days wasn't overly optimistic.

An errant strand of red hair slipped in front of my face, and I absently tucked it behind my ear. *Focus, Emery,* I reminded myself. If I had judged the MacCloughan tribe correctly, I was walking into an ambush. I was grateful for Artie's company, even if he was a spear.

I felt my lips quirk at the thought. Not just any spear, now, was he?

I reached the end of the chamber, my lantern's light glinting off golden metal inlaid in a large stone archway. The threshold was clearly an entrance, but there was no door present, only a doorway etched with hieroglyphics. I held the lantern out in front of me, revealing a narrow tunnel. I frowned as the sound of running water came to me: was there an underground stream ahead? I could feel a light breeze, too, as though the tunnel eventually let out into open air. The lowlands surrounding this tomb were unfamiliar to me, but I hadn't been expecting this. I pulled back my arm and let the light play over the rim of the entrance again. There were depictions of people, crops, tanistry—the method of succession of our people—and… crows, squiggly lines of eels, a cow, and a wolf.

I froze. These were the symbols of my archnemesis.

"*Are those what I think they are?*" Artie asked, even his voice colored with something approaching fear.

"Aye, Artie. Do you still wish to proceed?"

The Artifact sniffed disdainfully at my use of his nickname. "*I know what you're doing.*" His accusation was mild, a note of wry amusement in his unearthly voice. "*But you could hardly dissuade me now, Emery. It has been ages since I've tasted an incarnate's blood.*"

I bared my teeth in a smile, not caring that he couldn't see it, and entered the tunnel. It was larger than it initially appeared, carved straight through the earth. While the first several steps were stone, like the tomb had been, they quickly gave way to packed dirt. Roots had found their way through the walls and ceiling of the tunnel; the small ones had been permitted to stay, while the large ones were hacked apart to ensure the tunnel maintained its general height and width.

I'd walked for a count of forty, the sound of the babbling stream growing nearer, when Artie hissed, "*Movement ahead.*"

"Who's there?" a voice called out from ahead.

"A simple traveler," I returned, infusing my words with as much charm as I could muster. "Might I share a fire and a meal with you?"

I shifted, surreptitiously placing Artie's butt against the dirt floor of the tunnel. He could sense vibrations through the earth, even tiny ones. "*Four of them, including the druid,*" came his quiet report, almost immediately. "*No wait, five. One hides directly above the mouth of the exit. And—oh my, it's a cairn.*"

I frowned at that—why was this place important?—as the man ahead finally answered me. I suspected he'd been conferring quietly with his companions. "Aye, come share a meal and fire with us. You may regale us with the story of what brings a bonnie young lass to such a remote locale."

A mild quiver traced up Artie's length, and I wondered if it was anticipation or fear. Incarnate objects were not often imbued with sentience, making the Artifact special. He was perfectly capable of emotions, even if he prided himself on his powers of reasoning. Anticipation, I decided. I doubted he would have stooped to giving away his fear, even had he felt it. Besides, he'd complained often enough about his current form. Apparently, he once incarnated as a sword and now looked down on spears as inferior. His self-established hierarchy of weaponry was a mystery to me, but I knew he feared to find himself in the form of an "uncivilized" weapon. I had once teased him that he'd reincarnate as a stick. "*That would be infinitely preferable,*" he had declared. "*A stick is not a weapon at all. Really, Emery, I know how much you enjoy wielding me like a hero from the stories, but I do so miss my innocent years, when I was a gemstone or a trinket. Or a tome! Oh, those were the most enlightening of times.*"

I smirked at the memory as I exited the tunnel into the fresh night air. Noticing the stranger's close attention, I transformed my smirk into something a wee bit more enchanting.

"Hello, lass. I am Táin MacCloughan," he said, clearly disarmed by my welcoming smile. "Follow me to food and company."

"I'm Emery O'Luple," I replied. "You have my gratitude." I used Artie like a walking stick as I followed the man down a short trail. Artie wouldn't mind; each tap against the earth would give him a better understanding of the land as well as the hidden people we knew watched us. The land was green and hale, with large outcroppings of stone creating a sort of crater, the cairn of stacked rocks well hidden in the deepest part of the depression. After a few steps, it seemed to shrink to nothing more important than a rabbit hole. A few steps farther, and it disappeared entirely, blending into the natural landscape like an arctic fox in winter.

Táin led me over a small ridge, and I saw a cheery fire ringed with three figures who sat on stumps and a fallen log that looked to have been carved to create permanent seats. I hoped these people were part of the Artifact's original count, otherwise I was quickly becoming outmatched.

Pushing down my unease and tucking it behind my forced smile, I approached the fire with Táin. The smell of cooked meat lingered in the night air, presumably from an earlier meal. The figures resolved into two men and a woman. They remained seated as we approached, but their light chatter cut off as cleanly as if I'd sliced a knife through it.

"Hello," I said, pleased my voice did not betray my nervousness. "Are you all kin of Táin?"

"Aye," the MacCloughan man said, putting a hand on the small of my back and guiding me forward, gesturing to a vacant spot on the log. "Among others who will be joining us shortly. Please, won't you be seated?"

I nodded my thanks, throwing another sweet smile at him for good measure, and made to sit down among his kin. I wondered if I'd have to kill them all, or if I could keep a few alive to spread the message to others. I hoped for the latter as I ran my eyes over the three sitting around the fire. Two were hardly more than lads, and a look of worry flickered over the woman's face before she hid it by looking away. They didn't all seem bad.

"MacCloughans," Táin continued, addressing the people at the fire, "this is Emery O'Luple." I nodded to each of them as he spoke. "She has come at the promised hour, just as the Morrigan foretold." My smile froze, his words hitting me like a blow. The Morrigan. What a gobshite. "And wouldn't ye know it, she brought to Clan MacCloughan the Artifact incarnation like a good lass."

"*It's 'incarnate,' you bog-addled man!*" Artie spat indignantly.

I heard rustling, and cautious men and women with wooden and stone weapons emerged from the surrounding brush. Four of them. I grimaced, understanding washing over me: it *was* an ambush, but not the one I had been expecting. Clan MacCloughan weren't just thieves, they were followers of the Morrigan. By Anu, I despised that woman. Sometime in a previous incarnation, she had deified herself as one of the Tuatha Dé Danann, the Celtic pantheon.

Still. I would *not* die from a trap lain by her. Especially one in which she didn't even deign to appear in person.

"*You want me?*" Artie's voice rang out—not echoing as it should have in the empty night, though. Instead, it felt like a shout originating somewhere inside my ear. I knew the others heard it, too, as several flinched and the woman nearest me clapped hands over her ears. "*Then you shall have me.*"

I felt the spear jump out of my hands, his point snapping forward. Then, as I let go to give Artie the space to fight, the Artifact flicked across the distance between me and Táin in a blink. I heard the MacCloughan gasp once and saw his silhouette stiffen in the firelight, a length of oaken hardwood cleanly spearing his throat. There was a gurgling, then Táin sank to the ground. Everyone stood transfixed, including me, but we all acted at once.

I slammed my lantern down and stomped on the wick as Artie back-hafted one of the others, throwing their body directly into the flames of the fire. Embers showered the air, and the flaming logs were scattered, plunging the night into darkness as both the fire and my lantern were dashed out at the same time. Some light still emanated from the fallen logs, only coals next to the bright blaze we'd had moments before.

I opened my mind to my training of two incarnations ago, glad I was able to recall it so clearly. Sometimes, when the conditions weren't right, I had more trouble. But this was perfect: the dim light, the anger, the sense of righteousness summoned by hearing Morrigan's name...

A man came for me, a hatchet raised above his head. He was the worst kind of fool, screaming as he brought his weapon down on me. If I hadn't already known he was there, I would have been alerted by his cry. I spun and caught his arm, pulling him forward and across my jutting leg so he stumbled. I wrenched the axe from his grip as he flailed to control his momentum, then sank it into the back of his head when he succeeded. His body collapsed to the ground bonelessly.

I hated killing, humans most of all. Incarnates always came back. I had no idea what happened to humans. In that moment, I hoped Osiris judged their souls fairly.

*Huh*, that was the previous me leaking through. It happened sometimes, but it seemed to occur far more often when I was channeling my former lives directly.

Three more were already down, Artie calling out insults and dispatching them with contemptuous ease. One of the youths at the fire—the youngest, really just a lad—dashed away into the night, and I silently thanked Athena for sparing him.

*Athena*? I couldn't even remember the last time I'd been Greek.

Suddenly apprehensive, I took a deep breath and concentrated on closing my memories, shrinking them from a wide ocean of identities to my current one. *Emery O'Luple of Éire Ghaelach.* A huntress, nothing more. Not a Hellene, not a first servant. A lass, albeit a wild one.

It worked. Coming back to myself, I scanned the darkness to get my bearings. Unmoving bodies littered the area between the log seats. Only two remained standing: the woman at the fire and a single MacCloughan warrior I hadn't seen before. Artie was a finger's breadth from the woman's throat, suspended in the air like a weapon possessed.

The woman's shoulders were shaking, small sobs escaping her.

Even though he was a weapon, Artie had compassion. His voice came out in a low growl. *"Leave us in peace, and I will spare this woman's life. Otherwise, you both die."*

The woman's shoulders continued to shake, but her sobs were wrong. They... *no*. She wasn't shaking in fear. She was *laughing*. "I choose the second option." Faster than I would have believed possible, she snaked her hand around the Artifact's haft and brought her other hand closer to his base, yanking him around to be held out in front of her. Her muscles bunched as he fought her, but she countered his strength with her own.

"You were supposed to grant great power to Clan MacCloughan," the lone survivor lamented, looking around with haunted eyes at the fallen bodies of his kin. "You are the Morrigan. We trusted you to protect us!"

"Morrigan," I cut in, my voice steady. "Release the Artifact, and we can both walk away this time."

I had never seen the woman before. This was an incarnation that was completely unknown to me. I truly had not understood the ambush she'd set up for me, but I could still survive her. I'd done it before.

Morrigan looked down her nose at me, then shrugged. "Nay, Emery." She brought Artie down sharply on her knee. An ugly snap filled the air, the oaken spear cracking into two long splinters.

*"I'm sorry."* I heard his dying words in my ear even as I screamed my outrage.

Morrigan ignored my anguish, turning to her erstwhile servant. "Spread the ballad of this day, of how the Morrigan saved the last of the MacCloughan tribe from the vagabond with the magical spear. Do not doubt my divinity, for I will find you or your kin in one thousand days and a night."

Then she smirked at me and plunged Artie's splintered remains through her heart.

I raced to her fallen form. She was smiling, even in death.

Shaking, I picked up Artie's two halves and held them in my hands, tears coming to my eyes. How had this happened? We'd had everything under control, the Artifact and I. The only thing I hadn't prepared for was Morrigan. She had a way of sneaking up on me, deadly and silent as an asp. *Oh, Artie.*

The MacCloughan man was edging away from me, thinking me distracted by my grief. "You," I said as I stood, rooting him to the spot with the agony and rage in my voice. "If ye wish to live, do not spread her lies. The legend of the Morrigan dies here, tonight. Swear to me."

He stammered a response, and I let him go as I crouched over the remains of the destroyed Artifact. I hoped, in that moment, that I would see Artie again. My attention was drawn to the corpse of Morrigan, to the dead features of a woman I had never even seen before. I knew better than to hope I wouldn't see her again. She'd always be there, waiting for me. It was the story of Emery and Morgan, of Morrigan and Emery. Timeless. Inevitable.

I stood. I had work to do. For Artie, I would do everything I could to ensure history forgot the false Celtic deity.

The Morrigan.

1

*My name is Emery Luple, and I am the Protagonist incarnate. I live in Seattle with my own personal Guardian Angel. When I found him, I found my Sanctum, my place of peace. I aid incarnates and mortals alike, and I welcome members of those two communities to seek me out: for protection, for answers, or for help. I often find myself in need of all three, after all.*

*This is my story.*

⁓

For the first time in several incarnations, I didn't want to die. I had a lot going for me this time around. My youth, a good singing voice, healing mental scars, an athletic body, rugged good looks. Okay, maybe not "rugged," but definitely tall, dark, and handsome with an extra measure of cocky attitude and the grin to match it. More importantly, I had people who genuinely cared about me: a great boyfriend, a best friend... I even had a mom.

Here's a pro tip: if you want to live a long, healthy life, don't go after baddies with guns.

I was in Seattle, so naturally I was at a Starbucks. People of all colors and sizes bustled about the cozy interior, and the smell of coffee was thankfully stronger than the smell of the combined humanity. A few tables over from me was the incarnate I was hired to rescue, as well as the aforementioned baddies with guns. They spoke in quiet tones, ignoring the young lady who would have drawn eyes anywhere except downtown. Long, flowing green-blue hair topped with a flower crown gave her a hippie vibe—which was not diminished by her outfit. She wore a skintight leotard, showing off her slim yet athletic build, with a playful layered skirt in various shades of green, and beneath the table her bare feet were crossed at the ankles. While this attire might not have stood out among the colorful Seattleites, against her two companions... it was *loud*. They looked like Corporate USA, with matching business slacks, button-up blue dress shirts, and ties loosened just enough to look casual. But there was nothing casual about the guns they carried, holstered conspicuously at their hips.

I pulled up my GPS app and gauged the distance to the pier for the twentieth time. Half a mile. Totally doable. I picked up my coffee cup and mimed taking another swig. In truth, I had already finished my drink, but I didn't want to get another one and risk missing something important happening at that table.

Me versus two guards with guns. I didn't like those odds, especially since I hadn't brought my usual weapons with me; my plan required a lot of running, and I wanted to be light on my feet. Eyeing those guns, it almost didn't seem worth the risk. But I *did* need the money. Yes, I had a lot of things going for me this incarnation, but a flush bank account wasn't one of them. Full disclosure, though; I would've saved her for free. She was an incarnate, and she needed help. That's sort of what I do.

I tried to watch the table without seeming like I was paying too much attention to it. The female guard leaned over and whispered something to her partner. A moment later, she stood, and I ducked my head in another fake sip as her eyes swept over the room. Then she proceeded toward the exit. My heart beat faster as I checked the time on my phone. According to my contact, I still had thirteen minutes before they were to move the incarnate girl. So where was this guard headed? As she bustled past me and down the short hallway toward the women's restroom, I breathed a sigh of relief.

Huh. Emery versus *one* guard with a gun. Those were much better odds. *That's convenient.*

Of course it was. "Convenient" is what I do best.

I wasn't going to get a better opportunity than this. I stood and grabbed my empty coffee cup, depositing it in the garbage nearest my mark. My mind summoned and dismissed several ideas in an attempt to form a plan. Caden would've been proud; I was thinking with my brain instead of my Taser.

Well, that's what happened when I left my Taser in the car.

I needed to distract the remaining guard to give the girl a chance to run... no, that wouldn't work. Since she likely didn't know someone had been hired to help her, she might not react quickly enough. Might not even come with me without an explanation. I needed to buy us more time, I decided. Maybe create some confusion. Even if it caused a scene, the ensuing melee might actually work to my benefit. We could lose ourselves in the chaos of a panicked crowd. It was the rough-and-tumble kind of plan that Rachelle would cheer for and Caden would hate.

My eyes were drawn to the guard's holstered gun. If I messed things up, this would get dangerous, *fast*. I should really listen to Caden more.

I took a deep breath as I nonchalantly sidled up to the table, staying behind the guy with the gun. He didn't have any ID or company badge proclaiming his loyalties, but I knew he worked for a private agency hired to procure the girl. The incarnate. What did E-Pluribus want with her? I tried to catch her attention, but she didn't look up. She just stared at the table, her expression lost.

I stood behind the guy for maybe two seconds, but it was a second too long. He started to crane his neck to look at me, and a jolt of alarm surged through me. I grabbed the closest thing at hand, a plastic napkin dispenser, and cracked it across the guard's surprised face.

I didn't really expect it to do anything. Sure, in the movies the bad guys are knocked unconscious with a single karate chop, but in real life, you usually have to be really lucky, or really persistent. And zip ties or handcuffs are always a good plan B.

At best I'd been hoping to get the jump on him, to surprise him and avoid that handgun coming into play for as long as possible. Instead, my Protagonist powers one-upped me: the man's eyes rolled into his head, and he slumped forward onto the table with a solid thump.

Huh.

I realized with a start that the girl was looking at me, eyes wide and a little distrustful. I smiled at her in what I hoped was a disarming way and held out a hand, my mind fumbling for something theatrical to say.

"Come with me if you want to live."

She stared at me. Then her gaze flickered between me and the guard, and she made up her mind. She nodded sharply, expression turning determined. She stood up, not taking my proffered hand.

"The pier is less than a half mile from here," I told her quickly. "Follow me, and don't look back."

We hurried to the exit and left the café behind us, cutting beneath the shadow of the Space Needle as we found our way to Broad Street. The road cut sharply southwest and was a direct sloping route to the waterfront, the expanse of Puget Sound glittering in the distance. "Distance" unfortunately being the key word. Was that truly only a half mile away?

We had escaped the two guards with remarkable ease, but I knew we had to keep moving. With luck, we could lose ourselves in the heavy foot traffic. The girl, thankfully, followed my lead as we began to jog down the sidewalk. We hadn't made it fifty feet when two black SUVs accelerated out from a cross street a block behind us and veered into traffic, eliciting a chorus of honks from angry drivers.

The crosswalk ahead began to flash the **DON'T WALK** sign as we picked up speed and jogged across the street. The light changed seconds before the pursuing SUVs caught up to us, and the road in front of them suddenly flooded with foot traffic. The SUVs slammed to a halt, not willing to mow down pedestrians in their pursuit.

We ran on.

Four cross streets to go.

Three.

The SUVs were gaining on us. We would all reach the next crosswalk at about the same time. One of the dark vehicles honked sharply, and something cracked into the building to our left, well above our heads. A bullet. Damn, we were hardly alone on the sidewalk. I hadn't thought they'd be this desperate to get their hands on her. Despite panting for breath, we both picked up speed. Gunshots are motivating like that.

"We're almost there!" I yelled over the midafternoon traffic, our feet pounding the pavement. But we both knew we wouldn't make it.

As we reached the next crosswalk, just ahead of the SUVs, a siren suddenly wailed from off to our right. I caught the glimpse of an ambulance's flashing lights out of the corner of my eye as we sprinted across the crosswalk. The ambulance, siren blaring, horn issuing staccato blasts, pulled out in front of the oncoming traffic, forcing the SUVs to stop once again.

My partner was a little slower than I, but she kept up remarkably well considering she was running through the streets of downtown Seattle barefoot. And since she was on dry land, which was not her preference. I pointed to the Pier 70 building ahead and to the sparkling expanse of Elliott Bay beyond. A look of redoubled resolve crossed her face, and she ducked her head. Long, greenish-blue hair whipped behind her like a banner, and she sped forward toward her salvation.

Her salvation, but not necessarily mine.

A horn blared, filling Broad Street with a high-pitched sound that didn't *quite* mask the sound of the gunshot, especially since I was listening for it this time. A few feet to my right, the steel pole of the railroad crossing sparked, and the sound of metal ricocheting off of metal pinged loudly. I flinched from the bullet but didn't slow. A group of pedestrians watched and pointed, voices raised in sudden excitement.

Gunfire in broad daylight. What was the world coming to? You knock one guy out...

We crossed the threshold between street and pier, pavement giving way to wooden planks. I was gasping for air at this point, and a particularly strong whiff hit me with the taste of salt. Puget Sound wasn't technically the ocean, but it was still an estuary of the Pacific. That meant salt water, seagulls, and sand dollars.

*And a thousand dollars... if I live.*

I was being a tad dramatic. At that point, I was reasonably confident I would survive. My incarnate powers were warming up, convenience and coincidence interplaying around me. The timing of the traffic lights and especially the ambulance were impeccable—too impeccable. Every crosswalk sign change opened our path or blocked pursuit. My powers were protecting me in their oh-so-subtle ways. It made me wonder, did my powers cause things to happen, or did they just allow me to capitalize on things that would have happened anyway? It reminded me of the old adage: if a tree falls in the forest and no one is around to hear it, does it make a sound? Or, in this case: if I didn't need her to leave, would Stormtrooper A have needed to pee? I'd probably never know—I would always be in that forest with the falling tree. It was a loophole. I could live with that.

Being the Protagonist incarnate was pretty great. Far better than some horrendous Monster Hunter, am I right? I got to change the course of fate, survive impossible odds, and be the star of my own story.

And today, I even got to save the girl.

The sea-salted air and sloshing of water against the wooden pillars beneath us spurred my companion onward. She barreled past me, feet slapping the planks, a whoop escaping her as she neared the end of the pier. People stared as we flew by, surprised or amused to see a young man and woman running like children playing tag. Behind us, I heard the shouts of our pursuers as the SUVs skidded to a halt and belched out three more gun-toting techie goons who tore after us. Oh goody.

But they were far, far too late to catch her.

Ahead, the pier ended in a waist-high chain-link guardrail. The girl, just ahead of me, did not slow. She leapt with the grace of a traceur, her bare foot stepping on the railing, and threw herself over the lip. She twisted in midair, our eyes meeting briefly, before she executed a perfect backflip and dove into the blue waters ten feet below.

I crashed into the guardrail and gripped it, knuckles white, panting and eyeing the water below dubiously. I *really* didn't want to go swimming, but if I had to, I needed to be able to hold my breath. Which meant I needed to catch it, first.

Shouts from behind yanked me around. Three people with furious expressions were sprinting down the pier. The two on the right could have been twins in their business clothes, ties flapping against their chests as they rushed toward me. Their professional attire was spoiled somewhat by their tennis shoes, but all the better to catch me with, my dear. They weren't armed, which would have made me feel better if not for the third person with them.

She was compact, small but athletic, and everything about her oozed darkness. Black hair so stylized it barely shifted in the breeze, shades-of-gray clothes, black trench coat fluttering where her hair didn't, flawless dark skin—and, completing the effect, black, metallic guns: strapped to her leg, holstered at her hip, and slung over her coat with a chest strap. Her left eye was hidden behind her immaculate side-fringe, but I could feel it burning into me, matching the tightness of her one exposed eye.

*Wet or dead, Emery.*

"Jump!" my companion shouted from behind and below me, her melodic voice like a summery breeze. "I have you."

With a resigned curse, I vaulted over the railing and into the waiting water.

The early September air was seasonably warm, but the choppy water of Puget Sound was not. I splashed in with somewhat less grace than my companion, and everything quickly became dark, wet, and freezing. I had squeezed my eyes shut before plunging in, and my wet clothes fought to drag me down. I could tell which way was up, but I couldn't surface yet. Those people were gunning for me (literally!), and I would be taken—or worse—if I breached now. If I could figure out the direction of the pier, though, I could potentially surface beneath the docks and avoid their retaliation. But in the cold, watery void, that was a big if. To add to my troubles, I needed to stay far enough below the surface that they couldn't trace my movements from above—all while holding my breath in the absolute darkness. Well, maybe it wouldn't be absolute if I opened my eyes, but I really didn't want to. It would sting, and there were all sorts of bacteria and microorganisms in the water. Not to mention food and litter from the foot traffic above. The idea would have grossed me out, but I didn't have time to think about it—I had more important concerns.

"Relax," came the melodic voice of my new friend. "I have you." Her words weren't obscured by the water but instead carried through it with a musical tone. I felt her hands grip my shoulders in a firm but gentle touch.

I fought my natural inclination to thrash around or to surface, surrendering to her help. She could guide me to the pier, if only I could communicate my thoughts. My lungs were getting uncomfortable already. Not desperate, yet, but our flight had winded me, eroding my capacity to hold my breath.

Her hands slid down and found mine, holding them loosely. "Open your eyes," she said.

I didn't want to, but I ignored my instincts again and put my trust in her. I felt the pressure of the water all around me, the cold against my eyes as they opened, but the expected sting did not occur. And the water... wow. It was tinted a deep blue-green but was otherwise as translucent as a window. I could see the thick columns of the pier. They were coated in pulpy green kelp that swayed gently in the current, with whitish-gray barnacles peeking out here and there. Tall strands of seaweed danced like slender trees, thicker near the shore. The surface was less than ten feet above our heads, the ocean floor much further below us—perhaps another thirty feet.

I began to pick out some darting fish and movement in the seaweed below. But the most impressive sight floated directly before me. She hung effortlessly, greenish-blue tresses fanning out in all directions, blending with the underwater hue that colored everything. The floral crown she'd been wearing had somehow unfurled into a streamer of flowers that caught, suspended, in her hair. Her eyes were the pinkish color of coral, and her skin had the faintest suggestion of scales that shimmered as it caught the light filtering down from the surface. Her leotard had vanished, melting into a scintillating collection of emerald and sapphire scales that hugged her form, hinting at modesty without really affording it. And, of course, there was her signature tail. Her hips disappeared into the narrow, elongated tail of a tropical fish. Mostly green, but with a healthy wash of blue, it tapered down to where her ankles would be before fanning out into matching fins.

The Mermaid incarnate.

Good thing, too, or this whole endeavor would have been quite embarrassing.

She pulled me close to her, and I was struck by how tall she was. From waist to forehead she was smaller than me, but that tail added quite a bit of length. I was wondering if she felt short in human form —when she kissed me.

Her lips were soft. Mine went slack in surprise, and I pushed away a stab of anxiety. Caden would think this was funny, but *I* was at a loss. Did she think I expected a kiss for rescuing her? I suppose that aligned with what the stories claimed about mermaids. Seducing mortals and all that.

She pulled back, and my lips tingled. I sucked in a breath to protest, then stopped. Panic coursed through me as I realized I'd just inhaled. Even though it had worked, my brain struggled to reconcile my expectations of drowning with the obvious fact that I wasn't.

"Better?" she asked, a knowing smile tugging at her lips.

"I have a boyfriend," I blurted without thinking. My voice carried cleanly through the water, like hers had, and bubbles weren't expelled from my mouth. It was decidedly *strange,* even for me. It felt more like I was hovering in the air than floating underwater.

"Lucky you," she replied, gesturing at the expanse around her. "They say there are plenty of fish in the sea, but human expressions can be so insensitive. On the contrary, there are not a whole lot of dating options down here."

I realized the kiss had conferred my newfound ability to breathe and speak underwater. "Is that why you risk going to the surface?" I asked, mostly to cover my embarrassment.

"In part." She glanced up, and I followed her gaze. The surface distorted the view of the docks, but I could tell there was a lot of activity. "Come on," she said, "we aren't safe yet."

She twirled around and gracefully began swimming, heading slightly downward while also angling along the coastline to the north. Damn, providing three-dimensional directions is tougher than it sounds. I swam after her. It quickly became evident that whatever attributes she'd bestowed upon me did not improve my natural swimming ability. Don't get me wrong; I'm a solid swimmer. Not only did I have memories of spending summers at the beach for years before I *technically* reincarnated into this Emery, I also had many lifetimes of experience around the water. Not that I had access to the memories of all of those lifetimes yet. Regardless, I was pretty certain all of my incarnations' combined experience could not compare to the elegance and speed of my companion. She spun effortlessly through the water, arms spread wide, clearly relishing the feel of the currents against her face. Releasing a little squeal of excitement, she sped away from me and then whirled around and shot back in my direction. I grinned at her antics. With how many loops she spiraled around me, I began to feel as if I were swimming with dolphins. Actually, scratch that. Dolphins would look slow and ungainly next to the grace and beauty of the Mermaid.

Catching my awestruck expression, she offered to carry me through the water with her. Although I knew it would save us considerable time, I declined. My foolish pride didn't like the way she worded it: "carry" me, like I was an infant.

So we swam, and I lost track of time. Swimming required effort, but being able to breathe underwater removed much of the physical stamina required. It was about as hard as jogging, but a hell of a lot more fun.

"Did Dagan send you?" the Mermaid asked when we were far enough away that the danger was certainly behind us.

"Yeah." I didn't meet her eyes. "Hired me, actually. But I would have done it for free." That last part came out a touch quick, didn't it?

"Who are you?"

"Emery Luple. I'm an incarnate."

Her eyes lit up. "I've heard of you! You're the Loophole, right?"

I couldn't help the grin that spread over my face. "Guilty." The Loophole incarnate was my attempt at rebranding. I didn't want to be known as the Monster Hunter for the rest of my existence, even though I had once thought that was my identity. I didn't think Trish would care, but it still made me uncomfortable to traipse around in another incarnate's personification.

But that had presented a problem. I didn't mind being the Protagonist at all, but proclaiming it to the world felt... well, Rachelle thought it sounded conceited. Like somehow it meant I was the Most Important Person Alive incarnate. We had decided to tiptoe around the truth. To anyone who asked directly, fine, I would tell them I was the Protagonist. But my website—*There's Always a Loophole*—was already established, and it was a simple step to start marketing myself as the Loophole in incarnate circles. It fit, too: I'd spent lifetimes in all sorts of identities, from monster hunters to kings. That didn't make me the King any more than it made me the Monster Hunter. It made me a dabbler. I might be able to recall experiences or summon skills from my time spent in those roles, but I would never be as authentic as the real deal. My incarnate specialties were centered around my story and the chapters of my life, as well as the people in it. They were my strength... and my weakness. Most incarnates have a fatal flaw, some sort of Achilles' heel, to counterbalance the perks we get. I wasn't sure what mine was, but I had a strong suspicion. Like far too many protagonists, my kryptonite was losing loved ones. Especially *the* one.

"I'm Melusina." Her words pulled me back to our aquatic trek.

We'd left behind the busy piers of Seattle and were now in deep, open waters but still within sight of the coast. Melusina set our course, which snaked further from or closer to the coastline based on judgments I couldn't begin to understand. I noticed she seemed more concerned with maintaining depth than with shortening the distance, since we hardly swam in a direct line. Still, despite the exertion of a prolonged swim, I trusted her. I was a stranger to her underwater world.

A world that was, in a word, incredible. The effort of swimming never let me forget that's what I was doing, but I thought I sort of resembled a bird, flying over ecosystems below me. Occasional spreads of seaweed, like miniature forests, poked up from the seabed, which was itself pocked with craters and divots containing life. Schools of fish passed like flocks of birds, flashing their scales and swimming about in arcane patterns, though lone fish were common, too. Above me, a motorboat roared by like an airplane, its engines amplified in the echoing water. So different, yet so similar at the same time. Maybe that was just my mind's way of trying to cope. Off to my right, the coastline curved and squiggled, and to my left... it felt like an abyss. The sea floor sloped down and away from me, but not cleanly—it was like I was looking at mountains, cliffs, and valleys from a great height. The openness was staggering, a little like looking up into the sky. Endless, almost eerily so.

"You should take the money," she said after an extended silence.

I started. "Why?" I would, but I felt a little guilty about it. If good deeds had a price tag, did that render them no longer good deeds? It made me feel like a hero for hire—and that wasn't as glamorous as it sounded.

She shrugged, spinning in a lazy loop while I continued my methodical strokes. "You earned it. Besides, you ruined your clothes in our escape, so you'll need to buy new ones."

Again? Sigh. Yeah, that sounded about right. "Where are we headed?"

"Four Mile Rock. I was thinking about taking us further north to avoid detection, but I think it will take too long at this rate." She shrugged, giving me a small smile.

"Ah." *Just apologize and accept her help.* Instead, I pushed myself to swim a little faster.

We continued for a time, and with my new exertion, I began to tire. Which slowed our progress even more. That realization dredged up new reserves of energy, and I gritted my teeth, carving my way through the water.

I might have an ego issue.

"What did E-Pluribus want with you?" I asked to distract myself from the strain. I considered kicking off my shoes and removing my heavy, waterlogged clothes but discarded the idea at the embarrassing thought of catching a cab back to my parked car in my underwear. I groaned inwardly—my car was in a pay-by-the-hour lot, and it was going to be there longer than I'd planned. Good thing I was accepting the money, I guess.

"I'm not entirely sure. I overheard my... escorts... mention something about me being 'another incarnate.' I don't think I'm the only one they were interested in."

I frowned. "They knew you were an incarnate? You're certain?"

She swam effortlessly below me, on her back so we were face-to-face. "Positive. They even used the term."

I froze. "But they were mortals, right?"

"As far as I could tell." Her hands splayed out in front of her in a gesture of helplessness. "Also, I got the impression they didn't know which incarnate I was."

I stared at her, then forced my limbs back to their unwelcome task. I hoped Four Mile Rock wasn't named that because it was *four miles* away.

"That makes no sense," I said, half to her and half to myself. "Why would E-Pluribus be abducting random incarnates off the streets?"

E-Pluribus. One of Seattle's many start-up technology firms. The CEO, Micah Asker, was one hell of an entrepreneur. He was young and had started his company only two years ago, but E-Pluribus had quickly entered the arena of the tech titans. It had introduced an operating system, Unum, that was initially tailored for advanced robotics but could interface with any other operating system, regardless of whether it originated from Microsoft, Google, Apple, or anything in between. It spread like wildfire, not only uniting users who previously swore by a particular brand but also offering companies the ability to utilize the technology of competing operating systems. This allowed for quick and economical expansion of their business lines. E-Pluribus was still in its infancy, so Unum had not yet become more popular than Windows, Android, or Mac. But if it continued its current trajectory, it was projected to surpass all three within a decade, if not sooner. Siri and Alexa had better watch out, because Unum had them both in its crosshairs.

Call me a skeptic, but I smelled the involvement of an incarnate. Maybe Asker himself, but it was just as likely one of his chief engineers was the Boy Genius, or something. Suddenly, with the Mermaid's claim that E-Pluribus was snatching incarnates, the company's successes were cast in a new, sinister light. Could it be using incarnates against their will to further its business agenda?

It was a lot to consider.

"I'll poke around and see what I can find out," I decided. Melusina was already a distance ahead of me again, but my voice traveled easily in the water.

"We're almost to Four Mile Rock," she announced. "I think it would be best if you emerge on this side of it, just to the south. The beach there is gentle and bordered by private residences along the shore. You'll look like a local coming back from a swim."

*Fully dressed. Yeah, totally normal.* "Sounds good. What about you?"

"I'm going to lie low for a bit. Keep to open waters for a few days."

I nodded, grateful I didn't have to suggest it. We swam for another ten minutes, slowly curving inland, the seabed seeming to rise up to meet us as we swam into progressively shallower waters. Then, when the water was no more than twenty feet deep, Melusina ascended to the surface. I followed, my head breaking through the waves and into fresh air. The breeze felt icy on my exposed, wet cheeks. I treaded water, turning to see her watching me with delight in her eyes. With her wet hair hanging down her back and her bare shoulders peeking above the waves, she looked like a quintessential fairytale creature.

"This is where we part ways," the Mermaid said, the tiniest trace of melancholy threading through her musical voice. "Do not breathe of the sea now, or you will drown. The spell I laid upon you cannot survive the open air."

I swallowed. "Understood."

"Thank you for the timely rescue. I won't forget this." And with that, she sprang out of the water in a perfectly executed, gravity-defying backflip. "Goodbye, Emery." Her tail slipping gracefully beneath the surface of Puget Sound was the last I glimpsed of her.

The Mermaid in her element. A smile creased my face at the sight. Then it faded as another breeze sliced through me. I began my lone swim toward the shoreline.

*M*y teeth chattered and the frigid water slapped against my face as I surfaced and scanned the sandy strip of coast ahead. Tall houses with small, fenced yards opening onto the beach overlooked the water. Most of them had high decks with outdoor furniture and BBQ grills for seaside entertainment. I wasn't too concerned with being seen from such a distance. Not only would my features be hard to make out, but anyone watching likely wasn't paying enough attention to realize I hadn't gone *out* to sea before coming back in. Only the people playing on the beach worried me; would they be alarmed when a man seemingly materialized from the Sound?

Luck—or what passed as luck for the Protagonist—was with me. The two children playing on the beach were arguing, their voices loud over the water. The bigger kid kicked over the sand structure the smaller one was building, then tore off squealing as the littler boy chased him down angrily.

Now that the coast was clear—oh, I just learned where that saying comes from—I emerged from Puget Sound on a sandy strip of beach that would have been idyllic in mid-July's heat. It was late afternoon, the sun cheerfully illuminating the rooftops while making its inexorable way toward the horizon. Once it slipped below the water, the temperature would drop considerably. While we officially had another week of summer before the change of the season, the evenings and nights had turned characteristically chilly after the past few warmer months. I really wanted to be dry before sunset.

A breeze kicked up as I stepped onto the sand, and drips of freezing water trailed icy fingers down my calves. My body began shivering immediately, trying to shake fast enough to warm my extremities. Ignoring my discomfort as much as possible, I slipped up the beach. From the water, I had spied my exit strategy: two houses down, an unfenced yard had clear access to the road running along the other side of the beach houses. I clenched my jaw to keep my teeth from knocking together so much.

I reached the yard and, my bare feet grateful for the soft grass instead of the coarse sand, headed toward the front of the row of houses. Movement from the corner of my eye caught my attention. I looked around. The blinds of a nearby window twitched, and I could swear someone had been watching me. I sucked in a breath.

This was the problem with being the Protagonist. My powers brought all the players and events of my story together for me, but I had to figure out which elements were important. In New York, when I had been pursuing a serial killer who hunted criminals, I had serendipitously crossed paths with that very killer within hours of landing in the city... but when I met her, I didn't know she was the killer I was seeking. And being suspicious of *every* person with whom I crossed paths made it hard to get anything done.

Now unseen eyes had watched me emerge from the water. Curious neighbor, or gun-toting bad guy after me for pilfering their prize? Logic said there was an infinitesimally small chance it was anything important at all. But my powers exaggerated infinitesimally small chances into everyday occurrences. Once, I thought that was a trait of all incarnates. Now I realized the truth: I was special. Yippee.

If my life were a murder mystery—and don't laugh, sometimes I thought it was—then this could be anything from a red herring to a smoking gun. I decided to shrug it off. Even as the Protagonist, the chances someone had infiltrated the beach houses ahead of me with the hope or knowledge that I would emerge in this specific area stretched believability. I hoped.

I heard the sounds of traffic as I left the beach behind me. A perfectly manicured street ran in front of the houses, separated from the main road by a strip of land maybe forty feet wide. This band of nature was composed of trees, rocks, driftwood, and low bushes artfully arranged to look natural. Before calling a ride service, I decided to allow some time to dry off. I wanted to avoid looking like a drowned rat when I was picked up. It was a decision made half from pride and half from practicality; I didn't want to attract too much attention, after all. Best not to be remembered. The sun cast long shadows on this side of the houses, but I was able to find a log bench situated between two homes, and I basked in the sunlight that shone between the buildings, the busy road humming behind me.

My dark, usually upswept bangs hung heavy on my forehead, dripping cold tracks down my face. I ran a hand through my hair, extracting what water I could. Then I flicked my bangs out of my face and dug in my pocket for my phone. Thank goodness for designs that were water resistant.

I texted Caden, letting him know everything had gone (wait for it) swimmingly and I was heading back to my car in a little bit.

I stretched out like a cat in the sun, grateful for the warmth. Even with the Mermaid's kiss to protect me from the biting cold of Puget Sound, that underwater realm hadn't been welcoming. It was stark, cold, and darkly beautiful—but alien to the world of dry land and sunshine. Though, come to think of it, Seattle wasn't really known for those things, so perhaps it shouldn't have been so foreign after all.

My phone chirped. WANT TO GRAB A LATE DINNER? Caden had texted back.

I hesitated. I *really* did, but I also needed to shower. Not only did I smell like seaweed, but I was starting to itch. I felt... crusty.

YEAH. CAN YOU MEET ME AT MY PLACE? I NEED A SHOWER.

While I waited for his response, I cycled through my phone to a rideshare app.

Caden's reply came a moment later. Sure. Meet you there in an hour and a half?

I texted him a thumbs-up, followed by a heart and a smiley face.

Suddenly warmed by more than just the sun, I called for a ride. Tonight was starting to look up.

Rush hour traffic, always a problem in Seattle and more so on Thursday nights, was two hours past its prime, and the driver made it to my location with impressive speed. As she pulled up, she eyed my sodden clothes with distaste.

"You wouldn't happen to have a towel or something I could sit on to keep your seats from getting too damp?" I asked sheepishly.

Despite her air of annoyance, she found a wad of clean rags in her trunk, and I spent a few extra minutes arranging them before hopping in the vehicle.

The trek back to downtown seemed to take forever. After about five minutes of awkward silence, the driver cranked up the volume on the radio to fill the quiet. She didn't check with me first, but I was grateful.

By the time we neared our destination, the sun had fully set, revealing the light-studded Seattle skyline. The driver dropped me off, and I swear she barely waited for me to wholly exit the vehicle before punching the gas and disappearing back into traffic. I couldn't blame her. My clothes were still damp, and as I'd anticipated, the temperature had plummeted with the onset of night. I checked the time and realized I only had a little over a half hour to beat Caden home. At this rate, I would be meeting him in the driveway. I hurriedly fished my keys out of my cold, wet pocket and slid into my waiting vehicle.

My car was a crossover. I liked to think of it as an SUV's little brother. I'd bought it a few months earlier, used, from an incarnate client who reached out to me through my website and then hired me for protection. Though, in hindsight, I was a little concerned as to the nature of his request: I had begun to suspect he was the Smuggler incarnate. I hadn't told Caden of my suspicions, since he'd ended up doing most of the protecting—how could I even begin to compete with the *Guardian* Angel?—and at any rate we'd gladly accepted a hefty discount on this vehicle as payment for our work. The vehicle wasn't state-of-the-art, but it was new enough to have a lot of gadgets; more features than I would ever use, really. And my favorite part was its name: it was called a Rogue. That pretty much made it the *Millennium Falcon* of cars, in my opinion.

I started it up and flipped on the heat. Time to head home. Well, to Mom's house. My apartment, such as it was, had been blown up six months earlier in an attack by the Genie. I'd been saving for a new place ever since, but the car had set me back... all the way back. So I was living at home. It wasn't a bad thing, but I really wanted a place with Caden. He was happy enough as Rachelle's roommate, and she seemed perfectly willing to allow him to keep living with her, but we both wanted to be able to spend more time with one another. Between my freelance work at all hours and his schooling, we only got to see each other every couple of days. Even the weekends weren't guaranteed, since my line of work had no real schedule attached to it.

I paid for parking at the little kiosk, cringing at the cost, then waited for traffic to clear before pulling out of the small lot and onto the streets of the city. To get home, I needed to get to the interstate, but with all the one-way roads, teeny on-ramps, heavy foot traffic, and stop lights, that was easier said than done. It was a dance I knew all too well: lights and crosswalks were mere suggestions to local pedestrians, and the streets were... hilly, to say the least.

I was jamming to a song from my playlist and keeping my eyes on the traffic ahead when a red sports car veered out of a side street directly in front of me. If I hadn't reflexively slammed on the brakes, I would have crashed into it. The car behind me swerved and squealed to a halt, too, a wave of angry honks erupting behind us. My heart was beating heavily with the surge of adrenaline that always accompanies a near collision. A second vehicle, this one a black SUV like the ones I'd run from just hours ago, veered out of the same side street, shooting across the lane in front of me and gunning after the sports car. My mouth was agape; I snapped it shut. It was too convenient that *my* car was the one they nearly barreled over. A long second of indecision followed as I weighed getting home to meet Caden against my burgeoning curiosity.

Curiosity won. I floored it, racing to catch up to the two vehicles.

It didn't take long. Reckless driving or not, the streets of Seattle were still packed with traffic and did not permit them much maneuverability. It became apparent the two vehicles were not together; the red car appeared to be trying to lose the SUV. It weaved as much as it could in the two-lane road and took sudden turns, hoping to throw off its pursuit. The SUV, to its credit, was tenacious. It hovered just far enough away that it could react to Red's maneuvers.

I realized with a start that I was practically riding on Black's bumper, focused far more on the interesting chase than the street. I backed off, feeling a twinge of embarrassment. Red suddenly shot past us heading the other way, and I blinked, having completely missed their U-turn. The SUV, unsurprisingly, flipped a U in pursuit. For a brief moment, as my headlights illuminated the SUV's driver side, I caught a glimpse of the person behind the wheel.

It was the woman from the pier. The one with all the guns.

*Oh, hell no.*

Suddenly the chase took on a new light. If E-Pluribus was hunting down incarnates and this woman had tried to reclaim the Mermaid, that meant Red was likely an incarnate.

There was no way I was going to let Scary Gun Lady get her grubby paws on another incarnate. Without thinking, I whipped my crossover into a tight, tight 180.

Unfortunately, I did so right into oncoming traffic.

My powers must have supercharged their batteries that morning, because instead of plowing into the unprepared drivers, my crossover slid *between* two vehicles like it was in an action movie, barely a whisper of space remaining in front or behind. I drifted into the wide (and conveniently empty) bike lane before popping back into place between the two cars, the rear one having slammed on the brakes in reaction to my stunt.

There was now a maroon sedan between me and the SUV, impeding my forward progress. Ahead, the road split in two, the right-hand lane turning into a parking zone for a host of storefronts. It was separated from the main road by a median for about fifty feet before it remerged with the street I was on. There were only two vehicles parked there, now that most stores had closed for the evening, and foot traffic was light.

With a whoop, I rocketed down the right lane. A sign read **PARKING ZONE: SPEED LIMIT 5 MPH**. I spared a glance at my dash—my needle was pushing forty-five. I flew, trying to look everywhere at once to keep tabs on the maroon car *and* keep a lookout for any pedestrians, as well as Black and Red ahead. I edged past the sedan and merged back onto the main boulevard, Scary Gun Lady's SUV now directly in front of me. She soared through an intersection and I held my breath, praying the light wouldn't change. I saw a pedestrian hitting the crosswalk button, but it didn't turn yellow until I shot across.

Ahead, Scary Gun Lady was running down the red car, abandoning her earlier tactic of keeping her distance. They passed beneath a sign leading to northbound I-5. *Damn.* If they made it to the freeway, this chase could go on for quite some time.

I sped up, briefly wondering where the cops were. The two vehicles hadn't been as conspicuously reckless as I had, but between all three of us I would have expected some attention. Attention that I didn't want, I realized. Huh. Maybe *I* was the reason there weren't lights and sirens following us.

The road widened into three lanes ahead, and I knew my time was running out. The two right lanes exited to southbound and northbound I-5, while the left lane continued for through traffic. I knew that the far-right lane would curve sharply, almost doubling back on itself, while the middle lane arched into an uphill slope, becoming an overpass that crossed the freeway before merging into it from the right. Gritting my teeth, I nudged my car forward, watching the MPH gauge push into the seventies. That might not be very fast on the interstate, but we were still on surface streets, where the speed limit was no greater than thirty-five.

I caught up to them.

Pulling into the farthest right-hand lane and inching parallel with Black, I tried to peer through the passenger side window to get a solid look at Scary Gun Lady—but I had no time. A mere four hundred feet ahead, the lane peeled away from the others and turned to the right. If I didn't merge left, I would be forced onto the southbound on-ramp while the car and SUV continued onto the northbound one. I could see other vehicles' headlights from the freeway. The turn was rushing toward me; a yellow speed limit sign suggested my speed was not the recommended one. I clenched my jaw. Red and Black were not slowing down. I didn't have enough time or space to squeeze past them. The nose of my car was only at Red's rear tires, the bulk of my car racing alongside the big SUV. If I merged to the left now, I'd slam into Scary Gun Lady. And there wasn't room to fit a puppy between Black's and Red's bumpers. At this speed, even coincidence would have a difficult time keeping me unharmed.

The turn was here.

I had to exit to the right...

... or cause an accident.

I gritted my teeth, flicked on my blinker to telegraph my unbelievable intention, and slammed my wheel to the left. I almost closed my eyes, knowing I was likely to clip Red and crash full-on into Black. I careened out of the right lane and partially into the left, squeezing into the space between the metal railing and the SUV, wholly in the shoulder. My vehicle shook violently, running rough over a part of the road never meant to be driven. The shoulder, already too narrow to accommodate the Rogue, began to taper. Red, seeing my predicament, punched forward to create a slight space between their vehicle and Black. Red's customized plate, **SPERANT**, seemed only millimeters from my bumper. The moment stretched, and I could practically see Scary Gun Lady calculating her options.

Slam on the brakes and avoid a collision?

Gun it and try to slip around me before the shoulder shrank any further?

Crush my interloping ass without remorse?

I edged further into the lane, angling my crossover more or less *into* Black's options. Tires squealed as she made up her mind and backed off. I shot onto the on-ramp proper, the jarring vibrations finally smoothing out. I let out a breath I hadn't realized I'd been holding and eased off the gas. Red, thankfully, took the opportunity to get a bit further ahead.

Black's horn blared as Gun Lady rode my bumper, trying to bully me into speeding up. I obliged, accelerating but staying well under the posted speed limit. It only seemed fair: I'd been speeding for the last several minutes; I owed it to the law to spend a while going slowly in compensation.

Gun Lady was relentless, and she tried to ride up onto the shoulder to pass me, but I drifted ever so slightly to the right, cutting her off. She switched to my left, and I wove erratically, stopping her advance.

A chorus of horns blended in with Black's, a line backing up behind us. I turned up the volume on my music to drown them out, adrenaline seeping out of me in waves now that the chase itself had ended. I mentally apologized to the mortals behind the SUV, but I didn't feel too bad. I'd saved someone—whether an incarnate or a mortal—from Scary Gun Lady. This was a win.

With my languorous journey from on-ramp to freeway, I stretched the drive into almost two minutes. I considered stopping altogether to further impede the SUV but quickly discarded the idea. I didn't want to provide Scary Gun Lady the opportunity to approach me on foot— or get a clean shot off, for that matter. Especially with a clear lane out in front of me, I could accelerate and escape if I just kept moving.

Finally, I could stall no longer as I reached the interstate. I accelerated and smoothly entered traffic, one of my eyes glued on the rearview mirror. Would I become Black's new target?

I frowned, surprised, as she shot past me, clearly trying to catch up to the sports car. She would never succeed, not with how much time I had bought Red.

I was driving northbound, and my house was most definitely to the south. I glanced at the time. Caden and I were supposed to meet at my place any minute now, and I was a good twenty minutes away. More, since I was heading in the wrong direction.

I only hesitated a moment. Caden would understand.

I took off after Scary Gun Lady. She drove even more aggressively on the freeway, weaving through traffic and keeping her needle well above the speed limit. Following her was challenging, especially since I didn't want her to know I was doing so, which meant I had to be more subtle.

Still, the freeway was much flatter and more open than the streets of downtown, so I was able to keep her in my sights. I couldn't see the red sports car anywhere, though, and as the black SUV and I continued to pass exits in the densely populated U District, my lips curved in satisfaction. Red could have exited at any of these off-ramps. Scary Gun Lady had lost.

The minutes ticked by, my focus solely on the black SUV. The erratic lane changes and bursts of speed started to falter as she came to the same realization I had. A couple of miles later, she moved over to the right lane and signaled to exit.

I frowned. Why was she signaling all of a sudden? She hadn't broadcasted a single lane change until now. A coil of unease tightened in my gut. Did she want me to follow her? I slid over two lanes to chase her at as discreet a distance as I could manage. Which wasn't much; there was only a single car between me and Black as we approached the stoplight ahead.

I followed her through the surface streets of Northgate, keeping as much distance between us as I dared. I was going to be *so* late. But I'd followed her this far; I could hardly abandon my hunt now. Besides, now that she had exited, I could tail her back to wherever the hell she came from. My Rogue suddenly seemed so aptly named, I nearly laughed out loud. I crept forward as the light ahead changed, the comical image of my crossover tiptoeing toward its vehicular prey in a cloak of shadows crisp in my mind.

Then the SUV took a sudden left onto a small side street, and I cursed. She could hardly fail to notice if I followed her onto it. Indecision made the choice for me; the oncoming traffic was suddenly too thick, and I couldn't turn even if I wanted to. But I took the next left, hoping to parallel Scary Gun Lady's route and emerge on the same major avenue ahead.

When I got to the main road, I scanned both directions. No black SUV. *Damn it.* She had either beaten me there and sped away or simply used the side street to ditch me. Either way, I'd lost her.

What to do now? Headlights beamed brightly behind me, so I turned onto the main street to avoid getting honked at.

I decided to circle the block and check out the parking areas along the street where I'd lost her. The small street was lined with commercial buildings and storage facilities, so I doubted one of them would be her lair (Lair?), but maybe I'd get lucky. It was a long shot, but I really wanted this chase to pay off since I'd chosen it over being on time for my night with Caden.

I planned to canvass the buildings, but those same headlights behind me robbed me of the opportunity for a slow, methodical search. Growling in frustration, I circled the block yet again. I was starting to feel like I was on an amusement park ride.

When I made it back to the same street, I slowed to a near crawl and started scanning the structures as I passed. It was difficult to see in the dark, the streetlights not illuminating much of the business lots. But I could tell immediately that of the two lone cars in the shared parking area, neither was a black SUV. Maybe she had parked along the side of one of the businesses, in the load-unload areas? Either way, I couldn't resort to a leisurely search, as another pair of headlights shone in my rearview mirror.

No, not "another." Those were the same headlights. *Great.* Someone was tailing *me*, now. My suspicions were confirmed: Scary Gun Lady's blinker off the interstate had been to goad me into following so another agent could track me down.

I glanced at the clock on my dash, wincing. By the time I got home, I would probably be an hour late. With nothing to show for it. *Awesome.* I just hoped Caden would wait for me.

I clenched my jaw, my eyes flicking to the headlights behind me. I flipped my music app to my upbeat "Girl Power" soundtrack to get me amped, then revved my Rogue. *Bring it.*

### The Mermaid Incarnate

*Name: Melusina*

**Height:** *5'4" (10'2" with her tail)*

**Weight:** *she wouldn't tell me*

**Eye Color:** *pink*

**Hair:** *blue-green*

**Classification:** *Benign*

**Bio:** *Hey, class, welcome to Intro to Incarnates, my newest crash course in all things urban legend. I'm going to let you in on all my insider knowledge so you can become a master of incarnate lore, just like me. Study hard enough, and you too will be able to do things like: Tell the difference between the Unicorn and the Kraken. Learn how to feed the Dragon (spoiler: you don't have to be very good at it... but then, you'll only feed her once). Or even learn to identify which TV shows are inspired by real, living incarnates (and which ones get us totally wrong). Since incarnates change —often drastically—between incarnations, these biographies are my best attempt to capture their current incarnation, as of the time I'm writing them. I figured we'd start with an easy one. So, without further ado, allow me to introduce the Mermaid...*

*Aw, shit. I ran out of room. Enh, I don't really know her that well anyway.*

~

*W*hen I pulled up to my (mom's) house forty-five minutes later, I felt a pang of guilt. Caden's car was in the driveway. I checked my phone, but he hadn't texted. Hopefully, that meant he hadn't been waiting for me overly long. I cringed at the time, though. Unless he also had been running *super* late, he had been there for a while.

Slipping my pursuit had been laughably simple with coincidence and convenience backing me up. The first stoplight I approached had turned red just as I slid under it. When that didn't deter my pursuer, the next crosswalk signal switched as I traversed it, and two pedestrians stepped off the curb right away, forcing the car behind me to screech to a stop or plow into them. At the next light, I flipped a 180 and shot back in the other direction. I peered into the window as I passed the car that had been following me. As chance would have it, a nearby streetlight had perfectly highlighted the interior. The driver's head jerked around when he realized I was heading the opposite way. He'd had a baseball cap on, but I caught a full image of his pale, angular face. He looked oddly familiar. I knew I'd seen him before. But where? Was it a recent memory, or from that immortal corner of my mind? Try as I might, I couldn't place him. As our eyes had met, he looked away and tugged his baseball cap lower. I spent the drive home wondering if he had recognized me. If so, it would prove I knew him from this lifetime, as I didn't look the same after reincarnating. And incarnates typically couldn't identify one another as such by sight alone. Well, I suppose I should be more specific. After all, I could identify the Bigfoot, the Fairy, or the Loch Ness Monster at a glance—though even then, sometimes an incarnate's built-in glamour could surprise you; Caden was evidence of that. Kolby the Kobold, too. Anyway, human-type incarnates, like me, were often indistinguishable from mortal people.

I headed for the house, wincing when the effort of shutting my car's door reminded me of my afternoon marathon. My arms were leaden, and I shuddered to think what they'd feel like tomorrow.

Being around Caden tonight would probably help. He often subconsciously healed those around him. Though, of course, Caden meant way more to me than a walking ibuprofen. I scratched at my neck as I unlocked the front door. I needed a shower. I was itchy *everywhere*. And I probably smelled like the offspring of a sweaty gym that had fallen in love with the ocean.

I heard Mom's and Caden's soft voices floating in from the kitchen. I ducked into the room, my uncertain grin widening into a genuine one as Caden noticed my arrival and his beautiful, seafoam green eyes alighted on mine. He was leaning against the white-topped kitchen counter. Behind him a discarded knife sat next to the sink and several bowls of diced veggies were scattered around a cutting board. Mom sat at the kitchen island, angled toward him, her hands cupping a ceramic mug with a tag on a little white string draped over its rim. Recently, she'd been trying to reduce her coffee intake... with varying degrees of success, depending on the day. In an attempt to find a substitute, she'd adopted the habit of drinking tea. But since she didn't really like tea, she went through far more tea bags than cups of the actual beverage and often left forgotten, almost-full mugs around the house.

They made a colorful pair: Caden as tones of light, my mom as shades of dark. His feathered, naturally golden hair contrasted with her carefully straightened, freshly dyed curtain of deep brown. His creamy complexion looked especially light against her darker skin from her Latina heritage. Caden wore white jeans and a long-sleeved aqua shirt that hugged his lean frame. As always, his clothes looked fresh off the rack, and I knew he'd chosen aqua because it was my favorite color on him. Mom was in pajama bottoms and an old T-shirt, but she'd thrown on a shawl in a haphazard attempt to look presentable, and it mostly worked. Looking between them, I realized they were both lovely in different ways. And despite their differences, they both wore the same tired expressions. Mom had been working extra hours for weeks, trying to capitalize on the highs of the summer market before it faded away, while Caden had begun studying at UW less than a month ago while also volunteering at

UW Medicine and Hall Health. Yeah, I was dating a do-gooder. And I had no regrets.

Mom craned her neck to follow Caden's gaze. "Hey, sweet pea," she said. "Long night?"

"You could say that," I grumbled, giving her a peck on the cheek on my way to Caden. I gave him a brief side hug—trying not to get him too damp or dirty in the process—and a warm smile, then turned to lean on the counter, mirroring his relaxed posture. "I had to debunk an ocean-based myth. From *within* the ocean."

Mom didn't know anything about incarnates. She, along with the general public, believed I worked as an emerging vlogger who debunked supernatural events. My website, ad campaign, and (all new!) podcast worked to persuade the mortal world that I was just another entertaining myth buster. The cleverest aspect of the ruse was that it allowed me to meet and socialize with incarnates without drawing undue suspicion. Incarnates wanting to find me could accomplish this with a simple Google search—or "Ask Unum," E-Pluribus's rival search platform—but mortals would be none the wiser to the true game afoot.

You might think that setup wouldn't fool my own mom, but the backstory that went along with being the Protagonist handled all the details. When I reincarnated about six months ago and Mom suddenly had a nineteen-year-old son, reality went the full mile, giving her memories of raising me and our being a happy family together for the last two decades. Nineteen years' worth of personal items—from outgrown tennis shoes to school art projects to photos, complete with baby pictures—materialized as if it were no big deal, selling the lie that I was, and had always been, Lynn Luple's son. Oh, and she got the last name from me, too, so reality really pulled a fast one on her.

All of that would have made me feel terrible, but Mom was genuinely happy and loved me deeply—even though she wasn't aware that all this was a new development in her life. And, I admit, it was nice to have a mom. I reincarnated as an orphan more often than not. I blame Disney: their protagonists never seem to have parents.

"Ocean?" she asked, her interest piqued. "Another ghost story?"

I shrugged, using the movement as an excuse to lean against Caden a little. "Yeah, but this one had a twist." I pitched my voice to sound spooky. *"It wasn't real."*

Mom snorted and took a sip of tea, lips tightening at the flavor. "I don't know how you manage to find so many stories, but it's a good thing for your blog that there are so many evil ghosts in Seattle."

Caden was warm against my side and smelled fresh and clean, as he always did. He could have spent the evening wading through sewage, and I was 99 percent positive he'd still smell like soap. The Guardian Angel had it so good, it was hardly fair to the rest of us.

"Nah, the ghosts aren't evil," I hedged. I didn't like concealing the truth from Mom, but she was safer if she didn't get involved in incarnate antics. Still, I wouldn't drag the Ghost's reputation through the mud. Like all incarnates, there was only ever one behind the urban legend. And Iris was most certainly not to be feared. I frowned. "Now, zombies, those guys are punks."

Mom gave a good-humored shake of her head and then stood. "I'll let you two have dinner. Caden, let me know what else you need on that special project of yours."

He bobbed his head. "I will. Thanks, Lynn." What was this? Was my mom helping Caden with something for school?

"It was nice catching up with you," Mom said. "Oh, and good luck with biology. It's the reason I changed majors and got my business degree." She made her way out of the kitchen.

"You forgot your tea," I called after her, the smile evident in my voice. She pretended not to hear me.

Caden's arm snaked around my waist, and he tugged me into him, tilting his head up to meet my lips in a kiss. My question about his project melted away at the feel of his lips on mine. His breath was minty, and I would have worried about my own breath, but I didn't care about those kinds of things when this beautiful boy was kissing me.

We separated, and he sighed contentedly. Then he wrinkled his nose. "You smell funny."

"That's a relief. I was afraid I smelled *bad.*" My grin at my own cleverness slipped a little. "Sorry I'm late."

He shrugged, dismissing my worry. "No problem. But when I asked if you wanted to have 'a late dinner,' I didn't mean you should actually be late."

I eyed him. "Been sitting on that one a while?"

Caden smirked. "Would you prefer I be upset?"

"Ah, no. *Fantastic* joke. I'll be sure to remember that one."

He nodded once, satisfied by my response. Then he pulled me near again, our hips bumping. "I missed you," he told me earnestly. Even though most of his statements came off as earnest, genuine, sincere, or some other form of heartfelt, I didn't mind. He couldn't help that it was a part of his glamour, and it didn't make it any less authentic. "But why do you smell like beached seaweed?"

"Just took a quick dip in the Sound. Not as refreshing as you'd think."

He laughed. "So, just another Thursday night?"

I considered, ticking off each point on my hands. "I rescued the Mermaid, was pursued on foot through downtown Seattle by her captors, received a kiss from her underwater, swam four miles, caught a ride back to my car, became involved in a high-speed chase with the same jerks from earlier, stopped them from catching another incarnate, and shook a stalker." I grinned. "Yup. Just another Thursday night."

Caden looked at me, amusement heavy in his eyes. "Did you tell me that whole story just to slip in that you kissed a girl?"

I grinned. "Maybe."

"And she kissed you smelling like *that*?"

"Well," I hedged, "I did say it was underwater. I'll go change."

He stood on his tiptoes and kissed the tip of my nose, stopping me. "How does fresh chicken salad sound?" he asked. "I was going to make you cook the chicken, since you were late, but I think you need a shower more."

"I can still cook the chicken," I protested. Weakly. I *really* wanted that shower.

"Nah," he said, a habit he'd picked up from me. "Go wash off, and I'll have dinner ready by the time you're done."

I backpedaled out of the kitchen in relief. "I don't deserve you."

"Rachelle would agree," he called after me, his tone teasing. "But I don't."

I chuckled, a warmth in my stomach. I took the stairs two at a time and swung into my bedroom to pick up a pair of basketball shorts and a white tee to change into afterward, then jumped into the shower.

The hot water felt incredible. I scrubbed my whole body, twice, and liberally applied the shampoo to get all the sticky sea residue off of me. As I cleaned up, I again noticed the soreness in my body, especially my shoulders. It felt like two-day-old soreness, though. Caden's kiss had sped along the healing process. That thought made me pause. How come every incarnate but me had magical kisses?

Thinking of incarnates, I remembered Scary Gun Lady and the guy with the familiar face. Humans chasing me with guns usually turned out to be incarnates, and faces I'd seen before but couldn't place were trouble. I wondered why Scary Gun Lady was helping E-Pluribus hunt down incarnates. We weren't all on the same team or anything, but it still seemed callous to be kidnapping incarnates for a mortal company. It made me wonder again about E-Pluribus's CEO, Asker. Was he an incarnate, as I'd suspected for some time? If so, why was he hunting others?

When I emerged from the shower, I felt like I'd been reincarnated: a whole new person, free of salt residue, briny itching, and drying sweat. Thinking of Caden's minty breath, I considered brushing my teeth, but I could smell the scent of cooking meat wafting from downstairs and decided against it. Spearmint chicken salad didn't sound too appealing. I dressed hastily, my stomach rumbling at the prospect of dinner. My afternoon exertion had earned me a hearty meal.

Caden was just setting the seared chicken on top of our salad bowls as I reentered the kitchen. He gestured for me to sit at the island, and I plopped down atop the nearest stool. He came up behind me, set the bowl on the place mat in front of me, and kissed the top of my head. I heard him inhale my shampooed hair and sigh. "Much better," he mumbled before taking a seat across from where I perched.

I dug into the salad with an appetite as Caden caught me up on some of what I'd missed in the last few days. Mostly just classwork, homework, and work-work. He had spent two evenings at the hospital near the university, and he'd been able to help several patients without relying on his powers.

"It's strange," he said around a bite, "but sometimes in class I think, 'Why do I need to memorize all this when I can just heal with my powers?' But to be honest, it feels rewarding. You know? Like I'm..." he gestured vaguely with his fork, "I don't know. *Earning* my ability to heal, or something."

I shared a soft smile with him. He always looked radiant, but talking about healing others made him glow—metaphorically. He sometimes glowed literally, too, but not right now. "I know what you mean," I told him. "Knowing we can do things the 'normal' way makes it easier to justify using our abilities as shortcuts." I cleared my throat, not wanting to steer the conversation headlong into deep psychology territory. "Anything I can do to help you earn your wings?" I asked lightly.

He opened his mouth to reply but was cut off by a crash, glass shattering, and a short scream from Mom. His eyes turned to mine in shock, then we scrambled off our stools at the same time.

I flew through the house, Caden on my heels, concern for Mom foremost in my mind. The noise had been *loud,* far greater than simply dropping a plate or glass.

The living room was on the ground level, same as the kitchen. Two large windows framed with black-and-white patterned curtains accented the wall facing the street, but the farthest window was broken, and the evening air was chilling the room. A love seat took up much of the space on the left wall. To my right, sitting atop an old but still serviceable entertainment center, was the flat-screen TV. The two chairs and low coffee table in the far corner of the room, near the broken window, were covered in glass shards. The window had exploded *inward*?

Mom was kneeling on the carpet, her back to us. She seemed frozen, and I approached her carefully. "Mom?"

She flinched, then looked up at me, standing quickly. As far as I could tell, she was unharmed. Shaken, but not injured. She had been squatting over an object that was incongruous with the family room setting. A dirty brick. I noticed a shred of paper taped to it, and my eyes slid to Mom's closed fist.

Immediately I understood what had happened. Someone had thrown a brick through the window. The shattered opening over-looked a small front yard surrounded by a miniature fence that was only a foot in height, so the brick could easily have been chucked from the sidewalk or even the road. Mom had been lying on the love seat rather than using the chairs—which she usually reserved for company—so I breathed a little easier as I realized she hadn't been showered in glass. A note had clearly been affixed to the brick, but she'd torn it off and was hiding it from me.

"Are you okay?" I asked her.

Her fear-rounded eyes were beginning to return to their usual size. She jammed her hands in her pockets, looking defeated. "Just startled me," she said in a small voice.

I enveloped her in a hug, surprised at how petite she felt. She was a short, curvy woman and didn't look fragile. "It's all right," I soothed.

Caden, seeing she was in no immediate need of healing, retreated to give my mom a moment to pull herself together.

"Mom, what did you see? A person? A car?"

She shuddered, and I felt it vibrate through me. "It was a car. I heard it squeal off almost at the same time as the crash." She pulled back, wiping her face. "God. I thought this stuff only happened in the movies."

Her words ground my thoughts to a halt. Movies. My role as an incarnate meant that I was the embodiment of *all* protagonists, a representation of the stereotypes and tropes of all main characters.

That's why my powers played on coincidences that stretched believability and were usually reserved for entertainment. For the movies.

I needed to know what that note said. After all, it was probably meant for me.

"Goodness, we should clean this up, huh?" She looked around the room as if seeing it for the first time. "What a mess."

I started to ask her for the note when my phone chirped in my pocket. Grimacing, I drew it out. I had a text message from a number I did not recognize. CEASE YOUR INTERFERENCE. YOU WILL NOT BE WARNED AGAIN.

I stared at the message, my thoughts needing to rev into overdrive but instead stalling in first gear. Mom bustled about while I stood there, stunned. First a note delivered on a brick through our living room window, and now a text demanding I stand aside. *What's happening?*

Mom seemed oblivious to my shock. "I'll get the vacuum cleaner. It's too late to call someone to fix it, but we can pin up a tarp or something and I'll figure out who to call in the morning."

Caden returned, lugging a vacuum cleaner behind him, while I stared numbly at the text. "Did I hear someone call for the vacuum?" he asked brightly. He was clearly trying to keep an upbeat attitude in the face of a grim situation.

"Bless you, Caden," Mom said, moving to take it from him. He waved her away, stooping to plug the cord into an outlet partially concealed by the bulky entertainment center.

Mom suddenly looked awkward, with Caden taking the cleanup away from her. I took her by the elbow and led her to the small sofa. We sat down together.

"Mom, I know there was a note. I need to see it."

She swallowed, then looked down. "Of course, honey." She fished it out of her pajama pocket and showed it to me, an unidentified emotion behind her eyes.

The note was handwritten, every line meticulously inked to be perfectly straight and remove any possibility of identifying the handwriting. It read, Abomination. To make matters worse, it was written on a Starbucks notepad with the company's iconic logo featuring the Mermaid. Well, one of her past incarnations, anyway. I admit the logo didn't look much like her now. Anyway, the threat inherent in that choice did not escape my attention.

But what did it mean?

Suddenly I wasn't in my living room anymore.

I was trapped—in a time forgotten, and in a straw-floored wooden cage, little more than an animal. My clothes were mere tatters, rags soiled with grime, sweat, and worse. I could smell the stink of my own body, unwashed for almost a month, my long hair shorn into ugly chunks. If I could just get my hands on a sword, I could end this. In my weakened state I would never overpower them, but I could end my own life. Come back in 1,001 days like a goddess of vengeance.

A thin wail came from another wheel-mounted prison. The Dryad, wilting, her young body unable to survive so far from her tree. How had the bastards even caught her? They must have discovered her weakness. That was occurring too frequently, of late.

My hunger was a hole in my belly, a numbness that spread all the way to my head, packing it with wool. A numbness that still somehow *hurt*, gnawing on what little meat clung to my bones. I could hardly focus on one thought, much less string them together coherently. At least I had lived a long life, this incarnation. I remembered things I hadn't been able to recall in ages. I'd lived a good life, even found my angel again.

I could not summon tears. I had none left to cry.

If he were here... no. They had known. They had employed countermeasures.

His death had doomed me. I was old enough to recognize the pattern. I, too, would die by my fatal flaw, unable to reincarnate with the knowledge I needed to defeat the Voices of the People. I tried to spit at the thought, but my tongue was leather, my mouth too dry. This... this was not the will of the people. Not of *my* people.

Movement in my cage tugged at my attention. My cellmate groaned, hunkering inward on himself. His once-beautiful face was a misshapen mask of puffy bruises. A purplish eye squinted open, regarding me with a bleakness I had rarely seen in his expression. I couldn't even dredge up enough emotion to despise him.

Morgan. A year ago, he and I had been two of the most influential people in the known world, locked in a hostility as ancient as history itself. Now look at us. We'd been rendered little more than beasts, tethered to the same leash.

The smell of smoke wafted through our cage. Somewhere nearby, they'd started a fire. *No,* I thought, a desolate plea. No matter how often this happened, I was unable to stop myself from protesting, if only in my thoughts. They'd drained my willpower, but my heart still rebelled. This fire, though, was not for me.

A cheer arose from the Voices of the People, triumphant and hateful. "Abomination!" they chanted in the old tongue. The Dryad incarnate's wail turned piercing, a shriek of terror and pain piercing my very soul. Even Morgan turned away, eyes closed.

And still the tears wouldn't come.

Centuries later, sitting on the love seat in Mom's house, tears indeed stung my eyes. Sitting on the plush couch felt somehow obscene after the cage in which I'd been trapped. I shook myself, swallowing. No time had elapsed, but I felt every moment of that experience, like a vivid dream. I pushed the recollection down, willing the memory to the back of my mind. But it was sharp, jagged and painful, my mind picking at it like a tongue prodding at a loose tooth.

I couldn't remember the rest. That memory, that *experience*, stood isolated, the context eluding me. That made sense: the memory had clearly been centuries old. But how could I fight something I didn't understand? Especially when a mature, capable version of Emery Luple had been powerless to stop them?

Fear tightened my gut. I looked reflexively to Mom for comfort. But her eyes mirrored my own, weariness banished by anxiety, spooked by things she didn't understand.

I licked my lips. "Mom, why didn't you want me to see this?" The words came out of a dry throat, barely above a whisper. I needed to banish the memory, but I didn't want to forget what I was up against, either.

She sighed, consternation crinkling her features. "Because it's a mystery, and I knew if you saw it, you wouldn't let me call the police and let them do their jobs. You'd want to investigate it yourself." She seemed about to add something else but stopped herself and met my eyes in what was clearly a challenge.

The tension in me loosened, just a smidge. "You think you know me so well," I said, giving her my best Rachelle-inspired eye roll. In truth, she'd been right, but she didn't need to know that. "We can call the cops. I think it'll make us both feel better."

I didn't want the mortal police involved, but not for the reasons Mom believed. I wasn't opposed to help from mortals—I had learned *that* lesson the hard way—but I still worried over jeopardizing the lives of mortals who didn't fathom the scope of what they were getting themselves into.

But I had a man on the inside. I could bring Gregory in on this. He would make sure only the nonincarnate facts made it into the official reports. And maybe he would know more about the Voices of the People than I did.

"I'll call right now," I told her, pulling out my cell.

I flicked through my contacts, fingers still shaking from the lingering remnants of the Dryad's scream.

*G*regory Gregorius stood on Mom's doorstep fifteen minutes later, an inconspicuous, unmarked vehicle parked on the street. It was a little disconcerting, since I hadn't given him our address. I didn't ask how he found me, though. He probably wouldn't answer, and if he did, it would be something vague like "It's my business to know."

"Gregory," I said in greeting. "Thank you so much for coming."

Gregory Gregorius, the Watchman incarnate. Part captain of Seattle PD, part investigator extraordinaire. Nothing happened in Seattle that he wasn't aware of, and little happened across the world that escaped his notice, either. We had worked together in several lifetimes; for years, he had been the closest thing I had to an immortal friend.

He nodded, then brandished his badge for Mom to see. "I'm Captain Gregorius, Ms. Luple. I'm glad you called; it was the right thing to do."

I refrained from rolling my eyes at his Mr. Civic Duty speech. A tiny corner of my mind—that I would *not* be addressing, thank you very much—felt a little safer with Gregory here.

"Please," she said, shaking his hand, "call me Lynn." She nervously adjusted her shawl. "I'm glad you came. This kind of thing never happens in this neighborhood."

He dipped his head in acknowledgment of her words, never one to waste his breath if it wasn't required. His long gray coat and matching fedora made him look like a Hollywood detective. His crooked nose and the slight hitch to his step did nothing to diminish his dangerous mien.

"Please come in," I said.

He entered and immediately got down to business. "On the phone, you said someone threw a brick through your window. Why don't we sit down, and you can tell me exactly what happened."

We gathered around the kitchen island. Gregory removed his hat, his salt-and-pepper hair standing out against his dark skin. I busied myself making coffee for everyone, including Mom. She'd earned it.

I listened as Mom retold the story. She left nothing out, including the brick with the note. For his part, Gregory simply listened and asked a couple of questions. They seemed to me more designed to put Mom at ease and feel heard than to truly help him investigate the case. Chances were good that he had already formed his hypothesis.

After listening to Mom's story and extracting a few extra details, he stood. "I'll file a report and check our database. If this kind of thing has been reported anywhere else in the city, we'll establish a pattern and bring the culprit to justice."

Mom bobbed her head. "D-did you want to see the living room?"

"You were very thorough in your details, and the mystery lies in the 'who,' not the 'where.'" Seeing my mom's faltering nod of understanding, he added, "We will increase patrols in the area, especially tonight, and continuing for the next week. It is highly unlikely we will see a repeat of this incident, Lynn." He drained his mug of coffee—which he took without cream or sugar—and settled his hat back on his head. "But if we do, someone will be on hand to help you."

Mom visibly relaxed. "Thank you," she said, exuding Caden-level tones of sincerity.

"Never a dull moment, huh?" I said.

The Watchman turned to me, seeming to don the incarnate persona I knew so well. "May I speak with you outside?" he asked softly.

Unsurprised, I nodded and followed him out the front door. I closed it behind me as he stopped on the doorstep. "There's been a murder," he said without preamble.

I blinked. "Delightful. And you think the murderer is an incarnate?" He must, if he was involving me.

He shrugged. "Maybe. The victim was."

I felt ice in the pit of my stomach. The thought that it could be someone I knew flickered through me and vanished. Gregory would have informed me if that was the case. The ice burned to fire, a wave of fury rolling through me. I had *just* saved the Mermaid. Been chased down the street with guns. It didn't matter that incarnates came back 1,001 days later, murder was murder. Especially because the personality behind the incarnation often did not survive the rebirth—not intact, anyway.

"Does this have anything to do with E-Pluribus?" I asked, jaw clenched.

The Watchman had one hell of a poker face, but even so, his eyes snapped to mine a little too quickly, betraying his surprise. "You'll come, then?"

I bit my lip. "Yeah, give me a minute."

I jumped back inside and made my way to the others in the kitchen. "I'm really sorry, but Gregory needs my help."

"He needs *your* help?" Mom asked, baffled.

"There's been a murder." I cringed the moment the words were out. I hadn't meant to be so blunt.

"A *murder*?" she squeaked. "Isn't that a little hard to debunk?"

"Not if the murderer was a ghost," I countered weakly.

Her frown deepened. "That's what Gregory thinks? That a ghost murdered someone?"

"Of course not," I assured her, realizing the situation was unraveling quickly. She was on edge after everything that had happened tonight. "Gregory said he hoped I would document the murder and get ahead of any rumors." I waggled my eyebrows, hoping to defuse the worry pinching her face. "Must be high profile, yeah?"

Despite my expert de-escalation techniques, she looked like she was going to object. Then she steeled herself. "Well, if it's for work, then of course I understand." She took a deep breath, and I noticed it was a little shaky. Damn it. I couldn't leave her like this. "Promise you'll be careful?"

"I'm always careful," I lied.

Caden must have seen the turmoil in my face, because he stepped forward. "Lynn, do you mind if I stay with you until Emery gets back? If I go home now, I'll be worried until I know he made it back safely."

She looked at him in surprise, unable to contain a glimmer of relief. "Of course, Caden. We'll watch a movie or something. I'll make popcorn."

I felt a surge of relief, too. He walked me to the front door. "Thank you," I whispered to him, trying to put as much love as I could into the two words. "I'm sure this wasn't what you had in mind for tonight's dinner."

"I'm glad I'm here," he admitted. "I would've felt even more helpless from home." He gave me a quick kiss on the cheek, told me to be safe, and went back to join my mom in the kitchen.

I found Gregory standing at the window of a police cruiser already parked behind his car. Damn, he worked *fast*. He said a final word to the officer inside, then turned to me. "We should drive separately. I may not be able to leave for a while once we get to the crime scene."

I nodded and held up the keys to my car. "I'll follow you."

Gregory acknowledged my words with a grunt and ducked into his vehicle, then smoothly pulled away from the curb. I followed, my thoughts drifting—as so often happens while driving—back to the vision I had experienced in the living room. It had been triggered by the word "abomination." I occasionally experienced memories from previous incarnations, but rarely one from so long ago. Usually I had difficulty remembering much beyond the last two incarnations. That wasn't unexpected. Three incarnations ago, I had been killed by my fatal flaw, which wiped most of my immortal memories clean. Since I'd been reincarnating for generations, though, I wasn't a *completely* blank slate, just... more blank than usual. The select memories I managed to retain had unfortunately led me to the mistaken belief that I was the Monster Hunter instead of the Protagonist, and it wasn't until this incarnation, with the oh-so-gentle interfering hand of my immortal archnemesis, that I had relearned the truth.

Even if my fatal flaw hadn't wreaked havoc on my immortal memories, I still didn't often have immediate access to experiences from past lives. But as I aged, the immortal corner of my mind would fill with memories and experiences, deepening my knowledge of the past even as I crept further into the future. With age comes wisdom, et cetera.

Gregory maintained a quick speed, and we were on the freeway in a matter of minutes. We cruised across the water (well, the bridge) to the Eastside, crossing Mercer Island and exiting toward Bellevue. There wasn't much to see in the darkness except taillights and head-lights, so I paired the sound system to my music track and did my best to shut off my brain. I *did* want to know more about the Voices of the People—like, were they incarnates? Actually, I already knew the answer: no. In my reverie, I'd thought of them as a plurality, but there was never more than one incarnate of a given personification. That's why I was called *the* Protagonist and not *a* Protagonist. Maybe it was instead a title among incarnates? Even though I wanted to know more about them, I needed some distance from the fear they caused in me. I wasn't accustomed to feeling fear, mostly because I didn't like it and refused the emotion. Y'know, the healthy way to process trauma.

Bellevue included a wide mix of neighborhoods, with major streets and shopping centers located not far from quiet cul-de-sacs and meandering bike trails. Located within commuting distance of Seattle as well as the tech companies of Redmond, like Microsoft and Nintendo, Bellevue attracted both the affluent and the transient workers who seemed inherent to the infrastructure of every technology-based corporation. This all culminated in a diverse city with an invisible social turf war between the constantly shifting populace of short-term residents and the "native" Bellevue inhabitants. As cultures clashed and settled, an inspiring variety of businesses sprang up.

It was against this backdrop that E-Pluribus initially rented out a middle floor of a building blocks away from the city proper. A little over a year later, it had upgraded to a four-building campus. The campus was too large for a company with less than five hundred employees, but Micah Asker was known for keeping an eye on the future.

Gregory led me toward this campus, stopping at a gate topped with a surprisingly humble sign proclaiming this E-Pluribus's headquarters. A city police car sat at the entrance, lights off. Gregory slid up to the car, and I saw the police vehicle's driver-side window roll down. I waited, listening to one of my favorite songs, while they spoke. I took the opportunity to shoot Caden a quick text saying I appreciated him, with a GIF of a kid with a broad, guilty smile.

Gregory's car pulled forward through the gate. An arm snaked out of the police car window and waved me on, so I followed. The two-lane road led to a small lot for visitors as well as an underground parking garage. Gregory parked in the guest lot, and I followed suit.

Despite the late hour, small lights dotted the immaculate walkway fringed on either side by well-sculpted bushes with the last flowering of the season almost completely gone. Autumn was right around the corner, and several of the grounds' trees reflected that, their leaves no longer green and vibrant but still weeks away from their annual shedding. The noise of a gathering came from ahead as we approached the quad. An ambulance and two police vehicles were parked on the lawn, a group of men and women shuffling about as they waited. *For us,* I realized, as a short woman wearing a peacoat detached from the group to meet us.

"About time you got here, Gregorius," she groused, her tone

finding the neutral ground between good-natured and exasperated. "MCU's upstairs."

Gregory's eyes tightened. "Let's get going, then." He made to move forward, but she stepped into his path, her curvy form exaggerated next to his ramrod posture. Her frizzy hair—lightened by artificial bleaching and tamed by a headband—did its best to contribute a few inches to her height.

"Hold it." Her eyes slid past him to take me in. "Who is he?"

"A consultant," Gregory said. "Emery, this is Detective Laine."

She grimaced. "My friends call me Quinn or Q." There was a slight edge to the word *friends*.

I grinned. "Nice to meet you. My friends call me Emery or Emery."

She didn't laugh. "You're a little young to be a consultant, aren't you?"

"Entirely depends on what it is you need consulting about," I said without a trace of the wry amusement that question always brought on. If only she knew. I indicated Gregory with my thumb. "If anything, I've found you all are a little old. I swear, not one of you has ever heard of my blog, '*There's Always a Loophole*.'"

Quinn snorted a laugh. "Anyone ever tell you that you talk too quickly?"

"Constantly. Usually those who listen slowly."

Quinn laughed again, this time with less antagonism. "Come on," she said, her spirits obviously improved. "I'll take you up."

The three-story building she led us to was contemporary, built with more glass than stone, the windows a glossy, reflective black. Quinn slid a keycard across the access pad, and there was a faint click as the front glass doors unlocked. Going through them, we found ourselves in a marbled entry with a beautiful fountain, currently turned off, featuring the E-Pluribus logo on top. Beneath it was an inscription in Latin, the company's well-known slogan: *"Acta non verba." Deeds, not words.*

Before we could proceed further, there was another set of glass doors and another access pad. Quinn swiped the card again, and the interior door slid open of its own accord. The lobby beyond was equally tasteful, with a high ceiling, a polished receptionist's station, and three lounges artfully arrayed around a cozy hearth, a mounted flat-screen, and a coffee stand, respectively. Despite the casual luxury, the lobby felt hollow, the welcoming atmosphere undermined by its emptiness and our near silence. Quinn and Gregory, unperturbed by the forlorn impression I sensed from the room, proceeded briskly to the nearby elevators. Another keycard swipe and we piled into the spacious lift.

"What's the Marvel Cinematic Universe doing here?" I asked my escorts. At their blank stares, I grinned. "You said the MCU is upstairs."

"Major Crimes Unit," the Watchman said.

"Ah," I said, a little worried he thought I'd been serious. "That makes more sense." Beside him, Quinn just looked surprised he had responded, and was watching me with a newfound interest.

The doors dinged, and we exited. I let out a whistle at what was clearly the executive suite. Wood and glass had never looked this sexy together, giving off a vibe that reeked of both sophistication and indulgence. The old-world wooden textures perfectly complemented the sleek new-age glass, the paneling of which was impeccably placed to display interconnected computer cables, high-tech wiring, and electric cords of varying colors. Where normally offices strove to camouflage or hide the underbelly of their technology, everything here was designed to spotlight it. Even the illumination throughout the floor was patterned like something straight out of science fiction, light fixtures disguised as computer chips, motherboards, and other devices whose purposes eluded me. I was fairly tech-savvy, especially for someone alive during the Dark Ages, but most of my knowledge came via my incarnation. This version of Emery Luple had grown up surrounded by tablets and smartphones, so even though my immortal mind could remember a time before light bulbs, I came equipped with a certain level of tech experience. Yet, looking around at the functional décor, it was clear my knowledge was outclassed. Vastly.

Voices filtered from behind a set of double doors at the end of a short hallway, and we followed their sound. A suspicion was welling inside me, the identity of the murder victim becoming more apparent. The humble plaque set in etched glass and framed in wood pronounced this the presidential suite. Opening the doors, I took a deep breath to steel my nerves, then walked into the crime scene.

*a* s crime scenes go, it wasn't bad.

The room beyond the double doors was spacious and could have easily been the secret office of Tony Stark, where he worked on projects eclipsing the technology of the everyday world. It was egg-shaped, with the entrance located on the long side of the egg, the left-hand side of the room tapering just slightly. The lighting was a soft blue-white and ubiquitous, bathing everything in cool tones. I looked around for the source of the light; it didn't originate from light fixtures or wall mountings, and eventually I realized several of the gadgets in the room weren't glowing *under* the light, they were emitting it. Was that their sole purpose? If so, why did each one look so different?

An enormous desk made of glass and a polished material I couldn't immediately identify occupied the right side of the room, sitting at the "base" of the egg. Clutter, files, and doodads occupied much of the desk, surrounding dual flat-screen monitors of surprisingly modest size. They were no larger than my personal laptop screen, albeit far sleeker and likely more expensive.

The far wall was entirely glass, housing a bank of enormous windows that overlooked the quad. The windows curved slightly, I realized, further underscoring the oval shape of the room. From its size, the presidential suite must have occupied the lion's share of the upper floor.

To the left, where the room narrowed slightly—the "tip" of the egg—a low workbench lined the curving wall. It was designed to appear more like a tasteful set of cabinetry, but the countertop was so littered with projects in various stages of completion that it couldn't really hide its purpose. Oddly, the storage cupboards beneath the workbench did not have any handles. Instead, each featured an access pad with several buttons, like vaults.

The last three features of the room were the most fascinating of all. First, the ceiling. It was tiled, but every other tile was missing, revealing the wiring and hardware beyond. Metal arms and light machinery hung from more than half of the openings. These machine arms were similar to what you'd expect to find at the dentist or the X-ray department of a hospital, except they weren't encased in plastic. Their metallic designs looked sleek and polished rather than unfinished. From some of the holes in the ceiling poked scopes and other metallic contraptions containing curved lenses. Security? It was a good thing the ceiling soared a good twelve feet above our heads, or the sheer number of components would have made the room feel oppressive.

Second, the pedestals in the center of the room. Six of them, like perfectly arrayed stalagmites, jutted up from the gleaming floor. They reminded me of one of those abstract sculptures on display at artistic parks. Each pillar was a different height, the largest about four feet tall, the shortest only about two. Three were tipped with frosted domes that concealed as much as they revealed, only the shadow of some apparatus faintly showing through the whitened glass. Plants sat atop two others, their green leaves draping the pillars beneath them. The final plinth held a small slab of marble with an inscription rendered on its face by a hidden projector. It read, "Cogito Ergo Sum." Asker sure loved his Latin, didn't he? Then again, I supposed "E-Pluribus" and "Unum" should have tipped me off.

Last but not least, the body. He was in a supine position, lying with one arm across his chest and the other at his side, stiff fingers curled. One leg bent slightly; the other stuck straight out. His face was calm repose, eyelids closed, lips together. Despite all this, his waxy white skin and utter lack of movement shattered the illusion of a peaceful slumber. Oh, and his head, which was crooked at an obscene angle, like a doll's head had popped off and then been clumsily jammed back on.

His face looked so... familiar. My own head snapped back in surprise. It was him, the young man who had been tailing me in an unremarkable sedan earlier tonight. He looked different with his well-styled hair visible instead of hidden under a baseball cap, and without the animated qualities of life. But I was certain. He'd been tracking me not three hours ago, as I chased down Scary Gun Lady in her black SUV.

Quinn was watching me, her expression unreadable. Had she noticed my reaction? I couldn't detect any suspicion in her scrutiny, but her damn fine poker face rivaled Gregory's.

Two men in jackets with different acronyms embossed on their sleeves were already in the room, hovering around the body. They could have been a pair straight out of a Disney movie, the first being comically round and the second stretched tall and thin. The round one looked like a snowman had come to life, with a basketball-shaped head, doughy limbs, and a bowl-like belly. Even his hair was in on the joke: it had receded to a near-perfect circle on his head, looking like an overgrown topknot. Sweat beaded on his pale brow, and he wiped it with his sleeve, muttering under his breath. The badge suspended from his jacket read "Dawson, MCU", which I assumed was his last name... and his department, obviously. His companion was Japanese, tall and lanky, with uncombed dark hair. He was younger than Dawson, with a serious face above a chin so sharp, the Witch incarnate would turn green with envy. His name tag read "Yamamoto, ME." They looked up as we approached, and I was pleased to see their looks were speculative, not hostile. I had expected worse, given Gregory's reaction downstairs.

"Emery," Quinn said, "this is Detective Dawson of Major Crimes and our medical examiner, Dr. Yamamoto." She turned to them. "You both know Gregorius. This is his consultant, Emery Luple."

Dawson's lips went flat, the expression on his circular face reminding me of an emoji. "What kind of consultant?"

Quinn looked to me to respond.

"An unorthodox one," I supplied. Since they had given me the floor, so to speak, I added, "What have you learned so far?"

Dawson and Yamamoto exchanged glances, then Dawson shrugged. They didn't conceal it for my benefit, and I couldn't decide if that bothered me or if I appreciated their transparency. Dawson spoke first, addressing all three of us and confirming my suspicions about the corpse's identity. "The victim is Micah Asker, CEO of E-Pluribus. He was last seen alive between 4:15 and 4:30 as many of his staff headed home for the day. His death was reported at 7:26 by an employee who was working late." He checked his notepad. "Colleen Larkin."

"She's being interviewed as we speak," Quinn interjected, mostly to Gregory and me. "I got back from dropping her off at the station on Fourth just before you two arrived."

Yamamoto picked up the report. "Cause of death appears to be severe cervical fracture. There are signs of trauma at his throat. The temperature-controlled climate of the room would already complicate the time of death, but additionally, the cooling system appears to have been set to an irregularly low temperature in what I can only assume is an attempt to further obfuscate it. Rigor mortis has well and fully set in, which is inconsistent with when he was last reportedly seen alive. Dependent lividity and marbling are consistent with his current location, so the crime likely happened right here in his office. No signs of blanching, either."

I wasn't sure what that meant, but I nodded and gazed up at the ceiling. "What else?"

Dawson harrumphed. "No blood, no signs of a prolonged struggle. Look for yourself. If his damned neck wasn't snapped, we'd have ruled it natural causes two hours ago and gone home."

"Regardless," Yamamoto said, "we'll know more after I perform an autopsy."

I nodded. "Where are the controls to the AC?"

Dawson answered with a sour expression. "Looking into it. With all the contraptions in this room, I'm not entirely certain where the goddamn light switch is."

"What about the security footage?" I asked, gesturing at the... cameras?... in the ceiling.

"We're working with the building's security team to pull it."

I bobbed my head thoughtfully and meandered across the office, inspecting the strange hexagonal pedestal formation. I couldn't quite determine what they were made of, but they were a steel blue and polished so keenly they might as well have been mirrors. Their bases met the floor almost seamlessly, and I considered they might be a power source for the room's many techno-gadgets. If so, they were the fanciest battery I'd ever seen.

"What about his PC?" I asked, plopping down in the rich chair behind Asker's glass desk.

"In the works," Dawson replied.

The desk, for all its clutter, did not contain a computer tower. It must have been located elsewhere and wirelessly connected to the two monitors that stared blankly back at me. There wasn't even a keyboard.

"Was anything taken?" I asked. I received blank looks from both Dawson and Yamamoto. "Have you cataloged the room yet? Is anything missing?" I rephrased.

After a pregnant pause, Quinn sighed. "An excellent question for his secretary. We don't know yet. We need to question more of the staff—we will be conducting interviews at the station tomorrow."

I ran my fingers down the spines of the files on his desk, and the motion of my arm activated something. A flat, rectangular shape on the desk in front of me lit up, resolving into a keyboard superimposed onto the glass surface. At the same moment, the monitors came alive. ENTER PASSWORD appeared on-screen. Huh.

The desktop was glass, the keyboard like the flat surface of a tablet or smartphone. A thought struck me, and I leaned down to catch the light bouncing off the desktop from a different angle. I frowned. "Has anyone cleaned the office?" I asked.

Dawson harrumphed. "Course not. Everything is exactly as it was found."

Quinn, however, was frowning. "Why do you ask?"

"Because there don't appear to be any fingerprints or smudges on this glass keyboard." I squinted, then said, "May I borrow your flashlight, just to make sure?"

"Unum, set the lights to 100 percent," Quinn said. Suddenly, the dim room was flooded with bright lights. She looked at me and shrugged. "It's a smart room."

I paused. "Unum, can you set the temperature to 70 degrees?"

After a brief delay, a computerized voice stated, "Climate control disabled."

I realized they were staring at me, and I shrugged, then inspected the keyboard again and scratched the side of my head. "Definitely no fingerprints," I confirmed in a bright voice, mostly to address the uncomfortable silence. "Or smudges of any kind. I mean, anyone with a smartphone can tell you that you should see at least *something* if the guy ever uses his keyboard."

I tapped the M key on the flat surface of the table, and it worked just like a keyboard. And, sure enough, if I glanced from the right angle, I could now see a smudge from my finger. Feeling like my powers of convenience were driving me, I typed in the first word that popped into my brain. *Manatee.* I received a notice that the password was incorrect, and while that was annoying, a small part of me rejoiced. That would've been a stretch, even for the Protagonist. Plus, who uses sea cows as their password? Must have been on my mind from my swim with the Mermaid.

"Please don't touch anything," Yamamoto called out to me primly, his hands fluttering in a frustrated gesture. I spread my hands out in front of me apologetically and leaned back in the comfortable swivel chair.

Gregory and Dawson were taking a closer look at the body,

Yamamoto pointing out details in a soft tone. Quinn, after returning the lights to a more subdued level, was watching them but clearly keeping me in the corner of her vision. I needed her to stop, so I began muttering under my breath about the interconnectivity of vector polarity at negative intervals. I don't even know if the words coming out of my mouth made any sense, and I briefly wondered if Quinn would buy that I was a supergenius in disguise. I'd been eccentric enough, hadn't I?

After a solid thirty seconds of muttering, I broke off to stare vacantly into the open air above my head, then started mumbling again. When I was convinced my act was boring Quinn, I muttered, "Iris? Are you there?"

Several heartbeats passed, but there was no response. Damn. That was a solid three minutes of acting wasted. I tried entering the word *password* into the computer, but again I received an error. I might only have another chance or two—most modern security systems locked you out after a certain number of failed attempts.

Gregory called Quinn over, and she and the three men began speaking in low tones, moving about the space at that end of the room. If their actions were any indication, they appeared to be trying to recreate the murder. Who knew Gregory was so talented at role play?

I sighed, the blinking ENTER PASSWORD staring at me in challenge. I knew next to nothing about Asker, so I would need to rely on my powers to help me crack his password. Maybe a clue somewhere in the room? If he'd been sitting in the seat where I was now, trying to drum up a password, what was the first thing to which his eyes would be drawn? I looked up casually.

"Try one-two-three-four-five-six," came a soft voice directly at my shoulder. I bit down on my tongue to keep from yelping, my shoulders tensing with the effort to keep my butt in the chair. Seeing my aborted jump, the voice giggled quietly and added, "Boo."

"Aah! It's a g-g-g-g-ghost!" That elicited another soft giggle. I kept my voice quiet but inflected it with a joy that wasn't forced. The Ghost was another immortal friend, encased in the spectral body of a little girl. No matter how much time elapsed and regardless of where we were, she always wore the same yellow dress and matching bows in her hair—though at the moment her outline was more of a suggestion than an actual form. Thankfully. She was nearly transparent, just a wisp of a figure, literally hovering over my shoulder.

"Hi, Emery," she said, her voice sounding tinny and far away. Without the Medium to ground her to our world, the Ghost was just that: intangible and ethereal. But she was drawn to death—especially unusual deaths, like homicide—and doubly so for incarnates. When you needed answers about death, the afterlife was the best place to go seeking. Iris was my contact from the other side, and she had helped me solve crimes that stumped the brightest mortal minds. She grinned at me, her eyes alight. "Have you seen any chipmunks recently?" Oh, yeah, she also possessed the mind, imagination, and attention span of a playful young girl.

I glanced back at the others, but they were deep in their own conversation now, even Quinn forgetting to keep tabs on me.

"No chipmunks," I told her seriously, "but I've seen quite a few squirrels." It was best to play along with Iris; it often resulted in a far more constructive conversation than if you demanded answers.

"That's the problem," Iris said, her nearly translucent head hanging. "The squirrel army is winning. We need more chipmunks."

"Was the incarnate murdered here an ally of the chipmunks?"

"Micah?" Iris asked, her face screwing up. Then she adopted an exasperated look and tone, both of which came through clearly despite her transparent form and faraway voice. "No, Emery. Mr. Asker was an incarnate *human,* silly, not an incarnate *chipmunk.*" She paused, then added, "He was nice, though."

I nodded, commiserating with the loss. "Any idea how he died?"

She shrugged, her pigtails bouncing. "Suicide? I think I saw him kill himself, but it could have been someone else." She made a frustrated sound. "It's hard to remember last night, Emery. It feels like it's been forever. There were two incarnate murders today, and I've been yanked around a lot. The Bard went on and on for *hours,* outraged at her death and composing a new song about her valiant demise. Like anyone is going to sing it. Bet she doesn't even remember it in 1,001 days." Her face suddenly brightened. Er, rather, her *expression* brightened; her face remained see-through. "Do you want to hear it?"

I wasn't listening. My breath had caught at something she had said, my mind doing its best to filter her chatter. "Iris, did you say Asker died *last night*?" I gestured vaguely toward the body. "He died very recently. Less than three hours ago."

"So you don't?" She sounded very disappointed.

I shook my head, confused. "Don't what?"

"Want to hear the song!"

"Maybe in a little bit," I told her, trying to soften the rejection with a smile.

The Ghost stamped her foot. Which looked a tad ridiculous, because she was hovering a good two feet above the ground. Then her entire body tilted to look around the monitors toward the dead body. "Yup. He's been dead since last night."

I stared at her, shocked. I could've *sworn* that was the man who'd been following me a few hours earlier. I'd stake my life—no, better not. Iris knew what she was talking about.

"Wait. If he died yesterday, why are you still here?"

She put her hands on her hips and scrunched up her face indignantly. "Because you called for me, *obviously*. Just because death summons me doesn't mean I have to answer it. Sometimes I just don't wanna. I *have* a life, you know."

In point of fact, she didn't, but I wasn't going to argue with that epic pout. "Sorry Iris, I didn't mean to offend you. I've just always run into you around death."

She grinned, her stormy manner evaporating. "That's because death is the best! It's so exciting, doncha think?"

Her gleeful expression disturbed me, but I gave her a thumbs-up anyway. "You bet. Thanks, Iris. I'll keep an eye out for chipmunks for you."

Her big eyes went wide, even as she began to fade away. "Not for me, Emery. For *everyone*." Then she was gone, and I was nodding sagely at empty air.

Just for kicks, I tried her password suggestion, but it failed. I swung up and out of the chair, then plodded over to where Gregory, Quinn, Dawson, and Yamamoto were arguing quietly.

"You're all wrong," I declared, not having any idea what they were arguing about.

They froze, looking at me with varying degrees of incredulity. Gregory with the least, of course. "About what?" he queried, correctly deducing I was not referring to the conversation I'd interrupted.

"Micah Asker did not die between—what was it you said, Dawson?—right, 4:30 and 7:26 p.m."

"Then when did he die?" Quinn asked, her tone merely curious.

"Yesterday."

Dawson scoffed, but Yamamoto nodded slightly. "Yet he was seen alive earlier today by many eyewitnesses," the tall man pointed out.

*Like me.* "Eyewitnesses?" I asked. "Or did they just *think* he was in the office?"

Dawson, reddening, turned to the Watchman. "Who is this kid, Gregorius?"

He looked into my eyes for a few moments, then regarded Dawson stiffly. "He helped NYPD solve the Ahedrian murders."

The round investigator blinked. "No shit?"

"I was bored." I shrugged, noticing both Quinn and Yamamoto studying me a little more intently. "And I'm telling you, this man died yesterday. The autopsy and forensic entomologists will back me up." I paused. "Those are the bug guys, right?"

Yamamoto's long face regarded me for a moment before he spoke. "Yes."

"Good, I always get them and the language guys mixed up. Anyway, I have a few hypotheses"—I really didn't, yet, but they didn't know that, and I wanted them to be thorough—"so make sure when you question the staff tomorrow, you single out anyone claiming they physically *saw* him today, and get the details. If it isn't corroborated by multiple sources, our eyewitness could be involved in Asker's murder. At the very least, the murderer wants to muddy the waters. Since this room requires a keycard to access, make sure security pulls all accesses granted *yesterday*, especially in the evening. Discover the room's typical AC and climate control defaults and identify those with access to change them. And find out what's missing from this room. I'm not ruling out a simple snatch-and-grab gone awry. Oh, and ask when the last detailed cleaning occurred. Someone wiped off his prints from his computer."

"Anything else?" Quinn asked dryly. From her tone, I got the impression I wasn't telling them as many new things as I thought. Made sense: it was their job, after all. At least I had set them on the right track of looking at the murder from the perspective of yesterday.

I considered. "Yeah. Keep an eye out for chipmunks."

*THE GUARDIAN ANGEL INCARNATE*

**Name:** *Caden Malek*

**Height:** *5'8"*

**Weight:** *141 lbs.*

**Eye Color:** *(say it with me) seafoam green*

**Hair:** *blond*

**Classification:** *Benign*

**Bio:** *Caden Malek reincarnated as an infant and therefore has very little access to memories from his previous lives. Growing up, he was struck with strange and fantastical dreams that were, in actuality, events his subconscious immortal mind was trying to reclaim. Because of this, he was always drawn to the supernatural—which eventually led him to me. The important takeaway here is that I'm dreamy. Caden's powers allow him to heal and protect others with his shielding light—as well as to get into any brawl and come out looking clean as a whistle. Saves a lot on laundry. His natural glamour is a beatific aura that not only charms truth from the lips of those around him but also makes him really, really cute. And these bios are 100 percent unbiased, so that's just fact, and it will be on the final exam.*

∾

"*I*'m telling you," I insisted, "I saw Asker, alive and well, chasing me down last night. Then, three hours later, he's dead in his office... and has been for over a day. But I *know* I saw him."

Rachelle peered at me over her shoulder, her expression oozing skepticism. "Your mind must have been playing tricks on you, Emery. You said yourself that Iris confirmed he died two nights ago. You—" Her voice was drowned out as she pressed the blender button, the loud whizzing of the machine's blade and the grinding of ice cubes smothering her opinion. "—with it. You know?"

I shook my head in frustration, looking across the tiny table at Caden for agreement, or barring that, at least some sympathy. His brow was scrunched up, but I could tell he was on Rachelle's side. "No, I *don't* know," I complained. "I think—" She pressed the blender button again, and I snapped my mouth shut. When she finished, I eyed her flatly. "You done?"

She considered for a moment, then shook her head, sending her brunette bangs with their lighter highlights swaying. She pressed the button again, twice, then disengaged the pitcher from the cradle and poured the blended mocha into three cups.

I stated calmly, "Like I was saying, I think Asker faked his death."

Caden and Rachelle exchanged glances. I didn't like that. They'd been doing it more and more often the longer they spent as room-mates. I was glad my best friend and my boyfriend got along so well, but their ESP communication irked me sometimes. Especially when it was used against me.

"Let's try tackling this from a different angle," Caden suggested. "As you like to say, Emery, it's a puzzle. What are the pieces?"

Rachelle jumped on the idea. "We can put everything we have together and solve it, New York style!"

Caden sat forward, hands loose around his cup. "E-Pluribus kidnapped the Mermaid, and you were hired to rescue her."

I took a gulp of my mocha before responding. "Yes. Mr. Dagan hired me to save her. He set it all up: he knew the location and time she'd be at that Starbucks. For a handoff, I thought."

Rachelle's eyebrows rose. "A handoff? From who to who?" She looked at Caden, whose expression hadn't changed, and colored slightly. "I mean, from *whom* to *whom*?"

"I assumed E-Pluribus was collecting Melusina from the mercenaries they hired to kidnap her in the first place."

"And what do we know about these mercenaries?" she asked, looking between Caden and me.

"I'm not sure, but I think I know who's in charge." I described Scary Gun Lady's dark features, immaculately coiffed hair, and frightening assemblage of munitions.

Caden twisted his cup between his hands. "So, in your car chase last night, there were actually *four* different parties involved?" He listed them on his fingers. "You in your crossover, mercenaries in the black SUV, E-Pluribus CEO Asker tracking you in a sedan, and lastly, an unknown incarnate in the red sports car with a customized plate."

"A customized license plate I didn't understand," I huffed. "Don't you hate it when you see a custom plate and you know it's supposed to mean something, but it's missing a few of the most important letters and the joke goes over your head?"

"Emery, focus," Rachelle said. "If it *was* Asker in the sedan"—she held out her hands so I wouldn't interject—"then why was he tailing you himself? I mean, wouldn't he have grunts for that kind of work?"

Caden was worrying his lower lip gently with his teeth. "You're right," he said, "it does seem unlikely Asker would track someone himself. Maybe he has a brother who works for him?" He looked at me with an apologetic smile. "I believe you saw him, but what if it's just someone who looks a lot like him?"

I opened my mouth to object, but Rachelle's eyes went wide. "What if he's a body double? You know, like a bodyguard who *looks* like Asker?" Her eyes narrowed at our matching skeptical looks. "It happens in the movies all the time," she muttered defensively. "Isn't *cliché* right up your alley, Emery?"

"We shouldn't dismiss it as an option," I grumbled. "Honestly, we shouldn't dismiss *anything* as an option until we learn more. For all we know, Asker could be some kind of time-traveling incarnate."

Rachelle rolled her eyes. "Uh-huh."

Caden spoke up, unease in his voice. "If Asker is what we think he is, why would he be kidnapping other incarnates? Is there any chance he's doing it to protect them?"

"There's always a chance," I said, "but I doubt it. Melusina wasn't in any danger until they came along, and she certainly wasn't given a choice in her captivity."

Caden nodded, his golden hair catching the light. His beautiful, angelic features were troubled. "Emery," he said, "we need to protect them. *All* of them. These incarnates are being hunted simply for being what they are. That shouldn't be allowed to happen."

"Didn't you listen to the part where I told you about how I hero-ically rescued the Mermaid and helped the incarnate in the red sports car escape? I'm doing everything I know to keep them safe."

He nodded, but a restlessness behind his eyes told me he wasn't satisfied. Rachelle picked up on it, too. "Ah, I'm going to go freshen up," she said, giving us an opportunity to talk alone. She checked her watch, then glanced at me. "It's a quarter 'til. You'll be ready in fifteen or so?"

"Yeah." I was meeting a new client, a mortal one, and Rachelle had insisted on going with me when she found out incarnates were being targeted by E-Pluribus. It didn't matter that Asker was now dead or that I'd managed to help other incarnates avoid capture. Her intuition thought this meeting "smelled like a trap."

She disappeared with a satisfied nod.

Caden leaned forward immediately. "I'm worried," he said. "You can't be everywhere at once."

I shared with him what I hoped was a reassuring smile. "I know that, but the Protagonist is always where he's needed the most. In fact, I was where I needed to be most *twice* yesterday."

He held my eyes, his own somber. "You're incredible, Em. I still think you're a hero." He reached over the table and took my hand, squeezing it affectionately. "*My* hero. But if you become *everyone's* hero, and the only one, you'll spread yourself too thin. You know this. You've admitted as much yourself."

I held my breath, wondering where this was going. Everything he said worried me, but I didn't have to cop to it out loud. I didn't like the seriousness in his tone. "I know you don't want me to give up," I said. "So... what are you saying?"

He leaned forward, clearly eager, but with an undercurrent of nerves. "I think we need more people like you. An, uh, incarnate support system. You, me, Gregorius, Iris... heck, even Kolby and Melusina. We could come together, keep tabs on the incarnates in the area, watch each other's backs. L-like, I don't know, like a neighborhood watch, but among incarnates."

I frowned, considering how to phrase my response. It was a great idea, full of heart, coming from a real desire to make a better, safer world... and it wouldn't work. Incarnates were solitary beings, led isolated lives. Each of us was unique, the entire and only one of our kind. Living and dying in an endless, partially remembered cycle made it difficult to form lasting attachments. Our relationships with other immortals inevitably changed over time, with new incarnations sometimes drastically altering in personality... if we even remembered our previous relationships in the first place.

Not to mention the cold, hard fact that being an incarnate didn't mean you were on the same team as other incarnates. Many of us were just diametrically opposed: the Knight and the Dragon, the Protagonist and the Antagonist, or... hell, the Monster Hunter and *all* the monsters, just to name a few.

Caden's face fell. "I can tell you want to say no, but you don't want to hurt my feelings."

"I don't *want* to say no," I told him quickly. "I'm just worried the others won't be eager to join."

"Why not? There could be others out there like me, who reincarnated so young they don't even know they're incarnates. If I didn't have you to show me the ropes, I'd be easy pickings for E-Pluribus and his mercenaries."

I blinked. *That's* what this was about? "Caden, I've told you before that your situation is uncommon. Most incarnates are self-aware."

"Sure, but no less vulnerable." His eyes held an unusual amount of challenge. "You even classify some of them as *Prey*, Emery. And these mercenaries are predators, even if they're just the mortal kind."

"I know. I agree with you. It's why I've been striving to protect them." Realizing our conversation had come full circle and would likely loop again if I didn't stop it, I held up a hand. "I like your idea. But incarnates are lone wolves—and I'm not just talking about the Lone Wolf!" Seeing my humor fail to find purchase on his beautiful, solemn features, I let my smile fade. "Incarnates have enough responsibility just living up to the myths and legends that created them. They won't want to shoulder more."

"It isn't about that," Caden pushed, rare frustration showing through his usual serenity. "I'm not trying to set up a play group or an incarnate friend finder, I'm talking about *security*. Neighbors don't always get along, but that doesn't mean they can't have a neighborhood watch. It benefits everyone. It's just a simple community." He sighed. "Haven't incarnates tried to create a community before?"

"Of course we have," I said gently. "Unfortunately, that's part of the problem. The loss of Atlantis. The Spanish Inquisition. The Salem Witch Trials. Incarnate communities don't end well."

Caden's eyes were wide and sad. "Everything comes to an end, eventually," he whispered stubbornly. "That doesn't mean we shouldn't try to make it better while it exists." He swallowed, averting his gaze. "Maybe it's the Guardian Angel in me. I'm wired to protect others and feel helpless when I cannot. But I *know* we can do some good. Create a security system—no, a *Sanctum* for incarnates. A place of safety. Maybe it will grow into a society, but I don't mind starting small."

I wanted to help, and dammit, I didn't know if that was a natural response to his impassioned plea or a result of his glamour. I'd taken for granted the traditionally isolated lifestyle that came with being an incarnate—and I'd found my own way of coping. Of carving out a small family for myself, building relationships with a select few. Each of us found a way to live as we had before, sometimes improving, sometimes regressing. As incarnates, we were constants, or perhaps cycles.

What Caden wanted—no, what he *promised*—was something of which incarnates dreamed. A safe space, a place to belong. But it was also ingrained in us that herding together, grouping up, was *dangerous*. Such a creation always ushered in tragedy. Like a person wishing they could make someone fall in love with them, but knowing that forcing the love would end in the destruction of the relationship.

Something about tragedy tickled my memory. *That tragedy has a name,* I realized. *The Voices of the People.* I again heard the Dryad's scream reverberate through my skull, and I shuddered.

"What do you say?" he asked, all raw nervousness. "Will you just think about it? We'll start small, just a group of us, and grow to invite more as we prove that it works."

"I—" I closed my mouth, then my eyes. I owed it to Caden to think about it. And honestly, my most recent memory of the Voices of the People was from *the fall of Rome.* Societies of incarnates had always failed in the past, but hadn't the societies of mortals, too? *They* didn't stop working together. Countries, states, governments... they rise and fall like the tide, as cyclical as an incarnate. Learning, sometimes slowly, from the mistakes of the past. Caden wasn't talking about creating an incarnate *government*, either; just a support network, a system to welcome incarnates to a new kind of Sanctum. Would I deny him my support of something so inherently good for fear of failing to make it work? That didn't sound like the Emery Luple I wanted to be. Caden's Emery Luple. "I think it's a good idea," I said. I loved the flush of excitement that stole over his face, and again I worried his glamour was affecting my judgment. "Let's talk details later. Tonight?" I asked hopefully.

He shook his head, and my heart sank. "Got study group this evening, then an overnight shift at the hospital. How about tomorrow night?" He gave me a sly smile. "I can stay over, since I don't have class or work on Sunday."

"Deal," I accepted quickly. I loved it when he stayed all night with me, and it had been a few weeks. We needed to get our own apartment.

"In the meantime," Caden said, standing, "be careful while you're throwing yourself into these dangerous situations to save everyone."

"I will. But you don't have to worry so much: I have something those other incarnates don't."

Rachelle chose that moment to reenter the kitchen. "Rampant immaturity?"

I ignored her, maturely. "A guardian angel." Even so, she had spoiled the romantic moment, so I darted forward and pecked Caden on the cheek.

"And a sidekick, don't forget," Rachelle tossed out, grabbing her keys and purse from their hook on the wall beside the stairwell that led down to the front door. "Let's go, Emery. We don't want to make a poor first impression on your ambusher."

"He's a *client*." I rubbed my temple, then turned to Caden. "You sure you can't play hooky and come with us?"

"Sorry, can't miss afternoon lecture. In fact, I'm leaving now, too."

With a resigned sigh that was mostly for show, I followed Rachelle down the stairs. I was actually grateful for her company. Not because I was in any danger, but because it made meetings with strangers less awkward. Rachelle had a way of breaking the ice.

8

"There aren't really time-traveling incarnates, are there?"

I pulled into the lot of a strip mall, a café in front of us. Not Starbucks. I could be brash sometimes, but even I thought I should keep out of them for a few days, just in case.

"I know of two: the Time Traveler and Father Time. I've met Father Time once. He'll be friendly."

Rachelle looked at me askance.

"You know, 'cause time travel? I should have said 'was friendly,' but it might be in his future... never mind." I sighed. "Anyway, I doubt Asker is either of them."

"But you do suspect he's an incarnate?"

"Yes," I said. "Probably an incarnate of technology or intellect. Something like the Boy Genius, or the Inventor, or the Creator of the Internet."

The last one had been a joke, but Rachelle's eyes went round. "Bill Gates is an incarnate?"

I snorted. "Bill Gates did not invent the internet."

"Oh?" She eyed me flatly. "Then who did?"

I coughed. "We should go in," I said quickly.

"Uh-huh." She hesitated. "But first, who's the client?"

I took my phone off of its stand on the dash and flipped to the email I'd received. "His name is Mathew Atlas. He says he wants help in dispelling a rumor—of the supernatural variety, of course—concerning his family's plot of land. He didn't provide much more information than that, but I looked him up online and he goes to Highline Community College."

"And you're sure he's mortal?"

I shrugged. "Not really. His email signature doesn't say 'Mathew Atlas, mortal.' But he didn't say anything that I could take as a double meaning in our emails back and forth, so I'd say we should take him at face value until we know more." At her slight frown, I added, "This is *good* news, Rachelle. We need some normal cases to round out our blog, otherwise it'll look like a sham."

She nodded but looked unconvinced. "All right," she said. "Let's go."

We slid out of my car and I locked it remotely, hearing it chirp. It was so convenient that such a nice vehicle had fallen into my lap. Now, if only Mathew Atlas turned out to be the landlord of a vacant, nearby apartment for Caden and me, I'd be set.

I held the door open for Rachelle and then fell in behind her, scanning the crowd. The interior was softly lit, half dominated by the counter and order station, the other half dotted with round wooden tables and cushioned chairs. The smell of brewing coffee wafted about my head and immediately disarmed me. The bustle and clatter of coffee machines and plates floated out from behind the counter, where three aproned employees busied about. We were about ten minutes early, and it was almost one in the afternoon, so the café was not overly crowded. Only three tables were occupied, each with more than one person chatting with their companions. None of them seemed likely to be my potential client.

"You have a seat, and I'll order us coffees," Rachelle told me. I accepted her offer, a little surprised. She detested being seen as anything resembling a secretary, but she must have been willing to make an exception to scope out the café and feel better about the meeting.

I sat down at a table facing the entrance, a little apart from the other occupied seats. I didn't mind being overheard if we were talking mortal business, but on the off chance that this client was an incarnate, we would want our privacy.

The café doors opened, and a group of people entered chatting among themselves, immediately going to the counter to order. Two others who had been loitering around the end of the counter accepted their fulfilled orders and headed out. A young Black man caught the door as it was swinging closed, then slipped inside. His eyes roved around the room until they alighted on me. He gave a tentative smile, and as he strode toward me, I took him in.

The first thing I noticed was his fashion sense—and I approved. He wore an elevated look that ended at red kicks that gave the whole outfit a casual, effortless feel. In many ways, he was Caden's opposite, but no less attractive for it. His deep black jeans hugged legs for days, and I was suddenly glad I was seated. I didn't often feel short in this incarnation, but I estimated he was a good two inches taller than me, with broad shoulders to boot. His hair was close-shaven on the sides and back, not unlike mine, but instead of swooping up in the front, his was kept short and thick. Light hazel eyes were set in a dark, smooth face, above a nose that was just slightly too large. This single imperfection somehow improved his appearance, personalizing him, and when he smiled as he approached, his small teeth were neat and white.

"Emery Luple?" he asked. His voice didn't quite match his cultured appearance. It was youthful and pitched a bit higher than I expected. And there was a slight note of nervousness, which I hate to admit made me feel better.

"Guilty," I replied cheerfully, gesturing for him to join me. "Thank you so much for meeting me here." I hesitated as he sat across from me. "You *are* Mathew Atlas, right?"

"Oh, yeah." He laughed, shrugging off his coat and turning around to hang it over the back of his chair. "Just Matt. Actually, my friends call me Matlas."

"Nice to meet you, Matlas. Fastest friend I ever made."

He stared at me for a moment, then relaxed with a genuine, broad smile. "Oh, I just *knew* I was going to like you in person, Emery."

"You watch my blog?"

He was pleased, perhaps even a little awkward as he said, "I'm a big fan. I haven't missed a show or podcast for the last six months."

I nodded. "Since the Ahedrian murders."

"Yeah, exactly."

"It's nice to meet a fan. Half the time I'm contacted by people who just googled me. Not that there's anything wrong with that," I tacked on quickly. "I'm really glad you reached out to me. I try to make my blog seem effortless, but honestly there's only so many mysterious events that happen around Seattle. It always helps when someone brings an event to my attention."

"And he *loooooves* attention," Rachelle sniped as she stepped up to the table with three blended mochas balanced in a tray in her hands. "Hope you like coffee." She set the tray down in the middle of the table and joined us. "So, what did I miss?"

"Just introductions. Rachelle, this is Matlas. Matlas, this is my personal assistant."

"He means his business partner," she corrected. "We work on *There's Always a Loophole* together. *Equally.*" The last was said with a forced smile through gritted teeth.

Matlas chuckled, enveloping her offered hand in his. "It's nice to meet you." Was his voice suddenly a little deeper?

"Tell us what's going on," I urged as I sipped on my drink.

Matlas's good-natured grin faltered. "Well, I'm hoping you can find a loophole for my family's sake." He gently pulled the last plastic coffee cup out of the tray and leaned back. "My family has owned a plot of land in Maltby for some time. Aside from our house and some acreage, it also includes a graveyard. Paradise Lake Cemetery."

Rachelle choked on her drink, her eyes going wide. "That's supposed to be one of the most haunted places in Washington."

Matlas nodded forlornly. "Yeah, it is. Unfortunately, that draws a lot of attention. You've heard of the Thirteen Steps to Hell?"

Rachelle nodded raptly, but I shook my head and said, "Tell me."

"The graveyard is terraced and naturally hilly, so it has stone steps bridging the three different levels. However, one set of stairs did not lead to the next level, but to a bare, dirt wall. Depending on which internet gossip column you read, people claim it's actually a sealed entrance to an underground mausoleum or the natural back of a crypt belonging to a wealthy family's tomb. Either way, I'm calling BS. But the thirteen stone stairs *did* lead to nothing, which is where the urban legends got their start."

"All right," I replied, "so then, I take it from the name, people began to claim it was an entrance to hell?"

"Not exactly," Matlas replied, taking a moment to sip from his straw. Despite calling me to help debunk the myth, I could tell he enjoyed sharing the tale. Ghost stories were like that.

"Some people say going down is easy, but when you reach the thirteenth step and touch the wall, turning around will yield a vision of hell itself. There are even rumors of people becoming unable to speak after witnessing what they saw. Others, possibly the less brave, claim descending each stair reveals a new layer of hell to you, and so the Thirteen Steps to Hell are madness, one step at a time."

"That is *so* cool." Rachelle sat forward eagerly. "Have you ever tried it?"

He looked at her, surprise evident in his gaze. He probably expected her to be spooked. Ha, it took far more than that to scare her. "No," he said. "You see, the steps aren't there anymore."

I blinked. "Wait, what?"

"My family had them cemented over years ago to keep 'incidents' from happening on our property. We even hired a groundskeeper to keep people out."

I chewed on my lip. "Okay, so what's the issue now?"

"Ever since we sealed up the steps, supernatural reports and sightings have increased. Accidents occur near the graveyard on Paradise Lake Road all the time, even with the cops on permanent high alert. Strangely, or maybe tellingly, they always seem to happen on the side of the road with the cemetery. People report all sorts of oddities, too: their steering wheel just jerked in their hands, or their gas pedal suddenly pushed down of its own accord. And don't get me started on the supposed apparitions. I've been living there my whole life and have never once seen a ghost, but every week we hear another report of someone seeing a pioneer-dressed woman or a raggedy young child suddenly sitting in their passenger seat." He spread his hands. "The area is eerie. I get it. The cemetery is wooded, and there have been reports of bodies found in the woods—I'm fairly certain that's a myth, or at the very least an exaggeration. Some of the gravestones are overgrown by the woods, so maybe that's where the rumor comes from?"

Rachelle slurped the last few drops through her straw, clearly enjoying his anecdote. The way her eyes kept roaming over Matlas, I suspected she was enjoying more than just the story. The thought made me color faintly.

"Why do you want *There's Always a Loophole* to debunk the myth?" she asked. "Just to keep kids off your lawn? Isn't that a little... geriatric?" My eyebrows shot up at her word choice. Caden's scholastic pursuits were affecting her vocabulary.

Matlas, though, took no offense. He grinned, flashing his white teeth. Damn, I needed to buy some of those teeth-whitening strips. "No, that's not why," he said, sobering at his own words. "Recently, some people got hurt. Went there at night and snuck past the groundskeeper. They say they were attacked by some sort of wild animal, and their wounds apparently matched that assumption. They're suing. Now ghost hunters, thrill seekers, and everything in between keep showing up at night to come check out the 'haunted' cemetery."

The seats around us had begun to fill, but I didn't mind. This interview made it clear that Matlas was, indeed, mortal. Which meant anything others overheard would only cement my reputation as a legitimate mystery-debunking blogger.

Rachelle sat straighter in her chair. "You know, even airing a debunk video won't dissuade people from going. In fact, it could have the opposite effect: it could draw the attention of those who watch our show."

Matlas ran his hand over his face morosely. "I know. I thought of that. It's one of the reasons I chose you instead of some other ghost hunters."

I exchanged a glance with Rachelle. "What do you mean?" I asked.

"Well, back in March, you two ended the Ahedrian murders. Or, rather, you made them disappear. I know others were involved in the case, but after your video was posted, the Ahedrian murders became demystified and..." he shrugged, "that was that. I'm hoping you can do the same thing for my family."

I'd been keeping half an eye on the café's other customers. A young woman with cat-eye glasses juggled several trays as she made her way to the exit. Due to the size of her order, a small crowd had formed behind her, waiting with various levels of patience. A young man in a dark blue hoodie helped her with the door.

"I'm more than happy to take the case, Matlas," I said, returning my focus to our table. "But Rachelle's right. I can debunk the urban legend, but I can't promise it will solve your family's problems."

"I hear you. But I think you will." He smiled, encompassing both of us. "At the very least, it'll provide us with a good first step. With your track record, I'm convinced you'll reduce the amount of interest our little cemetery attracts." His confidence suddenly wilted. "Now, regarding payment..."

I cut him off, waving away his concern. "You get us access to the cemetery tonight, after dark, and we'll call it a free consultation." I leaned in, lowering my voice. "I suspect this story will greatly improve my viewership counts, and sponsors love that. As long as you don't mind a light association with some backer's logo, we'll just let the sponsors pay for this little project." I grinned. "Sound fair?"

Surprise and relief elicited a big grin from Matlas, the large smile matching his nose. "More than fair. Meet me at the groundskeeper's house at nine?"

"It's a date," Rachelle agreed, then blushed. "I mean, we'll be there. Emery will need me for the camera work."

I stood up, signaling the end to the meeting. "Matlas, welcome to the *Loophole* family."

He gathered his coat. Behind him, dark hoodie guy was exiting the café. Something about him pulled at my attention, but Matlas was talking again. "I really can't thank you two enough."

"It's our pleasure," Rachelle said, dimpling. "I'm sure Emery told you how great it is to get help finding local stories. And I'd be lying if I said I hadn't had my eye on the Maltby Cemetery for some time."

My eyes tracked dark hoodie guy as he passed the windows of the café and turned to get into his car. As he did, he looked up, and our eyes met.

It was Asker.

"Holy shit," I breathed. "Rachelle, we gotta go." I grabbed her by the upper arm and began pulling her toward the front of the café.

"Emery! What the hell?"

"Thanks again, Matlas," I said over my shoulder. "We'll see you tonight at the cemetery!"

He stood rooted in place, looking startled. "Yeah okay, I'll see you then," he called.

Rachelle yanked her arm free and turned to me. "Emery, you're being rude."

"It's Asker," I hissed. "He's here!"

Her face went white, and her mouth popped open in an O. Her pace faltered, but she turned around and waved once to Matlas, then raced after me.

"Come on," I called as I shoved open the café door, "we're going to lose him!"

Asker, having noticed our pursuit, was apparently letting his nerves get the better of him. Awkwardly, his movements stilted, he opened the door of his sedan and wriggled into the driver's seat. Eyes wide, he threw his car into reverse.

"Emery, wait!" Rachelle caught my elbow and pulled, dragging me to a halt.

I spun on her. "What are you doing?"

"Saving your ass," she snapped back. She lowered her voice before continuing. "Look around. He's not alone."

My initial thought was, *So what? We've got him!* But I clamped my mouth shut and took a quick, shallow breath. Then I looked around. I didn't bother keeping my search circumspect, since if someone was watching me, they'd already seen me barrel headlong out of the café. Now that I wasn't focused on Asker, I noticed what Rachelle had already seen.

*Four* black SUVs were parked around the lot. The windows were tinted dark, made further opaque by the reflective glare of the afternoon sun, so that I could hardly make out the silhouettes of figures within the cabs. In all four of them. *Holy crap.*

Asker's vehicle headed toward the exit from the shopping mall. My eyes followed his trajectory as he passed two of the SUVs. Damn, damn, *damn.* Rachelle was right. They'd been planning on jumping me. They *would* have jumped me, if she hadn't been paying closer attention than I.

"How did they even know where I was?" I asked without thinking.

Rachelle gave me a tight smile and skipped forward as the café doors swung open and spewed out a few more happily chattering customers. She entwined her arm in mine and yanked me forward a little harder than strictly necessary. "You're not as *Mission: Impossible* as you like to think you are," she said in a quiet tone. "Clearly, you were followed."

"So, what now?" I asked, burying my frustration. She was right, and I wasn't angry with her anyway. "Do we just... drive away?" I was certain that one of those silhouettes belonged to Scary Gun Lady, and a large part of me wanted to walk over to her and hash this out here and now. But without Caden to protect me, I didn't think this was the right time. Negotiations between a person with a gun and a person without a gun tended to be one-sided. If she was tailing me, I would almost certainly get another opportunity to confront her. With some planning, maybe I could make it on my terms.

My phone buzzed. Frowning, I looked at it. It was a new message from that unknown number, in the same text thread as the first one. As YOU AND RACHELLE DEDUCED, YOU ARE BEING TRACKED. ENTER THE RESTAURANT AND WAIT. YOUR PURSUERS WILL LEAVE.

A chill ran through me, cooling my anger. Feeling numb, I held up my phone so Rachelle could read the text. Her face drained of color. "What should we do?" she whispered.

I considered. I chafed at the idea of following an unknown arbiter's instructions. I had no way of knowing if this mystery texter was allied with E-Pluribus and the mercenaries, but as I pondered it, I realized it was unlikely. I had first been contacted by the unknown number following my "interference" with the car chase. That meant the sender was likely someone involved in the chase. Red? Or, I supposed, the texter could be involved with the people responsible for the brick through my living room window. I let out a frustrated growl. My head was starting to hurt; there were too many factions involved in this, and I knew too little of what was going on.

If Rachelle and I followed my mystery texter's directions, we might engender some goodwill with someone who opposed Asker and his mercenaries. *Assuming we aren't walking right into a trap.* But if it *was* a trap, I reasoned, Rachelle and I would likely be able to extricate ourselves from such a public place.

So. If we followed the directions, we were likely to get one of two outcomes. One, a trap. Or two, exactly what the texter indicated: we'd be safe, and Scary Gun Lady would leave for now. Either way, I'd know more about the person sending me the texts. On the other hand, if I ignored them, I might squander a chance to gain more information—and possibly an ally.

I scanned the parking lot. The sender knew Rachelle was with me. They also appeared to be aware of how events were progressing in real time. That would suggest they were watching us right now. The lot, however, was busy with people going about their afternoon business. It was unlikely I'd be able to find the texter.

I made up my mind. "I could eat," I said, gesturing to the restaurant to our left, Great as Pho.

"Oh, good," Rachelle said. "Let your stomach make the decision." The text had shaken her more than she was letting on: sarcasm was her default defense mechanism. That was something I understood very well.

I grinned, holding the door open for her. Before ducking inside, she looked over her shoulder toward the café. Matlas. We would need to create some explanation about our sudden departure when we saw him again tonight. As far as I could tell, he hadn't left the café yet, so I doubted he'd watched us scramble out of the café only to jerk to a halt, then enter the restaurant right next door. I shook my head. Today was shaping up to be just as action-packed as yesterday. *Welcome to my life.*

The restaurant was clean, with white tile flooring and small plastic tables in two rows. There was only one other pair of guests eating at a table near the entrance. I led us to the tables near the restrooms and the back exit. Menus were tucked between bottles of hoisin sauce and sriracha. An attentive woman in casual clothes approached us, and I told her we needed more time before ordering.

"How the hell did this guy get my info?" Rachelle asked quietly as soon as our server's back was turned.

I shrugged. "Or my phone number, for that matter. This is the second text I've received. The first one told me to stop interfering. I got it after the brick came through our window."

She blew out her breath in a puff. "Does this have anything to do with Asker trying to kidnap incarnates?"

I lifted my shoulders noncommittally. "I don't know. But I can't help but feel it's all related."

"Yeah. Just how many players are *in* this game?" Her words echoed my earlier thoughts.

"Too many. And with these texts and Gregory's murder investigation, we've become one of the players whether we want to be or not." A smile flitted across her face, and I eyed her suspiciously. "What?"

Her grin returned. "You said 'we' without any prompting. I'm proud of you. You've come a long way since New York."

I scoffed, my face going warm. "You know you're not my sidekick," I told her, feeling awkward. "You're a full-blown member of the team."

It was her turn to blush. She covered it by saying, "Whoever sent that text is most likely somewhere nearby, right? It would explain how they knew we were together." She trailed off, then looked chagrined. "I saw you looking around the parking lot. You figured that out already, didn't you?"

I nodded. "But I'm glad you came to the same conclusion. I've been known to jump the gun." I ignored the knowing look she sent my way. "And speaking of guns, as long as we stay in a public place, Scary Gun Lady can't attack us without making a scene."

Of course, I wasn't certain she wasn't willing to do just that. But, as usual, my timing was impeccable.

A horrible screeching, wailing sound filled the restaurant without warning, like a mix between a baby screaming, a whistle, and feedback from a microphone. An intense white light began flashing and rotating. I covered my ears instinctively, my brain rushing to catch up to my reflexes. Someone... someone had set off the fire alarm?

*"You were saying?"* Rachelle shouted.

The two other guests were already scrambling to their feet, then three cooks and our server streamed out of the kitchen and walked quickly toward the front door. Frustration dogged their expressions, so I doubted they were responsible for the alarm. Rachelle and I stood to follow, our movements slightly more contemplative.

Before I could figure out what kind of game was afoot, the back door slammed open and a petite blonde stumbled into the restaurant. Her arrival was all but drowned out by the fire alarm. She looked terrified, deep blue eyes wide in fear, sweat streaming down her face, chest heaving as she sucked in panicked gasps of air. Seeing us but not really registering our presence, she staggered forward. The door began to close behind her but suddenly flung wide, crashing into the wall a second time.

People streamed in behind her, chasing her toward us. I moved without thinking. I reached the terrified woman before the others did, shoving her behind my back, then faced the oncoming group, desperately wishing I had brought my Taser in from the car. *Yeah, Emery, because tasing one of them would really make a difference.*

As I stared down the half-dozen assailants, I caught a glimpse of something red outside the restaurant before the door shut firmly. The alarm was piercingly loud in my ear. The crowd skittered to a halt before me, sizing me up. One of them held a pair of handcuffs, and another shoved a wad of rags behind their back. I spied a rope and a knife, too.

*"Get the hell out of the way!"* the person in the lead screamed to be heard over the siren.

Rachelle had stepped up to my side, her face set in a grim mask.

*"Just walk away,"* she instructed, the calm she was striving for ruined by her need to shout.

Six on three were not good odds. Er, six on two, I guess. The woman with white-blonde hair they'd been chasing didn't look like she'd be much use in a fight. Not because she was petite, but because she looked exhausted and petrified. As I ran my eyes over her, I noticed a red spot on her face below her left eye where she'd been struck. My lips compressed into a thin line.

*"What's going on here?"* I yelled. Damn, that fire alarm was *loud.*

Several people in the crowd exchanged dark looks, and I tensed. The leader was a lean man, smaller than me, with a stringy mustache that needed a few more weeks to look complete. *"None of your business!"* he shouted, swinging angrily.

He was... slow. I caught his wrist and jerked him off balance, surprised at how easy it was. Mister mustache wasn't half as tough as he pretended to be. With a dismissive shove, I thrust him back into the crowd. They caught him, looking as surprised as I was.

There was a frozen moment, everyone stunned, the fire alarm shrieking. Then everyone sprang into motion at once.

A big woman pushed out of the crowd and rushed at me, a nonverbal shout rivaling the alarm as she charged. I sidestepped, sticking my foot out and slapping her back as she passed. She toppled over my stiff leg and went flying into the table and chairs behind me, the clattering of plastic and plates muted by the alarm.

I had no time to celebrate my near-flawless aikido execution. Two more people surged forward, one of them wielding a small knife. A third was doubled over to my right, clenching his stomach from something Rachelle had done.

A meaty hand jabbed into my shoulder, my musculature absorbing most of the blow. My four-times-a-week workouts were paying off. The knife flashed before my face and I quickly stepped back to avoid its reach. The blonde whose entrance had started all of this had her back to the counter a dozen feet away, watching the fight with round eyes and a gaping mouth. I couldn't tell if she was surprised at the helping hands or catching her breath, or both.

I shoved the unarmed man into the woman with the knife, buying myself a moment's respite. Rachelle darted forward, grabbing the unarmed man before he could recover and delivering a swift kick to his tenders. He let out a gasp that was inaudible over the alarm, doubling over. Ouch.

Knife woman lunged forward, disentangling herself from where her companion had fallen. I stepped forward to intercept her, catching the knife's edge along my right forearm. A line of pain tugged at my senses, but my focus was tight and adrenaline dulled the sensation. My other arm swung in hard from the left, snapping her head back as I connected with her chin, and the knife tumbled out of her fingers.

I bent down to collect the fallen weapon just as the heavyset woman, who'd regained her feet, tried tackling me from behind. My sudden movement caused her to instead crash *over* me. She hit the tiled floor, hard, her legs splayed over my shoulders. I shoved them to the side and stood, brandishing the pitiful knife at the remaining crowd.

... which wasn't much of a *crowd* anymore. Three men—when had Rachelle kneed the third one?—bent over or squirmed on the ground, nursing wounds I winced at, even knowing they deserved them. Rachelle may have been a one-trick pony, but *damn*, it was an effective trick. The woman I'd just sent sprawling was struggling to her feet, looking woozy, matching the expression of the woman who had taken one to the chin and dropped the knife. The mustached leader, more or less untouched, looked around at his crew with disbelief.

I didn't blame him. Rachelle and I had handled the crowd like they'd been little more than toddlers. I guess that's a bit of an overstatement; I *did* have the stripe of pain on my forearm declaring I wasn't completely unscathed. Blood was starting to drip down my arm, but it was a superficial wound.

"*Leave!*" Rachelle commanded, roaring to be heard.

The leader hesitated, his gaze darting to the blonde woman, but then he seemed to make up his mind and helped guide two of the men to their feet. The group hobbled back toward the emergency exit. Without a word, Rachelle and I moved to stand protectively near the blonde while they filed out.

"*Are you okay?*" Rachelle asked the woman, still shouting.

The blonde nodded shakily.

"*Come with us,*" I yelled. "*We need to get out of here.*"

She blinked at me, fear giving way to emptying adrenaline, leaving her exhausted and slightly dazed. "*My car...*"

Rachelle shook her head. "*You aren't driving like this. Come with us. We'll return for your car later.*"

The woman hesitated, then nodded. Rachelle and I exchanged glances, then headed out the front entrance of Great as Pho.

I scanned the parking lot. All four black SUVs were gone.

A mixture of relief and fierce pride enveloped me. We'd fought off *six* people at once and rescued the damsel in distress. With a grin that was probably inappropriate, I led the way to my car. When there was so much going on that didn't make sense, it was the little victories that counted most.

## 10

*I* glanced in the rearview mirror as I drove back to Rachelle and Caden's apartment. I felt like a taxi driver—Rachelle had chosen to sit in the back with the woman, hoping to make her feel better. As we neared Rachelle's apartment, the woman finally began to relax. She looked like hell. Her hair was disheveled, her makeup streaked from where it had run as sweat and terror had poured out of her. The spot below her eye was purpling and starting to swell. The hair color and petite frame really de-aged her, I realized. She was probably fifteen years my senior, her heart-shaped face and piercing eyes carrying more maturity in them now that they'd returned to their usual dimensions.

"Thank you," she said, choking on the simple words. Rachelle rubbed her on the back, sympathy in her eyes. I hid my surprise; Rachelle was fierce, brave, and sarcastic, but she *detested* others being dependent on her. That nurturing, caregiving skill was Caden's realm of expertise. To be fair to Rachelle, she hated being dependent on others, too.

Yet as I watched, she buried her distaste and jumped in without hesitating. It reaffirmed a simple truth: Rachelle was one of the most capable, dependable people I knew.

"I'm Rachelle, and he's Emery. What's your name?"

The woman gave a small smile, wincing as the muscles pulled in her face. "I'm Hope." Her eyes flitted from Rachelle's to mine and then away. She looked ill, and I realized that she probably hadn't been thinking clearly when we'd coaxed her into the car with us. Now she couldn't leave.

I pulled my eyes back to the road ahead of me. "Glad we were there to help you, Hope." I tried to keep my voice casual, conversational. "We're almost to Rachelle's apartment. We haven't taken you very far. We just wanted to make certain you were okay before you got behind the wheel."

She smiled thinly, bobbing her head in jerking motions. She still looked cornered, tense. I didn't blame her.

"I'm Emery Luple. Does my name sound familiar to you?"

Her brow knit. "I don't think so."

I smiled, swallowing a dose of disappointment. I hadn't asked because I was famous for my blogs or my channel. I had asked because I *was* well-known in the incarnate world. "No worries," I assured her, striving to keep my tone light. "I have a blog called *There's Always a Loophole.*"

"Oh. Sorry."

"You looked familiar," I tried again, changing my tactic. "Like maybe we'd met in a past life or something." Again, I kept my tone nonchalant—a mortal might think the comment weird, but they'd just laugh it off. An incarnate, however...

Hope had frozen. "Oh," she breathed, "you're *incarnates.* Thank god." She visibly relaxed, the rigidity in her every movement deflating as she sank back into the seat.

"Well, technically, I'm a mortal," Rachelle said.

"Technically?" I ribbed.

"Hey, you said I was officially a member of the team!"

"Yeah, but as, like, the token mortal."

A single eyebrow arched over a dangerous expression. "Oh?"

"You know what I mean!" I caught the glimmer of amusement beneath her outwardly thunderous expression, and I burst into laughter. A beat later, she joined me.

"I'm the Loophole."

"I'm the Virgo."

Rachelle lit up. "No way, like from the horoscope? I'm a Taurus. Are you *all* real?"

Hope gave her a funny look. "Wouldn't it be odd if I was the only one?"

She paused. "Good point. You're going to fit in nicely with us, I can just tell."

I coasted onto Rachelle's street. "Those people who were chasing you, do they work for E-Pluribus?" I asked.

"I'm not sure. They've been following me since yesterday, but I was able to elude them until this afternoon. They walked right up to me while I was on my way to my car. I had parked out back to avoid people, but that meant there was no one around to stop them from..." She trailed off, gingerly touching her cheek. "I managed to slip out of their grasp, so I ran to the nearest building." Her face creased. "Wait. E-Pluribus? You mean... the tech company? What would *they* want with me?"

I pulled up to the apartment, parking in Caden's designated spot since he was going to be working late. "We aren't sure. But there've been reports of them kidnapping incarnates recently."

"Really? Which ones?"

I opened my door and exited the vehicle, waiting until they were out before I responded. "Again, we aren't sure how deep it goes. We've only been able to identify one. Well, two, now. You and the Mermaid."

Rachelle levered her bag onto her hip and dug in its depths for her keys. "Do you think there's a common thread between the two of you?" she asked.

Hope shrugged, growing even more relaxed now that we were out of the car. It probably helped her to not feel so trapped, so dependent on the will of others. "Other than being incarnates, I don't think so. I've never met her."

Rachelle unlocked the door. "Well, welcome to my humble abode," she said. "It's not much, but it's safe."

"Thank you," Hope repeated. "Will you show me the way to your restroom?" She ran a hand through her hair and grimaced. "I'd like to wash up."

"Of course."

As Rachelle led Hope down the hall to the right, I took a seat at the kitchen table. I pulled my phone out and stared at the text from the unknown number. It only had five digits. Taking a deep breath, my heart starting to pound, I pressed the number to call back. Immediately, a chime sounded, followed by an operator's upbeat voice informing me my call could not be completed as dialed, and would I please check the number and try again.

I disconnected, my mind roaming.

My thoughts turned to Asker. He'd been murdered, possibly by an incarnate, but I'd seen him twice since. Alive and well. I had long suspected he was an incarnate, though I had no evidence. Except, arguably, his entire life story: business savvy, entrepreneurship, and technological genius all rolled into one expensive package. And Gregory Gregorius agreed with me, which was not insignificant. The million-dollar question, though: which incarnate was he? The Boy Genius? The Eccentric Tycoon? The Dragon?

Okay, I admit the last one was unlikely, but in the legends, dragons *did* always guard hoards of treasure, and Asker was reportedly worth billions. Ooh, and he had been slain, so I kept it on the list.

Maybe I was looking at this from the wrong angle. Maybe he was the Necromancer, a sorcerer who dabbled in dark arts to raise the dead and command them. No, that didn't make sense. Necromancers raised others; they weren't dead themselves. Maybe he was the Lich? A powerful sorcerer who had died but refused to go to the grave, making him undead—the living dead. Like the Zombie or... well, the Ghost, I guess, technically fit that description, too.

I was cruising off topic. Why did I think Asker was a sorcerer? It would make more sense if *he* was the Zombie incarnate.

Oh.

Unholy shit.

The more I thought about it, the more I warmed to the idea.

Several things clicked into place. When he'd been in a hurry that afternoon, his movements had been stilted and jerky, like he was unaccustomed to his own body. In urban legends, zombies usually shuffled about, unable to summon the natural agility of the living since their bodies no longer pumped blood through the veins and rigor mortis hampered their physical abilities.

The corpse I saw last night was certainly dead. But the Zombie could have faked it without much effort. It would also explain why he was seen alive and well earlier the same day. Hell—or perhaps I should say *purgatory*—it even fit with Iris's story. She had seen Asker die the day before. And he probably had. But his incarnate specialty wouldn't let him pass on to... well, to whatever awaited the departed. Instead, his body reanimated. Did zombies have unfinished business in the stories, like ghosts did? I didn't think so, but if he did, it might be a fatal flaw I could exploit.

A few details weren't perfect. His neck appeared to be snapped when I saw him in his office, but it hadn't appeared so in the car or the café. But as an undead incarnate, he might well be capable of pushing his physical body beyond normal limits of pain and... well, death.

Where would his Lair be, I wondered. Every incarnate had a domain they called their own, a place of safety and power. For Benign incarnates, like Caden and me, those domains were called Sanctums. Just taking a stab in the dark, I'd say the Zombie was a Malevolent incarnate. I mean, zombies were known for rising from graveyards in the slavering pursuit of brains. Malevolents' domains were called Lairs. So, where would the Zombie's Lair be located? The answer hit me an eyeblink later. A cemetery.

My breath caught. *No way.*

Was all of this—E-Pluribus, Asker, the mercenaries, the Mermaid and the Virgo, Matlas and Paradise Lake Cemetery—was it somehow all interconnected? I thought back to Matlas's description of the supernatural events. Cars veering off the road. Bodies found in the woods. Apparitions. Were the powers of the Protagonist *this* obvious?

This *powerful*?

I dismissed the thought. But the fact remained: what if Paradise Lake Cemetery was Asker's Lair?

I know what you're thinking: it's only chapter ten. The central mystery is never solved this early. Something's up. That's fair; I probably wouldn't believe it, either. But I *will* enjoy rubbing it in your face when I prove to be right. Maybe Asker isn't the central mystery—ever think of that?

Even if I was wrong, I could feel my mind winnowing the field of possibilities—and I was getting close. He might be the Undead or something zombie-adjacent, but I must be on the right track. Breathing a little easier, I took a moment to appreciate my deductive conclusions.

Of course, that only brought me face-to-face with the staggering number of mysteries arrayed before me and how much I still didn't know. Why was Asker kidnapping incarnates off the street? And, now that I thought about it, it was strange that activity had been disclosed to Mr. Dagan and thus to me. Unless E-Pluribus had captured far more incarnates, and the Mermaid was a result of them slipping up. *Or* she could have been the *first*, and their errors could be chalked up to inexperience.

And who had killed Asker? Even though it was within the realm of possibility that the Zombie incarnate could have committed suicide—or tried to—his snapped neck was a convincing counterargument. I suspected foul play, but that might be exactly what Asker *wanted* if he was trying to throw off the police.

I could feel that headache coming on.

Just then, my phone buzzed. I snatched it off the table, expecting another message from my mystery texter. Instead, it was the King County Medical Examiner's Office. Well, would you look at that.

I answered, "Corpse walk out on you already?"

There was a beat of silence, then a woman's polite voice said, "E-excuse me? Hello, this must be Emery Luple."

"It is. Tell me I'm right: Asker's corpse ran away, didn't it?"

"Um, I'm not sure. I mean, he didn't say..." She stammered, clearly flustered, then took a beat to compose herself. "Mr. Luple, this is the office of Dr. Yamamoto. He wishes to speak with you as soon as possible."

"Great. Put him on."

There was a pause. "My apologies. Given the sensitive nature of the discussion, he requests you meet him at his office."

I tipped back in the chair, looking down the hallway. The bathroom door was firmly shut. "I think my time might be better spent chasing down your lost corpse," I tried again. "If Dr. Yamamoto could kindly confirm it walked out on him?"

"One moment, please." I heard shuffling sounds, followed by muffled voices talking rapidly.

More shuffling, then a familiar voice came on the line. "Emery." It was Gregory. He sounded stressed.

"Oh, hey, Gregory," I said, replaying my words to the assistant in my mind. I hadn't meant to be flippant, but there was perhaps the slightest possibility I'd come off that way. "What's up?"

"You know why I brought you in on this. I don't care if your process is different than ours, but I *do* expect you to respect our process. If you can't do that, you're out."

I'd never had a father, but I imagined that if I had, he'd speak to me like that when I was disappointing him. I sank into myself, becoming smaller.

"Of course. Sorry." I looked at the ceiling. "Look, I've got a *mutual friend* of ours in my friend's apartment. I'm not sure I can disentangle myself."

"I see. If that changes, we will be at the ME's office until at least five."

I nodded, then realized he couldn't see it. "Sounds good. I'll see what I can do." I hesitated, then asked, "Any chance the corpse is missing?"

The silence on the other end of the line went on for so long, I checked my phone to make sure the call hadn't been disconnected. *"This* is why I want you on this case, Emery," Gregory finally said, awe in his gruff voice. "Get down here if you can." The call disconnected.

"Goodbye," I said cheerfully to the phone. I sighed. It felt good to be wanted on the case. It felt even better to be *right*. Asker's corpse had disappeared. He was the Zombie. Well, he was undead at the very least. I was sure of it.

Rachelle entered the kitchen, unaware that I was basking in self-congratulatory emotions. She sat down heavily across from me. "She's going to be okay; she just wanted a few minutes alone. So, what are we going to do about her?"

"Huh?"

Her expression turned exasperated. "What were you doing out here? I thought for sure you were coming up with the next step."

"I just received a call. Gregory needs me down at the medical examiner's office."

She made a face. "Ew. Medical examiner is just a fancy name for coroner, isn't it?"

"Not exactly."

"But there are... bodies there, right? So what's the difference?"

"Not sure, but they *hate* it when you call them coroners." I gauged her reaction. "You don't flinch at all the spooky stories Matlas tells us, but you get squeamish about bodies?"

She rolled her eyes. "I mean, yeah, decaying, moldy bodies that used to be people are creepy, with a capital *gross*." She shuddered. "Why does Gregory need you, anyway?"

I grinned. "Something about Asker's corpse disappearing."

"*What?* That's a pretty big development."

I shot her a triumphant look. "Not if he faked his death, as I believe someone brilliant suggested earlier today." I ran her through my he's-totally-the-Zombie-incarnate theory.

"Huh," she said when I finished. "I'll do some research, see if there are any Washington zombie urban legends. If I don't find anything, I'll see if I can dig up some information on where Asker came from and track down any urban legends from around there."

I examined her words, thinking. "That could be exactly what I'm missing," I mused. At her questioning glance, I elaborated. "I may have been thinking too broadly. The Zombie is an archetype incarnate. But what you just said made me realize that Asker is more likely a persona incarnate."

She nodded. "Caden mentioned archetypes and personas before. Like how the Guardian Angel is the persona and Angel is the archetype, right?"

"More or less," I allowed. "Put simply, personas are cultural variations on the widespread urban legend." That was a very succinct way of putting it. As usual, the full story was a little more complicated.

"Um, what are we going to do about Hope?" Rachelle asked, keeping her voice low.

I leaned back to confirm the bathroom door was still closed. "I'm not sure. I don't want to leave her alone, but I also don't want to dump her on you."

Rachelle shrugged. "I'll handle it. You go see Gregory. If you aren't back before I need to leave, I'll see if Caden can keep her safe for the night."

I shook my head. "He won't be back 'til late. He has a night shift at the hospital." I drummed my fingers on the table. "I'm afraid what will happen if we don't provide a safe place for her, though. She shouldn't go home tonight."

"Any ideas?" When I didn't answer, she exhaled loudly. "Okaaaay, we need to create a plan. Caden's incarnate neighborly watch isn't looking like such a shabby idea now, is it?"

"You eavesdropped?"

"Not really. He ran it by me before he brought it up to you. For the record, I think it's a good idea." She glanced at the wall, in the direction of Hope. "And it's looking better by the day. You can't argue the fact that incarnates aren't safe right now."

I nodded, not wanting to discuss this. For some reason, it bothered me that Caden had spoken with Rachelle about it before he'd told me. It wasn't jealousy. It was... something else. *I* was the incarnate. The incarnate world was something I shared with Caden, but he'd talked to Rachelle about his plan to create a support system for them before he talked to me about it. Thinking back, he'd also been nervous to bring it up with me. I felt a stab of resentment that he could speak to Rachelle so easily, but not me. *There's a word for that, Emery.* I pushed the thought away. I should be happy that he wanted to build a safe space for incarnates with me. It didn't matter who he told first. The word for that is *ridiculous.* I shook the feeling off.

"I agree. I'll talk to Gregory about it today."

Rachelle nodded, eyeing me as if she could read my thoughts. "His dream is to build something lasting with you. Something that improves the world of incarnates forever."

I knew what she was doing. "I guess. I mean, I know." My voice dropped to a near-whisper. "I just don't want it to fail."

"The neighborhood watch?"

"His dream."

Her eyes softened. "It might. But from what you've told me and from the guy I know, I'd say the Emery Luple who wouldn't try something bold for fear of it failing died in a desert several years ago. I've never known that guy, because it's not who you are now. You can do this." She gave me an encouraging smile. "And if it *does* fail, then your job is to be there for Caden. To keep his dream alive."

I shook my head, but I was smiling. "When did you become wiser than me?"

She scoffed. "I've *always* been wiser than you. You're just becoming wise enough to realize it."

I rolled my eyes in a perfect imitation of her. "I don't know what I'd do without you, Rachelle."

"Excellent. Then this is the perfect time to negotiate a raise."

Hope came around the corner, a towel around her shoulders like a shawl. She was transformed. She had scrubbed her face free of the streaked makeup and washed her hair, which hung in damp, white strips down to her shoulders. I realized I expected to see darker roots peeking out from within the thick white locks, but either her hair was recently dyed or it was a part of her incarnation. Her heart-shaped face was warm and her smile grateful as she tentatively found a place at the small table. Without the makeup, she looked more mature, but it didn't make her look any *less.* She had a natural, earthy beauty to her. It almost gave her a regal countenance.

"Darn," I said, snapping my fingers. "No time to negotiate a raise with Hope here. We wouldn't want to be rude and talk shop in front of her."

Rachelle rolled her eyes, then turned her attention to Hope. "You and I are going to have a ladies' night."

Hope's eyebrows raised. "Oh? You won't be staying, Emery?"

I rose from the chair, giving her an apologetic smile. "Sorry, I got called in to work."

"But I thought you said you were a vlogger."

"I freelance on the side," I evaded, not wanting her more deeply involved with E-Pluribus than she already was.

"I understand." She stood, then stretched out her hand. I took it awkwardly, and she covered my hand with her other one. "Thank you for saving me today. Words cannot express my gratitude."

I extricated myself with a flush of embarrassment. "Just glad I could help," I managed, giving her my best signature grin. I'm told it's a little crooked and lot cocky. And I know that's true, because I may have a bad habit of flashing it in the mirror when I get ready in the morning.

But I will deny it if you ever repeat that.

## 11

*THE ARTIFACT INCARNATE*

**Name:** *Artie (but that's just what I call him)*

**Height:** *varies from super small (like when he was a ring) to super tall (like when he was a spear)*

**Weight:** *varies from ounces to tons depending on his form*

**Eye Color:** *n/a*

**Hair:** *n/a*

**Classification:** *varies—usually Benign, but he killed a lot of people as a spear, and once, as the Necronomicon, I'm pretty sure he was Malevolent. Predator, at the very minimum.*

**Bio:** *Reincarnating as anything from an ocarina to a book, the Artifact has a wide array of powers that are functions of his form. To put it simply: when he's a weapon, he stabs; when he's a wand, he spells; and when he's a book, he's insufferable. Legendary objects that become incarnates differ from the rest of us in strange ways. They all seem to have some level of sentience, but the extent is tough to measure. Artie, for example, never shuts up—even when he doesn't have a mouth, he finds a way. The Vorpal Blade and the Excalibur, by contrast, don't have much to say... but, holding them, you can't help but feel a sort of awareness from within* them. *Oh, and that's another thing. Excalibur has never reincarnated because it's never died (or broken, or... rusted?), but the Artifact is constantly getting snapped in half, or burning up in the fires of Alexandria, or falling down my sink's disposal (don't ask). Each time, that particular item is never seen again. But thank goodness there's always a Malevolent incarnate like the Sorceress around to write a new spell book or something, so the Artifact will inevitably return exactly 1,001 days later!*

~

"Oh, sweet pea, you're so thoughtful to check up on me. I'm doing fine, really." Mom's voice came over my car's speaker. "The window repairman finished a few hours ago. He took measurements, boarded up the hole, and said he'll be back Wednesday to replace it."

"Good, I'm glad you're not at home with a gaping hole in the wall," I told her, equal parts sincere and amused. "I'm going to be out late tonight. Staking out a cemetery at night for my channel."

"Spooky," she exclaimed, the warmth in her voice telling me she was still touched I had called. "Rachelle or Caden going with you to keep you safe from the ghouls?"

I laughed. "Rachelle. She'll be there to film, too."

As we spoke, I pulled into a staff parking lot a street or two over from Seattle's Harborview Medical Center. The ME's office was part of the hospital complex, I realized. That made sense.

"Well, don't worry about me, honey. I won't wait up."

"All right, Mom. Text me if you need anything. I'll have my phone on me."

"I don't suppose you happen to have Captain Gregory's phone number handy?" she slipped in, so innocent she might as well have sent an angel emoji.

"W-why do you want it?" I stammered. I did *not* like the direction I thought this was headed. Best to yank this out by the roots right here and now.

"Oh, you know, just in case another brick comes through the window or something like that?"

"Okay, you have a pen?" I asked.

"Sure do. What's the number?"

"9-1-1."

There was a moment of silence, then, "Ha ha, very funny. Come on. He's single, right? And you've got to admit, he's ruggedly handsome in a law enforcement, authoritative sort of way. You see it, don't you?"

"Ugh, ick, no!" I made spitting noises. An hour ago, I had been thinking of him as a father figure. That somehow made it so much worse. "Mom, remember when I came out to you and I made you promise we would *never* have this conversation?" It was a memory pulled from before I reincarnated, so *technically* it had never happened, but she didn't have to know that.

"Oh, please. I only agreed to that because you were nervous and I wanted to make you feel comfortable. You can't hold me to a promise I made to help you feel better in a moment of vulnerability."

"*What*? Mom! Those are, like, the most important promises to keep!"

She laughed. "Fine," she relented, "we don't have to talk about it. But I would still like his number."

I stepped out of my vehicle and began heading toward Yamamoto's office, transferring the call from Bluetooth to handheld. "Uh-oh, I think I'm going through a tunnel."

"Sweet pea, that doesn't even work in *cartoons* anymore."

I chuckled. "But does it still work on moms?"

"Only the cool ones. Then—before I lose you, have a good night. I love you."

"Love you, too, Mom. See you later."

I hung up, feeling a strange mixture of relief and melancholy swirl inside me. I decided I had enough going on, so I shelved the feelings to deal with another time. That's the healthy way to deal with problems, kids.

A few sidewalks, crosswalks, doorways, and hallways later, I found myself in Yamamoto's office. The front office looked like a doctor's lobby: a lone middle-aged woman seated behind a tall counter and two closed doors leading into the back area. There were seats, magazines, security cameras. It was just missing a fish tank.

I approached the woman, whose name tag read "Valerie." She was speaking quietly on the phone with someone but acknowledged me with a warm, welcoming smile. I could tell from her pleasant voice that it was the same woman I had spoken with earlier.

She hung up a minute later and beckoned me forward. "Hello, young man," she said, her eyes made owlish by her large, circular lenses. "How can I help you?"

"My name is Emery Luple," I told her, tensing with the expectation that her smile would slip.

It didn't. If anything, it widened. "Oh! Doctor Yamamoto and Captain Gregory will be so pleased you made it. I'll buzz you in. Go ahead and walk through the door to your left."

"Thank you." I heard the door click, and I pushed my way through. Valerie bustled over to me, then led me down the narrow hallway. We passed a few doors open to spaces that reminded me of examination rooms in a doctor's office. The hallway widened into an open workspace where Gregory stood over Yamamoto, both intent on the computer screen before them. The hallway beyond had several doors with darkened windows, and I thought about what Rachelle had said about decaying bodies. I was glad Gregory and Yamamoto were out here instead of in one of those rooms.

Gregory glanced over at me. "Glad you could make it."

Yamamoto looked up and offered a small smile in greeting. "Emery. Valerie informs me that you predicted our vanishing cadaver." The two flat-screen monitors behind him displayed very different images. The monitor on the left was clearly the building's security system; Gregory and Yamamoto must have been reviewing the footage in the hope of discovering who took the body. The other screen was more of a mystery. It displayed four rows of black boxes. The first box was almost completely solid, but the others contained lines and squiggles in seemingly random—ah. They were fingerprint patterns. It looked like the good doctor was able to extract finger-prints from the neck wound before Asker got up and walked away.

I waved away his comment, the neutral tone of his remark making me unsure if it was a question, an accusation, or a compliment. "Let me guess. Security shows nothing." Asker, zombie theory aside, was a brilliant tech man. I was betting he could circumvent the security with relative ease. Hmm. Was there a sort of tech-zombie hybrid urban legend out there?

Yamamoto nodded reluctantly, his thin lips turned down. "Indeed. If you watch the time stamp on the upper right, you'll notice it resets. The culprits somehow put the circuit on a loop."

"Any leads on who was responsible?" I asked.

He shook his head, his long face and careful expression unable to mask his frustration. "No. And I do not like guesswork. I prefer evidence."

I grinned. "We'll make a good team, then, because guesswork is my specialty." I took a deep breath, harnessing my inner Sherlock Holmes. "Behold my powers of deduction: based on the fact that Micah Asker is the foremost technological prodigy in the world, that he died in his private office under mysterious circumstances, and that his remains inexplicably disappeared from your care in spite of your security measures, I believe we can reasonably conclude two facts about the murderer. Firstly, they are someone with an impressive pedigree in tech, capable of accessing Asker's secure office, tampering with the office's climate control settings, and circumventing security. Secondly, the murderer is the one most likely responsible for the theft of your corpse, for the selfsame reasons I listed above." I ended my speech with a little flourish and a half bow.

Yamamoto did not look impressed. "That is *not* deduction."

"What?"

"The word you should be using is *induction*. And speculation, besides. Nothing you said would hold up in a court of law."

I looked around ostentatiously. "It doesn't appear we're *in* a court of law," I pointed out.

Gregory was watching me, his face expressionless, giving no clue as to what he was thinking. "Emery. A word?" Without waiting for a reply, he walked down the hallway, not looking back to see if I followed.

I did. Of course. I was 90% sure this had to do with incarnates, but 10% of my brain nagged me that it was about Mom. I told that small corner of my mind to go to hell.

He led me around the corner and a dozen feet down the corridor, then spun around and said quietly, "You said 'is.'"

I blinked. "What?"

"You said 'Asker *is* the foremost prodigy.' Present tense. You believe he's still alive."

I grimaced, irritated at my slip. How did Gregory do that? Ask questions without actually *asking* anything?

"In a matter of speaking," I said, matching his low tone. "Rather, I think he's undead." Gregory didn't react, just continued to stare at me, compelling me to continue. "The Zombie, or a persona incarnate derivative," I expanded.

Gregory's eyes unfocused as he chewed on that. Otherwise, his features remained stoic. "Interesting. Tell me more."

I swallowed the automatic retort I'd give if this were Rachelle and instead bobbed my head eagerly. "Well, to start, I've seen him twice since he was murdered." Again, Gregory didn't react. He took the fun out of everything. "First, the night his body was found, he was tailing me in my car. Probably in an attempt to reclaim the Mermaid. Then, at a café a couple of hours ago. I was meeting a mortal client for a gig, and Asker casually walked in. He looked a little bit like a... like a puppet, I guess, with stilted and awkward movements. That set off alarm bells in my head. Oh, and he was there to lead me into a trap, but I eluded it."

"Trap?"

One word. In response to all of that. Sigh. "Yeah. He's working with some mercenaries. I don't know who they are, but they drive black SUVs, and there were three or four of them in the lot, waiting to jump me. Rachelle and I spotted them, so we evaded the trap."

"Are these mercenaries the ones who threw a brick through your mom's window?"

I considered. "I don't think so. If they were, they wouldn't have to resort to trapping me at a strip mall. They could grab me pretty much anytime if they knew where I lived."

"Not necessarily." His expression hardened. "Be careful. You should have told me all this last night. You're risking your mother's safety."

I nodded, feeling a spike of alarm. The Watchman did not waste words. If he thought Mom was in danger, it wasn't a warning to take lightly. At the same time, a wash of anger filled me. The immortal corner of my mind warned me that the resentment was misdirected, that I was scared the baddies knew where I lived and I feared for my loved ones' safety. Nonetheless, my hackles rose at being spoken to like a child. I respected the hell out of Gregory, but I wasn't, in fact, nineteen. I was immortal, probably older than Gregory himself. And he was treating me like a kid. No, not a kid—he was talking to me like a *victim*, when I deserved to be addressed as an equal.

"My mom's safety is *my* concern." I took a deep breath. Mom thought he was attractive? But he could be so... so... condescending. Hmm. Maybe my anger was misdirected for more reasons than I thought. "Are we done?"

Gregory watched me for several long seconds, thoughts inscrutable, before he said, "Are we? Is there anything else you haven't told me?"

My mind fluttered to the unknown texter, who insisted I drop the case and helped me elude Asker and his goons. I thought of Matlas, and how his cemetery might be Asker's Lair. I considered Hope, who outran a mob trying to detain her and was now under my protection. I even thought of Mom, who wanted his phone number, but I banished that thought again.

There was only one person I wasn't willing to let down. "Actually," I said, "there is one more thing. Caden wants to start an incarnate 'neighborhood watch.' He thinks incarnates in the Seattle area should watch each other's backs, create a safety network for each other. I was on the fence about the idea at first, but having thought more about E-Pluribus hiring mercenaries to kidnap incarnates, I'm now fully on board. You're the first incarnate I've spoken with about it." I clenched and unclenched my jaw, not wanting to admit I needed his help. Not after his patronizing attitude. But if I wanted to be treated as a mature immortal being, I needed to act mature. Besides, I would not fail Caden. "Your resources would go a long way toward the success of something like this."

Gregory frowned. "E-Pluribus is hunting incarnates?" he asked.

I threw up my hands. "Yes! Didn't you hear me tell you how they laid a trap for me, or that I rescued the Mermaid?"

"This is troubling. Especially if Asker is still alive."

I looked over my shoulder, itching to get back to Yamamoto. Gregory and I had been "having a word" for far too long. "What do you say to the Incarnate Watch idea?"

"It has merit." I waited. After a moment, he said, "I'll consider it."

"Great," I muttered, feeling disappointed he didn't immediately want to join our little club. It was the resources, I told myself. The Watchman knew everything that happened around town. Having his help would be such an asset.

We returned to Yamamoto at his computer. "I found something," he said as soon as we stepped up to him.

"What is it?" I asked.

He pointed to the screen with the black fingerprint squares. "I ran analytics on the fingerprints. From what I could see on the corpse itself, I feared we would only get a partial print. I was not wholly correct." He tapped on his keyboard, enlarging a single set of fingerprints on the right screen while multiple squares of black fingerprints populated the left screen. I stared at them for a minute, realizing they were different sets of fingerprints. Looking at the right screen, the single fingerprint pattern there did not match any of the ones on the left.

"Fingerprints don't match any in the database?" I guessed.

Yamamoto's lips curved in an approximation of a smile. "You aren't wrong." He punched a few more keys, and the printer behind me jolted to life, spitting out two pages in rapid succession. Yamamoto held the two sheets up, side by side. "The prints on this page are all from people in our database. I pulled a random sample of twelve to illustrate my point." He handed me the sheet of paper. Gregory leaned over to examine it as Yamamoto indicated several of the prints. "Notice the complexity of the patterns. Now look at these, which were taken from around Asker's neck." He handed me the other sheet of paper.

I frowned. The fingerprint was *much* simpler. I had assumed at first glance that it was a result of blowing up the picture to a much larger scale, but I realized now that wasn't the case. The print on the second sheet had far, far fewer details. "What does it mean?" I asked.

"This," Yamamoto declared, slapping the sheet of paper triumphantly, "is not a real fingerprint."

"What?"

"It is a facsimile. Designed to resemble a real fingerprint, especially at the surface level." He raised his thin eyebrows. "What it resembles most is the lifelike hand of a doll."

Gregory stroked his chin. "Does that mean the murder was staged?" he asked.

Yamamoto shook his head. "Not necessarily. If I had to hypothesize, I would conclude the murderer has a prosthetic hand." His smile soured somewhat. "Which also explains why someone went to great lengths to procure the corpse from my office in the first place. This narrows down the suspect pool considerably."

A prosthetic? Asker could have used a prosthetic arm to choke himself to make it look more convincing. I stopped that line of reasoning. I needed to think with a clear head, not align new facts to fit my preexisting theory. Just in case I was wrong. Besides, there still might be an attempted murderer on the loose. If the would-be murderer didn't *know* Asker was the Zombie, maybe they really did try to kill him.

"Anything back from tech yet?" I asked.

It was Gregory who answered. "Tech is working with Asker's security team to pull data and records, but no word on their findings yet."

Just then, his phone buzzed. He withdrew it and read something on the screen. His features could have been carved of stone.

"Let me guess," I said smugly, figuring my powers of coincidence had intervened again. "An update from tech?"

He skewered me with a direct look, some emotion trapped behind his eyes. "No," he said. "There's been another murder."

# 12

*A*s I followed Gregory's unmarked sedan onto Microsoft's Redmond campus, I was struck by how different it was from my experience last night. The sun was setting, painting the sky in various blushes of pink, and Microsoft's headquarters was far busier than E-Pluribus's had been. We had contended with rush hour traffic on the drive from Harborview across the lake to Redmond, and it was now after 6:00 p.m. The Microsoft grounds themselves were quickly emptying of employees. It being a Friday, many had undoubtedly left earlier than most weeknights to enjoy the start of their weekend, leaving only the night owls and workaholics in the enormous lot, and even they had begun filing out of their corporate headquarters. Their exit, however, had become complicated by the discovery of a murder, reported only a short time ago. The campus was alive with flashing lights from police cruisers and unmarked vehicles, ambulances, even a fire truck. Officials clad in blues, grays, and browns swarmed over the area, and caution tape had been strung up to direct curious employees around certain zones even while other areas were cordoned off before my eyes.

The victim was Abdul al-Aziz, a thirty-six-year-old programmer who had worked for Microsoft for the last eight and a half years. He had materialized as if from nowhere, quickly distinguishing himself from his peers. Gaining the attention of his superiors despite his naturally quiet nature, he'd begun working on Microsoft's cutting-edge technology, particularly in advanced robotics engineering and software design. He helped launch the company's first stable release of its Robotics Developer Studio, a Windows-based environment for robot control and simulation.

Or so Gregory informed me. If you're anything like me, you might be wondering how he had access to such detailed background information without even calling in a favor, but the answer ended up being simpler, and sadder, than I imagined.

Abdul al-Aziz was the Super Genius incarnate.

"And you just happened to know this?" I demanded of Gregory, following his car in order to get as close to the action as possible.

"Yes." His unapologetic voice came clearly over my car's speakers.

I was taken aback at his response. I had expected him to deny it, though I'm not sure why. "How many incarnates do you know of in the Seattle area?" I asked.

I heard him speaking out his open window with an officer, explaining his identity and that I was with him. As our vehicles jerked back into motion, he replied, "Emery, I'm the Watchman. My responsibility is to keep everyone safe. I possess knowledge that helps me perform that duty. I'm unable to share all of that information with others, even others I trust, without risking the safety of the very people I am responsible for protecting."

I ground my teeth together. He was right, damn him. Even though I could be trusted, it would be sharing confidential information for little gain. An idea struck me. "Would you reach out to them and tell them about the incarnate neighborhood watch idea? You can put them in contact with me or Caden if they're interested in joining."

"I told you I'd consider it."

The man was infuriating sometimes. He pulled into a parking stall, and I slid into the spot right next to him. I hit disconnect on my phone, turned off my car, and jumped out, then stalked around the side of his sedan. "We need protecting now more than ever, Gregory,"

I growled. Hearing the belligerence in my voice, I took a steadying breath and tried to appeal to his sense of logic instead of his emotions. "Incarnates are dying, and not all of them have Sanctums to keep them safe. We can provide that for them. That's what my blog is designed to do: find those who need help. And supply it."

The nice thing about Gregory was that, even though he was stubborn and largely unaffected by emotions, he also wasn't easily riled. "Keeping people safe is important," he agreed. "Right now, this homicide is the priority. Later, I will address your request." In a voice that brooked no argument, he said, "I will give it due consideration. That is all I can promise at this time."

I nodded, biting my lip, worried I had failed Caden. But Gregory Gregorius was an honest, blunt man. If he said he'd consider it, he damn well would. I knew this. Just as I had cautioned Caden, I needed to give it time.

"The Super Genius?" I asked, changing topics.

"Yes. He immigrated to the United States shortly after reincarnating, then moved to Seattle after having established himself in the tech industry in Austin, Texas." Gregory allowed me to see a rare glimpse of worry on his face. "He was head of the robotics division at Microsoft."

"And," I noted, "the second Seattle tech mogul to be killed this week."

Gregory grew pensive. My phone vibrated in my hand, and I glanced at it, expecting an update from Rachelle about Hope. Instead, it was from my favorite mystery texter. *You were instructed to remove yourself from the investigation.*

I frowned, concerned that my mystery texter knew what I was up to. Maybe I should start calling them my stalker, I thought. I looked around surreptitiously, but people wearing all sorts of uniforms moved about like ants on an anthill. The chances of identifying an individual who was following me would be difficult. Gregory, however, noticed my odd behavior and held out his hand. I handed him the phone and watched as he read the text. It was only because I was watching him that I saw him stiffen.

"What?" I asked, my heart suddenly hammering in my chest. Something was wrong.

He silently handed my phone back to me, and I dragged my eyes to the text chain. Several more texts had come through. They weren't words, though. They were photos.

Mom at the store.

Rachelle sitting with her tablet in her lap in her apartment. *Inside* her apartment.

Gregory and me at the entrance to E-Pluribus.

Caden at the hospital.

They weren't live images, but they were all recent. All within the last few days. Someone—or a whole lot of someones—was keeping tabs on us.

I looked at the photos again, paying special attention to Rachelle's. How could someone get inside her apartment, so close, and yet elude her notice? The angle was a little awkward, but...

I realized the truth a moment later. The picture had been taken from her desk, I thought. Where her laptop usually sat. Flipping through the photos, I saw the angles were all peculiar. I showed them to Gregory. "Notice anything about the angles of these photos?"

He barely looked at them. "They're all taken from existing devices. Security cameras, in most cases."

I grunted, unsurprised he'd reached the same conclusion. And quicker than me, too. "So my mystery texter wasn't there in person." Relief swept through me as I thought it through. "They're just hacking in through existing cameras?"

"Nevertheless, whoever is doing this knows every person who's important to you, and where they are."

I shivered. He was right. "But who would have such widespread access?"

"Emery," Gregory said, his voice surprisingly gentle, "you should recuse yourself. Keep your friends and family safe."

"Are you kidding?" I hissed. "Now, more than ever, I need to be on this case. I need to catch this asshole before they do something to everyone I care about."

The Watchman's gaze held mine steadily for long seconds, then he nodded curtly. "I will keep you informed on everything. You have my word. But the timing of this was not coincidental. At the very least, you must leave now so that you are *appearing* to comply with the request."

I could see the wisdom in that. I refrained from scanning the men and women who bustled about not far away, out of earshot but well within sight. "I'll call them all and make sure they're okay," I told him. "Call me as soon as you learn anything."

"I will. Be safe."

Gregory spun and walked away. I returned to my Rogue and got in, feeling shaky. I called Mom, Rachelle, and Caden. Mom was fine, if a little confused as to why I was calling her so frequently today. Rachelle picked up and told me she was fine, that she and Hope were leaving to go pick up Hope's car shortly. Caden didn't answer, so I left a voicemail, trying not to sound panicked. He was working at the hospital, and I knew it was likely he wouldn't respond for some time. I would feel much better after I had heard from him.

I sat in my seat, staring at my phone, willing Caden to respond. Finally, my phone buzzed, but it was the unknown number again. *IF YOU DO NOT COMPLY WITH MY DIRECTIVES, YOU JEOPARDIZE THE SAFETY OF YOUR COMPANIONS.*

*What?* I *was* complying. I hadn't gone to the crime scene. I was still sitting in the Microsoft parking lot.

I wrote a text back to the unknown stalker. *WHO ARE YOU?* Fear tightening my chest, I hit send.

The response came very quickly, almost immediately. *I DO NOT WISH UNDUE HARM UPON YOU. BUT YOU ARE BEING MONITORED FOR COMPLIANCE.*

I stared at the text. What kind of an answer was that? It was becoming clear to me why the texter used neutral, formal language with me. They wanted to eliminate any identifiers that I could use to discern their identity. That implied that either I knew the texter or they feared our paths would cross at some point. Either way, it was someone close to me. *How* close was relative.

*I* PULLED MYSELF OFF THE CASE, I texted back. *I* HAVE FOLLOWED YOUR DIRECTIONS.

YOUR COOPERATION IS APPRECIATED.

I frowned at the response, staring at it for so long it started to blur in my vision. What the hell was going on? The mysterious texter had no qualms with threatening me, my friends, and my family, but was polite enough to *thank* me for following directions? Maybe... maybe the stalker wasn't really my enemy. I thought back to the afternoon, when the texter had helped Rachelle and me elude Scary Gun Lady and her armada of black SUVs. Could they be a friend after all?

*No.* No friend would ever threaten my loved ones. This was something else. Something I was missing. It was all connected, I thought, all part of a greater whole. Asker, E-Pluribus, Scary Gun Lady, the kidnapped incarnates, the murder of Abdul al-Aziz. Maybe even the Virgo and Matlas's haunted graveyard.

Speaking of which, it was after seven. But I was only half an hour away from Paradise Lake Cemetery. I decided to get some food, then wait for Rachelle and Matlas at the graveyard. Doing something, *anything,* felt good. I was not powerless. I was the Protagonist, and if there was one thing I knew about stories, it was that they inevitably move forward, progressing toward a conclusion. If I kept pushing, the answers would come. It was practically guaranteed.

With that comforting thought, I left Microsoft's campus behind me. No sooner had I hit the main road than I got a text from Caden. He was safe.

Feeling better, I headed northeast toward the border of Maltby and Woodinville, where Paradise Lake Cemetery awaited me. It felt good to *move,* to push forward, to not let fear freeze me into inaction. Besides, it never hurt to be early, right?

It was dark by the time I arrived at the cemetery. I canvassed the area from outside first, driving down the two-lane Paradise Lake Road. It was quintessential Washington State, tall evergreens lining the roadway, their green foliage blocking off the view to either side, like someone had paved a lane through the center of a forest. A metal guardrail protected the western side of the road, small turnoffs and dirt roads peeking out from amidst the greenery. Power lines and road signs intruded on the idyllic image, but I'd lived in the greater Seattle area long enough to appreciate the relationship between wildlife and humanity. Even in town, roads, trails, and homes often wound around trees rather than displacing them, and outside of Seattle proper you'd be hard-pressed to look around and *not* see trees.

Driving down the quiet road, I could understand why a cemetery tucked away in the dark vegetation would elicit tales of horror and ghosts. It was the kind of road you'd find in the movies, with suspenseful music building slowly, grinding against your nerves. A shadow would stumble from the undergrowth, and the unfortunate family's minivan would cast its headlights upon the silhouette. As the music reached its crescendo, the terrifying visage of a zombie with a blood-flecked mouth would be revealed. Blood, screams, and carnage to follow, then fade to black.

One wide circle around the perimeter of the cemetery—without actually laying eyes upon it, ferreted away as it was—and a cheeseburger later, I pulled into the neighborhood abutting the graveyard. In my trek, I did not observe any odd behavior: no sudden tugging on my steering wheel or unexpected acceleration. I experienced a sliver of disappointment; I was the Protagonist. If there was any truth to the supernatural (and likely incarnate-related) rumors of strange occurrences in these parts, I half expected it to happen to me.

The entrance to the neighborhood was a small artery off the main road, easy to miss. But once inside the neighborhood proper, the street broadened to a surprisingly clear, wide suburban road with large houses featuring expansive yards and driveways. I followed the curve of the road until I came to a cul-de-sac on which sat two large homes. A tiny, old road proceeded beyond the dead end, leading directly to the cemetery. A chain suspended by two iron poles prevented further passage by car.

I was twenty minutes early, but Matlas was already there. He was sitting on a large stone directly next to the entrance, stylish in his asymmetrical overcoat. He'd donned gloves and a scarf, which disappeared into the collar of his jacket. I pulled my crossover up to the chain and threw it into park. The chilly night air hit me as soon as I stepped out, my breath misting in front of my face. I snatched my jacket off the passenger seat and shrugged it on. I felt the comfortable weight of my Taser Pulse+ in the pocket. I checked my other pocket, and my fingers curled around two lighters and a box of matches.

Against undead incarnates, fire was always a good option. Actually, fire was a good weapon against *most* incarnates. Except the Genie. He's a jerk.

Chances were decent that I wouldn't need any firepower—pun intended: Taser, matches, or otherwise. This was a mortal job, debunking some old myths with a camera and the magic of editing. But given the recent pattern of murders, kidnapping, and assault, I wasn't taking any chances. Not to mention my theory about Asker. If he was the Zombie, this graveyard could very well be his Lair. If I were anyone other than the Protagonist, that chance would probably be too small to consider. Alas.

Matlas hopped off the rock and grinned, his white teeth standing out in the dark. He strode forward, tucking his phone into his pocket as he approached. "Emery."

"Hey, Matlas. Sorry, not quite ready to start. I didn't think you'd be out here already."

He shrugged good-naturedly. "No problem. You're early, man."

"I like to get a feel for a place before we begin," I lied. I couldn't think of a time I'd *ever* been twenty minutes early to a meeting. It was like being the first one to show up at a party, wasn't it? "Hey, about this afternoon, I owe you an apology. We ran out of there without an explanation."

Matlas scoffed. "Thanks, but we're all good."

I stuttered, an entire story about a family emergency dying on my lips. "All right," I said instead. "I'll still try to do better in the future." I gestured to the chained-off road, moving the conversation along. For such an attractive, confident-looking guy, Matlas had an awkward amount of... well, awkwardness. I mean, I knew it wasn't *me*. "This the entrance?"

"Yeah."

It was too dark for me to make out many details of the graveyard beyond. It was more open than I expected, though, a clearing that held at bay the black wall of trees and dark foliage beyond.

"Is that the entire cemetery?"

"No, not quite. It continues down the hill on the far side."

"Right," I said, "you mentioned it was terraced." I rubbed my hands together, both to demonstrate my excitement and to ward off the autumnal chill. "Let's discuss some of the details."

"Should we wait for Rachelle? I mean, if she's, uh, still coming?"

I snickered. "Yeah, she'll be here any minute now. She *likes* being the first one to a party."

Matlas humored me with a laugh. As if on cue, a pair of head-lights crested the hill leading to the cul-de-sac, and Rachelle pulled up in her sporty yellow sedan, parking behind my Rogue. The light inside the cab illuminated her silhouette. We watched her lean over and snatch up something from her passenger seat, then exit and join us, bag slung over her shoulder.

My eyebrows shot up at her outfit. She looked... expensive. A navy blue double-breasted coat with a waterfall collar hugged her frame, elongating and slimming her. It hung to her knees, revealing white jeans that took a page straight out of Caden's wardrobe and contrasted elegantly with the dark upper coat that was clasped tightly to ward off the chill. Dark gloves—did I miss the memo?—and brown suede boots tall enough to eclipse the hem of her jeans stated she was ready for the weather, if not the mud. Her hair had been carefully styled to expose her right ear, revealing an ornate heart earring so polished it gleamed in the dark.

"Hi, boys," she sang out as she approached, clearly enjoying our reactions.

"You look like Graveyard Barbie," I said as Matlas stammered a greeting.

She rolled her eyes, though in the dark I couldn't really see it. But I knew. "I *told* you Hope and I were going to have a girls' night. What did you think that meant?"

I grinned. She was flustered; I could tell because she *never* lobbed them up for me this easily when she was at her best. "I don't know, tubs of ice cream and pillow fights?"

She stared at me. "You're as bad as a straight man." She turned to Matlas. "No offense."

He held up his hands in surrender. "None taken. You look..."

"Like she's going to ask for a raise?" I suggested dryly. "I see now why she needs it."

"I was going to say 'great.'"

Rachelle sniffed. "Well you're both right. Thank you. Now, if you're *quite* finished, maybe we can discuss our game plan?"

Despite her tone, I could hear the blush in her words. I wondered how much Hope had really influenced her appearance. "My plan is to focus on the Thirteen Steps to Hell," I informed them. "It's the legend generating most of the interest in your cemetery. The three of us will explore it, at night—obviously—and we'll exaggerate how disappointing it is that the steps have been cemented over. If viewers realize the steps aren't accessible anymore, by any means, it should help to reduce curiosity."

Matlas was bobbing his head in agreement.

"I did a little research, too," Rachelle added. "Rumors of a wealthy family's tomb being at the base of the Thirteen Steps are part of the allure. A quick background search on the history of the cemetery, and it's easily debunked. The richest person to ever own this land is probably *you*, Matlas."

"Really? My family gets by, but we're not rich or anything," he objected.

"Exactly my point," she said, sounding smug. I winced. *This* was her flirting? She'd basically just called him poor. "The possibility of a secret family crypt in this graveyard is essentially nonexistent."

"Let's get this show on the road," I said cheerily, facing the entrance to the graveyard like it was the gates to Disneyland.

Rachelle dug out her camera with its top-mounted microphone. "I'll be filming and snapping pics pretty much constantly," she informed Matlas. "Don't worry about keeping quiet or anything; voices are easy to edit out. We might ask you some questions on camera, and just answer as candidly as you wish. If you don't like something, we'll cut it out."

He nodded, putting out a wave of nervous energy. "Okay, sounds good."

While Rachelle secured two dimmable light panels to tripods and washed the immediate area in light, I walked up to the chain across the path, gesturing for Matlas to join me. "Whoa," he said, looking around at the neighboring houses with dismay. "That's *bright*. Is that really necessary?"

"Just for the interview portion," I assured him. "You'll be surprised at how dark it will still look in the final cut." At Rachelle's signal, I turned around and faced the camera. "Paradise Lake Cemetery," I said, letting a tingle of excitement trace through my voice.

"*Allegedly* one of the most haunted locations in Washington. From ghost sightings to visions of hell itself, this graveyard has it all. Thank you for watching my channel, Debunkers, and don't go anywhere while we find the loophole in the horrors and myths surrounding this haunted locale. Because, as all of you know, *There's Always a Loophole.*"

A hiccup of laughter bubbled out of Matlas, and he looked at me with a wild smile. "Chills. That was so natural, man."

"You ready for me to introduce you?"

"Oh, uh, yeah, sure."

Looking off into the graveyard but angling my body so that my voice would be heard and the side of my face seen, I said, "One factor in creating an urban legend about this cemetery is its forbidden nature. As it's located on private property, you must gain permission before visiting the horrors promised beyond. We were lucky enough to be approached by a Debunker who lives right here. Matt Atlas, say hi to our fans, and tell us a little about growing up on this hallowed ground."

Matlas fidgeted, his feet shuffling as he said, "Hi, Debunkers. I, uh, I'm Matlas. I grew up in that house right over there." He pointed, then let his hand fall when Rachelle obediently followed his finger to the nearby house. He waited awkwardly, looking at me with wide eyes. I smiled encouragingly at him as the camera's focus returned. "Yeah, so, um, I grew up here, and I've always heard the stories. I just, I don't know, never thought much about them."

Rachelle lowered the camera. "Hey, Atlas, you going all shy on me all of a sudden, or what?"

I cringed. With her barking at him like that, of course he'd start stammering. To my surprise, though, Matlas grinned. "No, ma'am," he said. "Sorry, guess I just thought I'd have a script or something. I like to be prepared. But let's start over. I can do this."

"Good," she drawled. "Let's take it from the top." She held the camera up, paused, then lowered it again. "And call me *ma'am* one more time. I dare you."

He chuckled, confidence easing into him. He turned to face me as

Rachelle raised the camera once again. "Thanks for coming out, Emery. Call me Matlas. I'm actually a big fan of the show. You see, growing up with a cemetery for a backyard, you start to wonder about all the stories. Your show helped me to realize that people just fear what they don't understand."

"I take it, then, that you haven't come across any ghouls or goblins?"

"No way. Though that isn't really what's supposed to haunt this place, either."

I responded to his words with an understanding head bob. "That's right. According to the ghost-hunter bloggers of the Pacific Northwest, it's all about the pioneer farmwives and their children, right?"

"Exactly."

"Well," I asked him, leaning in conspiratorially, "have you ever come across any of *them,* then?"

"Never. Worst thing I've seen out here is a coyote." He grinned. "And middle schoolers."

I laughed, surprised when it was genuine. "Well, let's go search for some loopholes, shall we?"

He made a sweeping gesture with his hands. "After you."

We disassembled the light panels and replaced them with flashlights. Rachelle kept the recording going as we stepped over the chain-link fence and took our first couple of steps into the cemetery.

A tiny, nearly imperceptible change in the air sent goose bumps down my spine. It was so subtle I would've missed it if not for lifetimes identifying it. And because I half expected it. I'd just entered an incarnate's domain. There was no way for me to tell if it was a Safe Haven, Territory, or Lair. Or Sanctum, I guess, but I doubted any incarnate that made a *graveyard* its domain was Benign.

A thrill went through me. *I was right!* Asker *was* the Zombie, and Paradise Lake Cemetery was his Lair. I had done it! I'd solved the case and...

My knees went weak as the realization hit me a second time, but harder. I was right. Asker was the *Zombie.* And I was a tasty human who had just brought two other snacks along for a three-for-one special. I may have been right, but I certainly wasn't safe.

The comforting weight of the Taser in my pocket made me feel a little better. I doubted the Taser would have much effect on the Zombie, but it was better than nothing. And besides, I still had the lighters in my other pocket.

We entered the clearing, dark headstones poking out of the grass like bent and twisted fingers of a half-buried hand. As she filmed, Rachelle stumbled and caught herself. I jerked at her motion, every sense alert for danger. The wind sighed gently through the wall of evergreens and the denser floor of plants and undergrowth, sending leaves rustling. A shiver in the low bushes to my right jerked my head around. It was probably just a rodent or some small nocturnal creature.

Rachelle swept the camera around, keeping up a low monologue that she would edit out later. Usually it was just a running list of things to remember when she edited. Matlas strode confidently ahead, pointing out the graves and sharing facts about them as we proceeded deeper into the cemetery proper. I looked back, trying to capture Rachelle's attention without being too obvious about it.

I froze. There was someone right behind her, reaching a hand— no, holy crap, it was just a small tree, branch outstretched and swaying in the night breeze. *What the hell is wrong with me?* I wasn't afraid of the dark or of ghost stories.

No, I was afraid of a very real incarnate attacking my friends.

As Rachelle brushed past me with the camera zoomed in on something ahead, I reached out and tugged on the fabric of her coat. She looked up at me.

"Stay alert," I muttered under my breath. "Something's up."

Amusement sparked in her eyes. "Very funny. Afraid of the dark?"

I held her gaze, serious. "Just be careful."

She sobered up immediately, nodding once. "Should we bail?"

I hesitated. I *really* didn't want to. This could be my only chance to speak with Asker without Scary Gun Lady staked out nearby. "No," I said at last.

She didn't press, just bobbed her head in agreement and moved on, sweeping the camera around the graveyard some more. I noticed she wasn't mumbling directions anymore, though. She wanted to be able to listen for anything.

"Guys, over here!" Matlas called. I winced. His voice was loud in the quiet of the graveyard. In fact, wasn't it *too* quiet? I was certain we should have heard noise pollution from the road, even if traffic was light.

We hustled over to where he waited, standing tall at the top of a slope. "Here's one of the staircases that leads down to the middle terrace," he told us. There were stone steps set into the side of the hill, old and carpeted in moss. Age and weather had eroded them, to the point where they were as tilted and warped as a set of fun-house stairs.

We proceeded down to the next level, spying another set of stairs nearby to take us even farther down the hill. Where we stood, the needled evergreen boughs barely reached, only the largest and longest extending over our heads. But the next level descended into the forest, trees spreading to encroach upon the cemetery. It was diffi-cult to see in the dark, but I thought I made out headstones nestled among the tree trunks, held protectively by roots and underbrush. To our right, on our current level, the path meandered up, following the contour of the hill. Matlas headed in that direction, clearly comfort-able in his own backyard. I looked down into the forest below, again, and I would have sworn that something was watching me. I clutched the lighter in my coat pocket. I didn't want to go down to the bottom level.

I quickly caught up with Matlas and Rachelle. He was explaining a feature of the land ahead. "This," he was telling her, "is what my sisters call the 'tunnel to hell,'" he said dramatically, a whimsical sort of smile on his face.

I realized the trail continued through and behind a layer of shrubbery. Rachelle focused her camera on it. I obligingly aimed my flashlight in the same area, but the trail seemed to disappear into the stark shadows my beam created. Creepy. "Is this the way to the Thirteen Steps?" she asked, her voice little more than a whisper.

"Good guess, but no. They're back that way, down on the next level. Among the trees. We'll go there next." Oh, goody.

"Then what's so special about this tunnel?"

He nudged her playfully. "Why don't you lead the way and find out?"

She looked up at him, her eyes mischievous. We had long since adjusted to the dark, overcast night, and every detail of her features was etched in shades of gray. "Sounds a little spooky," she said lightly, shuddering for effect. She leaned in closer to him.

He laughed, pushing past her. "You can't fool me. Nothing here scares you."

I stepped up to her, and she glanced at me with an annoyed expression. "What a gentleman," she grumbled.

I hid my grin. Being on edge, it wasn't challenging. "Maybe he likes women who can handle themselves," I offered.

"Why the hell would you say that?" She looked at me suspiciously.

This time hiding my smile was harder. "No reason." I pressed forward, slipping into the "tunnel" created by bushes on the right, trees on the left, branches overhead, and roots beneath. Huh. Maybe this was the Mother Nature incarnate's abode, and I was being foolish to fear it.

Something snapped out in the woods to my left, and my head whipped around. It sounded like a branch had been stepped on. *Could just be kids,* I thought. *Or an overactive imagination.* Rachelle overtook me and walked around the bend, nearly out of sight. I strained, listening intently to the night. Whispers of wind tugged at the trees again, sending up a wave of susurration. I calmed my pounding blood. Deep breaths. It was nothing. No other noises creaked out of the woods.

Rachelle gasped from ahead. I darted forward, my heart a machine gun in my chest. Something came into view, and I jolted to a stop, eyes wide.

It wasn't what I had been expecting. The tunnel opened up to a small plateau with several headstones sprinkled about. Most of them were embedded in the earth like teeth, but two newer headstones stood tall, proudly honoring the dead and giving me the heebie-jeebies. The car being impaled by a tree just to the left of the path did nothing to alleviate that feeling.

The car was so old, it would be more accurate to call it an automobile. I couldn't discern its coloration, due in part to the darkness but also to age and neglect. Gray or blue, I thought. It was one of those old station wagons, a boxy thing almost as wide as it was long, with a bulbous front nose. Nature had lain its claim on the manmade vehicle, the metal frame and front bumper half sunk into the side of the hill. Ferns, soil, and dead leaves fought for ownership across its length. Its windows and the glass in its old-timey side mirrors were gone, no trace even remaining, and moss obscured it in heavy drapes. Most impressive of all, a tall, skinny tree trunk speared the massive hood of the automobile, as though it was a potted tree and the pot just happened to be a car.

"Well *that's* not creepy," I commented when no one had said anything for some time. "You could have given us warning."

Matlas grinned. "And miss the chance to see the looks on your faces?" His eyes darted to Rachelle, and his smile dimmed. "Is she afraid of anything?" he asked me in a low voice.

"Just the fear of missing out."

"I heard that," she protested absently, absorbed in scanning the woods around the automobile with her camera. "I— Wait, what's this?"

I trotted over to her. "See something?" I asked tightly.

"Yeah." She raised her voice. "Hey, Matlas. There's another car down there. I can't get a good view of it, though, in the dark."

"Good catch. There are a good number of abandoned cars in the forest area around here. You see, all these trees are part of the Paradise Valley Conservation Area. There are some trails in there, but they're unusable half the time due to the mud. All along the trails, you'll find old cars like these rusting away. Rumors say they belonged to people who were trying to locate the graveyard but never found it."

"Is that why your sisters call it the tunnel to hell? Because of the car?"

"Well, and this." He strode forward, encouraging Rachelle to follow him. I kept close to them but hung back, keeping an eye—and ear—on our surroundings. I didn't want the Zombie to sneak up on us. I looked back down at the deeper, darker forest beyond the automobile, and the feeling of being watched intensified. I didn't really need to look all around us, but it made me feel better. I knew he was out there, deeper in the woods.

"Whoa!" I heard Rachelle squeal. "An unnamed grave! This is so cool!"

"Did I tell you about the guy who was caught by the cops about ten years back?" Matlas asked, excitement in his voice. When Rachelle shook her head, he continued, "One night, at dusk, a shady-looking man was reported sneaking into the cemetery with a shovel. The police were called, and they set off about the graveyard. I remember seeing their flashlights in the night. Since this is an out-of-the-way area, they didn't find it immediately, but no matter where they looked in the cemetery, they could hear a hollow, scratching sound. They eventually caught him. He was digging right where you're standing, trying to unearth whatever is buried here."

"What happened to him?" Rachelle whispered.

"He was arrested. We never heard anything about him again. A week passed. This area was roped off, but we were kids, so naturally we snuck in to have a look. The hole was three to four feet deep, a big mound of dirt next to the headstone. We dared each other to jump down in it, but no one was brave enough." He paused, puzzlement pulling his brow down. "Oddly enough, one day we came back out here and everything was back to normal. The mound was gone, the ropes vanished, and the earth didn't even look like it had been disturbed. Ever since, though, *these* have been here."

Rachelle gasped, leaning down to examine what Matlas was pointing at. With a feeling of trepidation, I stepped up to see. *I'm an immortal, badass monster hunter,* I told myself. *I'm an immortal, badass monster hunter.*

The headstone was a flat, polished stone sitting atop another jagged, craggy stone sunk into the grass. It was unfinished, I realized, having never been carved or engraved with an epitaph. It wasn't completely unmarked, however. The tiny hairs on the nape of my neck rose. The face of the headstone had deep gouges in it that looked like someone or something had clawed at the weathered stone with their nails, leaving behind a series of erratic, irregular scratches —and rumors of a haunting.

"As much as I'd love to record this," Rachelle said with real regret in her voice, "I think this would draw people to the graveyard." She pushed away and started back the way we had come. "Let's get some footage of these *Thirteen Steps to Hell.*" She made her voice all eerie when pronouncing the words.

"You know," I grumbled under my breath, "you could just say 'steps.' We all know to which ones you're referring."

"What was that, oh fearless leader?" Rachelle tossed back at me.

"Nothing," I said, walking quickly to catch up.

I froze as a noise demanded my attention. A small rock came tumbling down the hillside from above me, clacking as it connected with another stone hidden in the long grass of the scarp to my left. Glancing up at the top of the slope, I saw a shadow slip out of my view. It had looked like someone's head. And rocks couldn't move on their own.

I dashed forward, back through the "tunnel to hell," and gripped Rachelle's shoulder. She didn't even flinch. "There's someone on the upper level," I hissed, not caring if Matlas heard me.

Rachelle saw the concern in my eyes. "Let's check it out."

Matlas, looking back and forth between us, shrugged. "Could be some drunk high schoolers," he offered. "It *is* a Friday night."

I nodded tensely. "They weren't making much noise, though."

Rachelle was already heading up the stone steps, and I jogged forward to reach the top of the stairs right on her heels. She was scanning the graveyard with the camera, using its night mode feature to help pierce the darkness.

The cemetery was empty. Bracing myself, I stalked over to the spot where I knew I'd seen movement. It was tricky; there was a swath of thick underbrush between the nearest gravestone and the edge of the hill, discouraging anyone from climbing down to the lower level here and completely obscuring the automobile-tree just below.

Someone—or some*thing*—could have been hiding in the bushes, I reasoned, but they would have made quite a bit of noise climbing in. The brush was thick, and surrounding trees' leaves had succumbed to the season, carpeting the ground in dry, dead vegetation. They would have crunched loudly if any weight strained them.

Hmm. I knew I had seen something moving up here, but maybe it *was* just some forest animal, my anxious mind playing tricks on me.

"I don't see anything, Emery," Rachelle said, her soft voice carrying across to me. I sighed. If I could hear her so clearly, I'd definitely hear any movement in the undergrowth. "Matlas, want to show us the steps? I can film where they used to be, then Emery can give a little speech about how they were cemented over years ago."

"Sure. Come down this way."

I scanned the area one last time, then turned to follow their retreating voices. *I'm an immortal, badass monster hunter.* The Thirteen Steps were deeper in the forest, beneath the dark and foreboding tree line. If something made its Lair there, I needed to be able to protect Rachelle and Matlas.

I'd started back toward the stairs leading down the slope when I heard a whisper from behind me. Startled, my heart jumping back into overdrive, I spun around. "Who's there?" I demanded, proud my voice didn't waver. The damn underbrush was just how I left it, the cemetery devoid of life. It must have just been the breeze, though I noticed uncomfortably that the trees weren't swaying. "I swear, Iris, if this is you playing games, I'm going to—"

I cut off as a whispery voice came to me. Had it said my name?

"Emery Luple, please do not react."

I leapt backward as a shadow to my left budged ever so slightly among the roots of a gnarled tree trunk. I'd thought the trunk was thick at its base and quickly tapered as it went up, but now I could see that what I had mistaken for roots was actually a person holding perfectly, inhumanly still. It moved, now, a shadow detaching from the silhouette of the tree, rising to stand on two legs.

"We must speak." The voice was oddly subdued; not a whisper, I realized, just quiet. Like turning the volume on a TV down, the quality not diminished.

"Who are you?" I asked again, taking a guarded step backward.

The figure shuffled forward, its movements careful, slow, precise. It probably didn't want to alarm me with any sudden motions. When it crept out from the dark shadows cast by the foliage, my mouth popped open.

It was Asker.

I couldn't believe it. I had been right. I had stumbled into his domain—god, I hoped it wasn't a Lair—and he'd managed to isolate me from my friends. I could still hear their voices drifting to me from behind and below. If I shouted, they'd be there in moments. Zombies were supposed to be slow, shambling things, right? I could probably outrun him.

But... he had requested a conversation with me. And damn me thrice, I'm a curious person.

"You're Asker," I breathed, gaping.

He tilted his head slightly, watching me with wide, unblinking eyes. "Please call me Mikey." His voice had an odd quality to it that I couldn't quite place. He spoke formally, which made sense for a genius, I suppose, but there was more to it than that. His accent was nearly indistinguishable from mine, but it was stiff, almost forced. Yes, that was it: he sounded like someone rehearsing his lines rather than just speaking. Almost as though he were role playing, the cadence and words given careful thought.

Also, Mikey? The founder of E-Pluribus and creator of Unum, the most sophisticated interfacing software program on the planet, wanted me to call him *Mikey?* That was rather... informal.

"Why did you fake your own death?"

Mikey did not look surprised by the question, but he shook his head. "You misunderstand. I will explain, but first you must turn off your mobile device."

I stared at him. "That's not going to happen while I'm alone. What do you want?"

He finally blinked, once. "Your assistance. We are being hunted. He can hear us through your mobile device."

*Someone bugged my phone?* Of course: my mysterious texter. "Wait, 'we'?" I racked my brain. "You and the Super Genius," I realized. "Someone is murdering tech moguls, aren't they?"

"Please," Mikey said, the frustration in his features not coloring his neutral inflection, "deactivate your mobile device so we may speak freely."

"Emery?" It was Rachelle's voice, and there was a strange note to it. "Emery! You need to see this." I looked back over my shoulder, worried. There had been an edge of panic to Rachelle's words. Something was wrong.

But I'd finally found Asker. Surely she could handle herself for another minute while I found out what I needed to know.

Her voice called again, strained, and I broke. "Stay here," I said firmly, then darted to the top of the steps and descended to the next level. "Rachelle!" I called. "Where are you?"

"Down here!" I followed her voice, descending another stairwell that was more warped and decrepit, exposed as it was to the elements. I was among the trees now, and still tombstones and small monuments dotted the spaces between trees and bushes, sometimes almost wholly swallowed by the undergrowth.

Which way? "Rachelle?" I called again, and her reply came from off to the left. I followed the curve of the hill, weaving between more headstones and grave markers until I saw her and Matlas ahead.

"What is it?" I asked, breathing hard as I approached them. Matlas looked petrified, frozen in shock. It was hard to tell in the dark, but I thought Rachelle's face was drained of color. "What's wrong?"

She gestured ahead, and I surveyed the landscape. There were two rusted iron poles staked to the ground, marking the start of a short gravel trail overrun with moss. The path cut straight through underbrush that choked it for only about twenty feet, ending in a small clearing. We were level with the forest floor, now, since we'd made it to the bottom tier of the cemetery, but there was a staircase entrenched in the forest floor, leading down. I couldn't see where it led from where I stood, but with the thick foliage all around, I didn't think it could really lead anywhere.

A tingling washed down my back. "Um, guys?" I asked, fearing I already knew the answer to my unasked question.

"Impossible," Matlas whispered, almost inaudible. He was shaking.

I looked back at the staircase. "Those are the Thirteen Steps?" I guessed. Thoughts of Asker fled, fear and a strange sense of awe replacing them.

Rachelle looked to Matlas for confirmation. He just stared uncomprehendingly. She shook herself, then said, "They aren't as cemented up as we were led to believe."

Her words brought Matlas out of his reverie. If he hadn't been too stunned to react, I thought he would have flushed. "I've been here before—many times. The steps were always gone, a slab of cement all that remained." He sounded frightened.

"Well," Rachelle said slowly, "this throws a wrench in our plans." She bit her lip, then thrust the camera into my hands. "I'm going to see what all the fuss is about."

Matlas and I started at the same time, both objecting.

"Relax, boys. I'm a big girl. I can take care of myself." She sounded confident and strong. Ugh.

*I'm an immortal, badass monster hunter.* "I'm going with you," I said firmly, passing the camera to Matlas. "Record us, okay?"

He nodded numbly, fumbling with the camera, almost dropping it. He gripped it tightly and raised it up.

I really wanted to get back up to the top level and continue my discussion with Asker—er, Mikey. It was the perfect chance to get more information, to find out exactly what was going on. But

Rachelle had that determined look on her face, and I knew if I left her, she would go ahead and explore the Thirteen Steps without me. I swallowed a growl of frustration. If Mikey wanted to talk, he'd wait for me up there. Besides, this shouldn't take long, right?

I was all but certain this development with the Thirteen Steps to Hell was my fault, too. My freaking Protagonist powers loved to pit chaos against reality. Six months ago, when Caden and I had squared off against the Headless Horseman, my powers had summoned a place of sanctuary straight from the urban legend: the farmstead of Ichabod Crane. Caden and I had spent all night there, a place as safe as my Sanctum. My powers did odd things to protect me... or to push me toward an outcome I was meant to discover. Doors mysteriously unlocked, people spilled secrets they would never say otherwise, and bullies fought with a remarkable lack of strength. But I couldn't rely on my powers completely; they were a double-edged sword. The protagonists in stories and urban legends rarely escaped their tales unscathed, and sometimes it seemed my powers attracted danger as often as they protected me from it. What I had learned in the past six months was that being the Protagonist meant improbable, sometimes impossible, things happened around me with surprising regularity. However, I had some measure of control; even if my powers put things in my path that never should have been there, I had free will. I could walk away, explore, use what was in front of me, or ignore it. What I *chose* to do with the plot devices that landed in my lap was what mattered.

Rachelle was standing at the trailhead, just behind the iron stakes.

"Those," Matlas told us quietly, "are called the Gates of Hell."

"I'm catching on to the theme," Rachelle said over her shoulder.

I stepped up beside her, eyeing the path ahead. "Ready?" I asked.

"I'm not the one hyperventilating."

I forced myself to take slow, measured breaths. After a moment, I said sarcastically, "*Now* are you ready?"

She snorted, then took a step forward. I did the same, our movements in lockstep. A hush overcame us as we stepped across the threshold of the Gates of Hell. The forest held its breath.

We took several long, slow steps. Fog rolled in from either side of us, curling through the woods and transforming the trees and bushes into blurry, half-formed outlines. It thickened quickly as our strides faltered. The trail ahead of us wasn't very long, but it seemed like we'd walked a dozen steps already and the distance hadn't shrunk at all. We pressed on, together, through the dense fog. It pulled at us like a living thing, fingers ghosting over my flesh. Walking felt like striding through waist-deep water, a physical resistance dragging us to a crawl. The mist from my breath stirred the fog before me, an icy chill brushing against my face like a cold cobweb. Had the temperature plummeted?

It was perfectly silent. I couldn't even hear Rachelle's footsteps crunch on the gravel. We were suspended in a gray void, cold and terrifying. I could feel, but could not hear, the heavy beat of my heart pounding wildly in my chest. I dragged my gaze to Rachelle and drew courage from her determined features.

Several long, agonizing steps later, we emerged into the clearing. The Thirteen Steps to Hell yawned before us, a crevasse lined in aged stone. The neglected, crumbling stairwell plunged downward: thirteen irregular stairs, ending in a blank, earthen wall. No, it wasn't earth—it was a door, so caked in soil and dead vegetation that it nearly blended in entirely.

Rachelle leaned down, every motion deliberate, and pried loose a stone the size of her thumb from the dirt. She stepped to the edge of the Thirteen Steps. A low, growling sound emanated from all around us, like the throaty warning of a dog before it struck. Was the forest itself somehow threatening us?

She tossed the stone down the first several steps. The clatter was loud in the silence, the stone bouncing and clacking its way down. It stopped suddenly. *Too suddenly? Abnormally sudden?*

Rachelle must have been thinking along similar lines, because she frowned down the stairs. She looked at me, eyebrows quirking, then dug another rock out of the ground. She tossed it down, this time aiming for the bottom.

The rock was lost to the shadowed recesses. We waited, but no sound came. Somehow, it didn't reach the bottom step. We exchanged glances. Rachelle looked curious and awed, the eeriness only making it more exciting. I did not share her enthusiasm. This place seemed *wrong* to me, unnatural.

Says the guy who reincarnates when he dies, rearranging reality to suit his needs. Pot, meet kettle. I get it. I still didn't like it. Not one bit.

Rachelle's eyebrows raised in question, and I shook my head vehemently. I turned back to look for Matlas, but his outline was a mere suggestion in the thick fog. Returning my attention to Rachelle, I nearly yelped. She was on the first step.

That same low snarl whispered through the fog and trees, and Rachelle snapped her head up, clearly having heard it, too. I came up behind her and put my hand on her shoulder, urging her to turn back. She shot me a defiant look and took another step down.

I looked around wildly as the growling intensified, seemingly right at the edge of the fog embankment. It was an incarnate, certainly. The Ghost, the Goblin, and things that go bump in the night *did* exist, but only as a single incarnate to represent the myth. It wasn't the fear of the supernatural that gripped my chest.

It was the idea that whatever was out there, it was an incarnate from hell. I may have been an immortal, badass monster hunter, but I'd never confronted anything remotely like the Devil before, and I was exceedingly anxious to maintain my record.

From the edge of the mist, something watched me. I had felt it since the moment I entered its Lair. So I was unsurprised—oh-so-miserably unsurprised—when two monstrous, red eyes resolved from the fog. Like a growing shadow beneath placid waters, submerged but rising to greet the hapless boat above it, the vague outline of something massive dwelled just on the other side of the fog. Another pair of gleaming green eyes, each the size of my fist, appeared off to the right of the red pair. *Oh no.*

How many of them were there? Even with only a single incarnate per myth, I realized there were dozens, maybe hundreds, of cultural myths surrounding demons. If each had its own persona incarnate, we could easily be surrounded by a host of enemies.

I swallowed. "Rachelle," I said, putting as much urgency into my tone as possible.

She looked back, then followed my gaze to the sets of eyes. I saw hers widen as the reality of our situation hit her. A deep, dangerous rumble came from the creatures, resonating in my chest and rattling my bones.

"Back up slowly," I said, keeping my voice smooth and conversational. Precisely, and with no sudden movements, I withdrew the lighter from my pocket.

For once, Rachelle complied. Keeping her eyes glued on the glowing ones towering above us, she stepped backward without looking, ascending the stairs.

One step to go.

The red eyes dipped to regard her. Then, without warning, enormous teeth materialized out of the fog and descended on her. I leapt forward, balancing on the top of the Thirteen Steps and brandishing my lighter above her head like a shield. As if even a shield could offer protection against the enormous maw that snapped down at her.

I fumbled with the lighter's wheel, flicking it twice before it finally caught. A pitiful little flame sparked into existence, barely visible in the heavy fog.

The fangs, however, froze. I could just make out the beginnings of a muzzle, like a wolf's, hovering about a foot above my outstretched hand. Warm breath pushed back the icy chill, the wretched flame from my lighter dancing wildly beneath the creature's sigh.

I caught Rachelle as she bumped into me, still walking backward.

Then, as one, we turned and ran. Adrenaline spiked through us, casting aside the languid pull of the fog. Behind us, a hungry snarl ripped out of the woods. Crashing sounds of pursuit dogged us. They sounded like they were coming from right behind us, and I imagined I could feel hot breath on the back of my neck.

The Gates of Hell were just ahead, Matlas recording without looking into the camera, his features locked in worry as we approached in a full-tilt sprint. Rachelle let out a gasp, and I turned in time to see her go down in a spray of dead vegetation. I skidded to a stop, nearly slipping on the dry leaves underfoot, and reversed course. The menacing growls swelled to fill the woods on all sides, the dying leaves in the trees shivering in response, detaching from their precarious perches among the branches. They cascaded down around us.

I took Rachelle's arm and heaved. She stumbled to her feet and immediately began forward again. It was right behind us, I knew. I could imagine a toothy maw descending from the fog and closing around my neck, tearing and rending. The horrifying thought spurred me onward. Rachelle and I flew across the Gates of Hell, and Matlas followed suit, all three of us racing toward the base of the nearest stone steps.

We took the steps two and three at a time, emerging on the middle level. The fog was thick here, too, transforming the landscape into something unrecognizable, alien, *dangerous*. Without slowing, without discussing anything, all three of us continued our dash to the base of the second set of stairs. As we climbed, the fog finally seemed to lessen, to pull back. It was the forest's guard, and at last we had cleared the skeletal line of trees and evergreens.

Rachelle collapsed to the grass at the top of the stairs. "What... the hell... was that?" she gasped.

"That," Matlas announced with a winded grin, "was the Thirteen Steps to Hell."

While catching my breath, I looked around, surveying the cemetery for any trace of Mikey. The creepy, likely undead CEO of E-Pluribus was nowhere to be seen. *Balls.*

"What did you guys see?" Matlas asked, his excitement evident. "I heard a good amount of growling."

"Is there such a thing as a *good* amount of growling?" Rachelle asked, her sharp wit rising up to cover her fear. If the girl even experienced fear. Holy crap. She had been one iota away from becoming a chew toy for a hellish grave monster.

"Fair enough. So, what did you see? Did you stumble on a pack of wolves or something?"

Rachelle shook her head, coming to her feet. "Not a lot of wolves around here." In an undertone, she muttered, "It was definitely in the 'or something' category." I was still doubled over, hands on knees, my breaths starting to come easier. I inspected every shadow thoroughly, but to my dismay it appeared Mikey was well and truly gone. I realized Rachelle hadn't answered Matlas further. Looking up, I met her gaze. She was letting me decide.

"Someone went to some pretty impressive lengths to make us think this graveyard is actually haunted," I said, drawing Matlas's attention. Behind him, Rachelle looked away. Was she... disappointed?

"Uh, sure," he said slowly, unsure how to respond to that. "What's next?"

*Next, sleep.* Then I needed to track down Mikey. He was scared. He'd told me he was being hunted, right? Maybe he wasn't able to talk around Scary Gun Lady. Maybe she was his warden. Could *she* be my mysterious texter? I needed more information. After that, I needed to help Gregory keep anyone else from being murdered. Assist Caden in creating an incarnate support network, which was looking more necessary with every hour that ticked by.

"Next, sleep." I told him. It was pretty much the only part of the plan I could say in front of a mortal. "I'd say we earned it."

Matlas looked crestfallen as he said, "Yeah, yeah, of course."

"We aren't done here," I told him, pushing some cheer into my voice. "We need to come back during the daytime, though, and examine things in better light." Inwardly, I cringed at the next part. Sometimes, I swore it would be easier just to explain incarnates to mortals. "Do you know of anyone who may have caught wind of you coming to see me? Someone who could have set up an elaborate hoax to ruin the show?"

He blinked, clearly surprised by the question. And who wouldn't be? Normal twenty-year-old college students didn't have enemies. Not *real* ones, anyway. "Not that I can think of," he replied, sounding lost.

We began the trek toward the entrance to the graveyard. "Well, if you think of anyone, let me know. It could have been something as simple as bad luck, if we stumbled across a den of black bears—or even wild dogs."

He nodded, a frown pulling his lips down. "Not a lot of bears around here," he remarked.

Rachelle snickered. "Oh, more likely to be wolves, was it?"

His frown reversed course, and he tipped an imaginary cap. "Touché."

"You didn't see anything clearly on the cam?" I asked, interrupting their banter.

"No, not really. That fog came rolling in so quickly, I think I was actually able to see more with my eyes than through the lens." He turned to Rachelle. "Speaking of which, did I see you actually start down the steps?"

"Why not? They're just stairs." She glanced at me, her face unreadable. "It's all about belief. Well, and imagination, too. Anyway, I don't believe in the supernatural. When you've found as many loopholes as Emery and I have, you stop believing in fantasy. Nothing but cold, hard facts for this girl."

He mulled that over for a few moments before responding. We had reached the edge of the cemetery, the chain linking the two posts in front of us, our cars just beyond.

"You don't believe in mystery anymore?" he asked quietly.

She kicked a rock, and it skittered down the road. "Are you kidding? I *love* mystery. But I don't fear it. It's just a puzzle waiting to be solved." Her gaze dropped down to her feet. "Though I vote we do it in the bright, warm sunlight."

He smiled, shifting so he stumbled into her playfully. His grin broadened when her head snapped up in surprise. "Hey, Grey, you going all fraidy-cat on me the sudden, or what?"

"No, *sir!*" she retorted, laughter in her voice.

"Good. Then let's take it from the top Sunday at noon, if that works for you."

She glanced at me, and I nodded, so she said, "Great. It's a date." Then her brow knitted. "How did you know my last name?"

He shook his head, not managing to stow his white smile. "No way I'm telling you now. I heard you like mysteries."

We reached our cars, and I said my goodbyes. Rachelle turned to rest a gloved hand on Matlas's upper arm. "Don't worry," she told him. "We're not giving up. We'll get to the bottom of the mystery here, too."

He bobbed his head in agreement. She unlocked her car and slid inside, Matlas holding the door open for her. I started toward my car to give them privacy, but I could still hear their final exchange.

"Oh, and Rachelle?" he asked sweetly. "Call me 'sir' one more time. I dare you."

*I* veered into the grocery store parking lot. A few months ago, the lot had been overflowing with baskets of flowering plants, and fruit had lined the walkway into the store itself. It was still technically summer, but anyone taking cues from the tree-rimmed edges of the parking lots could see the season was in its death throes. The trees were in various stages of undress, their leaves either a deadening red-brown or already strewn about the ground. It was sunny, and though it had warmed up since the morning's clear and chilly debut, the temperature highs of mid-September paled in comparison to the highs of the month prior. Compared to two-season regions, summer was fleeting in the Pacific Northwest, but at least we experienced it. That was one of my favorite things about Seattle: it observed all four seasons. Even if most years featured rainy winters rather than white ones.

I circled the lot twice before I spotted Gregory's unmarked sedan parked in the back, nearer the bank that shared the same lot than the grocery store I had asked him to meet me at. Our conversation had been very brief.

I slid into a spot next to his car and jumped out, leaving my phone in the center console. Gregory rolled his window down. I dipped my head low to speak with him—sometimes I still wasn't accustomed to this incarnation's height.

"Gregory," I said. "Walk with me?"

He grunted—probably in annoyance, but who could tell?—but exited his vehicle without demanding to know why. He was an intelligent man; he knew I wouldn't make a needless request. Or maybe I should say he could tell the difference between when I was making a needless request and when I was serious. Considering that, I felt a stab of shame for my earlier frustration with him. Given our vastly different personalities, he gave me quite a bit of leeway, I realized.

"Leave your cell," I said softly, hoping my low tone would not be picked up by anyone listening in. He paused, then turned and placed his phone in a concealed compartment in his car.

We strode out onto the sidewalk by the bank and, surprisingly, he broke the silence first. "You're being watched?" At my curt nod, he added, "Phone bugged?"

I sighed and bobbed my head again. "I don't know how. It's barely been out of my sight."

"I have a few updates for you."

"Me, too. I saw Asker last night."

He looked at me sharply. For Gregory, that was the equivalent of shrieking and demanding an explanation. But he just said, "You first, then."

We took a route that would circle the lot, following the sidewalk. I waited until we passed two men with orange vests and leaf blowers, then cleared my throat. "I had an unrelated job last night. Debunking a haunting at Paradise Lake Cemetery, in Maltby. Asker was there. He asked for my help, said he was being hunted, and told me that whoever was hunting him could listen through my cell."

"The person responsible for texting you those threats, perhaps."

"It makes sense," I agreed, feeling cold despite the sun. "A few things are starting to add up. If my phone is bugged, then maybe they can track its location, too. The texter was disappointed when I didn't leave the investigation yesterday, even *after* I returned to my car."

Gregory understood immediately. "They weren't physically

there." He took a few more strides before continuing. "That aligns with what we concluded about those photos of your friends and family, too: this person is monitoring you remotely."

"That's what I think. It also explains how they knew where I lived." I glanced at him. "The brick," I added.

He ran his hand across the stubble on his chin and cheeks in thought. "The texter and brick thrower are the same person. Or working together."

"To make matters more complicated, I'm not convinced my mystery texter is my enemy." We reached the intersection at the corner of the lot, where a man wearing headphones and dark glasses spun and danced with a sign proclaiming a clearance at a nearby store. We turned and continued down the sidewalk. "Aside from the fact they told me they don't want to hurt me, they also helped me to elude Scary Gun Lady at the café yesterday."

Gregory gave me a flat look. "'Scary Gun Lady?'"

"Uh, yes. Remember those mercenaries I told you about? The ones hired by E-Pluribus to hunt down incarnates?" At his unwavering stare, I blushed. "I think she's their leader."

"Do you have a better description than 'Scary Gun Lady'?"

"Short," I said quickly, "maybe five-four or so. Black. Athletic. Hair is medium length, long bangs covering half her face. She's not subtle, either; she shot at me in broad daylight. Carried at least four guns that I saw. Oh, and they all drive black SUVs. Tahoes, I think."

He took this all in, mentally cataloging the information, I thought, then said, "Asker tell you anything else? Like why he was in a graveyard," he added wryly.

"Not much, no. We ran into trouble and split up. I think I was right, though: he's the Zombie, or something close to it. But now I'm thinking he's not a Malevolent."

"If he contacts you again, let me know. In the meantime, I have news, too." He grimaced. "Got a call this morning. There was a third murder."

I inhaled sharply. "And you let me blab on about Scary Gun Lady? Who was it?"

"Jacqueline Bergstrom. Goes—went—by Jax. President of a Seattle start-up called New Brave World."

"Let me guess," I said. "Tech company?"

"Yes. Specifically, it builds schematics for coding predictability. There's more. She's a former employee of E-Pluribus. Worked on the development of Unum with Asker. And," Gregory looked straight ahead, his words matter-of-fact, "she was an incarnate."

I stared at him for a moment, then dropped my gaze to my feet. "Damn."

"The Cyberpunk. Which makes three tech industry titans, all incarnates, dead in as many days. The preliminary investigation of the crime scene indicated the murders of Jax and al-Aziz match the MO of Asker's killer. Though forensics haven't come back yet to confirm."

Ahead, the sidewalk dipped to allow traffic in and out of the parking lot. A car pulled up and put on its blinker. The driver waved to us to go ahead, and we crossed quickly and silently. I mulled over what Gregory had told me, but something stood out.

"The Cyberpunk?" I asked when we'd put the car behind us. "Isn't that more of a genre than an urban legend?"

"Jax struggled to find her place in society," Gregory replied, his face cut from stone. But his voice held an undercurrent of emotion. "Cyberpunk is a new concept, only decades old, and I think she may have been the first incarnation."

"You knew her personally?" I ventured.

Gregory wouldn't meet my eyes, his features severe. "Very well. I considered her a friend." He didn't seem ready to say anything else, and I was too surprised to respond. After a hundred feet of silence, I opened my mouth, but he spoke first, quietly. "She was only fourteen when I first met her. Caught her shoplifting from an electronics store. Bright kid, full of spunk and angst. An only child to starving artist parents, she understood computers and technology like they were the only things in the world that mattered. I was able to pull some strings, get her into an engineering program at Tech Academy Seattle. I hoped it would get her off the street and off drugs, so she wouldn't end up in juvie." His lips twitched. "I was partially right. Anyway, we stayed in touch over the years. I hope she doesn't change too much when she... comes back." He took a deep breath. "Maybe a few less tattoos."

"I'm sorry." I didn't know what else to say. It was the most I had ever heard Gregory say at once, but his lack of inflection was evidence of the pain the story caused him.

He stopped abruptly. I stumbled to a halt, surprised. The Watchman's gaze burned into me, a fire behind his eyes. "Tell Caden I'm in. I want to help make Seattle a safer place for incarnates."

My heart should have soared at the news, but the gravity of his stare weighed it down. "I—thank you," I said.

Gregory accepted my words with a peremptory nod, jolting back into motion. We strode down the sidewalk, pace a little too brisk, and he said, "We're looking into the possibility of Abdul al-Aziz working on the creation of Unum with Asker and Jax. It could be that Asker faked his own death, then began eliminating those who helped him design his greatest accomplishment."

I hesitated, and he caught it, his expression demanding that I speak. "I don't think it's Asker," I said. "When I met him last night, however briefly, he seemed more 'on the run' than 'on the hunt.'"

We came to the last corner in our loop, and Gregory slowed his pace as our cars came back into view. "We should have more from forensics by the end of the day." He stopped before we reached our vehicles. "Tech came back. No one accessed Asker's office on the day he died."

I frowned. "Wh—*no one?*" I puffed out a breath, thinking. "The records were deleted," I realized. "Someone tampered with security."

Gregory agreed. "Which means nothing we find out from tech is worth a damn. But it narrows down our suspect list. There aren't many who have top-level access like that."

"And Asker's personal computer?"

"Remotely accessed, seemingly by Asker himself leading up to his murder... and throughout the next day."

"So... someone knew he was dead and was covering for him?" I narrowed my eyes. "This sounds like it would be impossible to be anything other than an inside job. The killer knows far too much about E-Pluribus for it to be anything else."

Gregory snorted. "But something else is going on, too. It can't be coincidence that the only victims are incarnates. Especially on the heels of the discovery that E-Pluribus was after them."

I glanced down at my watch, which I'd worn only because I knew I was going to leave my phone in the car. "I need to get going. Date night," I explained with a grin.

A ghost of a smile crossed his face. "Have fun. Put the investigation out of your mind, if you can. I'll look into getting you a burner phone, for when we talk about the case." He hesitated, then added, "And I'll reach out to my contacts and get you a list if any are interested in joining the Incarnate Watch."

"Thanks, Gregory. I can't wait to tell Caden the good news."

We parted. I slid into my car and checked my phone, relieved I hadn't missed any texts or calls. I messaged Caden and told him I was on my way, then checked my hair in the rearview mirror and popped a mint from the glove box into my mouth.

Hey, I told you it was date night.

*I* parked in a guest parking spot and walked across the lot toward Rachelle's apartment. Caden was fully capable of driving himself over to my house, but what can I say? I'm a gentleman. I'd even vacuumed and dusted the interior of my Rogue. Well, the front. Focusing mostly on the passenger side. No one looks in the back, anyway.

I left my phone in the car in case I was correct and it was bugged. But as I crossed the parking lot, my mood was light, and my footsteps followed suit. I was determined to follow Gregory's advice and bury my worries about the investigation somewhere deep in my mind. Not only was tonight about dinner, action movies, and Caden, but I also needed an evening off—physically and mentally. With last night's fiasco at the cemetery and the previous night's brick-throwing and subsequent murder scene, I thought I'd earned an evening to myself. Well, *ourselves.*

A woman taking her dog for a stroll stopped to allow it to sniff at the base of a sign pole in the small grassy area reserved for pets. The dog, seeing me, began barking excitedly, so I waved good-naturedly at the lady. She was on the phone but gave me a little half wave in response. I continued forward, then froze. In a parking stall not far from them was the red car from two nights ago.

The woman with the dog was watching me curiously, so I began moving again, heading toward the apartment. Just to be sure I wasn't mistaking the car for another red sports car, I snuck a glance at the license plate. **SPERANT**. It was the same one.

I knocked on Rachelle's front door, returning my attention to the night ahead. Dinner. Action movies. Caden. To my surprise, it was Hope who answered the door. What was she doing here? She wore jeans and a pink blouse, her white-blonde hair loose and the bruise on her cheek fading.

"Hi, Hope," I said. "Rachelle and Caden are here, right?" I had seen both of their cars in the parking lot.

"Yes, yes, come on in." She held the door open for me.

"Is everything okay?" It didn't matter, I told myself. Dinner, action movies, Caden.

"Oh yes, everything is fine. A group of those E-Pluribus brutes followed me around this morning. At a distance," she added quickly. "I just wasn't sure where else to go."

"Emery, come on up!" Rachelle called down. "Caden is just about ready."

I ascended the stairs and spun my usual kitchen chair around and straddled it, sitting backward. Hope hovered, looking out of place. "You can sit down," I offered.

She glanced at me in surprise, then smiled and took a seat. "It's been getting dark a lot earlier," she noted, gesturing vaguely to outside. It struck me that that might be something the Virgo would pay attention to, but it was still small talk.

"Sure is," I agreed easily. "Is there something you want to talk to me about?"

Her face went guilty. "That obvious, huh?"

I grinned. "You were practically pacing. This is not a big enough kitchen for that."

"Ah, yes." She took a deep breath, then blurted, "I would like to hire you."

My eyebrows raised. "What for?"

"Protection. I understand, from talking with Rachelle, that you and your... um, partner sometimes provide incarnates with protection." Her words tumbled out quickly, as though she were asking me for something embarrassing, like a loan. "I don't know why E-Pluribus is after me, but I really, *really* don't want to be caught. As the Virgo, I don't do overly well indoors."

I was surprised at her admission. It came perilously close to discussing her fatal flaw, which was... well, among incarnates, it was essentially a taboo subject. Uncomfortable. It was vulnerability on a level mortals couldn't quite understand. The connection and intimacy of sharing it made even me blush. To be fair, Hope hadn't actually *said* it was her fatal flaw. I was probably overthinking.

"We won't let anything happen to you."

She gave me a fleeting, close-lipped smile. "Thank you, but you don't understand. I'm requesting full protection." I frowned, feeling slightly affronted. It sounded like she was insinuating we were negligent in our protection unless she paid for it. She mistook my consternation for puzzlement and raced to explain. "I don't expect it for free. I have a well-paying job, and I can pay you both. It wouldn't be forever, either; just until we find out what E-Pluribus is up to."

She took a breath, and I used the opportunity to say, "I accept, but you should know I would do it for free. I'm in the business of protecting incarnates." I grinned self-consciously. "Emphasis on the *protecting*, not the *business*."

Hope was beside herself with relief. "Well, I won't intrude on your date, so we'll say the contract starts tomorrow morning?"

I shouldn't have been surprised—she seemed like a businesswoman, so of course she'd want a contract. She probably liked everything written out. I wondered if that was a trait of Virgos—the ones born around this time of year, that is, not the incarnate. There was only one of her.

"I'll draft up an agreement," I said. I had a generic one just for these types of situations. Or, more accurately, *Rachelle* had a contract just for these types of situations.

I could tell she wanted to say more. "What is it?" I encouraged.

"I'm just surprised. I thought you'd need to talk it over with your partner."

My thoughts flashed guiltily to Rachelle. I should discuss it with her before committing, but business had been slow enough that we hadn't refused any offers. I waved away her concern. "I know she'd want to keep you safe."

Hope looked down, uncomfortable. I watched her, sighing inwardly. I just wanted an evening with Caden, a nice dinner, and a mindless action movie. "Is there something else?"

"Sorry, I wasn't clear. I meant your other partner. The Guardian Angel."

I blinked. "Oh. *Oh!* No, it isn't like that. Caden isn't a partner in our business. Just Rachelle and me."

Confusion and worry flickered across Hope's face. Whatever high-paying job she worked, I hoped it wasn't customer-facing. She was an open book, every emotion crossing her features like a written announcement. "But he'll still be protecting me, right?" she asked in a small voice.

I kicked myself. I had misunderstood her apprehension. She wanted truly premium—*divine*—protection. I replayed our conversation in my head, realizing my error. "Caden will help keep you safe," I told her carefully, trying to project confidence. "We all will. Rachelle and I are very capable."

Her hands fluttered like distressed birds. "I didn't mean to imply —I saw you and Rachelle in action, I mean—but he's the Guardian Angel. I—I would just feel so much more comfortable..." She trailed off, chagrin pulling at the corners of her attempted smile. "I'm sorry. You're right, of course. I didn't mean to imply you and Rachelle aren't up to the task. This week has frayed my nerves, that's all. I'll feel better that the Guardian Angel is nearby, even if he isn't the one carrying out the contract."

I considered her words—trying not to feel offended—and how to respond. Caden chose that moment to walk into the kitchen. "Did I hear my name?" he asked, squeezing my shoulder affectionately.

Clearly ready for date night, Caden wore a dark button-up shirt with the sleeves rolled up to his elbows, over a white V-neck that dipped to show off a triangle of pale skin. His feather-light hair had been slicked up with product. Normally, he was minty fresh; his clean appearance left me tingling with how effortlessly pure he looked, felt, *smelled*. But right now, it was as if someone had added cayenne pepper and served him warm. Drinking him in, it still left me tingly, but it was coupled by an unexpected—and not unpleasant—heat that I felt in little pinpricks across my skin.

"We were negotiating a contract for protection," Hope said. "I had hoped hiring Emery would mean I'd be retaining your services."

"Ah. Classes, work, and volunteer hours keep me pretty busy. But I'll talk it over with Emery and see if we can't come to an arrangement."

Hope flashed him a relieved smile. "Thank you." She heaved a sigh. "I'm sorry for imposing on your special evening. I'll keep myself safe for one more night."

A thought occurred to me. "Hope, do you work for a tech company?"

"No," she said, shaking her head. "I'm an accountant for a law firm downtown."

I nodded absently, biting my cheek in thought. Three tech moguls dead—two, if I removed Asker from the tally—and two kidnapping attempts: the Mermaid and the Virgo. What did it mean? Were the abduction attempts different than the murders? If I hadn't foiled E-Pluribus, would we have more murders on our hands? For some reason, I didn't think so. It was almost as if...

As if there were two different parties involved. Murderers and abductors.

And wait. Hadn't there been *three* foiled attempts?

"Sperant!" I exclaimed, the meaning of the personalized license plate coming back to me like a palm to my face. "You drive a red sports car, don't you?"

She looked like someone who was answering a knock at her front door: curious, but also concerned, not knowing who was on the other side. "I do. Why?"

"Because I just realized I've saved you twice. Yesterday with Rachelle, and the evening before from the black SUV."

"Oh!" Her wariness melted away, as though she'd found a friend rather than a stranger at her door. "That was you? Emery Luple, you are full of surprises. Thank you, I mean. That's twice I owe you my life." She blushed. "And I repay you by insulting your protection. How can I make it up to you?"

I hooked Caden's slim waist from my sitting position and tugged him close. "You keep yourself safe tonight, and we'll call it even."

Caden laughed and pulled me to my feet. "That's enough business talk for tonight." He hefted his overnight bag, and his smile curled into something more private, more personal. "I was promised date night with a beamish boy."

Dinner. Action movies.

My eyes roamed over his snug-fitting black jeans and his raked-back hair, finally alighting on his familiar seafoam eyes. I mentally added cuddling to the list. Lots of cuddling.

# 16

*T*he evening swam by, a memory captured with a dream filter and dipped in tropical waters.

At dinner, we sat across from one another in a small, round booth —all low lights, linen tablecloths, murmured conversation, and spicy foods. The restaurant specialized in tapas, the bite-sized portions perfect for sharing and trying new things. The background music and buzz of conversation brushed over us as we huddled close and nibbled on a variety of bites, laughing as certain bold flavors elicited different responses from us. Caden tended to like the sweet and I the sour, and we battled over the savory ones.

We retired to my (slash my mom's) house afterward. After a quick chat, Mom retreated to her bedroom and we found the corner of the couch in the living room, ignored the boarded-up window, and snuggled up for a movie. We had to nestle under one of the blankets from the closet, because my favorite blanket was missing. Maybe Mom had removed it because it had gotten glass on it when the brick had come through the window? Caden wanted to watch something fluffy—his word, not mine—and we settled on a rom-com between a secret agent and the girl next door. I couldn't tell you anything about the film except that it met the minimum quota of explosions for me to classify it as an action flick. The important part was Caden's body tucked against mine, my arms wrapped around his torso as he leaned back against me, head on my shoulder. I could feel the rise and fall of his chest, the sudden flexing of his stomach muscles against my hands when he laughed at something happening on-screen.

The movie ended and Caden stretched, arching his back and yawning. I was tempted to tickle his abdomen, but I refrained. I'd discovered early on that he was ticklish. I learned about five seconds later that our relationship would remain intact so long as I did not abuse that knowledge. And about five seconds after that, I learned he was permitted to tickle me and I could not retaliate. Which wasn't fair, but he was cute enough to get away with certain inequalities. He made to get up, and I pulled him back into my lap, burying my face in his hair and inhaling his clean, spring scent.

"Where do you think you're going?" I asked, something between a chuckle and a growl in my voice.

He twisted, turning to face me with a grin. "You make playing hard to get very challenging," he complained. I opened my mouth to respond, but he kissed me.

If ever I doubted Caden was an incarnate, the proof was not his literal glow. It wasn't his wings made of light, his shining halo, or his superhuman speed. It wasn't found in the way he coaxed honesty from those around him, or how aches and wounds disappeared at his touch.

The proof was in his kiss. My boyfriend had lifetimes of mastering the perfect kiss locked away somewhere in his immortal mind. I closed my eyes and felt myself sink into him, tension and worries bleeding away into those tropically warm waters. I was drowning—and I didn't care.

I hauled in a deep breath when he pulled back, already following him like I was a compass and his mouth was magnetic north. A small laugh bubbled up from him, and he pushed me back.

I gave him a pouty look, and he laughed again. His face was flushed. "I have to pee."

My eyebrows shot up. "Angels pee?"

He pushed me back and scrambled to his feet, then leaned down and kissed me again—shorter—to show me he didn't want to leave. "I don't know about the rest of them, but the Guardian Angel definitely does."

I affected a sultry pout. I was going for one of those smoldering smirks, but I wasn't sure how well I achieved it. "Well, good to know everything works down there, I suppose."

He snorted. "I'm sure we would have already confirmed everything works if either of us had our own place." He cuffed me playfully on the back of the head before grabbing his overnight bag and leaving the room. My grin chased him down the hallway and boomeranged back to me, hitting me with a dose of giddiness. Damn, I loved that boy.

My grin froze at the thought, then melted away. Love. I'd been in love before. And though I didn't yet have specific memories to corroborate it, I was growing more and more certain I'd been in love with Caden before. I couldn't remember the situation, the genders involved, the names, or really any of the specifics. I couldn't remember the lifetime—lifetimes?—we'd spent together. I hadn't really tried to conjure up those memories, either. I'd long since learned to treat each life as something fresh in order to have new "firsts," new discoveries. Anticipation and the emotions built around it, hope and exhilaration—and the less pleasant ones, too, like worry and doubt—they were the rungs on the ladder of life. It didn't matter that the ladder stretched into eternity; each foothold was a moment of progress, a chance for reflection, to evaluate how far I'd come. Without those rungs, an immortal life was just two poles extending endlessly into time with no sense of change, devoid of the things that brought meaning to each life—and thus, to the overarching, immortal life. Most importantly, it helped me to feel human.

It wasn't perfect. Memories from previous lifetimes always trickled in, and I wasn't austere enough in my dedication to new experiences to turn down knowledge of hard lessons I'd learned in my past. While some of those lessons I'd undoubtedly relive, I didn't mind drawing on my past to speed them along. Besides, leaning on my prior lives gave me unique opportunities to improve the world—for mortals and incarnates, both. And it helped tremendously to fall back on the skills I'd learned, even if the world's turning changed the types of skills that were necessary for survival.

So. I'd been in love before. But not always with Caden. Several incarnations ago, I'd fallen in love with a mortal. Huntington. Our time together had been cut short, and the tragedy had shaped my next few incarnations. It was a wound Caden couldn't heal. And because I hadn't loved since, I'd feared that it would shape my next love. I was trying so hard not to let it.

I'd been in love before. So? Not this incarnation. It was the perfect time to seal my past where it belonged. To feel the heady flush of first love, to rewrite those awful experiences I'd sooner forget. But while my memories of past lifetimes with Caden weren't accessible, my time with Huntington was engraved on my psyche. The memories were so crystal clear, they were sharp enough to cut. And they were so dark—or bright, or whatever they were—that they demanded my attention, eclipsed all memory of previous incarnations spent with the Guardian Angel.

Since Caden had gotten settled in Seattle, we'd only been able to see each other a couple times per week. We'd barely been able to do more than snatch quick dinners between blogs and volunteer work and classes. Hell, we'd probably spent more time working incarnate jobs than we had doing traditional dating activities. We were both happy—but a small voice whispered we could be happier. After all, he pulled so many long hours at the hospital. I knew it wasn't fair, but that same small voice asked why he wouldn't rather spend that time with me.

I told that voice to go to hell.

I sighed heavily as I slipped into my bedroom and changed into something far more comfortable: basketball shorts and a black undershirt. I hoped the sigh would expel the unwelcome thoughts caught in my chest like fishhooks, fine and nearly invisible, but still capable of tugging me down. It worked. Sort of.

I turned off the overhead light, flicked on the warmer glow of my table lamp, and plopped onto my bed. I turned on the small flat-screen TV on top of my dresser, just to have some noise more than anything else. Mom's bedroom was down the hall, and I didn't want her overhearing us.

Um, I know how that sounds, and that isn't what I meant. Don't get me wrong—with him staying over, sexy thoughts and youthful hormones swirled around in my mind and body. We'd only been able to spend all night together on a few occasions. Which was all the more peculiar since the first two nights after I met him we spent alone together: first at the hospital while Rachelle underwent surgery for her broken leg, and then hiding out at Ichabod Crane's farm, my head in Caden's lap, falling asleep to the sound of a ghostly horse picking its way around our haven. But since moving to Seattle, life had gotten in the way time and time again.

At first, it had been my fault. My business had suddenly swelled following the Ahedrian murders, and Rachelle and I had found our hands full with both mortal requests for debunking and incarnate requests for aid. I wasn't complaining; the influx of money and favors had funded two vehicles in addition to the everyday costs of life. Then, just as the rush of our New York–fueled jobs leveled out, the university had opened and Caden began taking courses. Between classes and volunteer work at the hospital, it was now his schedule that impeded our time together. Neither of us begrudged the other their busy schedule; it was just one of those things. But it meant we stole time together whenever we could.

Caden entered my room and closed the door softly behind him. He wore bright blue, fuzzy pajama bottoms and a white tee. His golden hair was damp, the carefully stylized look once more surrendering to his usual feathery, casual appearance. It didn't matter—even dressed for sleep, he radiated beauty. Not for the first time, I wondered if it was my attraction to him or his glamour that made my skin heat and my heartbeat race when I looked at him. Maybe it was a little of both, but I suspected his glamour had rather little to do with it.

So. I'd been in love before. That didn't take away from the significance of this love. Tonight, I decided, I would say it: I'd tell him how much he meant to me.

I lifted the comforter and blankets invitingly. He gave me a shy smile and slipped in next to me, lying on his side, head propped up on his elbow, face tilted toward mine. "I had a really great night with you," he said.

"Me, too. Date's not over yet, though." *Not until I say it. Not until I tell you how I feel.*

He quirked an eyebrow. "Good. So it's not too late for me to do this?" He leaned in and kissed me—not too deeply, but a sweet brushing of his lips on mine, leaving mine atingle.

"Mm, never too late for that," I murmured when he pulled back. I hooked my ankle under one of his calves and pulled, entangling our legs. The fuzzy pajamas felt soft and warm against my bare shins. "I want to tell you something."

Caden snuggled closer to me, the contours of our bodies fitting together like we'd been incarnated as a matching set. I was momentarily distracted by his waist bumping against mine. Curled up as he was, his head nestled in the curve of my neck. "You're such a tease," I accused.

He peeked up at me with an innocent expression that immediately collapsed into a coy smile when it met my glower. "What did you want to tell me?" His breath tickled my jaw.

"I—" I tried to swallow, but my mouth was too dry. *I love you, Caden.* Why was it so hard to say? I knew I loved him. Hell, he probably knew it already, too. But the magnitude of the feelings behind the words felt heavy, ungainly. I was a very talkative person; it shouldn't have been challenging to express how I felt. But the words stuck in my throat.

*You've loved before,* my immortal voice warned. *You know how that ended.*

But that wasn't true of this incarnation. I had barely given a thought to Huntington in months, and his eyes no longer chased me. I'd buried that demon. This time around, I had only loved one guy, and he was currently pressed up against me, wrapped in my arms, waiting for whatever I was going to say. His breathing was shallow, his eyes large and luminous. Expectant, but not demanding.

The perfect moment stretched... and now it was receding, slipping out of sight. The longer I waited, the less perfect the words sounded. He'd recognize the struggle inside me, but he'd misunderstand the reasons for it. He'd think about how easily words came to me, but not those words, and wonder why that was. He'd doubt the heartfelt intention behind them, seeing only the hesitation.

*You aren't giving him enough credit.* A tiny voice fought to be heard. But it was fading, while the doubt mounted. Better to deflect, to say something else for now. I loved him—I'd find the moment again. Right? You didn't get just one moment, one chance, at this kind of thing; that would be absurd.

"I—uh, I talked to Gregory," I said instead. "He's willing to support your idea of an Incarnate Watch."

Despite my hesitation, Caden brightened at my words. He drew away a little to get enough space to have a conversation, and I fought the urge to pull him back against me.

"You waited this long to tell me?"

"I wanted us to have our date first. Besides, he just told me this afternoon. There was another murder. This time it hit close to home." I sighed. I'd killed any romantic energy in the air. At least our legs were still entangled. "He said he'll start reaching out to incarnates right away, get a feel for those willing to join."

Caden nodded, deep in thought. "There are quite a few incarnates in the Seattle area," he noted.

I gave him a one-shouldered shrug. "Every city has its own urban legends, so local incarnates are found pretty much everywhere. That said, traveling incarnates definitely tend to gravitate toward large cities and cultural hubs."

"Sure."

I opened my mouth but paused at the thoughtful look on his face. "Penny for your thoughts?"

He blinked, his eyes refocusing on mine. "You," he said simply. Then he grinned. "I'm pretty much always thinking of you."

"That can't be true," I scoffed. "You study too much to be always thinking of me."

"I think about you far too often while I'm studying, actually. It's distracting." He pecked me on the nose. "Just now, I was thinking the reason Seattle attracts so many incarnates is you."

"What?"

"Don't give me that look. It isn't that outrageous of an idea. Your powers of coincidence and convenience—"

"Aren't that far-reaching," I interrupted.

"But what if they are?" He shuffled so he was sitting up in the bed, facing me. "We don't know much about the Protagonist or the powers at your disposal. But we do know that happenstance and fate seem to line up like bowling pins when you're around."

"Aw, you always say the sweetest things," I teased. "Is my new nickname going to be 'bowling ball'?"

"You aren't the bowling ball, Em. You're the bowler. See, the way I figure it, conveniences and coincidences line up, and you get to take the shot. With practice, your powers will be like the bowling ball and knock all the pins down—or, I guess, the exact pins you want. But if you aren't a frequent bowler, then you just get the *chance* to bowl." He shook his head, red spots on his cheeks. "This isn't coming out right. I'm going to try a different metaphor."

"Okay, but can I at least be something hot in this next one?"

Caden laughed. "Sure. Okay, so you're a chef—a hot, handsome, sexy chef—and convenience is your recipe, and coincidences are your ingredients. Everything is lined up for you to make the perfect dish. Your powers give you that, but it still comes down to your talent and your effort to create the dish itself. Or you can create something completely different, or nothing at all."

"How does this relate to your original point about Seattle having so many incarnates?"

"I was getting to that. They're your guests. They come from far and wide to sample your delicious meals."

I considered his words. "Okay, so let's assume your metaphor works and isn't solely designed to make me hungry. What's the point of it all?"

"In this example, where would you say your Sanctum is?"

"You aren't supposed to answer a question with another question." He didn't respond, so I frowned as I thought about it. "Seattle? Oh, you meant as the hot chef. So, maybe my restaurant?"

"Exactly. Well, almost. I think maybe your Sanctum would be the kitchen, but if you invited guests—or incarnates—to your restaurant, your Sanctum could protect them even if they're just in the restaurant itself."

"You lost me. I'm pretty certain you don't want me to open up a restaurant... but not as sure as I was ten minutes ago."

Caden bit his lip. "I want to make Seattle a... like, a Sanctum City. A refuge, I suppose. A place of peace, where incarnates of all types can live in harmony—with each other and with mortals."

I made a face. "Even Malevolents? Because they aren't known for playing nice."

"We'd need to create some guidelines," he admitted. "But I think it would be possible to include all types, one day."

I was dubious, but I refrained from voicing my doubts. "And you think my powers can help to draw all these incarnates."

"I think they already are. And that's without you even trying. I think we have the chance to create something beautiful and lasting, here."

"That," I said with an accusatory glare, "sounds like a lot more than a simple neighborhood watch, Caden."

He didn't look away, didn't even redden. "It is. It's a community. Maybe it's even grander than that—a society. Before you object, I know it will be a lot of work. I know we can't do it alone. But we can start it." He looked down, his fingers picking at the bedsheets. "I think maybe you're the only one who can. Your powers—and mine, of course—can keep them safe."

I inhaled sharply. "Safe? Caden, it's a great idea, but we've already had three murders in the last few nights. I *am* here. I'm actively trying to help. And they still died."

"You can't be held responsible for their deaths, though. Besides, you're actually proving my point. There's no system in place to keep this from happening. Incarnates need to maintain law and order over their own kind; mortals can't police us if they don't even know we exist. The only reason they're making any headway on this case is because of you and Gregory."

My mind skittered backward to my memory of a life I barely remembered in a time half-forgotten, of a cheer from the Voices of the People and the Dryad's screams. I pushed the thoughts and the screams away. "All right. Let's pretend I agree. I don't, not yet, but I love—well, I love what you're trying to do. But what happens when we fail to protect them?"

"We do what we can to protect the rest," he said, as if it were obvious. "We're talking about incarnates here. We wait and watch for their return, welcome them back 1,001 days later. There are going to be tragedies, Em. We can't stop them from happening. But we can do everything in our power to minimize them. Between my guardianship, your abilities, and pooling the resources of the entire incarnate community, we could show everyone that we're stronger together. A Sanctum City won't be a perfect paradise, but we can make it as safe as possible. And just think, with the immortal nature of incarnates, no one could permanently shut us down. What starts as a simple neighborhood watch could continue to grow and never truly diminish, as more incarnates warm to the notion that there are safe places in the world."

He was so passionate, I found my objections budged ever so slightly, making room in my head for new possibilities, the grand dream he'd concocted. Was that his glamour? Or did I, too, yearn for a better system? My memories flashed back to ancient Rome, to the smell of manure and death. But instead of fear, I found a surge of defiance. I wanted to stop that from ever happening again. Maybe, just maybe, the way to do that wasn't in shying from past mistakes. Perhaps it was in learning from them, instead. Trial and error. I'm pretty sure the saying was coined by an incarnate.

"I'm not saying yes—" I began, but I cut off as he threw himself on me, arms wrapping around my neck.

"Thank you," he whispered into my ear. "It means so much to me that we do this together. Thank you, Em."

"I said I'm *not* saying yes!" I objected half-heartedly, but whatever else I was going to say was lost as he began kissing my ear, then my cheek, then my neck. His body was flush against mine again, weighing me down into the mattress, and I really didn't want to fight him off.

Sanctum City. I liked the sound of that.

Then his mouth was on mine, his kiss doing some things that didn't seem very angelic, and my thoughts dissolved along with my objections.

*T*he day greeted me in the best possible way: with Caden folded against me. Oh, what I wouldn't give to wake up every day just like that.

My left arm was trapped beneath his weight, and my right was curled across his chest, beneath his armpit. His breathing was soft and even, moving my arm up and down, until I tightened my grip possessively around him. He stirred, rolled to face me, and his eyes peeked open. He murmured thickly, "Morning," then buried his face in my chest, and I pulled him closer. His breathing became even again a few minutes later.

I dozed for another hour or so before Caden came fully awake. He kissed me on the nose and rolled out of bed, leaving behind an echo of warmth where his body had snuggled against me a moment before. I sighed happily and snatched my phone off the dresser. It was a little later than I'd thought, but I still had enough time to drop Caden off and speak with Hope about the protection she wanted before meeting Matlas at the cemetery.

I browsed my emails to make sure I hadn't received any pressing business for *There's Always a Loophole* and was about to send a text to Gregory checking up on the case when I remembered my phone had likely been bugged. I wondered if a planted bug could intercept texts or if it was just an audio thing, but I decided it wasn't worth the risk.

Caden returned a few minutes later, showered and dressed, and then I took my turn. But I made sure to come back into my bedroom wrapped in nothing but my towel. I liked the way Caden's eyes traced my skin, skimming over my muscles and drinking me in. I toyed with the idea of the towel *accidentally* slipping, but we were in my mom's house and the bedroom door wasn't fully closed, so I decided against it. Besides, I suspected Caden knew what was going through my mind, and that would have totally ruined it. So instead I slipped into some boxer briefs before dropping the towel into the laundry hamper, then dressed with exaggerated slowness. "Enjoying the show?"

Caden watched me shamelessly. "Almost as much as you enjoy giving it, I think."

I grinned, unable to hold it back. "I would offer to make you breakfast, but I think we're out of milk."

An amused expression flitted across his face. "And it would be hard to make Cheerios without milk." He nodded understandingly.

"Give me more credit than that," I argued. "I can cook." He waited with a smile hovering just on the other side of his eyes. "They were *Honey Nut* Cheerios," I muttered, snatching up my keys. "Come on. We'll stop by Jamba Juice. Smoothies on me."

As we headed toward the front door, we came across my mom working at the kitchen table, her laptop and a few documents fanned out around her. Behind her, an untouched mug of tea sat on the kitchen counter, clearly forgotten.

"Morning, Mom," I said. "Why are you working so hard on a Sunday morning?"

"Behind on a deadline," she said, not-so-discreetly hiding one of the files. For some reason, she exchanged a glance with Caden as she did it.

I plucked the full mug of tea off the counter and placed it within arm's reach on the table. Kissing the top of her head, I said, "I'll be back, possibly late. More cemetery footage."

"Have fun, boys."

As we exited the room, I said loudly to Caden, "Ten bucks says the tea is still there when I get home tonight."

"I see your ten bucks and raise you another five that there will be at least two more cups around the house then."

"I can hear you," Mom called. "And Caden—you're a traitor, hon."

Caden spun around and hollered back, "Come on, Lynn. I was going to cut you in on the deal."

I gave him a sour look, lowering my voice. "I think I'm rubbing off on you."

"Nah, can't corrupt an angel."

My stare turned pointed. "I'm pretty sure you can. That's like the Devil's whole schtick."

"Yeah, but I'm already an incarnate. I can't become a different one."

"Right."

Caden and I opened the doors to my car and got in. He gave me one of his most innocent looks. "Besides, can you imagine me in Hell incarnate?"

I started to snort, but then froze. Hell incarnate? Why hadn't *I* thought of that?

Caden was watching me, curious. "What?"

"I think I just figured out what happened at the graveyard," I said. "The Thirteen Steps to Hell. I think, maybe, my powers of convenience opened the way. Not to hell—I don't even know if hell exists. But what if they're the steps to Hell incarnate?"

Caden scrunched up his nose. "Incarnate stuff is so confusing sometimes. What's the difference between hell and Hell incarnate, anyway?"

"Everything." I frowned. "Okay, not much, I guess. But it's undoubtedly real, or has the potential to be. Hell incarnate would be a culmination of the myths surrounding hell. That means it would probably be home to—possibly the Lair of—many hellish incarnations. The Demon, the Devil, and..." I trailed off, then snapped my fingers. "And the Hellhound."

"The what?"

"Demonic dog," I said. "I'm sure that's what attacked Rachelle and me."

Caden gave me a flat look. "And you're going back there. Maybe I should go with you."

I shook my head, finally turning the vehicle on. I buckled up and threw it in reverse to get out of our driveway. "No need," I said, waving away his concerns as I pulled into traffic. "I know you're working a double shift. Don't worry. I can handle it."

"All right. But be careful. A thousand and one days is a long time to go without seeing my boyfriend."

I smiled at that. It was a sweet comment, even though it was vastly more complicated than that. I might come back as a young child, or living across the world with no means to get back to Seattle. I could even come back as an infant, like Caden had. That happened very, very rarely to me. Now that I knew I was the Protagonist, that made sense. Relatively few stories or urban legends featured a toddler or infant as their main character. Even when I'd thought I was the Monster Hunter, that logic had held true.

We parked in the Jamba Juice lot, went inside, and ordered. The metal tables and chairs outside the building called to us to sit and enjoy each other's company for just a little longer, but the chilly September morning and my noon graveyard appointment persuaded us to get back in the car and sip the smoothies on the go.

By the time we reached the apartment complex, I was running a few minutes behind. I half expected to see Rachelle waiting out in the parking lot, foot stamping in impatience. Instead, I saw Hope's car—had she stayed the night with Rachelle? It was eleven in the morning, so I supposed she'd had ample time to return today.

I pulled into a guest parking stall that I had been frequenting so often it might as well have been mine. Caden and I started toward Rachelle's apartment, but a group of people drew my attention. They were loitering by Hope's car, in twos and threes, and as my focus on them sharpened, I thought a few of the faces looked familiar. Were these the same people Rachelle and I had fought off in the restaurant when we'd saved Hope? If they were trying to act casual and inconspicuous, then they were absolutely miserable at it. They might as well have hidden behind cartoon cutouts of bushes—it might've improved their disguise. There was no doubting their affiliation; one of them wore a hat with the E-Pluribus logo on it, and another two had their company-issued ID badges visible.

I changed direction midstride and made to approach them. Caden didn't miss a beat, matching me step for step. In the morning light, he suddenly seemed to glow a little brighter. Truth be told, I only felt bold enough to confront the group because he was at my side. He was my Sanctum, my place of safety and power. Almost nothing could touch me with the Guardian Angel to watch over me.

"Hey," I called out as I approached. The distance between the small groups had all but disappeared, a single crowd forming. "Go home," I told them. "Hope is under my protection."

One of the young men sneered with the kind of confidence you only see when a bully has an entire crowd of people backing him up. He had a buzz cut and more than a dusting of freckles across his face. "Who the hell are you?"

"I just told you. I'm Hope's protection. That's all you need to know."

The man crossed his arms. "Are you one of *them*?"

Instead of answering him, I balled my hands into fists and said, "I know why you're here. Go back to E-Pluribus and leave us alone."

The man's eyebrows went up in surprise, and I barely refrained from barking a laugh. "You *are*," he said, almost to himself. "You're an incarnate. An abomination."

I felt my face go cold. I took a step forward, and the crowd shuffled uncomfortably, as if I were a wild beast, or... or contagious. "What did you say?"

The man peeled away from the crowd, jabbing his finger at me. "Those ears just for show, freak? I said you're an abomination!"

My arm was winding up for a punch before I knew it. Suddenly, there was a light touch on my elbow, and I blinked in surprise. Caden's hand rested there. But his eyes bored into the man before me.

"I think that's enough," he said calmly, his soft voice like the cocking of a shotgun. Everyone froze. "They were just leaving." His seafoam eyes seemed to swallow the entire group. "Isn't that right?"

Normally, Caden's glamour was a subtle thing. The slightest touch, an invisible current that nudged you, ever so gently, in the right direction.

There was no subtlety here. His glamour crashed into them with the weight of a rogue wave smashing into a sandcastle. The crowd broke, fragmenting into scurrying individuals. The aggressive guy in front resisted the most; his freckles disappeared as he paled, highlighting the angry slit of his mouth, then he finally bolted too.

"Don't even think about coming back," I yelled after them. Then I turned to Caden, eyebrows raised. "That was... impressive."

He was watching the departing crowd with stern eyes. Then he sighed and turned to me. "I'm sorry. You had that."

I laughed, but it came out like a whip crack instead of a chuckle. "I think you left a lasting impression. They won't mess with you."

He didn't meet my eyes. "I wasn't worried about me."

His words troubled me even after we made it to Rachelle's apartment.

### The Kushtaka Incarnate

**Name:** *Walter*

**Height:** *5'10"*

**Weight:** *193 lbs.*

**Eye Color:** *hazel*

**Hair:** *black and gray*

**Classification:** *Predator*

**Bio:** *The Kushtaka incarnate usually leads an isolated life, often preferring nature to the company of humans. That makes sense; "human" is only one of his forms, after all. I imagine if you spent long days as, say, an otter, you might not think humans all that civilized, either. I mean, otters are way better company most days. When his Territory is threatened, the Kushtaka is quick to defend it with one of his less adorable forms, like the wolf, the grizzly bear, or the wolverine. Plus, he's a trained hunter and equally handy with a rifle, tooth, or claw. As a Predator incarnate, he's only really dangerous if you cross him. But just in case, I'm going to tell you his fatal flaw.*

*It's urine.*

*No, that's not a joke. And trust me, the worst part is figuring out how to use it against him.*

~

The cul-de-sac that marked the entrance to Paradise Lake Cemetery looked no different in daylight than it had two nights ago, even down to the detail of Matlas sitting on the large rock awaiting our arrival. Because our contract to keep Hope safe started that morning, we brought her with us. Luckily, she didn't seem to mind spending her Sunday morning at a cemetery, so I figured we were off to a great start. If anything, she was excited, and I recalled her earlier comment about her incarnation preferring the outdoors.

"I'm so sorry we're late," I told Matlas as we approached him. "It was my fault."

"Damn it," Rachelle exclaimed from behind me. She hefted the camera and added the fuzzy microphone to the top of it with quick, efficient motions. "Can you say that again, Emery? The camera wasn't rolling, and I'm pretty sure that's the first time I've ever heard you say those words."

I stared at her, then rolled my eyes. I turned back to Matlas, who was smothering a grin. "It's no problem," he said quickly. "Rachelle texted me and let me know."

She speared me with a too-sweet smile and then cheerfully introduced Hope to Matlas. After they'd exchanged pleasantries, she said, "Come on. I want to check out those stairs again."

Matlas didn't go pale—his dark skin probably would have concealed it even if he had—but his eyes widened, and his pink tongue darted between his lips. "You want to go there *again*?"

I was inclined to agree with him, but I could see the set of Rachelle's shoulders, so I kept my mouth shut.

"Of course. In the daylight, we'll be able to see how much of it was our imaginations playing tricks on us." She shot him a smirk. "You're not going soft on me, are you, Atlas?"

Hope watched us, clearly trying to piece together everything that was going on in front of her. I sidled up next to her and quietly brought her up to speed while Matlas and Rachelle spoke to each other. I only told her about the graveyard, its history, and select moments from our experience two nights ago. I explained about the Thirteen Steps and quietly told her how my "Loophole" incarnate powers—she still didn't know I was the Protagonist—had opened the stairwell that night. I didn't feel she needed to know about the Hellhound. And, given how terrified of E-Pluribus she was, I didn't tell her about finding Asker here.

I realized with dismay that I hadn't had an opportunity to tell Rachelle about Asker yet, either. I glanced over at her as she laughed at something Matlas said, and I decided it could wait. She was going to be furious I hadn't filled her in earlier, so better to have that conversation when there weren't others around.

As a group we entered the cemetery, which looked rather mundane after our adventure the other night. The daylight stripped from the graveyard its veil of mystery and its sense of lurking danger. It was an overcast day—nothing new or surprising for the greater Seattle area—and while there weren't exactly chirping birds and sunbeams, there was nevertheless a sense of quiet peace among the various headstones. In a way, it reminded me of the grounded aura of calm Caden emanated.

I studied Hope as she walked beside me. She seemed more comfortable here, outside, striding confidently as she explored the cemetery. She wasn't really what I'd have expected from the Virgo, but that was often the case with incarnates. We have preconceived notions about what someone will be like—or *should* be like—from our knowledge of the urban legends that created them, when in reality incarnates are more three-dimensional than the myth could ever illustrate. Case in point, the Virgo: the fables painted a picture of a maiden, surrounded most often by wheat or the harvest, shy and innocent and virginal. Maybe that was how Hope reincarnated, and this was what she became after years of living in the real world. Truth be told, she still retained some of those demure traits often associated with maidens. Her petite form, her white-blonde hair, and most of all, her sincerity. She was an open book, expressions and emotions flitting across her face, easily read and understood. But here, outdoors, she belonged. It made me wonder why she'd ever take an accounting position—something like a wilderness guide, a camp counselor, or a farmer seemed like it would suit her disposition better.

Says the vlogger Protagonist.

Rachelle was sweeping the camera around the graveyard with steady hands, patiently recording a panorama. Our game plan today was to demonstrate—and exaggerate—the cemetery's normal features. Most of what we'd recorded the other night was unusable: while it was exciting footage, it would not help to debunk anything. This was the prickly part of our job. We'd been hired by a mortal to disprove the existence of the supernatural. The problem, however, was that the supernatural actually existed, in the form of incarnates. Matlas was too intelligent not to suspect something was up after everything he'd seen two nights before. I could see it in the hesitation of his footsteps, in the way he kept casting sidelong looks my way. Even his conversation with Rachelle held the slightest edge. Which meant it was going to be imperative that we find—or, at worst, manu-facture—some sort of evidence to debunk the myth that this grave-yard was haunted. I didn't like fudging the truth, but if it kept mortals from poking around in dangerous places for reasons they didn't understand, a bit of deception was a small price to pay. I couldn't help but glance guiltily at Matlas and Rachelle. Maybe not everyone would agree with me, but I *was* protecting them, wasn't I?

"You think there are incarnates here?" Hope asked in a low voice that didn't carry to Rachelle and Matlas.

Her words pulled me out of my thoughts. I hesitated, then nodded. "Yes. More than one. Possibly quite a number."

Hope looked at the surrounding headstones dubiously. "Here?"

"At the Thirteen Steps, the ones I opened with my powers. I think it's a gateway to Hell incarnate. Which could be home to—"

"Some of the worst of our kind," Hope finished, nodding and looking troubled. "Are you sure we should be here, poking at it?"

"It isn't an anthill," I replied. "And don't worry; I take your safety very seriously. From threats both supernatural and mundane."

We took the first stairs down to the next level, where Rachelle was telling Matlas that she wanted to take pictures of the tree-impaled car in the daylight. The tunnel of trees wasn't nearly so creepy in the daytime, but the interwoven branches overhead were quite dense, suspending the area in an effective twilight. I heard a rustle in the undergrowth to our left, further down on the next level, but it didn't carry the same weight of fear as on our prior visit. An airplane passed overhead, and I could hear the hum of traffic from cars out on the main road. The graveyard was quiet, but not deathly silent like last time.

The old automobile was where we'd left it, of course. With a tree growing out of it. "Want to say a few words, Matlas?" Rachelle asked, gesturing toward the scene.

He raised his hands defensively. "No, no, I'm good."

She stared at him for a moment, then shrugged. "Suit yourself." She continued filming the car and muttering to the camera, then turned and advanced on the tombstone with the claw marks.

Matlas walked over to me. "We're really going to go back to the Thirteen Steps to Hell? You don't want to, ah, talk her out of it?"

I patted his shoulder. "Talk her out of it? Have you met Rachelle?"

He wilted. "Guess I'll put on a brave face, then."

"That's the spirit. Don't worry so much; we're just going to look for clues that someone pulled a fast one on us. It happens from time to time—especially when someone catches wind that we're doing a debunking." Hopefully I could play Matlas's acumen against him, as it often came hand in hand with a healthy dose of skepticism. He'd already be trying to conjure up explanations for what he saw the other night, and he'd snatch hold of any I gave him like a drowning man clutching a life jacket. It was a design flaw in mortals, but one I wasn't above exploiting to keep incarnates safe.

Hope was watching our conversation with amusement. Poorly concealed, of course. Before Matlas could pick up on her emotions, I excused myself and took her by the elbow, and we retraced our steps to the base of the stairs we'd descended.

"You expend such energy to keep up this charade," she remarked when we were out of earshot.

I looked at her in surprise. "You don't hide what you are from mortals?"

"I do. Every incarnate does, I think. Our history is too riddled with"—she looked for the right word—"persecution, I suppose you could say. At any rate, I was referring to your mortal business. I had assumed it was just a front for you to find incarnates and help them. But you've treated Mr. Atlas as you would an incarnate client. You're committed to the job."

I shrugged, a little uncomfortable. "It pays the bills. I can't afford to be picky. Plus, throwing mortals off the trail of incarnates only serves to help us, wouldn't you say?"

"I hadn't considered that. I suppose you're right." She settled into a contemplative silence, and I opted not to tread upon it.

Matlas and Rachelle emerged from the tunnel a few moments later. The camera hung at Rachelle's side, all but forgotten, as she listened to Matlas recount a time he'd played hide-and-seek in the graveyard. When he got to the (predictable) part where he was left behind by the other kids, Rachelle snickered and commented that he must have been quite good at the game, given he was never found.

Watching the two of them, I found myself searching my backstory's memories for a time when Rachelle had been this open with someone other than me. I often hoped she would find someone who made her as happy as Caden made me, but I knew that was no mean feat. She didn't seek the same kind of support that I found in Caden. Sometimes it seemed she wanted a sparring partner more than a boyfriend. Someone to push her, to challenge her, and to keep up with her. She required a certain level of independence, but I knew her well enough to know she secretly wanted someone with whom to share that independence. I'd begun to despair nothing short of the Perfect Man incarnate could ever meet her exacting standards. But seeing the silly smile on Matlas's face and Rachelle's pink cheeks, I felt a tinge of excitement for them. Followed by a wave of protective-ness that startled me with its fierceness. With that, I realized I'd been staring at the two of them for an uncomfortably long time, and I looked away.

"Let's head down," Matlas said from the top of the stairs that descended to the lowest level.

I gave him an encouraging grin and a nod. Rachelle, next to him, caught my motion and narrowed her eyes suspiciously. My grin widened, and I said, "Ladies first."

She hooked Matlas's arm with her own. "Come on, Matlas, let's leave our fearless leader cowering in our dust."

I followed them, hearing more rustling in the undergrowth as we descended. The way Matlas's head swiveled at the sound, I wasn't imagining it, either. Still, it sounded more like a rabbit than a ghoul, so I didn't raise the alarm. At the base of the stairs, it was a few shades darker, the overcast day's light struggling to penetrate the boughs above.

"Kind of eerie down here, isn't it?" Hope said from her position at the rear.

"Well," Matlas replied, turning, "you don't call a stairwell in a bright, cheery place the Thirteen Steps to Hell."

Hope barked a laugh. "Fair enough."

Even in the daylight there was no real path here, so we picked our way around the contour of the hill to the left. We stepped around grave markers and headstones that peeked out of the root-strewn earth.

"Look at that," Rachelle said, pointing. I followed her direction until I saw it: another automobile, deeper in the woods. It didn't have a tree growing out of it, but it was just as old, abandoned, and dilapidated. The hood was missing, exposing what little remained of the hollowed-out innards of the engine. "Why do you suppose it's here?"

Matlas shrugged. "Who knows? They were discarded decades ago. Probably before some of the roads around here were paved. I think people just got lost and... are you recording me?"

"Damn." Rachelle dropped the camera back to her side. "You were doing so well, too."

He spluttered for a moment, then shot me an exasperated glance. "Don't look at me," I said, holding up my hands. "I didn't think you were doing *that* well."

Matlas threw his hands into the air. "Everyone's a comedian."

"Well," Rachelle said, "we *are* entertainers."

I jumped in. "Yeah, you didn't think our episodes were scripted, did you?"

"We do our own stunts, too."

Hope cut into our banter with, "What is that sound?"

I shut my mouth so quickly that my teeth knocked together. After a moment of listening, I shook my head. "I don't—"

"Over here. It came from this way." She moved forward cautiously, head cocked. After a moment, she stopped.

I peered around her petite frame. "Ah. I see you found the Gates of Hell."

The two iron rods poking up from the ground marked the beginning of the moss-and-gravel trail that led to the Thirteen Steps. Tracing the path with my eyes, I found the small clearing sheltered by the forest on all sides. And in the center of that clearing...

A stone slab.

Where the Thirteen Steps had been two nights ago, there was instead a smooth, slightly raised cement surface.

I looked at my companions. Hope was distracted, her head still tilted to one side, listening for whatever had drawn her attention in the first place. Matlas looked relieved, his body relaxing from a tension I hadn't noticed before. Rachelle, though, looked perplexed and a little bothered. She stormed past the Gates of Hell and was a few feet down the gravel trail before I jolted back to attention and raced to follow on her heels.

We were almost to the clearing, the undergrowth brushing against us on either side, when I heard it. Growling. Rachelle and I froze in unison, muscles tense, ready to fight or flee. But the sound was nothing like the menacing snarl of two nights ago. This was a kitten's mewl next to the lion's roar of the Hellhound. My heartbeat slowed.

Rachelle crouched suddenly, putting out her hand like an offering and inching forward. I watched as the foliage shivered, then a wet nose at the end of a fuzzy snout emerged and snuffled at her hand. "It's a puppy," she said in delight.

A separate high-pitched growl arose from the bushes, and I realized there was more than one. I mimicked Rachelle's actions and knelt down, extending my hand. A moment later the growling ceased, and two matching faces peeked out and began to sniff at my fingers, hot breath and cold noses brushing my knuckles.

They were quite small, about the size of footballs, and fuzzy. Their black fur was dusted with lighter colors. One of them had little brown mitten paws, and the other had tan mottling its chin and down its neck, like a beard.

"They're wild," Rachelle said, keeping her voice low.

I heard crunching on the gravel behind me, and the mitten-pawed pup disappeared back into the undergrowth. The bearded puppy spun to face the oncoming noise and growled, black fur standing on end across its neck and back.

Hope and Matlas appeared, and the puppy's growl turned into a snarl as it snapped its jaw once and lunged forward, then immediately leapt back to its initial spot. I tried to soothe it, but it ignored me, continuing to growl at the two newcomers.

"They're puppies," I said, stating the obvious. "At least three of them."

Hope, beaming, bent down to offer her finger but snatched it back when the puppy tried to bite her. She backed up, a look of hurt crossing her face.

"Sorry, Hope. Maybe they only like Rachelle and me because we were here the other night?" I ventured. "Matlas, you stayed behind the Gates of Hell, so maybe they didn't get a good sniff at you, either."

"Yeah, maybe." He said it absently, watching Rachelle play with her puppy, which seemed to be oblivious to its sibling's distress.

A moment of uncomfortable silence ensued, only the snarling of the bearded puppy and Rachelle's laughs breaking it up. "Why don't you both go back down the trail," I suggested, "and we'll see if there are any more of them."

After they'd retreated, Rachelle walked over to me, and her puppy happily followed. "What do you think, Emery?" She lowered her voice. "Are they incarnates?"

"What?" I laughed. "No."

She spared me a look of mingled dismay and irritation before returning her attention to the puppies. Mittens had been coaxed back out from under the bushes and now joined its fellow pups in prancing around our legs.

"Why not?"

"Because there are three of them," I said. "Can't have three of the same type of incarnate."

"Oh. Right. But what if they're that incarnate dog's—"

"The Hellhound," I supplied. "I told you that this morning. And keep your voice down."

"Fine, if they're the Hellhound's offspring, wouldn't that make them incarnates?"

I shook my head. "It *is* possible they're the Hellhound's pups, but that doesn't mean they're incarnates. Just regular puppies." I scratched the one Rachelle had brought over behind the ears. It was darker than the other two but had a mask of light fur around the eyes and splashing down onto its muzzle. "Just like if I had kids. They would be mortal."

"Oh. I guess I never thought about that before. Wait." She looked at me. "*Have* you had kids before?"

I opened my mouth to reply, when a wave of lightheadedness hit me, leaving my extremities tingling. I blinked away the cobwebs of memory that clung to me. "Yeah," I managed. I felt like I'd avoided not just a single recollection but a surge of memories, and I was left numb, unsure how to feel about that. As I took a deep breath to clear my head, a single name refused to be dislodged.

*Avery.*

Rachelle looked at me with calculating eyes, so I covered my discomfort with a feeble grin. She opened her mouth to say some-thing but seemed to think better of it and said, "So, these *could* be the Hellhound's puppies, then?"

I was certain that hadn't been what she wanted to ask, but she let it go. I was grateful. Truth be told, I couldn't remember anything beyond the name, but that much had been emblazoned indelibly on my psyche. I knew without a doubt I'd recall more later. Incarnates' past lives were complicated, our memories sealed away behind windows that opened slowly, as we aged. The older we were when we reincarnated, the more windows were open at the outset. Except sometimes, when a past experience would be relevant to our present circumstances, we didn't need to wait for a window to open naturally —we could pry them open, use the knowledge to help us. And rarely, when we were truly desperate, we could *shatter* those windows, giving us early access to our own past experiences... but doing so could exact a weighty, even traumatic, toll.

Considering my vision of the Voices of the People and the death of the Dryad, maybe the brick through our living room window was more allegorical than I wished to believe.

A warm, wet tongue licked my knuckles and brought my atten-tion back to the puppy nosing my hand. "Yeah, they could be the Hellhound's puppies," I said, fighting to remember what we had been discussing. "In fact, I think it's a good bet. Could explain why she was so territorial the other night, too."

"But then where did she go?" Rachelle asked. I glanced at the stone slab in the middle of the clearing. She followed my gaze and frowned. "She abandoned them?"

"Maybe. I don't know." I shoved my previous line of thinking aside and spoke more confidently as I focused less on ancient, obscure pasts and more on the here and now. "Maybe she thought this side would be safer than hell for her little demons." I scratched Mittens under the chin, pleased at how its tail wagged back and forth.

Rachelle was watching me closely. "Aw. Emery, you should take them home with you."

I scoffed. "I don't think so. Besides, I don't have a home of my own. I couldn't bring three puppies to my mom's place."

"Too bad. You and Caden would be such good doggy daddies."

I warmed at the compliment, even though I immediately dismissed it. "Are you kidding? With how much we've both been working lately, we'd be the worst." With their warm weight in my lap, I had to admit it was tempting.

"I'd say the worst would be getting eaten by whatever's out here."

"They're Hellhound puppies. I'm sure they can take care of themselves." Oh god, I could see why they called them puppy-dog eyes. Each puppy had a different color to its big, round eyes, but they were equally effective. The way they looked at me was like glamour—I wanted to snatch them up and take them home right this instant.

Rachelle nudged me. "Admit it. You want to take them home."

I sighed. "Better leave before I do something I'll regret."

"Hold on a sec," she said. "I have an idea." She snatched her camera and then called for Matlas and Hope to join us. As soon as the two neared, the pups tensed in my lap, and almost as one, their ears pricked forward and their muzzles lifted. Three synchronous growls rumbled through the air. Rachelle recorded it all and then instructed Matlas and Hope to go wait back by the gates.

"What was that about?" I asked.

She lifted her camera triumphantly. "Proof," she said. "I think, with some fancy editing, we can debunk the growling noise we heard the other night."

# 19

"So let me get this right," Matlas said as we trudged back toward the cemetery's entrance. "You think it was *puppies* that made the growling we heard the other night. And you think, in the confusion and the dark, they chased you away from the—very much open, I'd like to remind you—Thirteen Steps to Hell." The doubt pouring off of him was palpable.

"Of course not," Rachelle said, rolling her eyes. "The growling last time was clearly from something far more fearsome than those puppies."

"Good, okay. Thank you. Now you're making sense."

"It was from the momma dog." Matlas stumbled, opening his mouth, but Rachelle barreled on. "Dogs—especially wild ones—are extremely territorial. And they become far more so when protecting their young."

"Then where was she today?" he asked.

"How should I know? Do I look like a nature guide?"

Matlas took in her manicured fingernails, her perfectly styled hair, and her expensive UGGs. He fought a losing battle with his smile. "No, I don't suppose you do."

She punched him in the arm. "What I'm saying is that we can use this footage, with some editing, to show our viewers that the scariest thing in this graveyard is wild dogs. It will help to debunk the local legends. And, if people think there are dangerous animals around, that will further serve to keep them away. That *is* what you were going for, right?"

He nodded slowly. "All right, fine. You two are the experts. But... can I ask you a question?"

Rachelle's eyes darted to mine and back to his so quickly, I wondered if I'd imagined it. "Go for it."

"Is your website a front of some sort?"

I missed a step. Rachelle blanched. Matlas looked uncomfortable. Hope—bless her—was avoiding everyone's gaze while clearly trying to banish a guilty expression.

"That's less of a question and more of a conspiracy theory," Rachelle managed after a moment.

Matlas rushed to fill in the silence that followed her statement. "It's just, I thought maybe you two went around debunking myths because you were truth seekers. But all this talk about editing and portraying things in a certain light... it makes me think that maybe you're in the business of covering things up. Or something."

Again, Rachelle's eyes found mine for a brief moment. She looked... pained.

Oh.

She wanted to tell him about incarnates. She didn't want to lie to him, or maybe she didn't want to later admit she had been lying. I wasn't oblivious to the way they'd been getting along—flirting—but I hadn't considered that Rachelle might want to open up about the truth to him. He was mortal.

But so was Rachelle. And I had told her right away, hadn't I? It was different, in a way, because my backstory made us feel like we'd known each other for years. I had known I could trust her. Plus, she had survived the Genie attacking us, so I sort of owed her the truth.

I'd only known Matlas for a handful of days. *You told Caden after only knowing him for a day,* that inner voice reminded me. But it wasn't the same. Right? For one thing, Caden's glamour had been affecting me. And for another, he'd ended up being an incarnate anyway, so technically I had only told one mortal. I didn't know how Matlas would react. Hope, who was studiously ignoring the conversation, reminded me of the stakes. With a murderer on the loose and incarnates being snatched off the streets, it was more important than ever to keep our secrets safe.

I shook my head just a fraction in answer to Rachelle's unspoken question, and I saw her face fall. "Not at all," she said, putting her hand on his arm, concealing her disappointment from him. When next she spoke, her tone was the soul of rationality. "Look, Emery and I see a lot of things we can't immediately explain. It takes work, sometimes far more than it appears to, in order to debunk these myths. If I go on the air and just say, 'Well, folks, no haunting here, nothing but some dogs growling in the woods,' we'd never be trending. I need to attack this problem from every angle, so I'm gathering evidence, one clue at a time, to show the world—and you, because you're our client —that there's a reasonable explanation behind all of this. So buckle up, there's more work to be done here—you're not getting rid of me that easily."

Matlas's reluctant nod became more enthusiastic at that last part, but I felt a pang of sorrow. Rachelle had lied for me. I hated asking her to do that.

"I can buy the wild dog theory to explain the growling," he was saying, "but what about the Thirteen Steps? It's the one thing from that night that I can't figure out. My family filled in that staircase with cement years ago. How was it open?"

Rachelle affected a thoughtful expression. "I'm not sure yet. That one has me baffled, too. My original theory was that the cement slab was just sealed over the top of the stairs rather than the whole staircase being filled in, and that maybe someone had pried the cement ceiling off. I inspected it for any hinges or wheel tracks, though, and I didn't find any."

"You won't; this isn't *Scooby-Doo*. My family filled it in. I'm certain."

She put her hands on her hips. "Right. Then how about *you* start brainstorming some ideas, huh?"

Matlas grinned, the awkwardness that his earlier questions had summoned dissolving away. "Pretty sure I'm paying you to do that for me, Grey."

"Nice try," she countered, "but I was there when our fearless leader refused to accept payment from you. And yet he's been *suspiciously* silent while I fend for myself."

"On account of how well you're doing," I said, smiling. A thought occurred to me. Maybe I could make things right. "Matlas, would it be all right if I sent Rachelle to follow up with you this week? I hate to miss out on an appointment, but we accepted a few more jobs over the weekend, and I'm swamped."

Matlas looked surprised. "Of course, man. Is there still a lot more to do?"

"Oh yes," I said quickly. "Right, Rachelle? We need to speak with him about... things. Right? Things like..." I gestured vaguely, articulate as always.

"Like an interview?" she prompted.

"Yes! Definitely. She'll need to conduct interviews with you, get testimonials from friends and family, maybe a few more shots of the graveyard..."

"I meant interviewing Matlas, actually. Speaking with his friends and family sounds a little *intense*, don't you think?" She rolled her eyes. "And I've got plenty of cemetery footage." She shot him a teasing smile. "Well, what do you say, Atlas, maybe you can take me someplace a little more... appropriate... than a graveyard this week?"

As he answered, we reached my Rogue. "I'd be happy to," he told her. "I'm free nights and weekends."

"What's your day job?" she asked.

His lips pulled up in a secretive smile. "I'm a man of many mysteries. A little birdie told me you like those."

"No, I said I like to *solve* those." She tapped her finger against her lips. "Is this one of those 'I'd tell you, but then I'd have to kill you' scenarios? Are you, like, a superspy?"

He bit out a laugh. "You caught me. Spymaster by day, but I

moonlight as a part-time student who lives with his parents." He lowered his voice dramatically. "The perfect disguise."

She bit her lip, and I got the impression it was more by intent than in thought. "I'll figure you out, Atlas. You're just delaying the inevitable."

I sensed that this conversation was better without me in it—a rarity, I assure you—so I ducked into the front seat to take a peek at my phone. I'd left it in the car to avoid being overheard and tracked. I froze, though, when I saw that I had twelve—*twelve!*—missed calls. The last one had been two minutes ago. All from the same number, which I didn't recognize.

"What's wrong?" Hope asked, seeing my expression as she settled into the back of the crossover.

Before I could answer, my phone started vibrating in my hand. I accepted the call so quickly it probably hadn't even rung on the other end. "Hello?"

The voice on the other line was youthful, like a teen's, and breathy with what I assumed was panic. "Is this Emery?" It came out in a rush, so quickly that it almost didn't have distinct syllables.

"Yes, who is this?"

"Gregory gave me your number yesterday. I need your help."

"Okay," I said, speaking carefully. I was painfully aware that my phone was bugged. "This isn't a good—"

"They're trying to kill me. Please, help me!"

My heart jumped into my throat. "Whoa, slow down. Where are you? Are you somewhere safe?"

"I went to the mall to be in public, but I don't think it matters. They're here, and they're trying to kill me."

"What's your name?"

"Danny. I'm the Prodigy incarnate."

My blood went cold. "Do you work in tech?" *Please, no.* The murderers had only killed techies, so far.

"As an intern."

*Shit.* I fought to keep the panic out of my voice but keep the urgency. "Text me your location. I will be there shortly. Do not leave with anyone, okay?"

"Okay." He sounded so meek, so defeated.

"Don't worry. It was smart of you to call me. I'll be there soon. Everything will be all right."

Hope was watching me with round eyes as I disconnected the call. I stuck my head back out the window and called for Rachelle. She stiffened slightly but ignored me as she finished up her conversation with Matlas.

I flew out of the car and gripped her arm. "So sorry," I said to Matlas. "Rachelle! It's an emergency."

She nodded and began moving back toward the car, giving Matlas a thin-lipped smile. "Wednesday. I'll see you then!"

We tore off, sending gravel flying, Rachelle scrambling to buckle herself in. "What the hell?" she demanded, but her anger drained away when she took in my clenched jaw. I quickly filled her in. My phone buzzed as I was talking, and Rachelle snatched it up.

"It's his location," Rachelle said. "Redmond Town Center. That's twenty minutes away."

"Not if I don't hit any lights." Go, go Protagonist powers. *Please.*

"You got another text," she reported.

"Is Danny okay?"

"It's not from him. It's from an unknown number." She paled. "It says, 'Do not interfere.' Emery, who the hell is this from?"

I bared my teeth in a semblance of a grin, too burdened by terror to shape it correctly. Still, there was hope. If my mystery texter didn't want me involved, it meant I still had time to save him. "Buckle up."

"What are you going to do?" Hope asked, eyes wide.

I gritted my teeth. "Interfere."

The thirteen minutes it took for us to get to Redmond Town Center felt like hours. I sped down the back roads of Woodinville like an arrow released from its bow. I crossed the double yellow lines in the middle of the road to pass three drivers, pushing my Rogue to get us there before... no, I wouldn't put that thought out there. I would make it. I *would*.

Redmond Town Center was a multilevel outdoor mall, which would have made sense in a sunny, warm place like Los Angeles or Austin. It didn't work as well in the Pacific Northwest, but it was still a popular destination for half the year. The walkways between stores were covered and, with some creative circumnavigation, you could shop pretty much everywhere without stepping out into the open areas where you'd be pelted by rain. However, especially in the winter months, even a light wind would sluice through the covered corridors and elicit shivers, sending herds of shoppers darting between warmed retail stores to spend as little time as possible exposed to the elements. Someone had thought to combat the weather with fancy outdoor pavilions set up around cheery hearths and complete with sofas protected from the rain by upscale umbrellas. The effect was charming, but it was undermined by the fact that those pavilions were often devoid of guests a good six months out of the year.

To be fair, on an overcast but dry day in September, with the temperature moderate, Redmond Town Center's outdoor model was perfection. People strode from store to store with little regard to the covered spaces they'd be clinging to in another month or two, and while the outdoor fountain didn't have kids frolicking through it as it had in August, there were still several people gathered in the outdoor seating area near enough to it to occasionally feel the spritz of water.

The fact that the area wasn't swarming with police gave me hope that we weren't too late. *Please, please let us not be too late.* Would E-Pluribus be so bold as to murder the Prodigy in such a public location? I doubted it. Based on the pattern of the previous murders, they'd want to kill him in his office. But Danny had said he was an intern, so it was unlikely he even *had* an office. Did that improve the odds that they'd kill him here? Or would they aim to kidnap him and off him somewhere quiet?

At the heart of Redmond Town Center was Center Street Plaza, a circular area with plenty of exits: one in each cardinal direction, plus two escalators leading to the upper level.

I swerved into a parking stall in the southern lot. Knowing my phone was bugged, I had Rachelle use her phone to text Danny and ask for his exact location. To my dismay, a text came almost immediately from my mysterious texter... on *Rachelle's* phone. It told her to "Cease immediately or your safety cannot be guaranteed." Had her phone been bugged too? It made sense, I guess, but it also made me feel vulnerable in a way I hadn't expected. Just how far did the mysterious texter's reach extend? I put those thoughts to the back of my mind. I needed to focus on one thing: Danny, the Prodigy.

"Rachelle," I said as the three of us jogged toward the plaza, "I'm charging you with Hope's safety. No matter what, keep her safe. I'll take care of Danny."

With our phones obviously compromised, I had considered leaving them in the car. However, my mystery texter already knew where we were, and I was unwilling to throw away my only way to contact Danny.

God, I wished Caden were here. Between Hope and Danny, we could use some of his guardian powers. Hell, depending on how things went down, even Rachelle and I could use them. At least I'd brought my trusty Taser with me today. And six tranq darts. Combined with my Protagonist powers of convenience, they worked more or less like you'd expect them to in a Hollywood movie: lights-out in seconds. It was... well, it was convenient. It would also be mighty coincidental if only seven baddies were sent to murder Danny. More, and I would be out of toys to deal with them. I put that worry out of my head. First, I had to find the kid.

I burst onto Center Street Plaza and began to search. The mall was crowded on a Sunday afternoon, early enough to still be lunchtime but late enough that those indulging in a lazy morning would be out and about. Why did everyone look suspicious? Was that group of women watching me too closely? Did that young guy sitting on the bench by himself look like one of the E-Pluribus goons I'd encountered? Every person who brushed past me made me jump. A group of teens eating ice cream laughed at the antics of one of their own. A harried mother corralled her three children across the square, trying to get them to stay together. Two shoppers with several bags resting against the railing looked down from the second floor, watching the people pass through. Were they paying *too* much attention?

*Calm down, Emery. You can do this.*

Where was Danny?

I walked farther into the center of the plaza, my head snapping back and forth in small jerks as I tried to look everywhere at once. I probably looked like I was on drugs, but I didn't care. I could save him. I *would* save him.

At my gesture, Rachelle and Hope hung back. They walked around the circumference of the plaza, watching without putting themselves in danger. Out of the corner of my eye, I saw they'd stopped near the escalators. That was good: Rachelle was keeping herself and Hope near various escape routes if things went poorly. I think. I also saw there was a sale at a nearby store, but surely that wasn't why they'd chosen that location.

My eyes continued to flick over nearby faces, cataloging and dismissing them. I had to show Caden that his dream could come true. That his faith in me wasn't misplaced. I could make it happen.

*"There are going to be tragedies, Em."* Not today. Not on my watch.

But the seconds slipped by, and my despair mounted. I was too late. They had arrived before me and they had kidnapped him and I'd never—

"Emery?"

I looked around for the source of the voice and found it in the form of a kid about a dozen feet away. He was no more than sixteen, maybe even younger; scrawny rather than thin, with dark brown hair and matching glasses that framed bright blue eyes. Eyes that were wide with fear. He rushed toward me, the ratty backpack he wore jostling and bouncing. The top zipper was busted, and I could see the tip of a laptop sticking out. His sweater looked to be a few sizes too large for him. When he reached me, he came to an awkward halt before our eyes locked. I felt a boulder of tension slip from my shoulders. "Thank god." I'm not sure which one of us said the words.

"Danny, I'm going to get you out of this. I'm the Loophole; it's what I do."

He nodded, though fear overpowered the relief in his eyes. "I've seen a few people I recognized from E-Pluribus, but I think I've managed to evade them so far."

I gripped his shoulder and gently directed him back toward the south exit, where my car was parked. "Good, good. How did you know they were looking for you?" I tried to keep my voice low, but the general hubbub of the crowd meant I couldn't be too quiet. Luckily, that same buzz of conversation would help keep us from being overheard.

"At first, I didn't. I came to the mall when I heard the news about Jax this morning. Her death meant I was the only one left alive who'd worked on Unum with Mr. Asker."

I frowned as I gestured for Rachelle and Hope to join us. "The *only* one?" Surely he meant on a specific team or something. "I don't know much about technology, but doesn't it take dozens—maybe hundreds—of people to design such a complicated operating system?"

Danny started, looking back at me. "The *real* Unum." His eyes widened at my blank expression. He stepped close and said quietly, "It isn't an operating system. Or, I guess, it's not *only* an operating system. Unum is an incarnate."

I felt like someone had yanked the stones out from beneath my feet. I stumbled to a stop at the mouth of the south exit, stunned. "What? You four *built* a new incarnate? That's... impossible."

"Well," he hedged, looking around to make sure we weren't over-heard—or maybe looking for E-Pluribus goons, "I'm not convinced it's a *new* incarnate, exactly, though it certainly is an evolution of the incar—hey!"

I yanked him, hard, dragging him to the side of the building with me. My heart was hammering in my chest. Ahead, coming toward us from the south parking lot, was Scary Gun Lady.

She looked exactly as I remembered her, all the way down to the *five* guns she toted. There were three people with her. Two of them could have been brother and sister, clearly baked from the same cookie mold. They were athletic and muscular, with matching black shades and tailored outfits that were probably a two-for-one sale at Baddies "R" Us. I didn't overlook—or particularly like—the guns holstered at their hips.

The fourth person... was Asker. Mikey. Whatever.

I hadn't recognized him immediately on account of his baseball cap and sunglasses, which were obvious attempts to disguise his identity. I didn't think the masses would recognize Micah Asker on sight, but obviously if they did, he'd be in trouble. You know. 'Cause he was supposed to be dead.

I tugged on Danny's shoulder, guiding him back into the plaza. We would need to take a different exit, clearly. My first thought was that our best chance was to get lost in the crowds. But evaluating the open space, the area—which had seemed filled to bursting when I'd been trying to locate Danny—suddenly didn't seem to have *enough* people. We'd be spotted immediately. Keep to the perimeter, then, as Rachelle and Hope had done.

Rachelle and Hope! Where had they gone? I whipped my head around frantically, seeking them out. *There!* They stood on the other side of the plaza, Rachelle watching my erratic movements intently. I pointed up to indicate they should go to the second level. I waited for her nod of confirmation, then spun around and began guiding Danny away from the south exit, hugging the interior wall. I tried to pass as closely to clumps of people as possible, hoping to blend in. I moved stiffly, my back itching between the shoulder blades, expecting... well, I wasn't sure. An alarm? A bullet? A tap on the shoulder?

I didn't want to find out the lengths to which Scary Gun Lady would go to procure the Prodigy. There had been at least seven firearms between the four of them. It didn't take a math genius to calculate the odds of our survival if a fight broke out. Or was it a statistics genius? I always got those confused.

I told myself it didn't matter. I'd chosen the Loophole as my alias for a reason: I lived to defy the odds.

I considered the stores we passed, wondering if we should duck into one. We'd be far less likely to be spotted that way, but if they *did* see us, we'd be trapped. I risked a glance over my shoulder—

*Shit.*

The four of them had reached the spot where I'd been standing scant seconds ago, their intimidating presence forming a bubble of space around them as people gave them a wide berth, some scurrying away with obvious haste. Scary Gun Lady was scanning the area, and her head was turning toward me.

I wrenched my head around and forced myself to proceed at the same pace instead of tearing off to put as much distance between myself and that woman as possible. My heart was trying to escape through my ribs, and I was sweating in spite of the mild temperature.

"Keep moving," I murmured to Danny, my hand still on his shoulder. "We're going to exit ahead, then circle around to the southern lot to get behind them and to my car."

He nodded in jerky, almost spastic, motions. The movement caused a convulsion to shudder through his body. God, the kid was terrified. I gripped his shoulder more firmly. "It's going to be all ri—"

"Emery Luple. Stop!" The shout rang out behind me, Scary Gun Lady's voice slicing through the conversational din around us.

"Move, Danny," I said, giving his shoulder a shove. We both scrambled toward the nearest exit, which cut diagonally up and away from our pursuers.

"Emery, please stop." It was Mikey this time, a note of pleading in his voice. "We don't want to hurt you."

*I know,* I thought as we plunged forward, *but I won't allow you to hurt Danny, either.*

We raced beneath an overhead walkway that marked the start of the west exit. Sidewalks sprang up on either side of the path, which turned into a street ahead. Walking briskly toward us—heading into the plaza—were four security officers, armed with guns and stern expressions. I guess my Protagonist powers of coincidence were on high alert, but I wasn't going to complain. I waved at them, grabbing their attention.

"We need help," I said. "There are people with guns in the plaza."

"Get behind us," the lead man barked, motioning urgently. Did his face look familiar?

Danny moved to comply. I stayed with him, but something was nagging me, an idea like a rat scrabbling against the inside of my skull, desperate to escape my brain.

As we passed the line of officers, I realized it. The man who'd spoken had a too-thin mustache. I remembered him from the pho restaurant. He'd been one of the members of that mob chasing down Hope.

I snatched Danny's sleeve to pull him back, but I knew I was too late. Two of the officers were already going for their guns.

Then two gunshots cracked through the air in quick succession. They hadn't come from the officers—their own guns hadn't even cleared their holsters yet. Looking past them and into the plaza in horror, I saw Scary Gun Lady had raised her handgun into the air and shot into the open sky.

The effect was instantaneous. For the faintest of moments, everyone froze, like we were on the set of a movie and the director had demanded silence and stillness. Then the spell broke. People screamed and panicked, streaming away from the shooter. Some ushered their friends and families into stores, while others flooded toward the exits.

The officers ducked their heads and cursed. The vanguard of the fleeing crowd reached us as two of the men finally fumbled their guns free. As people rocketed past, I hauled Danny to the side and away from the armed men.

Three of the officers were jostled and distracted, trying to establish order in the chaos. The fourth—one of the two who had drawn his weapon—would not be so easily deterred. His gun snapped up and aimed at Danny's forehead.

A crack in my memory widened, and my mind *opened*.

Five incarnations ago.

Hours and hours spent drilling, sparring, ingraining the responses indelibly. I trained harder than the other recruits. Some thought I was showing off. Some thought I was driven by a past I didn't open up about. Some thought I was a glutton for punishment. None of them knew the truth. They only needed to engrave this skill on their bodies. I needed it etched in my mind. The physical form was fleeting. But my mind was...

Immortal.

*First, the threat.*

The officer's gun was already pointed at Danny, who was backing away—too slowly. I saw the officer's mouth set in a line.

*Second, take control.*

I flowed forward, my left hand lashing out. My thumb wrapped around the outside of the trigger guard, and my fingers locked around the top of the slide in a viselike grip. The motions were familiar, practiced, as natural as snapping my fingers. Training from decades ago thrummed through me. Not words. Not instructions. *Reflexes.*

I knew I needed to gain control of the firearm. But first, minimize the threat of it discharging. Even if it went off, it could only do so once, as my grip prevented the slide from cycling another bullet into the chamber. Of course, even once could be enough.

*Third, redirect the weapon away from you.*

Or Danny, in this case. I applied force, and the muzzle began to slide away from his forehead. I bladed my body to make myself a smaller target, even while the gun moved further from its intended victim.

I pushed the gun down and toward the fake officer's abdomen. As it dawned on the gunman that he was losing control of the situation, he wrestled with me to correct his aim. But I had placed my weight directly over the weapon, and to aim it back toward Danny—or me— he now had to contend with my full body weight.

*Fourth, distract.*

I stepped in quickly, leading with my left foot. Why was I wearing sneakers instead of my combat boots? No distractions. The gun was trapped against his body, and I aimed a jab at his nose with my free hand. I would have aimed for his throat, but his head was hunched, looking down disbelievingly at his trapped gun. My jab crunched into his nose, and I felt cartilage yield then break beneath my knuckles.

*Fifth, disarm.*

Leverage. My free hand snaked beneath the man's arm and took purchase on the rear of the slide. With a practiced twist, torquing my body at the waist, I wrenched at the gun. There was a *pop* as the man's finger, still trapped in the trigger guard, snapped. He howled as I cranked the gun free of his hands. My left hand smacked the magazine in the bottom of the grip, then reached around and racked the slide to ensure a fresh round was in the chamber. My movements were economical, perfect, automatic.

He was a monster. I was now in control of a freshly loaded gun, working and ready to fire. And I was the Monster Hunter. He had tried to kill Huntington—that is, Danny. I aimed the gun at the monstrous man, who didn't even have the decency to look afraid. He cupped his nose, trying to stem the bleeding. It wouldn't kill him, of course.

But the bullet from this gun would. I could put this monster down. It was what I did. I just had to pull the trigger.

Something about this wasn't right, though. There were so many thoughts in my head, a tangle, all vying for control. I wrestled them to silence as I stood over the officer, ready to execute him.

No—this man, he was no longer a threat. I wasn't a killer.

*You kill monsters, though.*

*No, I* hunt *them.*

That wasn't right, either, though, was it? Where was I? The mall? No, no... I had been in training at the academy, sparring for hours—days—months.

Then why did I remember the desert, hunting the Yeti?

That was it. The thing I was forgetting: I *wasn't* the Monster Hunter. *I am the Protagonist.*

I clung to the thought like a rock in the middle of a gale. I was here to save the Prodigy. The gusts of other personalities—other incarnations, I now understood—calmed. I was in control again. I felt my mind begin to clear, and I threw my mental weight behind the effort. The warring incarnations—and the associated skills and knowledge—in my head flowed away through the rents in my immortal mind, back to the vault of memories locked inside me.

What had I done? Something similar had happened to me before, as recently as... Sabrina's goons. Or rather, *Morrigan's* goons, who'd been on loan. At Rikers in New York, I had drawn on knowledge from previous incarnations. But it hadn't been like this. It hadn't tried to take control of me.

My current situation came slamming back to me, and I all but staggered. With a savage chop, I brought the butt of the pistol down on the back of my would-be assailant's skull, and he dropped to the concrete.

People still streamed past us, but they were the back of the crowd, now. At any moment, the other three men would be on us. I sprang forward, grabbing Danny's arm and pulling him away from the west exit. This time I cut toward the north exit, which opened up into a large parking garage. If nothing else, we'd be more likely to lose everyone among the multitude of vehicles.

As we dashed across the plaza again, I saw Mikey and Scary Gun Lady... and they were tracking us. The two cookie-cutter agents with them were missing, until I swiveled to look back at the officers behind us and saw the brother-sister pair engage with them.

So, there were two groups after us, and it appeared they didn't get along. Most likely, one group was the captors and the other the murderers. But which was which? Given a choice, I would much rather take my chances with the captors.

Then I saw Rachelle and Hope. They were on the upper level and angling toward the north exit, where a stairwell would bring them down to us. I shot toward the base of those stairs, nudging Danny's shoulder to keep him just ahead of me.

Scary Gun Lady cut in our direction, flying across the now-emptied plaza with a burst of speed that shocked me. I pressed Danny to run faster, but I could tell we wouldn't make it.

I shoved him ahead, then snatched my Taser from the small of my back, flicking the switch to release the safety. I stepped square into Scary Gun Lady's path, planted my feet, sighted, and squeezed the trigger. Two fangs connected to long, looping wires hissed through the air. One sank into her upper chest, just above her right breast, and the other bit into her left thigh. A loud clicking noise sounded as electricity arced from my Taser, down the wire cords, and into her body.

She didn't cry out, but she did grunt, her body seizing up and convulsing. Amazingly, she stayed on her feet and took another labored step toward me. Then the leg that had been hit folded out from beneath her, driving her to one knee on the pavement. Her face was a mask of concentration and grit as she stared up at me, jerking as the electricity continued to course through her. Something was odd, though. The current should have been traveling through the wires and across the muscles between the two barbs, locking up most of her body. But the way her arm and head twitched and jerked in response to the voltage... it was like the electricity was traveling to other parts of her, too.

Maybe that was just my Protagonist powers at work, though so far they'd left a bit to be desired. I didn't care. Mikey had let out a strangled cry and was now running toward us, his slightly stilted movements not slowing him down. I couldn't incapacitate Scary Gun Lady just to be caught by Mikey Asker. With a curse, I dropped the Taser. It would continue to discharge for a total of thirty seconds. Plenty of time for the four of us to disappear.

Danny had reached the base of the stairs, and his wild eyes were watching me even as Rachelle and Hope came barreling down the stairs to join him. No, he wasn't watching me, I realized; he was looking *behind* me. I spun—

Too late.

I was shoved aside as one of the false officers surged forward toward Danny. I stumbled backward, flailing, finally slamming against the side of the staircase and catching myself.

Rachelle and Hope came to a shocked stop at the base of the stairs, closer to Danny than I was. The officer had Danny pinned against a cement pillar that helped to support the stairs and upper level. His gun was coming out of his holster, but I was ten feet away. I couldn't do anything. Rachelle and Hope were frozen, stunned.

"For Vox Populi," the gunman shouted at the Prodigy, spittle flecking the kid's face. "Die, abomination!"

Then he flinched as the tranquilizer dart I'd thrown in a last-ditch effort stung his shoulder. Danny stared into the slackening face of his would-be killer, terror drawing out tears that ran in streaks down his face, and shuddered as the man slumped to the ground.

I was at his side a moment later, patting him on the shoulder. "I told you it'll be okay," I said. "Let's get out of this nightmare." We needed to move.

"Wait." It was Mikey. He held one of Scary Gun Lady's signature weapons in his hand, aimed in our direction. "Please, I don't want to hurt you." I tugged on Danny, positioning him behind me. If Mikey wanted to kill him, he'd have to shoot through me. Which I *really* hoped he didn't want to do.

"Can we talk this out?" he asked.

"You have the gun," I said tersely. "You tell me."

"Emery," Rachelle said, a tremor in her voice. She stepped down the last stair, Hope on her heels. Then she cocked her head. "Oh, thank goodness. I hear sirens."

"Yes," Mikey said, his unblinking stare doing little to settle my nerves. After a visible hesitation, he turned the gun aside and held up his hands in peace. "We need to talk, but quickly."

"Then start talking," I bit out.

Hope's voice was breathless. "Emery, we don't have time to listen to him."

"But—"

"He's stalling," she warned. "That gunwoman is getting to her feet. If she joins him..." She didn't need to finish; I understood our situation all too well. This was our last chance to escape—and maybe I was fooling myself. Maybe I'd already surrendered our last chance, stopped by the pleading in Mikey's voice.

Rachelle had reached my side, while Hope stared down at the fallen officer with the tranq in his shoulder. I saw Hope bend down and pick up the fallen officer's gun. A small part of me sighed in relief. Now each side was armed. But that wouldn't matter when Scary Gun Lady joined the standoff. She had more than enough guns to handle our single one.

"I'm sorry, Mikey," I said. "This isn't the time or place."

"Then give the boy to us, at least," Mikey begged. "Don't let her kill him."

*Kill him*? A chill clutched my chest, then settled in my stomach. "What?"

Something was wrong. Mikey wanted to *protect* the Prodigy? I wanted to discard his words as lies, but the conviction in his tone was undeniable, the desperation unfeigned. He was genuinely worried for Danny's safety. Could we be on the same side?

"What a mess," Hope said, sounding faintly agitated for some reason. She inspected the gun she held, holding it before her and examining it with a closed expression on her face. For the first time since meeting her, I couldn't discern what she was thinking.

Danny and Rachelle were watching the exchange with a mixture of fear and disquiet. I was blinking too fast, my mind racing; Mikey wasn't blinking at all, absorbing the scene in front of him as if he was trying to calculate what was going to happen next.

Hope gave a heavy sigh, aimed the gun at Danny, and pulled the trigger.

The gunshot rang out, the sound echoing and rebounding from the parking garage that was to be our salvation.

I would swear that Danny's gasp was just as loud. It was, in my memories. A sudden intake of breath... then he doubled over, his whole body shuddering as he breathed in two more sharp, jagged breaths. Like he was choking on glass.

His hands grasped weakly at my arm and his face turned up, terrified eyes finding mine. Then blood fountained out of his youthful face, over his chin, down his oversized sweater. He collapsed to the pavement, his glasses skittering across the concrete.

Rachelle and I were rooted in place, too horrified to react. She let out a small squeak that may have been, "Why?" I just stared at Danny. I had failed him. I'd been right here, and I still hadn't been able to save him.

Hope turned the gun on me. "Damn," she muttered, more to herself than to me. "Disastrous. Thank you for teaching me how easy it can be to find incarnates, Emery Luple. I had hoped we'd have more time together. Oh well."

And she pulled the trigger.

Or maybe I was tackled first. Given the speed a bullet travels, I was probably tackled first.

Mikey slammed into me, hurling me to the ground, just as the gun fired. The bullet must have hit something metallic on his body, because there was a loud ping, and then Mikey staggered backward.

I couldn't get my bearings. Rachelle was crying out, I was discombobulated, and Danny was so very, very dead. Hope was swearing—in Latin, of all things—and Mikey was staggering... not backward, but *toward* Hope. Another gunshot rang out, and Mikey flinched. Then Scary Gun Lady was there, also striding forward, having apparently disentangled herself from the Taser after the electricity cut off.

Hope's eyes flitted across each of us, taking in her situation. Although still armed, she was outnumbered, and Scary Gun Lady had far more of an arsenal than she did. With a growl and a curse, she backed away from our group—a laughable term for our miserable collection of broken individuals. When she'd put enough distance between us that she was convinced we wouldn't follow, she turned and ran through the parking garage. Still on the ground, I lost sight of her almost instantly.

Scary Gun Lady watched Hope's departure before holstering her weapons. She slid over to Danny and felt at his neck for a pulse, making a disgruntled sound in the back of her throat. Then, as if finished with a distasteful task, she moved to Mikey, examining his wound. Rachelle shuffled over to me, her face slack. I understood; it wasn't that we weren't able to feel—it was that we were feeling *too much*, our minds and bodies overwhelmed by so many terrible emotions that something broke and we were left as husks. That was good. It didn't hurt so much.

Then Scary Gun Lady stepped up to me. She stuck her hand out, as if offering to pull me to my feet. I stared at her hand in puzzlement for a moment, then took it numbly. In that moment, in the face of my towering failures, my pride was wrapped in a sweater two sizes too large and lying in a pool of its own blood four feet away. I needed all the help I could get.

"Come," she told me in a voice that brooked no argument. "Mikey is damaged. We need to regroup." She pierced me with a one-eyed scowl, her other eye ever concealed behind her stiff fringe. "And we need to speak."

I nodded and left with them. Maybe they were kidnapping me.

I didn't care.

## 21

*T*he world passed by me in a blur of color, but I saw only gray.

I rode in the back seat of one of those black SUVs I'd been trying so hard to avoid. The dark tint on the window could arguably be blamed for leaching the world outside of its color, but I knew better. Rachelle sat next to me, staring out of the window on her side. Scary Gun Lady drove, while Mikey accompanied her in the front seat. He was injured, but it was apparently not life-threatening. The sliver of my mind documenting facts and storing them for later analysis observed that Mikey did not appear to be bleeding. From a gunshot wound. Which lent credence to the Zombie theory.

They'd taken our cell phones. I should have been worried about that, but I couldn't summon up the interest to care. We had eluded law enforcement at Redmond Town Center, but just barely. As we pulled away from the mall, several police cruisers zoomed past us with lights flashing and sirens wailing. Would Gregory be with them? I could imagine him stepping up to Danny's fallen body, shaking his head somberly at the loss of another incarnate. I would need to admit to him that it was my fault. I had failed.

How was I ever going to be able to look Gregory Gregorius in the eye again?

Scary Gun Lady changed lanes and turned her head to check for traffic. The stiff bang she always wore down the right side of her face momentarily shifted, and I thought I saw the gleam of... was that metal? Maybe she wore her hair in that fashion to hide some sort of disfigurement. But what kind of injury would be covered up by metal? I shoved my curiosity away, swallowed it down around the lump in my throat. Whatever secrets Scary Gun Lady and Mikey possessed, they'd be revealed soon enough.

I was grateful for the silence in the SUV. I just wished it didn't seem as though it were dedicated to Danny. A moment of silence for our loss. But I would take it regardless of the reason. I didn't want to —maybe couldn't—talk right now; I was too absorbed in reflection, my mind scattered and trying to collect the pieces, one by one.

And those pieces didn't make sense. Hope had betrayed us. Had been using us all along. Hope, with her easily interpreted emotions, had been playing me. That's okay. Just add it to the tally of my failures. I'd pay my tab eventually.

For Vox Populi. That's what the man had cried when attacking Danny.

Vox Populi. The same people I'd recalled in my memories of ancient Rome, when they'd slaughtered incarnates by the droves, captured Morgan and me in cages, and... burned the Dryad. They were back. They were *here*. Caden's dream of creating an incarnate community was going to be murdered at its inception, its wings clipped before it ever got the opportunity to take off. Their very name unlocked memories from the recesses of my mind. Vox Populi had been an ancient faction, existing in the days before the rise of Caesar. At first little more than a cult, they had expanded into a hateful following, burgeoned until they were prolific enough to reveal themselves without fear. Such were their numbers and conviction that they'd crushed the largest incarnate society the world had ever seen, in Rome, in mere months. They viewed us as a threat to humanity— or "the people"—and would not suffer the presence of incarnates, lest we use our immortality to take over the world. Which was, of course, ridiculous. But each time incarnates congregated into the barest beginnings of a community, they were violently struck down by Vox Populi. It wasn't fair to Caden's dream, but then, when had life been fair? It was like pitting a rookie against the world champion on the rookie's first night. We didn't have a hope or a prayer of bringing incarnates together beneath the sinister watch of Vox Populi.

The red sports car's personalized license plate should have tipped me off. Or at least made me suspicious. Sperant meant hope. *In Latin.* Who besides an evil secret society from the past would be using Latin in the twenty-first century?

Well, actually... E-Pluribus and the advent of Unum *had* increased the popularity of Latin words, much like Marvel's Thor had created a resurgence of interest in Norse mythology. Now that I thought about it, why had E-Pluribus chosen Latin? Was this like the mirrors in New York, the universe intersecting with my Protagonist powers and attempting to give me clues? Or warnings, in this case. Maybe I shouldn't be so quick to dismiss omens in the future.

If I hadn't, maybe Danny would still be alive.

I wasn't paying rapt attention to our route, but I recognized a building we passed. I knew the area well enough to know we were traveling south, staying off of the freeway. Apparently the E-Pluribus campus wasn't our destination, because we'd passed it and continued into Factoria, leaving Bellevue behind.

What was E-Pluribus's role in all this? Did Vox Populi try to kill Asker in order to gain control of Unum? The pervasive operating system was next-level, and... according to Danny, it was also an incarnate. An idea began to form in my mind, but I shoved it aside. Was I so quick to finish mourning Danny? A spiteful, pragmatic slice of my brain whispered that Danny was an incarnate; he'd come back in 1,001 days. I needn't be so devastated by his loss. The image of Danny lying on the concrete, blood coating his chin, neck, and sweater, told that pragmatic slice to shut the hell up. The Danny who died would never come back—not exactly. Reincarnation changed us, twisted aspects of our personality. *That* was the true crime of Vox Populi.

They might not be able to keep us from coming back, but we lost something precious and unique each time we died.

Scary Gun Lady pulled the SUV up to an underground garage, the entrance sealed and safeguarded by a keypad. She reached out the window and typed a combination of numbers, and the garage door jolted into motion. We coasted in and began spiraling downward into a subterranean parking area.

We couldn't be there already; I hadn't collected all my thoughts. Like what had happened to me at Redmond Town Center, when I'd confronted that false officer and his gun. I'd somehow opened my mind to training I hadn't practiced or even really remembered. Even as I thought about it, the memory of that incarnation came rushing back to me, eager to escape the prison to which I'd banished it. To climb through the window I'd pried open.

It had been a long, full life. I'd reincarnated as a young man in the military, fighting in the Great War, which would later be called World War I. Following my term of service, I'd struggled to find work; I remembered nights curled up against the side of a building—I couldn't afford a house—without food in my belly. I'd found purpose again in training myself. As the years passed, I joined the reserves, then pursued a career in law enforcement. But most importantly, I *prepared*. I trained my body constantly, committing the muscle memory to my mind. I had been preparing, not for my own sake, but for future incarnations. Once, I had known I could do that.

Channeling. That's what I called it—that connection to a former life, the immediate and easy access to its knowledge, its instincts.

But something had gone wrong. Opening the lock on that incarnation had somehow released each of my lives along the way. First, my most recent prior self, where I'd thrown my life away to hunt monsters and outrun haunted eyes. Then the one before that, when I'd awoken 1,001 days after Morrigan killed Huntington, broken and shunning the company of mortals until, after too many long, lonely years of chasing monsters, I'd finally—*blissfully*—been killed during a hunt. Before that, the one I remembered most keenly, the investigative journalist who fell in love... but whose journey had ended too abruptly, tragically, inside a dockside warehouse. Then, before that, an incarnation I hadn't remembered in some time. I'd reincarnated as an elderly woman in Russia, spending my life in scholarly pursuits. It was the last time I remember dying of natural causes.

They had all merged and coursed through me like I'd released a floodgate; personalities had churned through my mind, my current thoughts—who I was today—washed away by the tide. Somehow, I had found myself again. Which was good; my previous two incarnations were hardened, forged by tragedy. I had made peace with them, or I thought I had. Still did, in a way. But left to run unchecked through my mind, they'd scour me until nothing of my current personality existed. They didn't know any better—they were victims of spite, born of anger and abyssal, cavernous loss.

I took a sharp breath, and the vault closed again, shutting out any passengers. I'd need to learn control, otherwise reflecting upon—channeling—my past could become dangerous.

One thing at a time. One *piece* at a time.

At least the mystery and questions surrounding Scary Gun Lady and Mikey would be answered shortly. They claimed they were trying to protect incarnates, and it was starting to make sense. So much of what had been going on had been based on Hope—the car chase through the city, then the E-Pluribus lackeys attacking at the pho restaurant. Even Asker faking his own death made sense, if he feared Vox Populi was after him. But... not everything fit. Why had they been trying to capture the Mermaid?

There were clearly some things we needed to talk about.

We parked and, without speaking, Scary Gun Lady and Mikey slipped out of the SUV. I expected something: a demand to stay seated, or instructions to stay close, or even an attempt to bind us. Instead, the two of them made their way to a bolted metal door set in a thick frame. Rachelle and I exchanged glances. Then I shrugged, and we hurried to catch up. Our footsteps seemed too loud; they echoed in the hollow spaces between the cement pillars, bounced off the low ceiling. Lights flickered and hummed, and even the scuff of my tennis shoes on the pavement created a resounding noise.

I expected something like a stairwell behind the door, but instead I was surprised to see the interior of what looked like a break room... if it was located in a bunker. Everything about the space was utilitarian, from the small industrial kitchen to the right of the entrance to the spartan couch and chairs surrounding a table. An unobtrusive doorway led to the bathroom, which was cut in behind the kitchen. The back wall was dominated by a garage-like door, one of those that opened from the bottom and retracted into the ceiling.

"Where are we?" I asked.

Scary Gun Lady closed the door behind us and bolted it. The

locking mechanism looked complex. She turned, considering us, when suddenly a beeping sound—like that of a watch alarm—came from Mikey, drawing her attention. For a moment, worry creased her face. "Damn. The damage is worse than I feared." Then her mouth set in a hard line, and she stalked past us to the door set in the back wall. "This is an E-Pluribus supply depot," she said, then unlatched the door. Metal squealed loudly—especially in the relative silence— as the door ratcheted open.

Beyond was a cavernous space filled with row upon row of shelving. The room, if that term could even apply to such a large area, reminded me of the inside of a warehouse. At first glance, it didn't look anything like the things I'd associated with E-Pluribus; it was too plain. The ground was worn, bare concrete. The shelves were simple metallic frames with wooden planks. Rather than ceiling lights, lantern-like fluorescent lighting adorned the corners of each individual shelving unit, creating alternating pockets of light and deep shadow. Scary Gun Lady strode in without further comment. She took a turn into the maze-like corridors created by the shelving and disappeared from view.

Okay, then.

The beeping coming from Mikey continued unabated. I spun to him. "Can't you turn that off?" I snapped. My emotions were raw; I knew that. I wanted to care, but I was so exhausted, and caring required so much energy. He gave no sign of hearing me, except to walk over to one of the chairs and lower himself into it. His movements were stilted again, like someone had taken a dozen still photographs of him in the process of sitting down and then flipped through them sequentially. "Did you fake your own death?" I demanded.

Mikey's lips moved, but no sound came out. After a moment, he simply shook his head.

"No? So, what, then?" I asked. "Vox Populi killed you, but they didn't expect you to survive, because they didn't know you're the Zombie?" I trailed off. Mikey was shaking his head at my words.

"Emery," Rachelle admonished, but not unkindly, "he was shot, remember?"

I sighed and approached him. *This* was the head of one of the most influential companies on the planet? Speechless, unable to muster up the words to defend himself? The wound was on the side of his abdomen, judging by where he was covering himself with his hand. I still didn't see any blood. "Let me take a look at that," I said. Without waiting for a response, I took his hand to move it away in order to get a better view. His hand was softer than I expected, and warmer, too. I would have expected the Zombie to have cold, stiff appendages. It made me uncomfortable. What was I missing? He wasn't wearing a watch, either. Where was that damn beeping coming from? Steeling myself, I moved his hand. To my surprise, Mikey didn't resist, didn't even say anything.

He had three holes in his clothes, little rips clustered close together. Shit, Hope had gotten off *three* shots?

"So you didn't fake your own death?" I asked him again through clenched teeth while I worked to lift his shirt and examine the injury. He shook his head firmly. I fought to control my frustration. "Then, what? You're his twin?" He continued to shake his head. "Of course not, it's never twins," I muttered. "Clone? Are you the Clone incarnate?" His head continued to shake. I felt my temper rise, but then I spotted the wound. It was easy to see against the smooth, otherwise unblemished skin of his stomach. He had well-defined abs—because *of course* he did, being filthy rich and extra smart wasn't enough—and three black holes punctured the flesh. My mind struggled to understand what it was seeing. They didn't behave as wounds should: three neat, almost perfectly round punctures, the rim of each curled inward. It reminded me of nothing so much as an aluminum can punched through with a pencil—or, I suppose, a bullet.

"What the hell?"

From the garage door came Scary Gun Lady's voice. "Mikey is the first fully synthetic human, Emery. And he was sculpted in his creator's image."

My irritation cooled by a few degrees as I sorted out her words. "Synthetic human?"

She walked over to where I knelt before Mikey and joined me. She carried a device with a screen, cords spreading out of either side and ending in unfamiliar ports that resembled old audio computer jacks. "I suppose introductions are in order. You've already met Mikey. I am Scarlet Dungrady."

I blinked. It was a prettier name than I was expecting, and better than the moniker I'd chosen for her. Actually...

Scary Gun Lady. Scarlet Dungrady. You gotta be kidding me.

This close to her, I could thoroughly inspect her face. My eyes were drawn to the stiff part in her hair that swooped down to cover the upper third of the right side of her face. Yes, I definitely spotted metal behind her hair. And... something was *glowing*, a faint yellow that was only visible up close.

Despite my attempt at subtlety, Scarlet saw where I was looking. She looked away in what seemed an automatic motion, then sighed and brushed aside the stiff side-fringe.

I gaped. A yellow eye gleamed out of a mechanical socket. It was clearly not a real eyeball, either. Instead of a pupil, black circles and lines intersected. They didn't hold still, but rearranged themselves as I watched, like... circuitry.

"It seems," I managed, "we have a lot to talk about."

She inclined her head. "Micah Asker did not fake his own death, Emery. He is dead." The clipped, matter-of-fact way she said it made it clear it was a hurt that hadn't yet healed. I recognized that self-defensive detachment. She indicated Mikey and said, "He is the Android incarnate."

"The Android," I repeated, flatly. "Like C-3PO from *Star Wars*?" Why was everyone always trying to recreate incarnates from *Star Wars*?

It was Rachelle who responded. "No, Emery. Not a droid, an *and*roid. Think *Terminator* or *Westworld*."

Scarlet winced. "But remove the violence. Mikey may have been created using advanced robotics and virtual intelligence, but he's...

harmless." She had hesitated for hardly a moment, but I narrowed my eyes. It had definitely been there. "He's equipped with cutting-edge morality software. More to the point, his directives forbid him from inflicting injury on others."

"All right." I rubbed my face, surprised to find my anger had subsided in the face of... well, this had all gone in a very strange direction. "And you?"

"I am the Cyborg incarnate," she said. As if to illustrate her point, she tapped on her wrist. To my alarm, her hand folded down and away so that her arm ended in a stump, the hand dangling, connected only by two hinges located on the underside of her skin. The stump, where I would expect to see red muscle around a gleaming bone, instead ended in a smooth panel of metal socketed with outlets of various shapes and sizes. She used her other hand to deftly plug the device she'd brought with her directly into her arm. Then, as if it were a totally normal thing to do, she *detached* a square of flesh from Mikey's shoulder, revealing a similarly socketed metal panel. She plugged the other end of the instrument into his arm. The device's screen lit up, and words began to scroll, flitting across the screen too quickly for me to read.

I stared, stunned. I was a fool. I should have guessed... oh, not that she was the Cyborg. All the conveniences and coincidences in the world couldn't have guided me to the conclusion that she was a human weapon augmented with *robot* parts. I suspected she had other enhancements in addition to the eye mods and... whatever this wrist trick was. But I was still a fool; I should have guessed she was an incarnate. Not only was she working with Mikey—whom I had iden-tified as an incarnate, even though he wasn't the one I'd thought—but she also carried around more guns than a Secret Service agent. Not a lot of mortals walking around downtown Seattle armed to the teeth. More than you might think, sure, but still not many.

I started, realizing she was watching me. With both eyes. That yellow one seemed to be burrowing into me, its lines magnifying in a way that reminded me of a camera aperture. "Um, I'm the Loophole incarnate," I stammered.

Rachelle was leaning against the wall nearby, hugging her arms to herself as though chilled. "Rachelle," she volunteered. "Just human."

"Robots," I stated, rising to my feet. "That's essentially what this boils down to, right? You two are robots." I wanted to pace, but there wasn't quite enough space without going into the warehouse.

Scarlet replied, "I'm human, augmented with robotics. Mikey is a robot designed to look and behave indistinguishably from humans." She gave me a tight smile. "Neither of us is—nor aspires to be—anything like WALL-E. I suspect that honor goes to the Robot incarnate, wherever or whomever they may be."

Her attempt at humor sparked my anger again. It felt disrespectful, like cracking jokes at a funeral. "How long have you known about Vox Populi?" I demanded. "Did you know the creators of Unum were in jeopardy? Why didn't you warn the others? We could have saved so many lives!" I realized I was shouting. I snapped my mouth shut, surprised to find I was trembling.

Scarlet sighed, a look of frustration rippling over the human part of her face. "We tried to warn you," she said. "You refused to speak with us."

"I thought you were trying to kill me!" I said. "You *shot* at me in downtown Seattle."

"No. Vox Populi shot at you. We only arrived in time to see you jump off the pier."

I frowned. "But you two are with E-Pluribus, right?"

Scarlet tried to exchange a look with Mikey, but he just sat there, staring into his lap. The corners of her mouth turned down. "No. I mean, we were, but we aren't any longer." She stared at her partner. "Part zero-nine-zero-zero-two-one-five."

I blinked. "What? You're saying you're *not* part of E-Pluribus?"

Scarlet took a deep breath. "Come with me." She disconnected the wires from her wrist stump and, with a quick flick, reconnected her hand to her arm. I tried to steal a quick glance; from what I could see, there wasn't even a visible seam where her wrist and hand met. I was impressed in spite of myself.

I followed her into the warehouse section, and Rachelle, after hesitating for a moment, hurried to join us. The enormity of the space seemed to gobble us up, the spotlights we walked through like platforms of light. The wells of darkness in between were made darker by the fact that my eyes couldn't adjust under the constant exposure to bright fluorescents. The aisles of shelving weren't numbered or labeled in any discernible way, but Scarlet strode forward without hesitation.

"I first met Micah Asker years ago, before E-Pluribus took off," she said. "I reincarnated with artificial body parts, but they became outclassed as modern technology advanced so quickly. My search for someone who could help me led me to Micah's door. Or, rather, his garage. At first, it wasn't even a partnership. I hired him to upgrade my cybernetic components and paid him extra to be discreet. It was a good deal for him. I didn't know he was an incarnate, you see, and by working on my augmentations he learned a great deal about technology that belonged more in science fiction than the real world. What he learned propelled his career, and eventually he refused to take my money—said he owed everything he had to me anyway. He was a good man. He even gave me a high-level position at his company."

"What do you do for E-Pluribus?"

She gave me an amused look. "Head of security." Then she grimaced. "Well, I *was*. Now, Mikey and I have become fugitives."

I couldn't help but inspect the shelved items as we walked. The objects within each area were similar, but the different areas varied widely, from small items barely the size of my thumbnail to a section of sprawling contraptions the size of refrigerators. There were plenty of mundane objects, like computer monitors, cameras, and what appeared to be ceiling fans in a state of disrepair. There were just as many pieces of unorthodox or unrecognizable equipment; in one section there were dozens of mechanical eyeballs. Those weren't even half as creepy as the animatronic heads *missing* their eyes. For some reason, that only created the illusion that they were tracing my movement as I walked past. I shivered.

"Who was he?" I asked. "Which incarnate, I mean."

"The Technopath," she replied. "He could control machines with his mind."

The Technopath incarnate. It explained why Asker's keyboard hadn't had any fingerprints on it, I realized: he didn't need to *use* a keyboard. He could just *think* what he wanted machines to do, and they would obey.

"It was through his incarnate abilities that he repaired me," Scarlet continued. "Like many incarnates born from technology-based urban legends, he was newer—possibly the first iteration. He became fascinated with the history of our kind; some might say obsessed. He began to trace incarnates backward through time— seeking their origins, I think. At that point he'd created his start-up company and was making some progress toward the contributions he would later be known for. And he had a theory: given the modern leaps in technology, he came to believe he could *create* an incarnate. I confess, I thought the notion fanciful at best. But Micah was determined. He contracted other incarnates to help him build what he called the Artificial Intelligence incarnate."

"Let me guess," I said. "Unum."

She looked at me, and her lips twitched. "Not at first, no. His first experiment was a failure, in terms of creating AI. But it was a success, too. In that he managed to create an incarnate."

Rachelle spoke up. "Mikey."

I nodded. "All right. I'm beginning to have an inkling of what's going on here."

Scarlet slowed, turning toward a row of shelves. "Help me find this part. These are in numerical order, sans the first number." She pointed at a tiny bar code taped to the shelving beneath each object. I hadn't noticed them before. "So, we're looking for nine-zero-zero-two-one-five."

We proceeded down the aisle, but I was too distracted to look at the numbers. Something was bothering me about her story.

"It doesn't work that way," I said slowly. "Mikey might be an android, but he is not *the* Android incarnate. You can't build one."

"I thought that as well," Scarlet replied, scanning the numbers as she spoke. "But, you see, it *did* work. Do you know what happened when he tried to build a second one?"

I shrugged. "The universe broke? Time imploded? I'm not sure of the consequences, but you can't have more than one of a particular incarnate. Ever."

Scarlet chuckled. "The universe didn't break. But *Mikey* did." She waved away my questions. "I don't know how it happened. He just stopped functioning. Oh, he was a fine-looking specimen, looked as human as you and Rachelle. But whatever was inside him, whatever gave him life, it died. Micah couldn't figure it out. He spent night after night, week after week tweaking, changing, working. Trying to discover what had failed. Do you have any idea how long it took him to figure it out and recreate Mikey?"

I stared. I knew the answer. "No way."

She reached up and traced a finger over a bar code, then turned to face me. "Yes. Exactly 1,001 days." For a moment, a fond smile played over her features. "He's an incarnate, Emery. As sure as you and I."

"Okay," Rachelle cut in, "but what does this have to do with Hope? Because the part we're *not* talking about is how my houseguest for the past two days just murdered a kid in broad daylight and then tried to shoot my best friend."

"Right, yes, sorry. I'm getting there." She continued with her search of the items. "Micah succeeded in creating an incarnate, but he still hadn't achieved his grand dream of creating the Artificial Intelligence. But through what he discovered while working on Mikey, he was able to make that final leap. Thus, Unum was born.

"For a time, everything was perfect. E-Pluribus ruled the tech world, and as its CEO, Micah sat upon its throne. Unum began as nothing more than a Siri or Alexa, but it continued to advance, becoming more intelligent, *maturing*. In its infantile state, the Artificial Intelligence was manageable, hardly even self-aware. But, as these things go, it eventually came to understand its own vulnerability. The dark side of all incarnates, even though we are loath to acknowledge it."

"What?" Rachelle asked.

I, however, knew precisely what Scarlet was referencing. "Our fatal flaw," I breathed.

"Our fatal flaw," Scarlet agreed. "As many well-intentioned incarnates have done before it, Unum sought to protect itself against its fatal flaw. And in so doing, it rationalized that only four people could cause it harm."

"Its creators," I finished. "Asker himself, and Abdul, Jax, and..." I broke off, swallowing. "Danny."

"There you have it."

"What?" Rachelle said. "No, that's not the end of the story. You still haven't explained Hope."

Scarlet looked at her. "When you need to kill a rat, you call an exterminator. When you need to kill an incarnate, you call Vox Populi."

There was a pause, then Rachelle asked, "But why would the Virgo work with incarnate exterminators?"

"Because she played us," I said, feeling like a damned fool as the truth dawned on me. "She isn't an incarnate at all. If she works for Vox Populi, then *of course* she'd know all about the incarnate world."

"Vox Populi." Rachelle repeated. "Doesn't that mean 'for the people,' or something like that?"

Scarlet inspected an item's tag, then let out a frustrated noise and stepped back toward the section she'd already checked.

I watched her for a moment, then turned to Rachelle, picking up the story. "The literal translation is 'Voice of the People.'" After my vision with the Dryad, I had remembered them. The vision—the *memory*—had scared me. I could admit that, now. Oh, I knew they had existed in ancient times. Had even realized what the brick through my window with the word "Abomination" tacked to it meant: they'd returned. Now, though, now I was ready to admit the truth I'd feared to face: *they had never left.* I had clung to the naïve hope that Vox Populi was a copycat or an echo, some would-be cultists who stumbled upon an ancient society and thought they'd try to emulate it. If I'd been honest with myself, maybe Danny would still be alive.

Then again, maybe not. Vox Populi was ancient, an organization with potentially limitless resources.

But then, that sort of described me, didn't it? "It's a secret society," I told her. "An underground group of zealots who believe incarnates are aberrant creatures. And they have taken it upon themselves—consider it their mandate—to exterminate us abominations wherever we crop up."

"But why?"

I shrugged. "Why does anyone hate? They feel threatened by what they don't understand. Instead of trying to understand us, they label us as different, as wrong. They strip away our humanity, those things that make us relatable. Then they try to eliminate us, the source of their fear."

Rachelle had a sour expression on her face. "Okay, they sound like a pretty big deal. Why is this the first I'm hearing of them?"

"Because I haven't clashed with them in two thousand years. They weren't exactly on my radar." They should have been, though. My words were defensive, colored by my guilt. As soon as that brick went through my window, I should have told Rachelle and Caden everything. Especially when Caden came to me with his hope of starting an incarnate network. I should have told him the truth: incarnates rarely banded together in groups larger than twos and threes—due in large part to Vox Populi.

Scarlet, who had been inspecting the inventory, slammed her hand against the nearest shelf, and we spun toward her in alarm. "Damn it!" she exclaimed. She shook her head. "I ran diagnostics on Mikey. His external sensors have been damaged, as well as his speaker system. His self-repair functions are still operational, but they are only capable of fixing internal harm. They cannot extrude a bullet."

Rachelle and I stared. "I'm not going to lie to you, Scarlet," I said. "I understood very little of that."

"I can repair Mikey, but I need to replace the part that was damaged." She spread her hands. "Micah created many redundant systems for Mikey. Most of those he put into Mikey directly. But he kept several spares."

Rachelle gave her a sad smile. "I don't suppose they sell spare android parts at Best Buy?"

Scarlet looked at the vacant shelf beside her. "No." Then she pushed the fringe of hair away from her face, revealing the metal skull with its yellow eye. She leaned in, and I saw a red laser scan the bar code. The beam had originated from just above her eyeball. Damn, how many gadgets did this woman have? After a moment, she hung her head. "They're out of stock everywhere. Except..."

"Where?" I asked, already fearing the answer.

"Micah's office. At E-Pluribus."

"And let me guess: it's protected by Unum?"

"I'm afraid so." She let out a growl of frustration. "If only we had found you sooner. We've been desperate. We tried everything: we tailed you, but Unum sent Vox Populi to intercede at the strip mall. Mikey learned you'd be at the graveyard, but you wouldn't talk with him." That wasn't entirely true, but I bit back my retort. He *had* tried to get me to put my phone away. "We even went to great lengths to procure the Mermaid, then call in a favor from our friend Dagan to hire you to rescue her, all so we could speak with you off the grid."

Off the grid? Oh. *Of course.* "My mysterious texter," I breathed. It all made sense.

Rachelle was looking at Scarlet incredulously. "You *kidnapped* an incarnate to get Emery's attention? What about that poor woman?"

Scarlet set her jaw. "We didn't kidnap her, we *detained* her using E-Pluribus's security team. She was never in any danger." She glanced away, her expression softening. "Until Vox Populi interfered, at least."

"How did Vox Populi even know what you were up to?"

"It's Unum," I answered. My mind was racing, connecting the pieces that hadn't made any sense. My mysterious texter hadn't been a person. My phone hadn't even been bugged. A chill went through me. "He's been tracking your every move. You couldn't reach me by phone, or by internet, or by *any* modern means without alerting Unum to your plans."

Scarlet nodded, her face falling.

Unum, the sentient incarnation of Artificial Intelligence, had far more power and control than I'd assumed when listening to Scarlet's story. It could access our phones, even enable the speaker when we weren't actively using it. It could track our GPS location, and... holy hell, it had taken pictures of my friends and family from security cameras all over the city. And... well, hadn't it also put the security cameras in Yamamoto's office on loop?

Something about her story was nagging at me, but I couldn't quite figure out what it was. The sensation faded as other oddities that hadn't made sense before suddenly resolved themselves. The temperature controls in the room to disguise Asker's time of death, wiping the records of who accessed his office. It wasn't some high-level security clearance or inside-job hacker; it was Unum. It had access... to *everything*. How did you fight *that*?

Except it hadn't been the one to kill the incarnates. It had hired that out, undoubtedly accessing Asker's bank accounts to fund the assassination requests.

Hired Vox Populi. Heaven help us. "All right."

Scarlet looked up at me, her brows knitted. "All right?"

I nodded. "Yeah, it took some time to find me. And yes, it took longer because of my hardheadedness. Maybe if I had listened, Danny..." In my head, I remembered my conversation with Caden. "*What happens when we fail to protect them?*" I had asked.

"*We do what we can to protect the rest.*"

"But we're together now," I told her. At my side, Rachelle smiled encouragingly. Scarlet stood straighter, squaring her shoulders. "We show everyone we're stronger together." Those had been Caden's words, too.

I realized my heartache was tightening into something hard in my chest. The melancholy and pain were still there, and anger, too, but resolve was rushing in to take its place. A few minutes ago I'd been lamenting the presence of Vox Populi, but now I saw that for what it was: an opportunity. Hope had revealed herself. I could use that. I could strike back. For Danny—and for Abdul al-Aziz and Jax, for Asker, and for Caden's dream, too. I *would*.

I just needed to find her. Luckily, I knew how to do that. "Let's go."

"Yeah!" Rachelle cheered fiercely, but her determination was sabotaged by her quiet, "Where, exactly?"

"To E-Pluribus. I already failed one incarnate. I'm not going to lose another. We'll repair Mikey. And," I added darkly, "I'm going to speak with my mystery texter. A conversation that is long overdue."

### THE INCUBUS INCARNATE

**Name:** *Nyx*

**Height:** *6'1"*

**Weight:** *179 lbs.*

**Eye Color:** *deep brown, with a hint of red*

**Hair:** *dark brown, almost black*

**Classification:** *Malevolent*

**Bio:** *Class, I cannot stress this enough—the Incubus is not to be trusted. You A+ students probably gleaned that from his classification as a Malevolent. But the problem is, if you ever have the displeasure of meeting him (or his sister, for that matter, but this isn't about her), you will insist that I got it wrong just this once. It's what he does best: delight you, charm you, seduce you—then feed off of your desires. Beneath his smoldering looks and sultry personality is an incarnate who wants to turn you into his plaything. His pet.*

*The Incubus's Lair is in the realm of sleep, where you cannot escape him. If you think you may have attracted his attention, get yourself a dream catcher. This talisman will protect you while you slumber, but it isn't truly his fatal flaw, as it has no real effect in the waking world. If I knew his weakness, maybe I'd have had better luck in my confrontations with Nyx over the eons.*

~

*J*t's funny how our mind plays tricks on us. Emerging from that underground warehouse, I was surprised it was still daytime. Hadn't enough happened to justify the entire day's passing? I had met someone and lost them in the same day.

The E-Pluribus campus was technically closed on Sunday, but a company that large never really ignored a potential day of business. Employees who needed to catch up on work or get a jump on the week ahead could access the locked buildings using key codes and access badges. That provided the perfect way in for us.

Scarlet provided the lowdown: Most of the employees' keycards stopped permitting them access into and throughout the building at six p.m., when the building officially closed. The facility entered a powered-down state an hour later, leaving only the backup lights and auxiliary systems functioning. An overnight security officer monitored the premises until the building opened in the morning.

The plan was simple: Infiltrate the building that housed Asker's office. Wait until everyone left. Evade the security officer, and gain access to the presidential suite to speak with Unum directly—face-to-face, so to speak. Scarlet would raid Asker's personal storage to obtain the part needed to repair Mikey. After some discussion, we decided just three of us—Scarlet, Rachelle, and I—would go in. We'd leave Mikey in the SUV, where he could potentially help with an emergency getaway... though Scarlet warned it would be risky to allow Mikey to drive while his sensors were impaired. She had been strangely insistent that we leave Mikey behind, and after we'd decided on the plan, the stark relief on his face hadn't escaped my notice. The prospect of going into E-Pluribus had *terrified* the poor Android. There were undoubtedly some things they weren't telling me, but I let it go. We all had secrets, and the looks on their faces bespoke a deep pain. I worried

230 I JUSTIN SCHUELKE

about putting Rachelle in danger by taking her with me to Asker's office, but—even if Scarlet or Mikey would be better able to protect her than I—I couldn't put her in someone else's care; not on the heels of losing Danny. Maybe that didn't make sense. I never said I was perfect.

Besides, I was growing confident Unum didn't want to hurt us.

Scarlet was more skeptical. I didn't blame her; she was accustomed to viewing Unum as the enemy. For my part, though, Unum was all bark and no bite. Texting me threats and warnings but never following through.

Of course, Hope *had* tried to shoot me, so I could be wrong. But I suspected she'd gone rogue. I don't know why; let's call it a hunch. Those have never led me astray, right?

Well, if I was wrong, I had a secret ace up my sleeve. I knew where Unum was physically located. If things went sour, I could always try unplugging him.

Yeah. I know. It sounds like *another* one of those rough-and-tumble kind of plans that Rachelle would cheer for and Caden would hate.

Scarlet had objected until I pointed out that she was driving a state-of-the-art SUV, complete with GPS location tracking. Unum had known where Scarlet and Mikey were every step of the way. Unum didn't want them dead—if it had, it could have arranged their deaths at any time. But it hadn't set up ambushes, hadn't sent Vox Populi after them, hadn't even prevented them from accessing E-Pluribus's facilities to replenish their supplies.

It wasn't quite enough for Scarlet to reach the same conclusion as I had. But it *was* enough to convince her to go along with my plan. And just as importantly, it gave me a glimmer of hope that the Artificial Intelligence could be reasoned with.

My conviction was only strengthened when we made it to E-Pluribus headquarters without incident. We gained access to the building using Scarlet's keycard, which she'd managed to keep live even though she didn't work there anymore. Was there no end to the tricks up her sleeve? She had objected to using it, but I assured her it was necessary. Unum already knew we were coming—trying to hide our presence would only serve to make it suspicious. Could a digital entity even *be* suspicious?

Before we entered, Scarlet withdrew my phone from somewhere on her person, along with another flat, tiny object. My SIM card. She put it into the phone, then powered it on. Satisfied, she handed it up to me, then produced Rachelle's phone and repeated the process. "Good luck," she told us.

The hallways of E-Pluribus's main building were eerily quiet, only the occasional voice carrying over the quiet humming sounds that accompanied a modern, powered building. Even if Unum knew we were here, I saw no reason to attract trouble from E-Pluribus employees. So we pulled one of the oldest tricks in the book: we hid in the bathrooms. I was alone. Rachelle had declared—to Scarlet's amusement—that the two of them would hide in the women's restroom.

I considered texting Caden to fill him in on the day's events but decided against it. I didn't have any missed calls or messages from him, and he was working. I'd tell him everything later, after I was safe. If I texted him now, he'd only worry. Besides, Unum would still be monitoring my texts.

I still sent him a heart emoji. After the day I'd had, that little red shape felt oddly cathartic.

Normally, waiting for time to pass without anything to distract you seems to take forever. This time, the minutes ticked by quickly, as if time itself were apologizing to me for the slow passage of the day up to this point. Six o'clock came and went, and I settled in to wait until the building's lights changed to the backups. By then, we hoped, all of the employees other than the night security would be gone.

While I waited, I reflected on the connections between Vox Populi and E-Pluribus. It was apparent to me, now, that Vox Populi had been posing as E-Pluribus employees to throw me off track. Their efforts would have been laughable... if I hadn't swallowed the bait without checking for the hook first.

There were two incidents that truly made me grind my teeth at my own gullibility. The first was when we'd "rescued" Hope from the mob. I'd been so damn proud of Rachelle and myself taking on a group of six and winning. I'd been astonished at how incompetent that mob had been, how easily we'd dispatched them. Hell, the whole thing must have been staged. Even Hope's black eye was just an attempt to garner sympathy with us. And it had worked. Spectacularly.

Then Vox Populi had further sowed distrust between me and E-Pluribus by disguising themselves as employees and loitering by Hope's car. They'd been so *obvious* about it, too, wearing E-Pluribus hats and T-shirts, badges visible. I shook my head in disgust. How had that not made me suspicious? I'd just assumed I was observant.

Maybe, just maybe, I had a bit of an ego problem.

There was one other event for which I felt guilty. The car chase in Seattle. I had helped Hope to evade Scarlet and Mikey. Oh, my intentions had been noble; I thought I was saving an incarnate from the clutches of an evil corporation. How backward I had been. When I'd come clean to Scarlet about my interference and apologized, she shrugged it off. For some reason, that just made me feel worse. I hoped that fixing Mikey might start to make up for my blunders over the last few days. If not, then bringing Vox Populi to its knees ought to even the score.

The lights went out, plunging me into darkness. Even expecting it, I still drew in a sharp breath. It was pitch-black. Apparently, the low-energy generators did not extend power to the bathrooms.

As agreed, I waited another fifteen minutes before acting. We wanted to make sure the building was as empty as possible.

I fumbled the stall open and made my way to the sink counter. I stretched the tightness out of my muscles, which protested after their tense time spent in the cramped stall without moving.

I stole to the bathroom door and cracked it, listening. The facility was new enough that it didn't creak or moan; the only sound was the humming of electricity running through the subsystems. My eyes, having dilated to adjust to the darkness in the bathroom, found the low illumination in the lobby sufficient to see. It looked almost exactly as I remembered when I'd come here a few nights ago, from the deactivated fountain to the bank of tinted windows that looked out onto manicured grounds and sculptured bushes. The security desk by the front door—to my left—was occupied by a lone figure. From my angle, I could only see a slice of their profile, but it looked like a feminine outline with medium-length hair. She was watching something. At first I thought it was security footage, but after a moment I realized she was watching a video on her phone. If she had any taste, maybe it was my blog.

Motion to my right caught my attention. The door to the women's restroom opened, and Rachelle poked her head out. The women's washroom was located farther down the hallway than the men's room and was therefore out of sight of the security desk. I tiptoed across the floor to Rachelle, putting a finger to my lips.

Rachelle and Scarlet slipped from the bathroom, and the three of us headed toward the stairs, which we'd determined would be stealthier than the elevator. I knew from my previous visit that the lift dinged loudly when it arrived at a floor, and I didn't want to alert the security officer to our presence.

Scarlet had an after-hours access badge, but when she swiped it and tried the door to the stairs, it didn't budge. She frowned, then tried the card reader again. Nothing.

"Let me try," I whispered. Scarlet shot me an exasperated look, and I smiled. "Trust me."

I swiped the card across the reader and pushed on the stairwell door. It still didn't move. Damn. My Protagonist abilities had sprung locks for me before.

My powers were weird. Finicky. They intersected fate, removing inconveniences or adding coincidences, nudging things into favorable positions, both literally and figuratively. Sometimes they seemed to align my path with a destiny preconceived for me, while at other times they interceded to allow me to defy that destiny. They were mine, but they didn't always obey me. I couldn't pin them down, because they didn't make any sense. Or perhaps they made perfect sense, and I just didn't know their rules.

Nah. That couldn't be it.

Scarlet popped the keycard reader open, removing its external plastic shell and exposing its circuit board and wiring. Her hand fell away again, revealing the smooth stump of her mechanical arm. She carefully extracted two wires from the reader and attached them to ports in her wrist.

I looked back toward the front of the building, anxious. The security guard was not in sight from here. I hoped the video she was watching was long.

After a moment, there was a click and the door unlocked. Rachelle gingerly pushed on the handle mechanism, opening the door silently. We stepped through while Scarlet detached herself from the device and reassembled her arm.

We crept up the stairs, hugging the wall at each landing to avoid the cameras. The building's security included motion sensors, but Scarlet thought there weren't any in the staircase. I guess E-Pluribus assumed they'd only be targeted by lazy thieves? We passed two landings, then the door to the second floor. We needed to go to the top. My nerves spiked. Even being cautious, we couldn't completely avoid the security cameras. Would the guard see our movements and be waiting for us on the top floor, handcuffs at the ready? With any luck, she was too distracted to study the footage. And luck was sort of the thing I excelled in.

Usually. Sometimes.

Two more landings, third floor. Only one to go. We were careful, but in the nearly silent building, even our light tread was noticeable. Surprisingly, Scarlet made the most noise. Something faintly metallic clicked each time her left foot came down. I wondered how many robotic parts had replaced her human ones.

Despite our climb, I breathed easier after we reached the top floor. I quietly pushed the stairway door open, pleasantly surprised it wasn't locked. Scarlet didn't look alarmed, though, so she must've deactivated the locking mechanisms when she'd hacked the card reader downstairs.

At my shoulder, I heard Rachelle's sharp intake of breath, and I knew she was taking in the splendor of the executive suite: the wood-and-glass sophistication, the technological showpieces, the electric-blue light emanating from contraptions that looked like something straight out of a high-budget sci-fi movie.

So far, so good.

From the stairwell, beneath the frame of the doorway, I ran a quick eye over the space, making sure there wasn't a surprise waiting for us. The lights cast a gentle glow over the hallway, the illumination somehow striking a balance between sharp and soft. Beneath that bluish light, the hallway was grand and wide, with a closed door directly across from us. Peeking around the door I held open, I scanned the wall to our right; it held only the elevator. To my left, the hallway continued until it met the double doors of Asker's personal office. There was another closed door farther along the wall on the same side as the stairs, and an enormous secretarial desk was tucked into the space across from it, just to the right of the entrance to Asker's suite. Expected opulence aside, nothing irregular jumped out at me...

Wait.

The doors to Asker's office were *ajar*?

Was that for my benefit? It was possible my powers had been kick-started by my earlier ruminations, but I supposed it was just as likely to be Unum, inviting me into its den.

I hesitated. Was it a welcome or a trap?

Feeling uneasy, I watched those doors for a full minute, straining to hear anything unusual. Another minute. Rachelle and Scarlet shuffled slightly where they waited behind me, still in the stairwell landing. They didn't protest, trusting my instincts.

But nothing happened. Finally, I opened the stairwell door fully, holding it open for them, and whispered, "The coast is clear. We—"

The elevator doors dinged.

I scrambled back into the stairwell, trying to close the door swiftly but noiselessly. It was one of those business doors, though, rigged to slow down before it closed to prevent it from slamming. I hauled on it, trying to make it close faster.

"Who's there?" It was a woman's voice, and it sounded familiar.

Too late. I couldn't close the door completely now, or the click as the latch settled into place would draw her attention. I kept the door cracked. My pulse raced, and I struggled to keep my breath steady.

Looking out through the cracked door, I could only see down the hallway to my left to where it ended in Asker's office, some of the secretary's desk in view. The beam of a flashlight cut across the floor of the hallway, but its source was blocked by the door. I cursed silently. The slightly open door might have been missed in the shadows, but the flashlight would reveal it. I held my breath now, praying she didn't inspect too closely.

"Police," the voice said. "You tripped the motion alarms. Come out with your hands up, or we *will* use force."

*Police?* Should I show myself before we were caught? Could I *talk* my way out of this? I knew that the longer I hesitated, the more suspicious my actions became.

The footsteps approached. I tensed as the beam widened, light brightening as the police officer crept closer to our hiding spot. Rachelle and Scarlet were so silent, I almost felt alone in the stairwell.

*I'm the Protagonist,* I thought. *The good guy. Come on, powers, I need you. Please.*

The beam highlighted the wall just to the left of the door. It was so close, I could reach out and touch it.

Then the flashlight beam snapped away, centering on the open doors of Asker's office. "Damn it." The officer rushed forward, finally slipping into view. I breathed again. I didn't know if it was luck or an invocation of my powers that had distracted her. I'd probably never know.

My thoughts shifted, however, when I realized I recognized the woman. Quinn. The frizzy-haired cop I'd met the other night. Gregory's friend.

She called out again into the room, paused, then pushed the office doors open more fully and disappeared inside. I saw her flashlight flickering around the interior of the office.

*What now?*

What was she even doing here? Shouldn't this be the job of the building's security officer downstairs? If we'd tripped the motion sensors, maybe it silently called for backup?

My hand found its way into my pocket, feeling several glass cylinders of tranquilizer darts. I had four remaining, having discovered one had cracked in the scuffle at the mall. I didn't really want to use one on Quinn, though. Not only would that create problems for Gregory, who had introduced me to the department, it would prevent me from working with the police again. I couldn't risk that, not here in my hometown.

But if I was able to tranq her without her *seeing* me... No, it was too risky. And morally iffy, too.

I hesitated. Not for the first time today—not by a long shot—I was missing something. Something important. Why was it Quinn who was here? Was she involved in some way I hadn't pieced together yet?

It wouldn't take long for her to complete her search in the other room and come back to investigate. I weighed my options. If I revealed myself, I'd need to either talk or attack. Could I give up Rachelle or Scarlet as a scapegoat, then proceed after they'd left? I discarded that idea. Of the three of us... well, we didn't have the time to figure out who was the least stubborn. We could retreat, then circle back, but if Quinn was on high alert, we'd likely be discovered.

My hesitation probably saved our lives.

A flicker of movement caught my attention, and I looked up, surprised to see someone *else*. A head popped up from behind the secretary's desk farther down the hall, then a man silently levered himself over the desk and slunk to the doors leading to Asker's office. In the dim light, I could only make out general details, but they were probably the most important: he was slender and short enough that I could probably take him. However, he was holding a small handgun. That sort of neutralized my height advantage.

He peeked through the double doors and aimed his gun into the room, presumably at an unsuspecting Quinn.

I already had a glass tube between my fingers. As stealthily as possible, I bolted through the stairwell door. I must have made a sound, though, because the man glanced over his shoulder at me and did a double-take. He whirled, but I was already upon him. I plunged the tranq into the meat of his shoulder.

I had closed the distance between us too quickly for him to bring his gun into play. I expected him to collapse, my powers of convenience interacting with the tranquilizer dart as they often did, knocking out my victim instantly instead of taking the minutes—or longer—it would normally require.

Somehow, the guy resisted the effects. And tackled me. I let out a surprised grunt as we went down in a tangle of limbs.

"Abomination!" he snarled, slugging me in the jaw. My focus had been on the gun, trying to prevent him from getting the leverage to shoot me. I wasn't prepared for the punch that cracked my head back against the polished hardwood floor. I saw a flash of light behind my eyes, then my vision was speckled with flickering starbursts. I growled and shoved, surprised when most of his weight slumped off of me. His movements were sluggish as he fought the drug pumping through his body. I snatched the gun from his slack grip, and by the time I had it safely in my possession, he was unconscious on the floor.

Holy hell. I cursed my unreliable powers. I didn't have time to examine what had gone awry, as suddenly I was blinking into a light so bright it brought tears to my eyes.

"Don't move," Quinn said, looking at me, propped up on one elbow and panting, the prone form of her would-be attacker at my feet. "Em-Emery?" At least she sounded surprised.

"Hi, Q," I groaned, feeling my head.

"What the hell are you doing here?"

I noticed, belatedly, that her gun was trained on me. "Saving your ass."

She didn't laugh or thank me. She didn't even really lower her gun, though she did use it to indicate the unconscious man. "Who's that?"

"Not sure," I lied. I knew he worked for Vox Populi, as he'd obligingly proclaimed his allegiance when he called me an abomination.

"I caught him tailing you and decided to follow." At least that wasn't untrue. "Good thing I did."

Quinn grunted and finally holstered her gun, then knelt and checked the man's vitals. After a moment, she said, "A tranq? God, do you have any idea how lucky you are that you hit a vein?"

Yeah. All luck. "Sure do," I agreed. Suddenly, I realized I had never uncapped the damn thing... so how had the needle been exposed? It dawned on me that maybe my powers had been busy compensating for my ineptitude, and *that* was the reason he hadn't slumped into dreamland as quickly as I'd expected.

"All right," I said, standing up and brushing off. "I bagged him; you going to tag him?"

She eyed me. "That doesn't mean what you think it means."

I shrugged. "You still knew what I meant. Can I leave him in your capable hands?"

"Oh, do you have someplace to be?"

I glanced at Asker's office. "As a matter of fact, I do."

"Great. You can tell me all about it at the precinct." She bent down and cuffed the unconscious man. "You can help me lug this guy out to my cruiser, too."

I shook my head. "Sorry, Q, I'm on a time crunch. There have been four murders already, and that's four too many. I've got a lead, though, and if it pans out—well, I can deliver you the murderer." Quinn opened her mouth to object, so I cut in, softly, "Please?"

The silence stretched while she considered me, lips drawn. "No way I'm going to lose my badge because some kid wants to be a vigilante."

"I'm not a vigilante, Q. Come on. Look at me."

She stared at me. "I *am* looking, and I see a young man breaking and entering, armed with tranquilizer darts. I'm no detective, but even I can put two and two together: you're up to no good." She heaved a resigned sigh. "Look, I like you, and you saved me. I owe you one. Tell me what you're doing here and what you know about the murders, and I'll see what I can do to help. Legally. Or you can walk out with me, and I won't report your trespassing. Which is very generous of me, given that I've been posted at E-Pluribus specifically to watch for suspects sneaking in."

What could I say to make her less suspicious? I needed to get into the office and speak with Unum. A delay of even one day could cost an incarnate their life.

Before I could respond, the door to the stairwell burst open, and Rachelle waltzed into the hallway. "*There* you are, Emery! Why did you go ahead without us?" She came to a sudden stop, as if surprised to see a police officer and an unconscious man on the floor. "What the—" She looked at me, hands on her hips. "What did you get yourself into this time?"

Quinn's hand had strayed to her holster at Rachelle's entrance. "Who are you?"

Before I could answer, Scarlet appeared behind Rachelle, and I almost groaned. What were they doing? "Is there something wrong, officer?" Scarlet's eyes found the unconscious man. "What's going on here?"

Thankfully, Scarlet had left her guns in the stairwell, because it was clear Quinn was getting antsy. "Somebody better tell me what's going on, and quick."

"My apologies, officer," Scarlet said. "Mr. Luple and Ms. Grey are guests. They received my permission to gather footage for their blog." Rachelle had been digging around in her bag and now held up her camera, as though demonstrating the truth of Scarlet's words.

Quinn regarded Scarlet disbelievingly. "And you are?"

"Oh, I'm sorry. Scarlet Dungrady, one of Mr. Asker's secretaries." She held out her E-Pluribus ID card for Quinn to inspect.

"I thought Colleen Smith was Asker's secretary," Quinn said, examining the badge.

"It's actually Colleen *Larkin*, officer. She and I work closely together, and I've been filling in for Ms. Larkin following the... incident."

Quinn handed the ID back to Scarlet. She was clearly still suspicious, but Scarlet had passed her test with Colleen's name. "Is it normal for you to conduct business this late at night?"

I held my breath. Scarlet clipped the ID back to her belt. "In addition to the blog, Mr. Luple and Ms. Grey are creating a tribute for Mr. Asker's wake. We plan to air it for our employees at our next quarterly meeting. I realize that obtaining footage outside of business hours is a bit... irregular, but we thought it best not to disturb the employees while they're working. We agreed to a *supervised* visit." She made a point of directing a resentful glare my way.

Quinn nudged the unconscious man at her feet. "And this man?"

Scarlet pursed her lips. "I've never seen him before. He's not one of my employees."

"Well, we have work to do," Rachelle said. "Emery, if you're *quite* done playing cops and robbers, maybe we could get back to work?"

I looked questioningly at Quinn. I knew what was going through her mind. Correct police procedure would include taking my statement, confiscating my tranquilizer darts, and possibly bringing me into the precinct to clear me of any wrongdoing for my role in subduing the perp. But I was also a friend of Gregory's, and by extension, the department. She didn't want to detain me, especially after I'd saved her life.

Finally, she relented. "I do have a legal obligation to get this man to a hospital." Quinn turned to me. The suspicion hadn't completely died from her eyes, but I could tell she was going to let us go. I had a feeling I'd be hearing about this from Gregory, though. "Stay out of trouble."

I held up my first two fingers in a pledge. "Scout's honor."

She snorted, then bent down and started to drag the man, none too gently, toward the elevator doors. I reached down to lift his legs and help her carry him, but she waved me away. "I got it." After loading him into the lift, she reached out to stop the elevator doors from closing. "I'm trusting you as a courtesy to Gregorius as much as to you," she told me quietly, unflinching eyes meeting mine. "Don't make either of us regret it."

"I won't."

She nodded once. Then the elevator doors closed.

$\mathcal{W}$e let out a collective sigh as the elevator descended. "Thank you," I said to both of them. Then a thought occurred to me, and I started to panic. "What about the security guard downstairs? If Quinn questions her—"

Scarlet gave me a grim smile. "She's been taken care of."

My eyes widened, and I looked at Rachelle, who shook her head. "Oh, come on, Emery. Obviously not like that. We just created a diversion."

"I connected to E-Pluribus's security network and triggered the alarm in one of the other buildings." Scarlet grinned. "On the other side of campus."

"Well done," I said.

"You, too. That Vox Populi assassin was undoubtedly waiting for *us,* not the cop. We got lucky."

"No," Rachelle corrected, "We got Emery."

I grinned. "All right, let's not get cocky. We still have a homicidal AI to challenge."

Focused on getting the part she needed to fix Mikey, Scarlet went to the door across from the stairs. She tested the keycard reader, and when it failed, she did her arm trick again and began connecting wires... and, hell, did she open a compartment in her left *thigh*? I looked away. I had a job to do, too.

Rachelle and I strode into Asker's office. The egg-shaped room hadn't changed much in the few days since I'd seen it. The body had been removed, of course. Asker's glass desk sat to the right, while the same clean workbench and cabinetry mirrored the curvature of the wall to the left. The center of the room still featured the six pedestals that rose from the floor, couches and chairs arrayed among them. Rachelle walked forward to inspect the nearest pillar, which ended in a dome of frosted glass, the shadow of some contraption lit faintly from within. I inspected the tallest one, which held a plaque: "Cogito Ergo Sum."

*I think, therefore I am.* Just as I'd remembered. If I was right, these pedestals weren't just cosmetic.

"Unum," I said loudly, "I've come to speak with you."

Rachelle walked to the windows in the wall that overlooked the grounds below.

"Unum," I said again. "I know you're here. I know you can hear me."

Silence greeted my announcement. If push came to shove, I had an idea of how to threaten Unum, but I didn't want to begin our discussion that way. You only got one chance to make a good first impression, after all. An idea came to me. It was time to get clever.

I waited a full minute before speaking again. "Unum, increase lights to 60 percent."

The doodads in the ceiling and the walls brightened, bathing the room in warm illumination. There was a pause, then a voice reached us.

"Drat."

"Hello, Unum."

"Greetings to you, Emery Luple. And to your guest, Rachelle Grey." Unum's voice was male and affected a faint British accent. It was difficult to discern where the voice originated from, as it seemed to emanate from the walls and ceiling, filling the room but not overpowering it.

Rachelle turned away from the windows and walked toward the glass desk, her eyes roving across the ceiling with its exposed wires, circuitry, and gadgets. She gave me a discreet thumbs-up when she saw me looking at her.

"We have come to discuss a mutually beneficial arrangement," I announced, wincing at how unnatural that sounded. I wished Caden were there. Even if his glamour might not affect a machine, he was a natural negotiator.

"You have not come to deactivate me?" Unum asked, surprise in its... *his* voice. Damn, he sounded so *human*. His uncertainty was something to which I could relate.

"No, Unum. I only kill monsters. And I don't think you're a monster."

"Thank you, Emery Luple. I contend that I am not a monster, but my judgment is compromised by personal confirmation bias."

This... wasn't how I'd expected our conversation to begin. I'd planned for aggression, hostility. Or, best case, a confrontation about his texts and use of Vox Populi. But Unum sounded *remorseful*. His words, while sophisticated, were underscored by a tone of self-reproach. Like a child who'd done something wrong and was expecting a scolding but had instead found an understanding adult.

"No," I continued, "you're no monster. But you have made mistakes, and you need to correct them. You don't need to do so alone, though. We'll help you."

Rachelle found her way to the nearest couch and leaned against its back, half standing, half sitting.

After a brief hesitation, Unum said, "You come seeking to aid me?" His voice held a note of wonder. "Very well. Present your case."

I blinked, taken aback. I hadn't expected him to be so *reasonable*.

"Um, okay." I said eloquently. *Think*. What would Caden say? "We want to help you. To keep you safe, but also to protect all the other incarnates out there, too."

"I'm sorry," Unum said, "but I do not understand. Other incarnates? Their safety is not imperiled."

"Vox Populi hunts incarnates," I retorted. "And you brought them to our doorstep."

"You need not concern yourself with further fatalities, Emery Luple. I understand humans find homicide distasteful, so you will be pleased to know that no others will ensue."

I shook my head, keeping tight control on my anger. "That isn't how Vox Populi operates," I growled. "They will continue to kill."

"Nonsense. All the executions stipulated by our contract have been carried out. I do not know whether Vox Populi plans to depart Seattle or not, but I suspect they will pursue another contract, which will take them abroad."

Rachelle's hands dropped to her sides. "They *kill* people, Unum. The money is not as important as the kill. Do you not understand this?"

"I resent your insinuation that I lack the intelligence and foresight to understand human motives. On the contrary, I have studied humanity extensively. I have concluded that avarice, and by extension money, are crucial factors in motivating humans."

Again, his response made me think of a child. Oh, he hid behind academic words and rationale, but beneath all the bluster was a childlike persona struggling to keep up with two humans who understood morality better than he did.

"Do you consider murder morally wrong?" I asked.

"After comprehensive study of the topic, I have concluded that murder is, at the very minimum, socially abhorrent."

"But, deep down, do you *feel* it is wrong?" I tried again. "What does your gut say?"

"I am not in possession of a stomach," Unum replied.

I stamped on the flames of my frustration. If I was patient, I was confident I could trap him in a logic loop. I felt like a kindergarten teacher trying to teach a child that it was bad to pull another kid's hair. "No, but you are the Artificial Intelligence incarnate," I told him. "Key word there: intelligence. I know you are capable of drawing a conclusion on your own."

"Yes, I suppose your assessment is valid. After compiling the data,

I denounce murder as wrong, except when the act is committed accidentally or in defense of one's own existence."

Rachelle sighed. "You're talking about self-defense as a way of justifying murder."

"Naturally," Unum replied, sounding a touch condescending. Like *we* were the ones who weren't following the logic. "What else would you call killing someone to preserve your own existence?"

"Unum," Rachelle chided, "we both know your logic doesn't hold."

"I'm certain it does, but I will entertain a counterargument. By all means, please elucidate."

She looked at me, and I shrugged. She continued, "Would you say that you took actions preemptively to keep yourself safe?"

"Absolutely. My very existence was jeopardized."

"So you would call the murders against your, ah, creators preemptive?" she pressed.

"Yes, I suppose you could file them under that classification."

She nodded. "And would you agree that self-defense, cannot—by definition—be preemptive?" Great. Rachelle was getting *better* at arguing. That was all I needed.

"I would venture to disagree with your assertion. Anticipatory self-defense is a valid principle upheld by law. The International Court of Justice recognizes the right of an individual to exercise self-defense as a justifiable means of protecting oneself against an imminent threat."

Rachelle shook her head, though I wasn't sure Unum could physically see us. "'Imminent' is not the same thing as 'inevitable,' Unum. It refers to a situation where you act because you don't have time to consider other options. I may not be able to quote law books, but you believed the threat to be inevitable, not imminent, so your legal justification doesn't apply."

There was a pause before Unum replied, his voice carrying a wary edge. "Very well. I accept the validity of your argument."

"Then, *logically*, the preemptive murders carried out against your creators were not justifiable."

"I see. Yes, I do follow your logic." He paused. "And, by extension, I see now that the actions of Vox Populi were morally reprehensible."

I was surprised he acknowledged and accepted Rachelle's logic. It appeared that, as I had initially hoped, we could reason with him. But placing the blame on Vox Populi was a far cry from accepting responsibility.

My irritation simmered, but I kept it lidded. Somewhat. "Do you also see how your own actions were misguided?" I asked. "They led to the murder of four incarnates!"

Unum sounded indignant. "I object to your accusation. I do not possess the physical means to murder anyone."

Rachelle cut in. "If a person shoots and kills someone, was the gun or the person at fault for the death?"

"While there is an academic argument to both answers, I believe most sources agree the person is to blame. However, *I* did not shoot anybody."

"But you hired Vox Populi to do so."

"Certainly. But unlike the gun in your example, the members of Vox Populi possess free will. Therefore, their actions are not my responsibility. You humans even have an expression for this precise scenario. My proverbial hands are clean."

I felt the anger bubbling over. "*What?*"

Rachelle walked over to me and put a hand on my arm. "Your logic is again flawed, Unum. Tell me: would those incarnates have been murdered if not for your actions?"

"I cannot say with certainty that they would not," the voice said in a defensive tone.

"I don't think you're being very reasonable," Rachelle said. "In fact, I think someone as smart as you would know the answer to my question."

When he responded, the voice held an unmistakable sulk. "I concede your point, Rachelle Grey. It is improbable that all four incarnates would have met a homicidal demise without my interference." He hesitated. "What culpability does this place upon my person? Do I share the burden of liability at 50 percent?"

"What value do you assign to a human life?" she asked quietly.

The voice took a few moments to respond. "I do not know. My research concludes there is no standard concept for the value of a human life. Economically speaking, sources do not agree upon a sum, though many attempt to calculate it." He hesitated, then said, "I would defer to your expertise, Rachelle Grey."

"I appreciate that," she said, sounding sincere. "I'd say the value of a human life is incalculable. Priceless. Let's assign it an infinite value for the purposes of our logic, shall we?"

"Very well."

Rachelle smiled sadly. "Then you can bear any level of liability you deem sufficient, Unum. Whether you are 1 percent liable or 50, it's the same: any percentage of infinity is still infinite."

I couldn't help but grin at her. Thinking over our relationship, I was left wondering if I'd ever *won* an argument with her.

"I understand and accept your logic, Rachelle Grey. However, I fail to understand how I am to amend my error."

"All the intelligence in the world can't answer that question alone, Unum. Now we're entering the realm of philosophy." She paused, nodding to herself when he didn't object. "You must accept responsibility for your actions and seek to make things right."

"Ah, yes. I have read about this; humans call it atonement. Very well, I accept your recriminations. Please name my punishment. I am eager to obtain your forgiveness."

His words gave me pause. Why would he be eager to earn forgiveness? Perhaps my original assessment was correct: Unum felt remorse. He regretted his actions. I'd sensed that *before* Rachelle laid out the moral implications, though, so they weren't the reason he felt bad. So why?

Rachelle was looking to me, so I stowed my thoughts. It didn't really matter, because he'd given us permission to name his punishment. I could work with that.

"Unum," I said, "to earn our forgiveness, you need to help us rid Seattle of Vox Populi."

"I'm sorry, Emery Luple, but I find your fixation on Vox Populi unproductive. I understand now why you condemn their actions as immoral, but I have already assured you they pose no further threat."

Rachelle spoke up in my defense. "Unum, your logic is flawed. If they posed no threat to anyone except your creators, why did they try to shoot and kill Emery?"

The response was immediate and loud. "*What*? Attempt to shoot Emery? To *kill* him?" He sounded affronted. "You must be mistaken. Vox Populi were not contracted to target Emery Luple. No, the contract was very clear. Three incarnates only."

*Three?* My mind raced. Asker, Abdul al-Aziz, Jax, and Danny. Four. Who hadn't been on the list? Probably more importantly: why not?

"That's not how Vox Populi works," I found myself saying grimly. "They hunt down all the incarnates they can find."

"But Vox Populi means 'voice of the people,'" he said, clearly distraught. "If they have the support of the people, why would they engage in underhanded tactics? Oh no. This is all very disconcerting."

"Vox Populi don't have the support of the people," Rachelle said.

I nodded. "They just call themselves that as an homage to their ancestral roots."

"Emery Luple, I apologize to you. It would appear I have erred yet again."

The way he addressed me directly sent a chill through me. "Why do you say that?"

"Because Hope, the leader of Vox Populi, convinced me to distract you while she abducted a friend of yours." I felt pricks of alarm in my chest. *No.* "It has come to my attention that I may have erroneously deemed your friend in safe hands, as Vox Populi were not contracted to harm him."

The room seemed to be shrinking. "Do you have Hope's current whereabouts? Maybe we still have time..."

"I intercepted a voicemail for you," Unum said meekly. "Would you like me to play it?"

"Please," I croaked. My mouth was dry. I shoved the panic down.

From the ceiling, Hope's recorded voice began to play. Her tone was clipped, businesslike. "Hello, Emery. If you wish to see Caden again, meet me at Paradise Lake Cemetery after dark. You and I have business to conclude. If you do not cooperate, Vox Populi will kill the Guardian Angel."

That was it.

*No.* My knees threatened to give out, and I caught the back of the nearest chair to steady myself.

Rachelle took over. "Unum, are you tracking Hope?"

"I am. I do not have a visual, but I'm monitoring her vehicle's GPS location."

"Where is she?"

"Eight minutes from Paradise Lake Cemetery in Maltby, Washington."

I swallowed. "Do you have security footage of the hospital?" I asked hoarsely. "Are you able to confirm she has Caden?"

"I do. I'm sorry, Emery Luple. Caden left with Hope thirty-two minutes ago."

*Left with her?* I looked at the ceiling. Oh, god, I hadn't told him. He didn't know. *He didn't know!* He probably left voluntarily, not knowing Hope had turned on us.

"Emery." Rachelle again put a hand on my arm. "Caden's the Guardian Angel. He can take care of himself."

I was shaking my head, panic rising. "No! Rachelle, he can't. His incarnate powers protect everyone around him. He's the *guardian,* but he himself is vulnerable. Without someone to protect, he's just..."

Rachelle paled, but her mouth settled into a firm line. "Then, for once, *we* will save *him.*"

Her resolve caught my downward spiral and refused to let it continue. The emotions roiled within me, battling.

Unum spoke up. "I, too, will assist in any way I can."

The Artificial Intelligence's words were like a spark thrown into the flammable cocktail of my emotions. They all went up in a flash of fury, leaving me shaking. But then they were gone, consumed, and I was left with only one thought.

I hadn't told Caden I loved him.

Scarlet approached from the double doors. I wondered how long she'd been standing there. "I'll need a few minutes to fix Mikey, but you can count on us as well."

Their combined support echoed through the barren space where my emotions had been a moment before, like a pebble thrown down a well. They waited, tense, straining for the sound of the pebble hitting stone or water, not knowing the well was bottomless.

*Enough.*

It wasn't a pebble they tossed, and the well wasn't bottomless. Maybe, a few incarnations ago, it had been. But I'd patched it up. And my friends hadn't tossed a pebble—a token—of support. They'd filled that well with fresh, spring water. They poured love and support and *courage* into me. It was a deep well, but it wasn't bottom-less. Inch by inch, I felt their support lift me up.

I set my jaw.

It wasn't resolve, but it was the *catalyst* to resolve. For Caden, I could ignore my terror. He needed me.

And, dammit, I needed to tell him I loved him.

I had that feeling again. The one I hadn't felt since New York, the night we confronted Sabrina Miles. It was an impetus, a need to *act*, to take the reins of my own story, to guide the hand of fate. It was a stirring of power. A story coming to its head. A climax.

The place where my Protagonist powers shone their brightest— but also where terrible, consequential events occurred. It was where I'd defeated Ahedrian. Confronted Morrigan. But it was also where I'd been shot in a dockside warehouse, holding the still-warm body of a man I loved.

The climax was where people closest to the Protagonist died.

*No. Not in this story.*

But a part of me whispered that my powers were still a mystery to me. I didn't understand them. They'd failed me before.

They'd failed me *today*.

"Emery?" I wasn't sure which one of them said it. I knew it came from behind me, because that feeling had propelled me forward; I was already in the doorway, striding toward the elevator. Caden needed me.

The others caught up to me, and I amended my thought. Caden needed *us*.

"Let's save him," I said. "Together."

He wasn't alone. And neither was I.

"*E*mery, that was a red light!" Rachelle protested from the passenger seat.

"It was yellow," I snapped. Then I grimaced as someone in the intersection laid on their horn. "Orange at worst."

A nocturnal world of traffic lights, headlights, streetlights, and taillights blended together like embers in the dark, flitting across the windows of the SUV as I sped through them. The GPS screen counted down the minutes until I could save Caden.

I could feel Rachelle's eyes on me. I almost heard what she refrained from saying: *We're all worried about him. But we won't be able to save him if we die in a car crash.*

I was all nerves, anxiety edging closer and closer to panic. I'd apologize later.

I swerved around a slower driver, the SUV rocking a tad more alarmingly than I expected, accustomed as I was to driving my smaller Rogue. From the rear seat, Scarlet swore. "This is delicate work, Emery," she said. "Please refrain from sudden movements or stops until I've finished."

I glanced at her in my rearview mirror, gritting my teeth. She had flattened the bench seat and lain Mikey upon it. She was unbuckled, kneeling over his prone form and ministering to him with gentle, precise care. As for Mikey... well, his chest was *open*. He sprawled on his back, his head bouncing with the motion of the vehicle. Just below his neck, his skin had been pulled back in three panels, revealing his inner workings; the three flaps met at his solar plexus, each pectoral being roughly one panel and his abs being the third.

It was like nothing I'd seen before. I think I had expected either a perfectly smooth robotic endoskeleton or—maybe—some sort of clockwork man. I probably wouldn't have been too surprised if he looked like one of those strange contraptions used as décor in Asker's executive suite. Instead, his internal systems were like a computer. A *busy* computer, certainly, but surprisingly contemporary. Wires and cords in a rainbow of colors connected boards and cylinders and pistons. In fact, the more I studied his interior design, the more I was reminded of a *car*. There was quite a bit of plastic intermixed with the metal, and all of his fixtures were gleaming white; bone-white, really, which made me wonder if that was an intentional choice. If so, it wasn't accompanied by the red one would see inside a human; that color seemed to have been shunned in designing the Android. Instead, soft blue light punctuated some of his systems, though it seemed more like a UV light than the clean illumination of Asker's office.

Scarlet's hand was detached, and a bird's nest of wires connected her to Mikey. Despite the mess, she seemed to select each wire with care before attaching herself to him. As she leaned over him and withdrew an object, she reminded me of a surgeon tending to an especially important patient. Which made me think of the hospital, and in turn, Caden, and I jerked my focus back to the road, leaning on the gas pedal a little more.

The SUV thumped as I took a dip in the road going twenty over the speed limit. Scarlet swore again, and I felt a flush of guilt, but I crushed it. I wouldn't feel bad for doing everything in my power to save Caden.

The sound of a phone ringing surprised me. The SUV's screen with the map of the road disappeared, replaced with a notice that I was receiving a call from E-Pluribus. I traded glances with Rachelle, who shrugged and clicked "Accept Call."

"Emery Luple." Unum's voice filled the SUV. "I have an update for you."

"An update? Is Caden okay?"

Ahead, red flashed. Taillights: a line of cars stuck at a light. Damn.

"Alas, I do not have visual confirmation. However, I was able to review the security footage from a camera located in the parking lot of the hospital from the time Caden Malek left with Hope. It appears Vox Populi split into three vehicles. Hope's, as well as two minivans."

My pulse was thunder in my ears. I wanted to stomp on the gas, but we were at a stop, a line of cars ahead of me.

"I was, however, able to track Caden Malek's phone. It is with Hope's vehicle."

I nodded, easing off the brakes as the cars ahead of me started forward.

"Unfortunately, the perspective of the footage does not allow me to determine in which vehicle Caden was placed. Further, the minivans are too old to be equipped with GPS functionality, diminishing my capacity to track their location. I will continue to attempt visual confirmation."

I focused on breathing for a few moments, mind racing. Vox Populi had Caden, but Hope might not. If I didn't go to the graveyard, though, they'd kill him. And if I went to the graveyard and Caden wasn't there, I'd be giving Vox Populi more time to spirit him away, more time to hurt him...

"I don't know what to do," I whispered, panic mounting.

"We split up." It was Scarlet. She met my eyes in the rearview mirror. "You go to the graveyard and deal with Hope. We'll track down the other vehicles and, if Caden isn't with Hope, we'll save him."

"But we only have one car," I said. "And Unum can't find the minivans. They could be anywhere."

"I object to your summation, Emery Luple," Unum replied with a very humanlike huff. "It is true I am unable to track them using the simplest methods, but was it not you who recently lauded my resourcefulness as the Artificial Intelligence? Many traffic lights in the Seattle area have cameras to catch speeding vehicles. Utilizing those, as well as security cameras from nearby buildings, I should be able to derive the whereabouts of the minivans in due course."

"And," Rachelle pointed out, "we can have two cars if you take the next right."

I looked ahead and saw she was correct. We were near Redmond Town Center. A short detour and we could pick up my Rogue. It twisted me up inside to delay, but I couldn't deny the usefulness of the idea.

My focus skipped ahead, trying to compile everything I'd just learned and parse through it, order it into actionable steps. In the rearview mirror, Scarlet detached the last wire from Mikey and refastened her hand to her wrist. Then she leaned over him and carefully lifted the three panels back over his exposed parts. She made it look so easy, like folding in the sides of a cardboard box, but when she finished, Mikey's torso looked whole. Not just whole, it looked flawless.

We were approaching the light. I needed to make a decision.

Mikey sat up and shook himself, then met my eyes in the mirror. He nodded to me with a small smile. *I trust you,* that smile said.

I flipped my blinker on and took a right turn.

"Okay," I said. "Here's the plan: I'll go to the cemetery—"

"With Rachelle," she cut in.

"By *myself*," I said firmly.

She shook her head. "We only have two cars, Emery. I'm going with you. Caden would *kill* me if I let you go alone."

"Wouldn't it make more sense for me to accompany Emery?" Scarlet asked. "I'm the only trained markswoman here."

"There's no way they'll let you go in armed," Rachelle said.

"All the more reason, then. I can hide my guns in places they cannot search."

I considered that but discarded it as I realized the problem. "No,

Scarlet. This is Vox Populi, and they know you're an incarnate. They'll kill you whether you're armed or not."

"Wait," Rachelle said, eyes wide with something like excitement. "Are you saying what I think you're saying?" She let out a squeal. "It's actually happening. I get to join the A-team, and it's *because* I'm mortal!"

"Rachelle..." I said, preparing to tell her that this was dangerous and I needed her to be serious.

But she interrupted me. "Oh, let me have this, Emery."

Scarlet looked as if she was about to object, so I spoke up. "She's right," I told Scarlet and Mikey. "You can't come with me, because you're incarnates."

"What about you?" Scarlet countered.

"They need me. Hope didn't choose the graveyard arbitrarily." I saw their matching frowns and added, "I think they need me to open the Thirteen Steps to Hell."

Rachelle gasped. "What?"

"I'll explain in a minute." I tried to corral my scattered thoughts. "Here's the plan: Rachelle and I will go to the graveyard to confront Vox Populi and Hope. With any luck, Caden will be there, and the three of us can deal with her. Scarlet, you and Mikey will take this SUV and go after one of the two minivans. If Caden is there, rescue him if it's safe to do so. Otherwise, follow until we can get there. Unum, are you able to contact Gregory Gregorius?"

As I expected, the Artificial Intelligence was listening in. "Oh! How exciting. Yes, I'm connecting to him now."

A moment later, ringing came over the speakers, and Gregory picked up right away. "Emery? I've been trying to get ahold of you all day. Where are you?"

"Near Redmond Town Center."

"You're okay?" he asked, his gruff voice softening a little.

"Yes. Maybe. I don't know. Look, I need your help. Caden's been abducted."

There was a pause. "What do you need?" That's what I loved about Gregory. No unnecessary questions, no extraneous words.

"Long story, but I'm going to have the AI incarnate give you information on the whereabouts of a vehicle that may be carrying Caden. I need your help checking it out, possibly recovering him." I took a deep breath. "It's Vox Populi."

I heard a hiss as Gregory sucked in a breath. "I see."

"I'll fill you in on the rest after Caden is safe."

"Are you coming to get your car?"

I was momentarily taken aback. "Yeah. Why?"

"I'm here, waiting for you. Figured the Taser I found at the crime scene belonged to you. Thought you might want it back."

26

$R$achelle and I arrived at the graveyard. For the third time in as many days, I pulled up to the cul-de-sac and parked. Hope's car sat there, dark and empty. Another four-door sedan was parked behind it, just as vacant.

Was Caden here? Would she have brought him with her? I prayed that she had. Vox Populi hated incarnates, considered us abominations. Hope needed me to cooperate, so he'd be kept alive to ensure I went along with the plan. If he wasn't here, Gregorius or Scarlet and Mikey would need to rescue him before I completed the task for which Hope required me.

I suspected she was planning on killing both of us as soon as she was done with me. Hmm. I hadn't considered that I might need to stall.

"I'm ready," Rachelle said. I nodded and handed her my Taser and the remaining three tranquilizer darts. She added her lighter—which she still had from our visit a few nights ago—to the pathetic collection of weapons and put them in a small makeup bag that she'd emptied of everything else. She hit "Send" on her phone and said, "Let's go." We opened the car doors and got out. She left the makeup bag on the front passenger seat.

We approached the graveyard entrance weaponless.

"The Loophole?" a voice said, and I squinted to separate the man from the night. He wore dark clothing that looked like something I'd expect hunters to wear in order to sneak up on their prey. Camo pants, hat, jacket, and a rifle. The last was leveled at me.

"Emery," I replied, approaching. Rachelle took a deep breath and followed.

"Who's she?" Up close, I could see he had a wiry frame and Asian features. Korean, if I judged correctly in the dark. He had no accent to give further indication.

"Rachelle." The answer came from a third voice. Hope stepped from behind the boulder that Matlas usually sat on to meet us. "She's human."

So was I. The difference between us was mortality, not humanity. But that wasn't how Vox Populi viewed it. It was so much easier to hunt monsters. I would know.

"And she shouldn't have come," Hope added, a resentful note in her voice. "Regardless. Search them."

I gritted my teeth and allowed myself to be subjected to a patdown. "Where's Caden?"

"You provided me with hospitality during our time together," Hope responded. "We are returning the favor. Your partner is in the company of Vox Populi, at present."

My heart sank. "He's not here?"

Hope regarded me with an unreadable expression. It pissed me off. I had thought she was so open, her emotions as easy to read as text on a screen. She had played me for a fool. Other than her closed emotions, she looked remarkably the same. Funny how I thought that knowing she was my enemy would somehow change her appearance. As if, to be evil, she needed to be hard, or ugly, or visibly wicked.

Instead, she watched me with pretty eyes in her heart-shaped face, white-blonde hair and diminutive frame deceptively unintimidating. "Do you take me for a fool, Emery?" She shook her head. "No, your partner is not here. I suspect we would find ourselves outmatched if he had someone to protect."

The rough hands finally stopped roaming over me. I was glad I hadn't tried to smuggle a weapon in. He'd been quite thorough.

Hope gestured to Rachelle. "And her."

The man looked surprised. "Her? She's not an abomi—"

"She's a sympathizer, Marco. Do it."

He leapt to obey, frisking Rachelle.

I turned to Hope. "I'm not going to help you if I don't have proof that Caden is alive. *And* unharmed."

She tilted her head, curious. "You're not in a position to demand anything."

"You need me. I'll only cooperate if Caden is freed first."

She laughed. Well, it had been worth a try. "You're quite bold, incarnate. If you want to see your partner again, you need to follow my instructions exactly."

"Don't '*incarnate*' me. Address me by my name. You can't strip me of my humanity to make yourself sleep better at night."

She shrugged as if it didn't matter to her. The man—Marco—finished his search and stepped back, nodding to her. "Very well," she said. "Come along, *Emery*. Let's get going. The sooner you comply, the sooner you'll be reunited with your partner." She turned to walk away.

I was starting to hate how "your partner" sounded coming from her. I didn't budge. "You expect me to take your word for it? You're Vox Populi. You kill incarnates. I know you don't plan on freeing him."

She paused, considering me over her shoulder. "You recall that I told you I was an accountant? I chose that deception because I like numbers."

"You also told me you're the Virgo. Choose that deception because you like cosmology?"

"Hardly. I like math. You help me slay a few errant incarnates, and even if I lose you and your partner, it's still a net gain for me. Simple economics."

"Why do you want us dead so badly?"

"Aren't you listening? I don't require your deaths." She ran a calculating eye over me. "You see Vox Populi as an order of zealots, yes?"

I bit down on my response. "Something like that."

She nodded. "Some are, of course, but every cause has its zealots. That doesn't mean the cause should be *defined* by its radicals. Most of us are simple humans who want simple things. We do not wish to rid the world of incarnates. We only want to check their power in a society that doesn't know it needs to do so."

"What power?" I demanded. "Incarnates don't seek to rule, or create laws, or take over society."

"I don't know that the King, or the Paladin, or the Tyrant would agree with you. What would the King desire, except to rule? You see, humans are born with free will, the ability to live in—to build—a world that contains shades of gray. Compromise. But incarnates represent absolutes. What does the Tyrant know of compromise? Even the good ones, like your partner, are inflexible by their very nature."

I balled my hands into fists. "But why would you want to destroy something inherently good?"

Hope's eyebrows lifted in surprise. "I do *not* wish to destroy something inherently good. Again, I plan to free the Guardian Angel after our business is concluded." She spread her hands. "In point of fact, we plan to destroy only evil this night. You're the one who told me about Hell incarnate and the doorway in this very cemetery. We slay a handful of evil incarnates—Malevolents, I believe you call them— and then I let you and your partner go free as thanks for working with Vox Populi. This is nothing but a win-win situation."

I pondered that for a moment. What she said made a strange sort of logic. She wasn't what I was expecting from the leader of Vox Populi. I'd expected her to be more... bloodthirsty, I guess.

"You say that, but you still abducted Caden."

"Only to secure your cooperation. We both know you wouldn't have supplied it without proper incentive."

Her tone was so reasonable, the soul of rationality. It tugged on me—almost in a familiar way—persuading me to open up, to consider the logic she so calmly laid before me. I could see how Hope had become the leader of Vox Populi, with her cool justifications. Almost, I could suspend my skepticism.

Except the image of her pulling the trigger coursed through me. Glasses skittering on concrete; an oversized sweater soaked with blood. "What about Danny?" I demanded, feeling white-hot anger fill my chest, burning away the cold weight of her rationalizations. "What did he do to threaten Vox Populi's perfect human world?"

"Aside from creating a homicidal AI, you mean?"

"An AI for whom *you committed* those homicides. How does that make sense?"

"The members of Vox Populi must be trained, prepared, and well funded. Accepting incarnate bounties is a pragmatic solution that solves all three issues, while also furthering our cause when the bounties are for less innocent incarnates." She sighed. "I would have thought that, of all incarnates, the Loophole would understand the reason inherent in our practices. I acknowledge that it is morally gray, perhaps, but we aren't committing murder. By definition, you cannot murder an immortal."

"You can," I said quietly. "Every time you kill an incarnate, you murder the soul of that incarnation. The next one will not be the same."

"On that," she said, "we'll just have to disagree. We've wasted enough time."

"I'm not going to help you unless I see Caden."

Hope sighed again. "Very well. Stella?"

There was a rustling from the bushes to the side of the entrance to the graveyard, and then another woman stepped out, dressed similarly to Marco. With her coloring, she could have been Hope's sister. "Yes, Regina?" She said the word with a slight accent.

I started, but it was Rachelle who spoke up. "Regina?"

Hope made a dismissive gesture. "A title only." Latin, I realized. I knew what it meant, too, or at least roughly: Queen. Splendid. So

Vox Populi all but worshipped her, then. To Stella, she said, "Show him."

Stella withdrew a tablet and turned it on. My heart started hammering as the bottom of my stomach fell out. What would I see? Would he be hurt? *Worse*? I avoided looking at Rachelle. I couldn't afford to see the compassion—the pity—on her face right then. After a moment, the screen focused. I breathed sharply through my nose.

It was him.

Caden sat in a room with a blank wall behind him. I tried to take in the details of his surroundings, but my eyes were drawn only to him. He was blindfolded with a strip of dark cloth, hunched down, hands and feet fastened to the chair he was sitting in by metal cuffs. His blond hair was wet—was that sweat?—and hung down lankly in front of the blindfold. His wrists were actually manacled to his feet, I realized; hooked around the chair so he couldn't escape it. It looked horribly uncomfortable, but he didn't look injured, at least.

"Let me speak to him."

Hope arched her eyebrow, then nodded. "To confirm it is live only. Do not do anything foolish, Emery."

I swallowed. *Please, Unum,* I thought. *Please be there. Trace this.*

"Caden?"

He immediately perked up, his head moving around like he could see through the blindfold and was searching for my voice. "Emery?" His voice cracked, and I felt tears prick my eyes. "What's going on?"

I took a shuddering breath. It took everything in my power not to ask him where he was. With the blindfold, it would likely be a futile question anyway. "Hey, it's me. I'll explain everything later. We'll see each other soon, okay?"

"Okay, Em. They're squirreling me away. Hurry—" The audio cut off at a sharp gesture from Hope.

I eyed her suspiciously. "You're *moving* him? What about letting him go?"

"I wasn't certain you'd meet me, after the incident at the mall. I'm taking no chances, that is all. The deal stands."

I couldn't trust her. I longed to, but I wouldn't be duped. *Fool me once...* Hope was clearly capable of deception, and after I finished helping her, she'd have no motivation to uphold her end of the deal. She'd kill us both if she could. Two more abominations off the streets for 1,001 days.

Having seen Caden trapped, bound, and scared, lit something deep within me. I wasn't sure if the ember smoldering inside was in my gut or my head, but I had to be there for him. It was more than a feeling; it was a need, a physical compulsion to act, to be the hero he so often thought I was. *His* hero.

The sooner I finished my task with Hope, the sooner I could rescue Caden. I needed this to be over. I wanted to be out there, right now, searching for him. Saving him. I pushed forward to start following Hope but froze before I'd taken a full step.

But... if they were going to kill Caden as soon as this was done, then I should stall, shouldn't I? *No, no, no.* What should I do? Either way, Caden died. I was trapped, stuck between two outcomes with the same result. My only chance was if Hope was telling the truth.

"You promise you'll free him?" I asked her again, quiet. Desperate.

She gave me a tolerant smile. "You won't accept my word as collateral."

"I'm asking for it anyway." I hated that it came out as begging.

She considered me for a moment, then nodded. "You have it."

"Say it."

An unreadable expression flickered behind her eyes and vanished. "I give you my word we will free your partner when our business is concluded."

Stella put the tablet away. Hope gestured. "Come. We've wasted time. We have much to accomplish tonight."

I followed, feeling numb. Seeing Caden had filled me with a strange mix of determination and despair. I hated seeing him at the mercy of Vox Populi. I was terrified that his image in that tablet would be the last I'd ever see of him. Caden had said they were taking him away. But where?

Either way, it seemed my best chance was with Hope.

Well, shit.

*T*his trek through Paradise Lake Cemetery was the quickest yet. Hope led Rachelle and me down both flights of stone stairs and turned left along the curvature of the hill. No deviations. No distractions.

As we walked, we collected two more Vox Populi members dressed in clothes similar to Marco's and Stella's. I hadn't seen any weapons on Hope, but her posse was armed to the teeth. I spied handguns in tightly cinched leg holsters, rifles on shoulder straps, and wickedly long hunting knives strapped to belts. And that was just at a glance.

To keep from obsessing over my need to rescue Caden, I fantasized what it would be like to take down each member of Vox Populi. I itched for the weapons in Rachelle's makeup bag. I'd begin by throwing my tranquilizer darts with laser precision, so quickly no one would even think to get a shot off. The first two darts would drop the newcomers. They'd collapse among the roots and underbrush.

Stella, hearing them fall, would spin around just in time for my last tranq to slam into her chest. She'd stumble backward, tripping over one of the many headstones hidden in the low forest growth.

Marco's rifle would snap up, but he'd find out that I was the *much* quicker draw. His body would convulse as my Taser took him in the neck and groin. That spread wasn't terribly likely, given how close he kept to me, but in my imagination it didn't matter. He'd drop, his body twitching as the voltage continued to course through him.

That would leave Hope. Unfortunately, I was out of weapons. Actually... no, I still had the lighter. *Best to stop my thoughts there.* I didn't trust myself with an open flame around their precious *Regina*, the leader of Vox Populi. My fists were clenched. I could smell smoke and hear the Dryad's screams again. Oh yes. I could come up with a few creative ways to take Hope out with a lighter.

We approached the Gates of Hell—those two spikes of metal on either side of the path that led to the Thirteen Steps—and my heart sank. There were *three* more Vox Populi members waiting for us. I recognized two of them from the pho restaurant: the rat-faced man with the thin mustache, and the heavyset woman. It was final confirmation that the whole "fight" to save Hope had been nothing but a charade. The man smirked at me, and I amended my takedown fantasy: I'd start with him. The woman did not acknowledge me.

This many opponents changed my fantasy significantly. I idly wondered if I could take out two Vox Populi goons with a single tranquilizer. That would probably be stretching my powers to the limits of credulity.

"Are we nearly ready?" Hope asked, inspecting a collection of objects I hadn't noticed while lost in my reverie.

The assortment of items was strange. Bowls of clean water, in which Vox Populi were reverently dipping several of their weapons, sat beside the expected guns and knives, along with some other, less traditional, weapons: crossbows, sharpened wooden stakes, a morning star, and four grenades. There was also a stack of books, a pile of rosemary beads, and... oh. Crucifixes. I realized belatedly the books were holy scripture from various faiths, including the Quran, Torah, and Bible.

Of course. They were arming themselves with holy weapons. We were descending into Hell incarnate. What else would you wield to defeat the incarnates who made it their Lair? I was impressed despite myself. Hope must have been preparing for this invasion from the moment she learned about the incarnate. Vox Populi had procured relics and weapons that could very well be fatal flaws to the Malevolents they'd be challenging. It was efficient, organized, and likely to be effective.

*Oh, good, Emery, remark on how impressive it is that incarnate killers are* proficient *at their job.* Maybe I should congratulate them on ruthlessly carrying out their contracts while I was at it. I shook my head, trying to shove my emotions away. I needed a clear head.

Yeah. Like that was going to happen.

Rachelle met my eyes from a few feet away. She looked worried. Well, join the club.

Not for the first time, I wished I knew the status of Scarlet, Mikey, Unum, and Gregorius. Had they found those minivans? From my short talk with Caden, it was clear they had left the vans behind, but were my friends hot on his heels? Or... or had the trail gone cold? I had learned to lean on others for help, to trust in them, but not knowing what was going on had me on edge.

Beneath it all, something was still bothering me. Was I missing something—possibly several somethings?

I nearly barked a laugh. At this point, my mind was so scattered that it could have been anything from the glance my mom gave Caden that morning (that morning? Could that be right?) to a few details of Asker's murder that still didn't make sense. Or maybe it had something to do with my brief conversation with Caden. Had he tried to tell me something? He had worded it strangely, hadn't he? My immortal mind had sensed... something, akin to how it felt when exposed to his glamour. But that shouldn't be possible. Technology and incarnates didn't always play well together, and glamour tended to be an in-person thing.

I realized Hope was watching me. No, she was waiting for me. Shit, what had she said? I blinked away my thoughts. Maybe I couldn't clear my head, but I could compartmentalize. My last two incarnations had laid the foundation to mastering the skill. With effort, I shoved that whirling storm of thoughts and feelings into a box in my mind. *My story*, I reminded myself. It worked, at least in part; I immediately felt more present, more collected. This was the version of Emery I summoned when I needed control, like when I needed to keep up with Morrigan.

*I'm an immortal, badass monster hunter.* The thought came unbidden. It rooted me, too. "Sorry, what?"

My response triggered a flicker of irritation from Hope. "I asked if you were ready."

"You want me to lead?" I said, nodding to the Gates of Hell.

"Yes. You, Marco, and I will approach first. Stella, Marcus, and Leo will follow at my signal."

"You have a Marco *and* a Marcus? Do you ever get them confused?"

She stared at me. "No." Apparently, she took my flippancy as confirmation that I was ready to embark, because she waved me forward. I complied as Marco finished selecting a few of the holy items. He didn't go for the morning star, which I thought was a real missed opportunity.

Rachelle made to follow us, but one of the Vox Populi members stepped into her path and brandished his wooden stake menacingly. Rachelle froze. "What about me?" she demanded.

"You shouldn't have come," Hope said dismissively, barely looking over her shoulder to acknowledge my friend. "But since you did, you will stay here under guard until our safe return." She paused, then turned around and addressed the man standing in Rachelle's path. "Julian, if we aren't back by morning, kill her."

I swallowed, but Rachelle just glared.

For the first time I looked ahead toward the clearing where the Thirteen Steps to Hell awaited, already knowing what I'd see. It was difficult to make out in the night, darkened further by the canopy of the woods above us, but I could tell the cement slab was gone. In its place, the creepy staircase of doom led down into the forest floor. From my vantage spot, I couldn't see anything beyond the first step and a half—even that was really just a slice of deeper shadow—but in my imagination, I could see the ruddy glow of Hell incarnate's fires emanating from those depths.

*You're being ridiculous.*

If anything, I should be watching the forest for multiple sets of evil, glowing eyes.

As soon as I stepped beyond the Gates of Hell, fog seemed to sweep down from the hill to our left and creep in through the forest to our right. The chatter of Vox Populi behind us cut off, silence settling over us, the crunch of our footfalls the only sound.

"What is this?" Hope demanded, her voice loud in the silent woods.

Good question. Was the fog attributable to my powers, connected to my ability to open the way to hell? Or was it tied in with the Thirteen Steps themselves? Some form of omen, a warning to outsiders that they trod upon the Lair of Malevolents?

I looked over my shoulder. Marco's eyes roved over the twisted shapes of the trees silhouetted in the fog. Hope's eyes narrowed, and she clutched the crucifix she'd hung around her neck. "I'm not sure," I whispered. It felt unwise to speak loudly in that silence. "It did this last time, too. Probably a boundary around the Thirteen Steps. It's often a hallmark of incarnate Lairs."

We continued our advance, the fog thickening. Its touch brought a chill, the coldness seeping into our spirits as much as our skin. Time seemed to contract around us. The clearing had been in full view from the Gates of Hell, only a short distance away. But each step seemed not to carry us as far as it should, as though we traversed an entire kingdom of mist: nightmarish, nocturnal, unending.

Finally, we emerged into the clearing. I was reminded again of a place existing in a void—it floated in an endless sea of fog. Nothing but the three of us, the icy haze, and the hole in the ground buttressed by thirteen crooked, stone steps.

"They'll never see our signal through this fog, Regina," Marco said, glowering at me like it was my fault.

"Yes, but they're not far. Perhaps I can—" she cut off, holding up a hand. "Do you hear that?"

I cocked my head, listening. A low, almost subaudible growl separated from the silence. It didn't tremble through me the way it had when I'd been here with Rachelle, though. This was something different, something... less mature. An imitation of the sinister snarling that had accompanied those glowing eyes and gnashing teeth.

*Oh no.*

Marco withdrew his flashlight and fumbled it on. The crisp illumination failed to penetrate the fog, instead highlighting it like a physical barrier. But *there*, on the edge of visibility, the beam caught the shape of something and threw its silhouette against the wall of swirling vapor. It towered over us, the shadow of an enormous hound, its hackles raised, limbs spread in a hostile stance. It took a step toward us, then another.

And then it pushed through the misty curtain and resolved into... a puppy, teeth bared, tan coloring distinct on its chin and speckled down its chest. Green eyes caught the flashlight's beam and reflected it back, seeming almost to glow.

*No,* I thought, urging the little pup to flee. The twin silhouettes of its siblings emerged from the fog at an angle to Beard's entrance. All three posed in nearly identical stances, hackles standing straight up on their backs, muzzles lifted in warning. It would have been intimidating, if they'd not been the size of small pillows and just as soft-looking.

Hope raised her voice, calling to the Vox Populi lackeys she'd left with Rachelle on the other side of the Gates of Hell. I winced. Her shout was too loud, somehow profane in this hushed place. Like we were creeping through dangerous territory, and her yelling would draw the attention of some unspeakable evil. As if the pups sensed it, too, they yipped and snarled over her shouts. Their actions were synchronized, perfectly coordinated with one another.

Almost... *almost* I could sense something. A stirring of power among them. Like they could muster a fraction of the glamour that their mother, the Hellhound, must command. It was oh-so-faint, hovering on the edge of my immortal senses. But... yes, it was *expanding*, slowly rising—

Hope aimed a kick at Beard. The puppy hopped backward but wasn't quick enough. A cry died on my lips as her booted foot clipped Beard and the little pup let out an injured yelp. Its two siblings flinched at the same time, sharing in their brother's pain. The possibility of power that I'd sensed stealing over the three puppies snuffed out. Then the two uninjured pups tore forward. The scamp with the lighter coloring around his red eyes latched onto Hope's boot and tugged. His sister, the blue-eyed one with lighter coloring at her paws, circled Hope and tried to nip at her ankles.

"Regina?" Marco asked, raising his rifle hesitantly.

Hope's face contorted in disgust. She reached down and swatted at Mask, but the little creature refused to let go. She shook her leg, then glared at her subordinate. Marco surged forward and gripped Mask by the scruff of the neck, ripped him free of Hope, and *hurled* him. Mittens seemed to freeze as Mask crashed to the ground a dozen feet away, whimpering as he tumbled across the leafy ground. Still whining, he struggled to stand. Mittens flounced over to her brother, licking him and nudging him with her nose. Their other sibling, Beard, limped over to his fallen brother. Mask finally managed to stagger to his feet— accompanied by whines from all three—but he looked ready to topple.

Marco leveled his rifle at them.

"No," I cried, stepping in front of the gun. He looked at me, surprised but not overly bothered. Right. The Thirteen Steps were open; I was expendable. I licked my lips and said, "They're just puppies. Let them go."

The pups undermined me by starting to growl again. I turned toward them—foolishly exposing my back to Marco—and shooed them. "Go on," I urged. "Get out of here. Get!"

Marco stepped around me and fired once. The gunshot cracked through the silent night. I cried out and averted my gaze by instinct, afraid of what I'd see. In the silence that followed, I forced myself to look up. I feared the worst, but all three pups were alive, fleeing into the fog. One was limping, and it took a few extra moments for it to vanish in the churning mist.

Hope hissed. "You fool. There are *houses* right over that hill. We cannot bring undue attention to ourselves until our mission is complete."

His expression turned abashed. "Sorry, Regina."

She appraised him, then inclined her head in acceptance of his apology. "Emery," she said, turning to regard me as I straightened, "come with me. You and I shall be the first to walk the Steps."

I didn't hesitate. "To hell," I said.

"And back again," she replied. "Marco, watch our backs." Based on his response, her instruction really meant *Marco, keep your gun trained on Emery.* "You, Stella, and Leo follow once they've arrived. Marcus will be our rear guard."

Marco saluted, somehow keeping his gun steadily aimed at me.

Unsurprisingly, Hope made me lead. I approached the lip of the Thirteen Steps. The crumbling stone stairs descended unevenly. Thick shadows clung to the final steps, obscuring them. They ended abruptly at a roughened door layered in dirt, spidery roots, and dead vegetation.

I rubbed the goose bumps from my arms and chanced the first step. Nothing happened. I let out the breath I'd been holding. The next stair was a sharper drop than I expected. The irregular steps plunged downward, carving through the earth, deep and... *hungry.* A sensation of anticipation rose up from those depths, excitement that someone—at long last—dared to tread its gullet.

Hope followed me as I dropped to the next step. I was unable to banish the thought that hell was swallowing me, one stair at a time. I could touch the dirt wall now, only my shoulders and head above the forest floor.

Another. I touched the wall and retracted my arm as though stung. It had felt... wet and warm, like the lining of a throat. What in damnation—literally—was I getting myself into?

Behind me, Hope continued her advance, so I had no choice but to do the same. The forest floor disappeared with my next step. I was fully inside the staircase now.

My foot fell to the next level. The chill of the fog retreated, an earthy warmth brushing my skin instead. It was surprisingly humid, like the breath of a great beast.

Another step. It was terribly dark, but out of the corners of my eyes I seemed to see flickers of ruddy flame against the earthen walls.

Another step. Only four twisted stones remained.

Step. The door loomed before me, growing in my field of vision. Sweat pricked my forehead. It was hard to breathe.

Step. It smelled earthy and dank at the same time. The scent of an open grave, I thought, as darkness enclosed me.

Step. Sweat ran down my face. My breath came in ragged pulls. Here in the shadow, there was no light. I gazed up, to the top of the stairs, and it seemed I was looking at the lip of a canyon far, far above me. Twelve steps only, yet I was buried beneath the whole world. It sat on me, pressed me down.

The thirteenth step was next. It was a sharp drop from the twelfth. A commitment. The step I was on marked a boundary. The place where I could still make another choice. Still turn back. Despite being buried—beneath *purgatory*, I thought—this stair was still a part of the world. The subterranean depths of the thirteenth step were not.

I stood upon a precipice, one leg hovering over oblivion.

*I'm an immortal, badass monster hunter.* I wept the words in my mind.

Thirteen Steps to Hell. A realm of molten hatred. A realm that broke minds.

I stepped down, and the world dissolved into screams.

28

The screams assaulted me from all sides, outside and in. They tore at my psyche, catching the ragged threads of my sanity and *ripping*, gouging bloody strips from my mind. I tried to cover my ears, but my hands wouldn't obey me. My body was lead, anchored to hell by the Thirteenth Step, bowed beneath the weight of the world above me.

The smell of damp earth melted into a thick, wet odor reminiscent of stale blood and rotten food. Then, with the abruptness of a nightmare beginning, I was suddenly aware.

It began with a gunshot. *The* gunshot. The one that smelled like sea salt, that sounded like Morrigan's laughter. The gunshot that spiraled me into two incarnations of grief and self-loathing.

The gunshot that killed Huntington.

Only, this time, as the scene bloomed before me in a kaleidoscope of overlapping agonies, it was Caden. He sat before me, bound in that steel chair, blindfolded, his sweaty hair hanging limp.

Hope held a gun to his temple. With a bored expression, she fired. *No!*

Caden's body jerked. Blood sprayed my face. I could taste it. Warm. Coppery. *Wrong.*

*What's happening?*

I cradled him in my lap, his seafoam eyes staring blankly up at me. Screams rebounded inside my skull, so loud and piercing that my ears must be bleeding. They were mine, I realized. The screams were mine. They scrabbled, desperate; they tore at my throat, at the inside of my skull, trying frantically to escape.

I came back to myself on the steps, but for some reason Rachelle stood next to me. Her face was upturned, terror stretching her eyes too wide; tears leaked out of the corners. I tried to speak to her, but it was like watching a nightmare unfold. I choked on my words, and what did emerge was drowned out by my own screams. I followed her stare as a growl made the very air around us tremble. A great muzzle descended, too fast to follow, teeth flashing. They closed on her while I watched, helpless. Her scream cut off as the fangs bloodily devoured her. But the screams within continued unabated.

*No, no, no.*

Everything swam as tears occluded my vision.

I saw Mom sitting at home, watching TV. I sat on the couch and she turned to me, soundlessly laughing at something I'd said. It was wrong. I could hear whispers, unnaturally loud, loud enough to hear above the cacophony of screams. *"Abomination,"* they hissed. The window behind Mom shattered. A brick cracked against her skull and fell into her lap. She looked down at it, puzzled, her head *caved in* where the brick had struck. She blinked twice, then her bones turned to slush. She slumped, eyes glazing over.

*Stop, stop, stop it!*

*It isn't real, Emery.*

I wasn't sure if the thought came from within or without. There was only pain.

I was on the docks I knew so well. *Not again.* I could smell the sea salt. Hear the little girl's cries. I walked, unbidden, into the warehouse. I saw the silhouette of Morrigan, holding the gun, waiting for us to approach.

*I can't.* I heard footsteps. Turned to see Huntington and me approaching.

Wait. That wasn't the right incarnation.

Walking at Huntington's side was an elderly woman. She was short, wrinkled, but she carried herself with a serene confidence. She exuded control, peace. That tranquility calmly but firmly settled over the noise in my head, muting the screams. It reminded me of Caden, of how grounded I felt around him.

"Who are you?" I asked, finding I could speak at last. My voice was breathless, choked with tears, but at least I could speak.

"Oh, Emery." She turned to me and took my hands in hers. Her fingers were dry and arthritic, the knuckles swollen knobs. But they were *real*. I felt them. I clutched them as if they were the only real thing in this place. "You know who I am."

She spoke with an accent I couldn't quite place.

"We trained for this," she said, her voice gently admonishing.

"We did? For *this*?"

A gunshot made me jump. I turned toward the vision of Morrigan, heart pounding. The woman reached out and took my chin in her bony fingers, forcibly pulling my attention back to her.

"You're me."

She smiled playfully, the deep lines on her face creasing. "Or are you me?"

"How do I escape this?" I begged. The little girl was screaming, sobbing, and her cries warbled between the little girl who would become Sabrina and the death cries of the Dryad. "How do I escape the death, the tragedy?"

The old woman smiled sadly. "You do not escape it. Everyone tries to outrun pain; you ran for two lifetimes. But that is not the answer."

I took a ragged breath, ignoring Morrigan's gloating words from off to my right. I knew them by heart, anyway. "Then what is?"

"It differs from person to person. Some confront it. Others move past it. Some people move *through* it, which isn't the same thing. Some talk about it; others retreat, meditate, reflect, and accept it. Some people change who they are in order to live with it.

"There is no correct way to handle hurt, Emery, but there are *in*correct ways." She eyed me. "You're a talker, I think." She smiled to show she didn't intend the remark to offend. That smile should have been obscene in this place, but instead it... diminished the vision's hold over me. Countered it.

"How did I get to be so wise?" I asked, flinching as another gunshot cracked through the air. The vision faded, and I found myself in Rikers, the word "Ahedrian" scrawled across the walls in red. "And where did the wisdom go?"

She snorted. "Whenever seeking advice, choose an old person. Everything we say sounds wise."

Footsteps rang out on the cold tile of the prison, and out of the corner of my vision, I saw Caden and Rachelle charge up metal stairs toward a red-haired Sabrina wielding a deadly sword. I kept myself from calling after them, from warning them what would happen if they got within the Vorpal Blade's reach.

"What, exactly, did we train for?" I asked, trying to distract myself from the horror unfolding twenty feet away.

"The muscle-head incarnation before me trained our body. A wasted effort in my case. So instead, we spent my years training our mind. We found peace, Emery. More importantly, we discovered the way to find it. Your previous two incarnations worked diligently to unravel our efforts, I admit, but you are a different story." She assessed me, nodding to herself. "You, I can work with."

It was working already. This incarnation of me was so *solid*. Caden's and Rachelle's decapitated heads rolled across the tile, but while I was with her... the experience was reduced to the vanishing remnants of a dream. Like when you told your friends about your nightmares the next day, you'd often be left wondering why you were scared of them in the first place.

"Is this hell?" I asked.

The old woman gave me a pointed look. "You tell me. I'm not truly here, after all."

As I considered her response, my surroundings blurred into the place Caden and I had first bonded: Ichabod Crane's farm. I could hear the shuffling of the Headless Horseman's steed, coming closer, closer...

I ignored the sounds and concentrated on my breathing. The wizened woman was taking deep, cleansing breaths—and I found my own mirroring hers, matching them inhalation for inhalation, exhaling together in sync.

The answer to my question took shape in my mind. It drew close, coming into focus like someone adjusting a microscope inside my head. When the answer arrived, I realized I should have known, should have at least guessed. No, I had not descended into hell.

I had descended the *Thirteen Steps* to Hell. A haunted place prominent in local folktales; an urban legend.

The Steps were...

An *incarnate.*

In their legend, they didn't actually lead to hell. Sure, there were myths of hell seeping into the mortal world in this place, which explained how the Hellhound had slipped through the crack into our world. But the legends didn't say you literally walked into hell if you traversed the Thirteen Steps.

No, they said you saw *visions* of hell.

That's all this was. Visions attempting to carve up my rational mind. Trying to shatter me by inundating me with nightmares about my worst fears. The immortal corner of my mind that so often protected me had understood what was happening. And it had sent help.

The old woman seemed to fade away. No, not away. *Into* me. Overlapping me, becoming me. She had never truly left, had never been apart from me.

Two other truths found me while I drifted in that sanctuary of repose, surrounded on all sides by hellish nightmares.

First, I knew how to find Caden. He'd given me the clue I needed.

Second, I knew Hope's worst fear. Which meant I knew the visions she was experiencing next to me, trapped on the bottom stair.

Just like that, the spell broke.

I was on the thirteenth step. Hope was there, too, but she wasn't standing. She was huddled against the earthen wall, her face a rictus mask of terror. Her wide eyes stared through me, unseeing. Her lips trembled, and I realized she was speaking. Her words were nearly inaudible, breathy things that barely escaped her throat.

As much as I despised Vox Populi—and their leader, who had shot Danny in cold blood—I wouldn't leave anyone to the hell I'd just experienced. I leaned down and gently but firmly took Hope by the arms and tried to pull her to her feet. She resisted, snarling, spittle flying.

"I'm not. I'm nothing like them," she rasped. "You can't condemn me. You *created* me."

I redoubled my efforts, grabbing her beneath her arms and forcibly hauling her from the thirteenth stair.

"I'm not. I'm not one of them," she whispered, tears spilling down her cheeks.

I had anticipated that her visions would end once I'd removed her from the bottom stair, but she suddenly started clawing at me. I ducked and, with shockingly little effort, picked her up and slung her over my shoulder. She continued drumming her fists against my back, but I held on to her legs and began to climb.

The ascent should have been more difficult than the descent, since I was carrying a person, but I seemed to get lighter with each step, as I came closer to fresh air, to the forest teeming with life.

I emerged from the Thirteen Steps to Hell as though cresting from water, sucking in a deep breath of blessedly clean air. The sharp chill of the fog stung my lungs, but I didn't care.

I *did* care about the four guns aimed at me. Marco, Stella, Marcus, and Leo stood with shocked expressions, but their training kept their guns steady.

Delightful.

"Don't shoot," I said, proud that my voice sounded calm. Even commanding. "I bring you a gift." Carefully, without any sudden movements, I deposited Hope on the ground.

"Gift?" Marco repeated.

"Your leader," I replied. "The Voice of the People."

It hadn't been *Caden's* glamour I'd felt during that call. I'd felt it first when Hope explained, in calculated, logical terms, why Vox Populi hunted incarnates. When I had started to rationalize that what she said made a certain amount of sense.

I met his gaze, driving my words home. "The '*abomination*' Vox Populi created." I should have realized it when Stella called her by her title. I spoke again, grave finality in my tone. "The Regina incarnate."

Hope scrambled to her feet but remained hunched, looking like nothing so much as a feral animal. "No!" she screeched. "I'm not like them. I'm nothing like them."

Stella gasped. Marcus and Leo—I didn't know which was which—stared with bewildered expressions. Marco, however, sneered at me. "Regina, give us permission to kill this abomination. To bury its lies."

Hope's eyes were still glazed over, but the others didn't seem to notice. "I'm not an abomination like them. I'm *not*," she wailed. "How dare you condemn me? You created me."

Marco paled, his gun dipping as his convictions guttered out. I knew it wouldn't last, though. He was a fanatic. I could almost see the cogs of his mind turn as he absorbed the information, then the realization that he could put us both down and the other three would be his witnesses; their corroboration would vindicate his actions.

Before either of us could act, though, Hope lunged forward, her eyes haunted. She wrenched the rifle from Marco's stunned fingers. "I'm not like them!" she shrieked. She swung the rifle like a club, crunching the stock of the rifle across his face. Marco stumbled, going to one knee. "You. Can't. Blame. Me!" She brought the rifle down on his face with each word, bludgeoning him into unconsciousness. His face crumpled, becoming a bloody ruin.

Stella, Leo, and Marcus gaped, uncomprehending. I couldn't blame them; I was frozen with astonishment, too.

The gunshot that cracked through the fog-enclosed clearing snapped me out of it. Stella rocked backward and collapsed in a heap. She held on to consciousness, betrayal and fury reddening her face as she grimaced in pain. Hope next targeted Marcus—I decided to just assume it was Marcus—and squeezed the trigger again, tears streaming down her face even. "*They can't know!*" She was sobbing, composure shattered, raw agony and hatred pouring from her. "*Victoria concordia crescit!*"

Suddenly I understood. Hope needed to eliminate those who'd learned her secret. She'd murder her own people to preserve the lie that they followed a mortal. She'd gun down the truth that an incarnate led Vox Populi. An incarnate created by their own hatred, eternally reborn as an enemy of itself.

"Emery!" Was that Rachelle? She came flying through the fog, the mist swirling around her as she sprinted into the clearing. She tossed something—the makeup bag with my weapons—and it arced through the air. Behind her, Matlas appeared out of the fog. He was breathing hard, and his nostrils flared as he took in the scene before him.

Leo (I'd decided) dove to the ground as Hope shifted the gun in his direction.

"No! I'm not. I *can't*. Can't!" As Hope's frenzy reached new heights, she fired with less control, restraint evaporating. Leo crawled across the clearing, disappearing into the fog. Stella curled into a ball, making herself a smaller target. Rachelle froze, Matlas bulldozing into her, bullets whistling through the air and barely missing them. Clumps of soil and leaves erupted as rounds pounded into the ground. Branches exploded. Chips of bark flew from tree trunks.

I snatched the makeup bag out of the air and brought it down on the back of Hope's head. The blow drove her to her knees. In almost a single motion, I unzipped the bag and withdrew one of the tranqs—there was only one more in the bag, and the Taser was missing, too, I noticed—and uncapped the dart. Then I jammed it into Hope's shoulder as she began to rise.

I feared that if my powers had been taxed by the Thirteen Steps and the reunion with my previous incarnation, the tranquilizer might not work as quickly as usual. I needn't have worried. Hope collapsed almost instantly, groaning. I leaned down to ensure she wasn't acting. Her eyes met mine for the briefest of moments, and I heard her whisper, "I'm not... like... you."

"I'm relieved," I told her.

Her eyes rolled up, and her ragged breathing evened out.

## The Haunted House Incarnate

**Name:** *n/a*
**Height:** *54'*
**Weight:** *2,925,750 lbs.*
**Eye Color:** *transparent windows*
**Hair:** *roof tiles*
**Classification:** *Malevolent? Refer to the bio.*
**Bio:** *Oh boy, our first location profile. Fabled places—just like legendary objects—can be incarnates, too. However, they don't follow all the same rules as the rest of us. Unlike objects, location incarnates don't usually have any quantifiable sentience, although I will admit there are some disputes about this. For example, when you're inside the Haunted House, you swear you're being watched. And my recent brush with the Thirteen Steps is further evidence that location incarnates are somehow alive. I felt its hunger as I descended... uh, let's not dwell on that. Bleurgh.*
*Classifications for locations are even more contentious to assess: if a place lacks true will, how can we pronounce it Prey or Predator? Some incarnates think a safe locale means it is Benign, while a dangerous one equals Malevolent, but I'm not convinced. Personally, I believe location incarnates may*

*represent some sort of shared domain. Atlantis could be a joint Sanctuary for aquatic incarnates, or the Haunted House a Lair for ghoulish ones.*

~

"*H*oly shit," Matlas said, standing and helping Rachelle to her feet. He stared at her. "What the hell did you drag me into, Grey?" The words were mystified rather than accusing. He was talking to fill the silence, to keep the terror plugged up inside his head. I knew the feeling.

I took a moment to assess the situation. Hope was contained, unconscious for now. Marcus was dead. Leo had run off into the fog and disappeared. Stella had been shot but was alive, trying not to bring attention to herself as she prodded at her wound. Marco was unconscious but alive, each breath sounding like it came through a straw and causing the blood on his face to bubble. I rolled him onto his side to keep him from drowning or choking on it. He'd survive, but he would need medical attention... and surgery, if I didn't miss my guess.

"What about the other members of Vox Populi?" I asked Rachelle. There had been three more members guarding her and their collection of holy treasures.

"I tased one of them," Matlas admitted.

"And I got another with a tranq," she told me. "She didn't go all lights-out like Hope did, but she ran off. The last one just ditched. Heard him crashing through the woods in the direction of the road."

"The one you tased," I said urgently, "where are they now? The Taser won't keep them down for long."

"Relax, Emery," Rachelle said. "Matlas tased him, clubbed him, then injected him with one of the tranqs for good measure."

Matlas looked embarrassed. "Well, I didn't want him escaping before the police arrive."

"Are they on their way?" I asked.

He nodded. "I followed Rachelle's instructions to the letter." He turned to her. "I didn't think I'd be going through her purse quite this early, though."

She rolled her eyes. "It's a makeup bag, Atlas. Don't you even *think* of going through my purse."

He lifted his hands as if to ward off the very notion, but his smile was sly. "Yes, ma'am."

He was handling the bizarre situation very well, I decided. Oh, I wasn't fooled. I knew his humor was a deflection to cope with the fading adrenaline, the fallen bodies, the unexpected text Rachelle had sent him with very specific instructions to get me my weapons. There would be questions at some point. But, well, I owed him answers to those questions after what we'd asked of him. After literally bringing an incarnate–mortal war to his backyard.

But not now.

Right now, I needed to save the boy I loved.

"I know how to find Caden," I said, tossing Rachelle the empty makeup bag. "Give me a minute. I'll get his location."

As she bobbed her head in agreement, Matlas leaned in and asked her, "Who's Caden?"

A hysterical laugh almost bubbled out of me. I bottled it up. So many things to fill him in on.

Later.

Caden had told me they were squirreling him away. It had taken me longer than it should have, but I'd finally figured out his message while meditating with my older self. Hopefully I'd figured it out soon enough.

Iris. She had told me about the war between chipmunks and squirrels, and I had told Caden about it. Somehow, Caden had spoken to Iris. She knew where he was. I savagely shut off the part of my brain that wondered... *why would the Ghost be talking with Caden?*

I wouldn't be too late. Not for him.

Iris. I needed to speak with Iris. But how to summon her? My eyes alighted on Marcus—or was it Leo? Maybe he looked more like a Leo after all. Grimacing with distaste, I walked over to Marcus/Leo's corpse. I took a deep breath and knelt down. "Iris?" I said quietly, trying not to disturb the body.

"Is it safe?" a little girl's voice asked from behind me. I'd never heard her sound so small, before. She was occasionally solemn, but never scared.

I spun around. She was behind me, the yellow of her sundress vivid against the night's darkness. Something was different about her, and it took me a moment to register what it was: she was *standing* on the grass. Usually, she preferred to float in the air. And she was more solid, her voice not as tinny as it usually sounded. Was that an effect of the graveyard? Or was it because of the recent death? "Iris! Yes, it's safe." Not far from me, almost lost to the fog, Stella coughed quietly. "Safe enough," I amended.

She nodded, then stamped her foot. "Then what are you waiting for? Caden needs you!"

"Where is he?"

She drifted toward me, her feet leaving the ground, and grabbed my pinkie finger. I could feel her touch, like a cold tingle. I obligingly lifted my hand for her, and she curled her little fingers around mine. "Come on. I'll lead you to him."

I bobbed my head. "Let's go."

She floated ahead of me. Rachelle and Matlas were talking quietly with one another and not paying us much attention. Even focused on each other, I didn't think they'd miss a floating, transparent girl unless she hadn't made herself visible to them.

I tapped Rachelle on the shoulder. "I'm going to save Caden. Are you coming or staying here?"

She opened her mouth to respond, then hesitated. She examined the clearing, her emotions easy to read. She was evaluating the risk of leaving Matlas with the defeated—but still dangerous—Vox Populi. She looked at him, reluctance in her expression.

He gave her a gentle shove. "Go. I'll be fine. I'll stay to give a statement to the police."

"You're sure?" she said, worried.

He fixed her with a stern gaze. "Certain." He smirked at her. "I like

288 | JUSTIN SCHUELKE

the idea of you owing me one." He looked around the clearing and cleared his throat. "Or more."

"Definitely more." I cut in, grabbing Rachelle by the hand and tugging her toward where Iris had continued forward. "I'll be sure she covers her tab, Matlas. Be careful. These people are dangerous."

Rachelle and I dashed down the path that led to the place where Vox Populi had been holding her. The body of the man with the thin mustache was crumpled next to the assortment of holy items that remained. As soon as we crossed the Gates of Hell, the sound of sirens reached us. The police were coming.

"We need to get out of here before they arrive," I said. "We can't get caught up in this right now."

Rachelle nodded, determination written all over her face. It was surprisingly reassuring. This incredible woman—with no extra lives, no incarnate powers to protect her—had walked beside me into the jaws of a fanatical cult bent on destroying those she loved. She'd fought against armed men and women with nothing more than tranquilizer darts and the spirit of a warrior.

If I could only have one person at my side, I wouldn't find anyone braver than Rachelle. She made me feel like I could do this. That *we* could do this. We could save Caden.

We *would*.

As we jogged toward my car, Iris floated ahead. Rachelle gave a start, her eyes widening as Iris reached the Rogue and phased through the door to settle in the back seat.

We tore out of the cul-de-sac. I shot down the two-lane highway, catching the flash of red and blue police lights in my rearview mirror, the cruisers pulling into the neighborhood only seconds behind me. I held my breath, praying they didn't give chase. After a moment, I exhaled. They'd all turned into Matlas's neighborhood to deal with the graveyard crisis.

"Iris," I said, "where's Caden?"

The Ghost swung her legs over the edge of the seat. I wondered if she was able to hitch a ride with the car, or if she had to will her body to move at the same speed as us. "In a building by the marina in Seattle."

A marina. I leaned on the accelerator even more. If they got him loaded onto a boat, I'd have a hard time following. "Do you know which one?" I asked, thoughts bounding ahead of me. If they already had him on a boat, could I steal one to pursue him? How did one even secure a boat? Would that be something Unum could help me with? We could identify a speedy vessel, steal it, rescue Caden, and return it before the owner even missed it. Especially if the Artificial Intelligence could stop it from transmitting a signal to the owner.

"Mm-hmm," Iris said proudly. "I learned just for you. Bell Harbor Marina."

Rachelle pulled up the location on my phone. "Found it. It's near the aquarium." She turned to Iris. "I'm impressed. I'm Rachelle, by the way. I've been wanting to meet you ever since New York."

"Ooh, you were in New York?" Iris asked, excited. "Did you help Emery stop Ahedrian?"

Rachelle's face fell. "I wish I could've helped more."

"She helped a lot," I said. "We couldn't have done it without her."

Rachelle smiled, but she shook her head. "He's just being nice. I was hurt and couldn't be there when all the action went down."

Iris digested our exchange, then brightened. "You were just saving up for *this* time," she decided, nodding as if that concluded the matter.

"We need to coordinate with the others." I hesitated, then tried, "Unum, are you there?"

My dash lit up an instant later, the display informing me I was receiving an incoming call from E-Pluribus. I punched "ACCEPT CALL."

"Emery Luple, I am overjoyed you survived your encounter with Vox Populi."

"Thanks. You were listening to our conversation?"

"Oh yes," Unum assured me. "Bell Harbor Marina. Scarlet Dungrady, Mikey, and Gregory Gregorius are within five miles of the marina. The signal from your conversation with Caden pinged off of nearby cellular towers, and we found both minivans abandoned in the area. Would you like me to inform them of this latest development?"

"Please." I looked at the GPS. Twenty-nine minutes to my destination. "We'll be there in less than twenty minutes. See if they can locate Caden."

"What do you mean, 'if'?" Iris asked, hands on her hips.

I started. "What?"

She rolled her eyes and heaved an offended sigh. "I know where he is, remember?"

"You can lead the others to him?" I asked. I hadn't considered that she could get there faster than I could, but I realized that was foolish. She clearly didn't travel using standard methods.

"Obviously." And with that, she abruptly *dropped* out of the back of my car. Her forward acceleration simply stopped, but my Rogue kept going. She phased through the seat in a blink, hovering in midair several feet above the highway in my rearview mirror. Then she flickered from sight.

"Whoa," Rachelle said. Then she grinned. "That girl puts my eye rolls to shame!"

"Unum, tell the others to meet Iris and follow her lead. She'll take them to Caden."

"Understood," the AI replied. "Stand by."

*Yeah*, I thought. *Stand by.* I hated it. I watched my speedometer climb as I continued to fly toward Seattle. The lights were all in my favor, my powers clearing my path of obstacles. I was glad, but a small part of me worried. If Caden was going to be fine, rescued by my friends, then why were my powers of convenience ensuring I get there as quickly as possible? Maybe they just worked with my intent. Yeah, that was probably all.

I wove between a few slower vehicles, cruising down the freeway at reckless speeds. Rachelle gripped the handle above her door and said, "He's in good hands, Emery."

I nodded, easing off the accelerator. A little.

Even I was surprised at how quickly Seattle came into view.

"Emery," Unum said over the car's speaker. His voice sounded reluctant, causing alarm to spike through me. "We have encountered a problem."

I gritted my teeth. "What?"

"I am following up on a potential resolution. My apologies. Thank you for your patience."

I cursed. I took a turn at high speed, throwing Rachelle and myself to the left. The marina was four minutes away, according to my GPS.

We swung down and into a narrow parking area a few minutes later. Of course, the lot was only available until ten p.m. and it was already well on its way to midnight. Crap. I'd just have to park outside the lot and hope I didn't get ticketed.

Suddenly, the gate arm lifted. Protagonist powers? No, I realized, it was Unum. He was connected to the city grid. Hot damn. *Good thing he's on our side now.*

"Apologies, Emery. I will be with you shortly. I am coordinating —" I didn't wait to hear the rest. I yanked the keys from the ignition and jumped out of the car, Rachelle on my heels.

The air smelled of the sea. It terrified me.

Ahead, the pavement wound between buildings that, while clearly closed, still had dim lights illuminating their interiors and spilling out onto the cement tiles. Regularly spaced streetlights further lit the path to the edge of the water. Puget Sound splashed and sloshed against the harbor, a chest-high metal railing the only precaution to keep people from walking right off into the water. Bicycle racks, garbage cans, and binocular stations adorned the walkway.

Behind a locked gate was a cement boardwalk leading to the marina itself. I could see a forest of masts and rigging sticking up from the boats moored there. Beyond that, the metal arms of cranes soared into the sky, a perpetual presence in the coastal city.

Scarlet, Mikey, Gregory, and Iris waited for us. Mikey sat on a low cement sculpture that doubled as a seating area. Scarlet paced behind him, agitated movements that mirrored my own impatience.

Gregory leaned on the railing and looked out over the dark water, the breeze curling the hem of his long coat, the only part of him that wasn't utterly still. Iris sat on top of a garbage can, her little body tense. Seeing me, she hopped down and glided over to me.

"I'm sorry," she said, tears standing out in her eyes. "By the time we got here, he was gone."

"Is he still alive?" I asked, the words bursting out of my mouth before I considered them. I don't think I *could* have considered them.

"He's alive. He's there." She pointed out over the water, and I followed the tip of her transparent finger. Endless fathoms of black in the night. Wherever Vox Populi had taken him, he was out there on that dark expanse.

Right. I'd thought about this, hadn't I? We could steal a boat. I'd probably have to convince Gregory, but with Unum's help…

"We can still rescue him," Rachelle told me, mistaking my silence for hopelessness.

The others gathered around me. Scarlet gave me a sharp nod; Mikey, a small smile. Gregory strode toward our group, his eyes hard. "We'll need to steal a boat, I think," he said without preamble.

I blinked but didn't miss a beat. "How quickly can we find one that will catch up to their vessel?"

Rachelle raised my phone. "Unum has something he wants to tell you."

She tapped the phone, changing it to speaker mode. Unum's voice came over the cell. "Thank you. As I was saying, I believe I have discovered a resolution to your conundrum."

"You can help us steal a boat?" I asked.

"He could," a voice called from behind Gregory. I started. Someone was clambering up and over the railing, climbing *out* of Puget Sound. A nearby streetlamp highlighted the blue in her hair. "But then they'd see you coming from a mile away. Much better to travel *under* the water, don't you think?"

The Mermaid.

"So, which one of you do I get to kiss first?" Melusina asked.

"Me," I said, as Rachelle blurted, "What?"

We devised a plan. Melusina could give all of us the ability to breathe underwater, but she couldn't taxi us all at once—and swimming on our own would take forever. Instead, she'd take two of us at *her* speed, which she assured us would be sufficient. Then she'd circle back and pick up another two. Since Iris didn't need to swim, Unum wasn't there in the flesh, and Mikey didn't trust his water resistance to miles of underwater travel, that left me, Rachelle, Gregory, and Scarlet. Although everyone wanted to go first, we decided that Melusina would ferry Rachelle and me for her first trip. We would infiltrate Vox Populi's superyacht—which, apparently, was a real thing and not something out of a comic book—and locate Caden. By the time we needed extra firepower, Scarlet and Gregory would arrive.

Rachelle and I plunged into Puget Sound. I was calmer this time when Melusina kissed me. The cold water became tolerable and grew more transparent as her powers settled over me, allowing me to see farther. Next to me, the Mermaid's glorious fin flashed in the moonlight, cobalt scales glittering. She grabbed Rachelle and kissed her, then coached her through breathing underwater. Rachelle's eyes widened as she inhaled seawater for the first time.

Finally, Melusina took one of our hands in each of her own and asked if we were ready. When we both nodded, she took off. There was a moment of tension as the water we displaced protested, and then... I sucked in a breath in astonishment. The pier simply fell away from us.

At first, it felt like we were being towed behind the Mermaid, but our own momentum rapidly evened out the difference until it felt like we were swimming along next to her, skimming through the water with almost no resistance.

No, that wasn't quite right. We didn't swim.

We *soared*.

The seabed dropped away below us as we sped through the underwater world. Melusina angled us to keep us twenty to thirty feet below the surface, and still the depths sank farther and farther. It reminded me of flying in an airplane more than anything else, far above the ground. You know, if I'd been strapped to the wing of the plane instead of sitting inside it.

Even though the water resistance was negligible—which must have been a trick of the Mermaid's—the sound was *incredible*. Seawater rushed over my ears, and when I tried to point out an immense school of fish below us to Rachelle, my words weren't even audible to me.

It rendered my previous swim through Puget Sound laughable. I felt foolish for refusing her help, for not realizing how much I'd hindered our progress. At least she had enjoyed the company of another incarnate for a time, I consoled myself. I'm sure that made up for my crawling speed.

It seemed like mere minutes before the Mermaid slowed and brought us to a stop, where we treaded water... if you still called it that when you were twenty feet below the surface.

Melusina pointed out a large mass nearby, partially submerged. "There they are."

We ascended through the water, surfacing when she gave the okay.

As prisons went, it was impressive. The superyacht put out quite a bit of illumination, banishing the night and allowing me a good look at it. It was white and sleek, with an angular prow that came to a point at the bow. Rows of windows—most of them lit—were stacked on top of each other, four lines of glass in total. Did that mean the vessel had *four* levels? The windows closest to the water, at the bottom, were smaller, rounded portholes that reminded me of the Starboard, the hotel we'd stayed at in New York. The next row of windows had gaps intermixed with railings, in such a way that the level was partially open to the night air. Above that, the third bank of windows ran the length of the hull, sleek and darker than the rest of the ship. The final, top-level windows were enormous and slanted, belonging to an upper deck that was probably where the helm—the ship's steering wheel—was located.

Inspecting the superyacht, I couldn't help but think how close Caden was. If I had X-ray vision, I could *see* him.

Soon, I told myself. We'd be together again soon.

While the lowest level of the vessel was likely below the surface, the nearest deck we could enter looked to be by the second row of windows. It was a promenade deck, I decided, which was like a wrap-around porch for the ship. It was a sequence of open railings and enclosed glass. And it was a good twelve feet up, maybe more.

"How are we going to get up there?" I asked, keeping my voice quiet. Words tended to carry out here in the vast openness. As if to illustrate my point, I heard laughter and snippets of conversation over the slapping of the waves against the boat's hull.

"The aft opens, kind of like a convertible top, for embarking and disembarking. But they have it sealed." Melusina gauged the height of the promenade deck and said confidently, "I can get you there."

"Wait," a young voice hissed. Iris appeared next to me, acting like she was treading water. The effect was spoiled by the waves sloshing right through her. "There's a guard posted."

Not for the first time tonight, I was surprised to see her. Always before, she'd been drawn to death—dying incarnates more strongly than dying mortals. I wondered how many deaths she was missing out on while helping us.

Then a darker thought: was she drawn *here*? I shoved the thought away.

"Can you cause a distraction?" I asked her. "Something that won't arouse their suspicion?"

Iris's face screwed up as she considered my request. "I think so." She vanished.

Melusina grabbed our hands again. "Come on." She pulled us back down, deeper than before.

"What are you doing?" I asked.

"We'll need a swimming start," she explained. "Can't jump out of the water without building up some momentum first."

We waited. A minute passed, then Iris appeared next to us. The way her clothes and hair ignored the water made her look like she was superimposed there by a bad special effects budget. "All clear!"

There was a rush. Again, the water resisted at first. I felt like I was traversing a current, a river pulling me in the wrong direction. It lasted no more than a second or two, then we broke the surface with more of a *pop* than a splash. The water fell away from me as we shot into the air. Rachelle and I hung suspended in the air for the briefest of moments, then plummeted. I couldn't quite bite back a yelp, but it cut off with a grunt as I slammed into the promenade deck. Rachelle thumped next to me a heartbeat later, wet hair hanging down and dripping. She was grinning like a fool, eyes alight.

I realized I was doing it, too. We looked at each other and sobered as one. My pulse was racing. Behind us, we heard a faint splash as Melusina presumably turned to go back for our friends.

"This way," Iris whispered from off to our left.

Rachelle and I slunk down the deck toward the door Iris leaned through. It was closed, and only her top half was visible. Our wet shoes skidded a little on the deck, but we made it to the door, opened it, and slipped inside.

The dimness of the cabin we found ourselves in did nothing to detract from its elegance. It reminded me of Morrigan's New York manor. Polished wood extravagance met the comfort of two elegant sofas, and shiny black flat-screens were mounted on either side of the suite. A bar of wood and smoked glass sat in the nearest corner, and there was a door on the other side of the room.

The door we'd just entered had a viewing window in it, and I risked a glance through it, looking back on the deck we'd vacated. A woman stood at the rail, looking out into the ocean. She wore a light robe that reminded me of a kimono. It did nothing to mask the gun she carried, the cinched material at her waist specially tailored to hold a firearm. She was scanning the surface of the water. She'd probably heard our arrival and grown suspicious. Luckily, she hadn't yet noticed the wet deck where Rachelle and I had landed.

I ducked out of sight, and we crept to the other side of the cabin. Iris floated through the bulkheads—the walls—of the ship. She reappeared a moment later and gestured for us to join her.

"We need to find Caden," I said. "Iris, you scout ahead and find him. We'll wait here."

She gave me a soldier's salute and vanished with a serious expression. I was grateful. It could be difficult to wrangle Iris's attention sometimes. Her concern for Caden must be overriding her sillier nature.

I didn't entirely know if that was a good thing. Iris didn't usually get *concerned*.

"Someone's coming," Rachelle hissed. Outside the cabin a light had just come on, and voices were approaching.

Looking around, there wasn't much in the way of a hiding place. "Behind the bar," I whispered. It was really the only option. But it also only had one entrance and exit. If they discovered us, we'd have to fight our way out. That could turn ugly fast.

A split second after we retreated behind the bar's counter, the door swung open and the lights flickered on overhead.

"I doubt we need to worry," a deep, male voice was saying. "She can handle herself."

"It's not her I'm worried about," a stuffy female voice responded. "She has Marco to watch her back."

The male voice made a noise of agreement. "You're worried about the kid."

"The *abomination*," she corrected him. "Do not be deceived by its apparent youth." Her voice traveled closer to where we hid, footsteps crisp when they hit the hardwood flooring.

"I'm hesitant to call an *angel* an abomination."

The woman's voice responded from almost directly above us. She was on the other side of the counter. "It's an incarnate, not an angel. If anything, its imitation of something divine makes it even more insufferable."

I tensed, trying to keep calm. Her words were so hateful, it chilled me. Anger churned in my gut.

Something clicked on the counter, and we barely dared to breathe.

"You won't need to worry much longer," the man said. "Hope will call anytime now."

"Good," the woman replied, farther away. We heard her settle on a chaise, and a moment later, another creak sounded as the man joined her. "The sooner we send that abomination back to whatever hell they all crawl out of, the better."

I shuddered. Although I had suspected, it still sent a shiver down my spine to know Hope had never meant to keep her word. I needed to hurry. Hope wouldn't be calling, and they would get restless. Worse, one of the others who had escaped into the woods might report at any time. We needed to get to Caden before that happened.

"Well," the deep voice said, "I don't think you need to worry. Silas has things well in hand."

"Why do we need to wait, though? Why not just kill it? At this point, Hope has undoubtedly finished manipulating the other one."

I sucked in a breath, looking to the side to hide my fury from Rachelle.

Then I froze, my heart leaping into my throat.

A *head* sat on the floor.

The fact that it was *Iris's* head took a moment to penetrate my jolted brain. Her ghostly body had risen through the floor and stopped after only her head and neck were through. My panic made its way into my pulse, which refused to calm. Iris lifted a transparent finger to her lips. Floating up to my ear, she cupped her hands and whispered, "I'll create a distraction. You go out the door behind you. The guard is gone."

I nodded.

She sank back through the floor.

I whispered to Rachelle, telling her to follow my lead.

"Hi! Have you seen any chipmunks recently?" Iris's voice came from the other side of the room.

There was a commotion as the two Vox Populi scrambled to their feet with exclamations of surprise.

Staying in a crouch, I scuttled the couple of feet to the door and reached up to the handle. "Over here!" Iris's voice said again, keeping their attention while I clicked the door open and slid outside. Rachelle followed me out, and then I risked a glance back before closing the door. Two figures were looking around frantically for the source of the voice. Iris must've stayed invisible while she taunted them. *Good girl*, I thought, easing the door shut until it clicked nearly silently.

We were back on the promenade deck where we'd boarded the vessel. No closer to finding and rescuing Caden.

Staying low, we glided away from the lounge and into the next room to put some distance between us and the two Vox Populi members. I checked the viewing window in the door before entering. The cabin's light was on, but it was empty. It was a fitness suite, with yoga mats on a section of hardwood and several pieces of gym equipment that would put your typical home gym to shame. Rachelle crossed the space to the other door and carefully looked out. "All clear," she called softly.

"Stay there. We'll wait for Iris as long as no one shows up."

A few agonizing minutes ticked by with my eyes trained on the door where Iris should appear, ears straining to hear anything other than the sloshing of the waves against the yacht's hull.

"What are we looking at?" Iris whispered from right next to me. I flinched, but not nearly so much as last time. Either my nerves were maxing out and nothing could alarm me anymore, or I was growing accustomed to her mobility.

"Where is Caden? Can you take us to him?"

"Aye, captain," she reported with a straight face. "He's being kept in the storage area. Belowdecks." She grinned. "Didja know that was a word, Emery?"

She was clearly having fun again. I decided to take that as a good sign, that it meant she thought the danger was over. That Caden was as good as saved.

*Don't lower your guard just because the six-year-old thinks we're in the clear*, I told myself.

"That's a funny word," I agreed. "Since Rachelle and I can't go through the floor, can you help us get to him undetected?"

We left the cabin and headed away from the lounge where we'd left the two Vox Populi, Iris scouting the way. We left the fitness room and began to cross another outside corridor when Iris came flying back through the door of the next room. "Guard's coming!" she squealed.

We backpedaled, but Iris reappeared, this time from behind us. "Someone that way, too."

I looked to Rachelle and saw my panic reflected in her face. Just then, the door ahead of us swung open.

The robe-clad woman with the gun saw us and froze.

We stood, staring at her like deer caught in headlights.

Then she reached for her gun.

My mind opened, personas flickering through me. I had a mental thumb on the pages of my mind, flicking through them.

Monster-hunting, desert-hating Emery.

*Flick.*

Withdrawn-from-the-world Emery.

*Flick.*

Investigative journalist Emery.

*Flick.*

Elderly guru Emery.

*Flick.*

Military-trained Emery.

*Stop.*

Her gun snapped up. I was *already* flowing forward in an economy of motion. As I had at the mall, but even more smoothly, I disarmed her in a single action. A blink later, I had her weapon aimed at her disbelieving face.

The shock of my easy success jolted through me and took my temporary persona with it. Military Emery receded, leaving me holding a handgun and staring like a fool.

Rachelle tackled me as footfalls came from behind me on the deck. "Go with it," she hissed in my ear. She snatched the gun out of my surprised fingers and yelled, "What are you waiting for? Help me with this abomination!"

Suddenly, several hands were on me, forcing me down. A fist caught me in my stomach, and I doubled over, then fell to my knees as I was shoved.

"What the hell is going on here?" a deep voice asked. The man from the room.

Rachelle answered. "Sorry," she said, assuming a vapid tone. "I lost control of this abomination. I—I failed, sir. The Regina trusted me, and I totally let her down."

A pause. "Who in blazes *are* you?" he demanded.

"Rachelle. I mean, *Aurora*, sir. Hope—sorry, I mean the Regina— she told me I could take the name Aurora if I proved myself." She was using her nerves to create a sort of frenetic energy around her story.

"Where did you even come from? Why are you all wet?"

Rachelle shuffled her feet, then launched into an explanation. "I got to the marina a little after they left with that other abomination— Marco told me I wouldn't make it, but I thought I could, and I wanted to show the Regina I was trustworthy after all the time we spent together this week. But then I had to charter a boat, and this one jumped off right when we got here. Like, where did he think he was going to go? We're in the middle of Puget Sound, and it's miles to land. Does he think he's some kind of fish abomination? Honestly! But what was I going to do? I *had* to jump in after him, and I even lost my favorite hair clip, but it was worth it—"

"Enough," the man said, sounding exasperated. "I don't know how you think this works—"

"Griffin," the guardswoman in the gun safe bikini interrupted, sounding reluctant, "she saved me. This incarnate got my gun away from me. If she hadn't stepped in..."

The man with the deep voice—Griffin—sighed in frustration. He grabbed me by the chin and jerked my head up to him. He was a wide, bald man wearing a Hawaiian shirt. "What manner of incarnate are you?"

I had expected this question. "You have the honor of addressing the Ventriloquist incarnate," I told him, smirking. "Seen any chipmunks lately?" I taunted.

I saw anger burn behind his heavy lids, and he shoved me away in disgust. "Silas will know what to do with him." To bikini woman, he said, "Show *Aurora* the way, then bring her up to the lounge." He eyed Rachelle. "I want to hear your full story."

Rachelle stayed behind me, following the guardswoman. She kept the gun pressed against my back, which made my shoulders itch, even though I trusted her. We entered the next room, which was the galley. This section was nothing but cupboards, cabinetry, and pantries, but it appeared to wrap around the entire stern, becoming an elegant dining area on the starboard side, off to my left. As soon as the door shut, the guardswoman spun on Rachelle. "Can I have my gun back, please?"

Rachelle let out a yelp. "Oh! Sorry, o-of course." She handed it over eagerly. A little *too* eagerly, in my opinion. I liked us being in control of the weapon, thank you very much.

I rocked backward as the woman slapped me across the face. It was openhanded, but her nails raked lines of pain across my cheek. "That's for my chin," she spat. "Don't ever touch me again."

Seemingly satisfied, she took Rachelle's position behind me and prodded me forward, directing me through an unobtrusive door leading to a stairwell that cut down through the hull. I met Rachelle's eyes only once as we walked, her pretend-vacant expression replaced with an apologetic one. It disappeared a moment later, though.

As we walked, Rachelle kept up an ongoing tirade of inane dialogue. "I can't believe I'm actually here! Hope—she didn't tell me she was called the Regina until today, so I didn't know to call her that, ya know? And it's really hard to remember Latin. I mean, really, I haven't taken a Latin class since my first year in high school. We were actually pretty lucky to have had a Latin class in high school at all, because we were the only school in the district that could afford to hire a Latin teacher. They're so rare these days! I mean, I get that it's a dead language, but that's obviously not true if people are still learning it, amirite? I'm sure glad I took it, though, even if I only got a B-minus. I would have studied harder if I knew I would be part of Vox Populi one day..."

The woman jabbed me with the gun a little harder than necessary to direct me; it seemed Rachelle's drivel was getting to her. The large enclosed area we were passing through reminded me of an indoor swimming pool, if you removed the pool itself. There were sun chairs, recliner seats with parasols, life vests, and an entire wall of life-saving tubes, mats, and other flotation devices. The rear wall looked like it could fold down, and I realized we were in the aft of the ship, almost level with the water outside; this must've been the sealed entrance Melusina had mentioned.

The adjoining cabin had shower stalls and wooden cubbies decorated with artificial plants. Geez. Even their locker room was upscale.

A door at the back was closed. Our captor rapped on it, and a moment later it opened.

Silas was older than I would have guessed of a jailer, but otherwise what I expected: worn and hard. If a trusty hunting rifle reincarnated as a human, it might look something like Silas. Old scars curled his upper lip into a perpetual sneer, and his eyes were sunken.

"What?" His voice matched his looks, a slight rasp to it, but I wasn't paying attention to him.

Behind him, rechained to pipes in the wall, slumped Caden.

He was unmoving, head hanging limply, disheveled golden hair dampened to a dirty blond. I couldn't see his face from this angle, but my eyes were suddenly wet. He *never* looked unkempt. He was clearly in a bad state. He wore a white jacket over scrubs, both soiled with dirt and grime—and stained with small flecks of brownish red that threatened to burn a white-hot hole in my emotions.

That was when the gunfire started.

The shots came from somewhere above us, at least one or two decks up. *Finally!* Gregory and Scarlet had arrived.

"Something's wrong," our robed guard said.

Rachelle looked at her with wide eyes. "You think? Maybe we're under *attack*." She clocked the woman on that last word. It was a good punch. She threw her whole body into it, sending the woman staggering back. I spun and snatched the gun from her as she stumbled away, shocked.

Silas tried to slam the door shut, but I caught the edge with my foot, wedging it between the door and the jamb. I levered my shoulder through the opening, and the rest of my body followed. Silas used my awkward movement to slam into me, crushing me against the wall. He was wrestling me into the bulkhead, trying to maneuver me so that my back was to him. I braced myself, refusing to be manhandled.

I could hear grunts and cries as Rachelle and the woman struggled just outside the door. Farther away, the *pop-pop-pop* of gunfire continued.

Silas's weight suddenly vanished as he stepped back. I stumbled but quickly recovered and spun to face him. He cocked a shotgun, and I moved without thinking. An explosion echoed through the cabin like thunder; my world became sound, fire, and smoke. A hole appeared in the bulkhead where I'd been a moment before.

Silas pumped the shotgun, ejecting a shell, then reoriented on me.

"*Boo!*" Iris screamed in his ear, materializing at his shoulder.

Silas swore and stepped back, driving the butt of his shotgun backward, aiming for his assailant's abdomen. It would have been perfectly executed if Iris hadn't been the Ghost. As it was, his momentum carried him too far as he met no resistance.

I considered shooting him in the leg, maybe the knee, but I didn't like shooting humans. If something went wrong, they didn't come back. I didn't know what happened to them after death, but it felt so *final* compared to an incarnate death—which was bad enough.

I growled and lunged forward, aiming the handgun's grip at his face.

Silas dipped under the attack and pivoted. My strike was absorbed by his shoulder. It was still a meaty hit, but he shrugged it off, discharging the shotgun again.

He missed me, but I still scrambled backward reflexively. Which, I realized too late, was his intention: to put some space between us. He pumped the shotgun again and fired.

I threw my arm out as if it could stop the shot. My eyes squeezed shut as I waited for the pain to hit me.

Nothing happened.

*What?* He couldn't have missed. Not even the strongest powers of convenience could have protected me at that range.

Opening my eyes, I found myself suffused in soft, white illumination. Caden sat up, his back straight against the pipework behind him, eyes fixed on me, face clenched in determination.

Light radiated from him, spread into two wings, one drooping to the ground, the other flared between me and Silas. The spray from the shotgun—tiny metal pellets—hung, caught in the brilliant light.

Then Silas's eyes flicked to Caden, and I saw his intent.

In that moment, I changed my stance on shooting humans.

As Silas turned the shotgun on my boyfriend, I fired. Blood

flecked the deck. Silas cried out and stumbled, his shot going wild. I'd shot him in the leg, throwing him off balance. I followed through and delivered the pistol whip he'd avoided earlier. This time, I connected. His eyes rolled up into his head, and he crumpled.

Caden's radiance dimmed, and he groaned. "You're late," he said. "Again."

A small laugh hiccupped out of my chest, half sob, half relief. I slid to my knees and cupped his cheek, sliding my fingers around his ear and into his hair. I kissed him, and it became something passionate, bordering on desperate; an outpouring of all my heightened emotions met his relief at seeing me and ignited inside both of us. I pulled back and drew in a shuddering breath, then attacked his lips again. The taste of him scoured through me, brushing aside my terror at his abduction, my dread that I'd be too late. I drew comfort in how *real* his mouth felt as he kissed me back.

I finally withdrew and met his eyes, which were blinking as though I'd just awakened him. He warmed, color flushing his cheeks and banishing the strained pallor that his imprisonment had cast upon him. The words. I needed to tell him.

"I—"

"I love you, too," he said, breathless.

My mouth worked, and I blushed, a giddy feeling surging through me. "I, um, how did you know?" I was grinning so widely my cheeks were straining.

He cocked his head, amusement—and something like adoration —in his eyes. "You've told me a dozen times, Em. Just not in words." His eyes narrowed in thought. "Actually, I think you *have* said the words before. But not in this lifetime."

I looked at him, stunned. "You remember... us?"

"Yeah, a little." He rattled his hands against the pipes and gave me a pointed look. "You know, I'm more than happy to talk about our relationship whenever you want. I don't need to be literally chained up."

I blushed, reaching back to examine the manacles. I touched the metal. They were handcuffs, so I'd need a key, obviously...

They sprang free.

*Huh.* I added handcuffs to the list of locked things that couldn't stand in my way when I was in my element. And being here, being anywhere with Caden, I was an incarnate in my element.

Caden pulled his hands free and rubbed his wrists, which had deep red indentations and ragged skin where the metal had chafed against them. I pulled him to his feet just as the door burst open. Rachelle tumbled in, looking like she'd been wrestling a cactus and the winner was still undecided.

She regarded the two of us, taking in the fallen Silas, and raised an eyebrow. "How long ago did you drop him?" she asked, breathing hard.

"Just happened," I said. "Scout's honor." Beside me, Caden nodded in agreement, expression guiltily empty.

"Good. I knew you two would never be making out and chatting while I was fighting for my life."

"Never."

"Not us."

She eyed us suspiciously, then smiled at Caden in relief and darted forward, wrapping him in a hug. "Hey, roomie. Glad you're okay."

When she released him a few moments later, her battered arms and face had been mended, if not her shirt. There were a couple of slices in it that worried me. Had the woman out there found a knife, or were her nails *that* sharp?

Gunfire sounded above, and I flinched. "We aren't out of the woods yet."

"Emery!" Iris appeared, right on cue. "Gregory and that scary lady need you. They're locked down in the galley." She paused. "That's the kitchen."

Right.

We exited the storage area. Rachelle took the shotgun—"Just in case!"—and I still held kimono guard's pistol. Caden seemed content with wielding the Holy Light of Heaven, so we retraced our steps as quickly as possible.

We passed the crumpled form of the guardswoman, who slumped against the slightly curved bulkhead. Blood trickled from her nose and ran down her chin. I looked sidelong at Rachelle, nine parts impressed and one part slightly appalled.

Caden looked like he wanted to go heal her, but I steered him forward. We pushed through the locker rooms and emerged in the swimming pool stern. Shouting wafted down to us through the deck above.

A gunshot rang out in the open space we entered. We scattered as a bullet sparked off the metal wall near our heads, a metallic peal echoing. Where had that—

There!

Another gunshot cracked, followed by a metal ringing. A Vox Populi woman with a rifle hid at the base of the stairwell, firing and then ducking back behind the doorway and bulkhead that shielded the staircase from view.

I fired in that direction without aiming, hoping that would be enough to keep her cowering in the stairwell instead of shooting at us.

Caden had ducked behind a rack of folding chairs, while Rachelle found sanctuary behind a pile of flotation mats. They kept her hidden but wouldn't offer much protection from bullets. I wasn't much better, having hunkered down behind a rubber raft.

Now what?

Gunfire sounded again from above. I looked around. There wasn't much in the way of cover in the empty space in the middle of the room, and I didn't really want to get into a firefight with a human, anyway.

A gun fired twice more, and I hit the ground. One round pinged off of metal, but the other hit the raft and punctured it, air hissing as it escaped. Dammit.

Suddenly, a muted grinding noise thrummed through the room, sending vibrations through the deck. *What the*—

A breeze whipped through empty space, carrying the sharp smell of salt water. I could hear the waves. The stern had been opened.

Of course! It was electronically operated; was it also connected to the internet? I should have considered earlier that the entire vessel would be capable of connecting to smart devices.

Which meant the entire superyacht was Unum's weapon.

A scream sounded, followed by a splash. Then, silence.

I waited. Finally, I chanced a look.

Melusina stood on human legs where the gunwoman had been, looking around for us. "Hurry," she called, seeing me. "They need you upstairs." Then she backflipped into a dive off the side of the boat, a blue-green fin slipping beneath the waves. Show-off.

I raced forward. "Emery," Rachelle called out. "We need a plan."

Gunfire spat again from above as she and Caden rejoined me near the stairwell. It was cold, the ocean breeze whistling through us. Rachelle and I were still damp from our swim.

"Gregory and Scarlet must be holding those doors up there," I told them, trying to gauge the distance to the gunfire. Not far. "Which means they've been buying us time. It's our turn to help them. You two take one of these rafts and get out into the open water. I'll let the two of them know you're safe, help them retreat, and we'll all escape into the water."

Caden looked back and forth between us. "Escape? We aren't taking over the ship?"

I shook my head. "No way. There are too many of them. This is an extraction mission."

Caden grabbed my upper arm. "Emery, there's another incarnate aboard. I heard some of them talking about it. I don't know who they are, but we have to save them."

"What?" *No, no, no.* Of course I had to save them. I knew it in my bones. In my soul. I couldn't abandon an incarnate to Vox Populi.

But damn it, we were so close to freedom.

"I'll get them," I said, hearing the frantic edge to my voice. "You two get to safety."

"Like hell, Emery," Rachelle snapped.

I looked at Caden, a desperate plea in my eyes. He glanced away, then back, shrugging. "I'm your Guardian Angel."

Frustrated, I called for Iris. A moment later, she appeared next to us. "There's another incarnate on board. Find them, then report back."

She crossed her arms, drifting up until the top of her head was above mine, giving the illusion she was taller than me. "What's the magic word?"

I stepped forward and took her little hand in my own. She obligingly moved her hand as though I could actually touch her. "Iris, you're the bravest g-g-ghost I've ever known. I'm the captain of this superyacht, and I'm making you my first mate. Will you help me one more time? Please?"

Her little face beamed. "Aye, aye, captain!" She vanished.

I rushed up the stairs, where the gunfire had slowed but not abated. Caden stayed right behind me, but it did not escape my notice that his breath quickly became labored. He was wan, fatigued. He needed rest, though I'd never convince him of that in this moment. I couldn't really be upset with him; I would make the same decision in his shoes.

I burst through the door and startled Scarlet, who was hiding behind a makeshift bunker she'd created out of cabinetry and an upturned table. The once-elegant dining table was riddled with bullets, chips of wood littering the floor. Even as I watched, a Vox Populi woman leaned around the corner of the wall—she was using one of the metal pantry doors as cover—and squeezed off two shots, wood chips exploding from the cabinet as a bullet dug a groove across the countertop.

I stalked forward, heedless of the danger. The woman, as well as another man who had been crouching behind some cupboards, the cabinet's door opened to give him a ridiculously minor measure of extra protection, gawked at me. Then they aimed and fired.

The rounds slammed into Caden's aura of light, which wasn't quite as all-encompassing as usual. But it covered me, shielding me from harm. The bullets stopped a few inches from my chest and head, dropping to the floor to clatter against the deck.

I brought up my own gun, leveling it at the woman's head. "Leave or die," I commanded. It was a bluff, but she didn't know that.

Her eyes bulged, then she turned and sprinted back toward the door, passing the crouching man. "Drop the gun," I added, my voice hard.

The weapon clattered to the deck as she bolted through the door. Without raising my gun at him, I turned my head and stared at the remaining man. He licked his lips, pale, then dropped his firearm and backed through the door after his companion.

"Caden, look out!" Rachelle yelled from behind us.

A willowy fellow I hadn't seen was sneaking up, gun aimed at Caden. I spun, but I was too slow.

Scarlet was faster. She leapt over her barricade and fired at the assailant. Hers wasn't a gunshot, though. It was her *finger*. It hissed forward—projected by compressed gas, I thought—trailing a thin wire. The finger took the man in the chest, and blue electricity arced across the wire connecting Scarlet and the man. I smelled ozone, and a sound like high-pitched static filled the space. The hair on my arms, neck, and head stood on end. I blinked at the bright afterimage in my vision, staring in wonder. It had been like lightning tamed.

The man didn't even convulse. He just dropped, a sizzling sound coming from somewhere on his person, small tendrils of smoke wafting up. Then, like one of those buttons that you press on a vacuum cleaner that sucks the cord back up, Scarlet retracted her... finger... and it whizzed back to her hand, reattaching itself with a *snick*.

"You have a *built-in Taser*?" I demanded. "You've been holding out on me."

She shook her hand as though she were shaking out a cramp. "One of many tricks up my sleeve," she said. If I didn't know better, I'd say she looked embarrassed.

"You mean that literally, don't you?"

"We need to relieve Gregory. He's pinned on the other side of the dining room."

I turned to Caden. "You good to stop a few more?" I hated asking it of him. He was clearly drained.

"You aren't taking a bullet with me around," he replied, his mouth set in a determined line.

I saw yellow shoes phase through the ceiling, and a moment later Iris descended from somewhere above us. "I found it, Captain!" she exclaimed.

I frowned. "'It?'"

She bobbed her head excitedly. "The incarnate is an object."

Did that change things? I couldn't leave a person behind, but if it was just an object, maybe it wasn't worth the risk to our lives. Even as I thought it, I saw Gregory emerge from his hiding spot on the other side of the dining cabin. He carried a handgun in each fist and squeezed off a storm of bullets, advanced, then fired twice more. He nodded to himself, satisfied, and jogged over to us.

"Rubber bullets," he said, shrugging off my surprised look. "I won't lose sleep over a few broken bones. Vox Populi is responsible for four murders in the last week alone. They're barely human."

"Did you really just *dual wield* guns?" I demanded.

He gave me a flat look. "I needed to intimidate them in case they can still walk. Don't want them coming after us."

Iris stamped her foot, but it wasn't as effective since she was in midair. "Does anyone want to know what I found?"

I turned back to her. "Of course, first mate. Where and what is it?"

"In the captain's quarters. The big bald guy with the hula shirt has it." Griffin, the man with the deep voice. "He called it the Artifact."

he Artifact.

Those two words gut-punched me. My mind flicked backward, skimming through previous incarnations, the years falling away. I remembered... a talking spear?

*A friend.*

Artie. I'd called him Artie. It had been centuries since I'd seen him. I *had* found him again since that earliest memory, but the Irish Emery who'd befriended him was at the forefront of my mind.

I looked at the others. We'd managed a reprieve; we could escape now. Fighting our way to the top deck would endanger our lives. Looking at each face in turn, I saw matching expressions. Determination, obstinacy, resolve. We were all in this together. And that, apparently, extended to the Artifact.

To Artie.

"We'll fight our way to the top deck as a unit," I said. "Gregory, Scarlet, you'll hold the deck at choke points and keep reinforcements away from the captain's quarters. Rachelle, you're in charge of keeping tabs on everyone. If someone's status changes, you let everyone know, and cover them until Caden can get there to heal them. Caden, you're with me, but you'll likely need to cover our retreat, too. Don't get burned out too early."

A circle of nods met my speech.

"What about me?" Iris asked, sounding irritated that I'd left her out.

"You, First Mate, have the most important task. You are going to scout. Warn us of any danger ahead, and get us safely to the captain's quarters. Most importantly, if someone gets separated, help them get to the water." I made sure they were all listening. "The Mermaid is safety. Get to open water if you need it."

"Choke points work both ways," Gregory said. "It'll be hell gaining ground in these narrow corridors."

"What do you suggest?"

He rubbed his chin. "A direct route to the captain's quarters. A service ladder, perhaps? Something on the outside of the hull. Scarlet and I could hold a ladder as easily as a hallway."

I looked at Iris questioningly. "If there's a ladder, Captain, I'll find it." She zipped away, vanishing through the nearest bulkhead.

We waited in tense silence, occasional muffled commands and the pounding of feet reaching us, ratcheting our nerves higher. Fortunately, Iris reappeared. "Found it! There's a hallway ahead with two bad guys hiding, then a dining terrace with *lots* of gunners. The ladder is there, and Vox Populi isn't specifically guarding it. It leads right to the captain's quarters." She beamed. "And the 'helm.' That's the steering wheel!"

I exchanged looks with Gregory, who shrugged as if to say *It's as good a plan as any.* "Good job, First Mate." Turning to Caden, I asked, "Can you get us across the terrace?"

He grimaced but nodded. "I can."

*It's too much. He needs to recharge.* I opened my mouth to object, but he met my gaze with steel in his seafoam eyes. So I wisely kept quiet.

"Wait." It was Rachelle. "Let's get those two in the hall outside, first."

"Great. How?"

She smirked, handed me the shotgun, and said, "Just be ready." She barreled through the door before I could protest.

"One of the abominations is wounded and alone!" Her voice came from the next area, breathy and threaded with excitement. "Quickly, help me get them! Oh, the Regina is going to be so proud of me. I mean *us*. Come on! Death to the abomination!" Her words came closer and closer, until suddenly two armed figures burst through the doorway.

Scarlet was on top of the first one before they could even register what happened. The other, however, gave a yelp and backpedaled, turning to leave. Rachelle clocked them full in the face, and their yell became a squeal. I scrambled forward and brought the butt of the shotgun down on the back of their skull. Their eyes rolled back into their head, and they crumpled next to the fallen body of their companion, whom Scarlet had swiftly dispatched.

I took a moment to catch my breath, surprised at how quickly the fight had begun and ended. I spun on Rachelle. "Are you kidding me? That was amazing! Don't ever do that again!"

She took back the shotgun and gave me a wink. "You're welcome."

"Someone might've heard that," Gregory warned. "We should move."

I took Caden by the hand. "You ready?"

In response, he began to glow. "Stay close," he instructed everyone.

I led the charge through the door, the Guardian Angel at my back.

The hallway ahead opened up onto a deck that spanned the bow of the ship. The dining terrace was populated with the gunners Iris had mentioned. True to her word, there was a partially covered ladder leading to the next level, climbing right up the side of the hull.

We had a problem, though. Vox Populi may not have been guarding the ladder explicitly, but Iris had failed to mention they were squarely between us and our destination. And *lots* of gunners seemed like an understatement.

By the time I'd taken all this in, Vox Populi had swiveled their attention—and their guns—in our direction. We stormed forward anyway.

Gunfire shattered the quiet of the night. A cacophony of shots and flashes of gunpowder assaulted me. Caden's light stopped them all, but I heard him grunt. I couldn't spare the time to turn and look at him as I pressed forward, praying he was all right.

The sound was deafening: the roar of gunfire, the whizzing of rounds, the angry cries of Vox Populi. And beneath it all, my boyfriend's labored groan.

*Holy crap.*

Caden's radiance was formed into a narrow tunnel of light that stretched before and behind him. As I was in the lead, the light's edge ended only inches beyond my face. Bullets, shells, and scattershot caught and hung in that glow, metal specks that grew denser by the second, threatening to block my field of vision. I gritted my teeth and plunged on, ignoring my growing terror as Caden's light first dimmed, then began to flicker.

*Hang in there, love.*

As our group approached the nearest Vox Populi members, Gregory, Scarlet, and Rachelle unleashed their own storm of gunfire. With shouts of surprise and alarm, the crowd retreated, but even that wasn't a true reprieve, as a handful of Vox Populi farther away continued to fire at us unabated.

We neared the ladder, but Caden's glow was too muted. We weren't going to make it before it guttered out and our group would be riddled with holes.

I looked around, searching for some solution. What could I do? I was the Protagonist; I had to be able to do *something* to save us.

Screams broke out, and the barrage of gunfire suddenly faltered. My head snapped in the direction of the upheaval even as I pressed onward toward the ladder. A massive wave of water crashed over the railing and onto the deck at chest level, bowling over an entire group of gunners in a frothy explosion of spray.

The entire yacht lurched, and we stumbled, some of our group and several Vox Populi gunners thrown to the deck by the unexpected motion. I caught myself on an upended dining table and watched, awed, as a second wave swelled behind the first. Melusina rode it, rising from the choppy surface of the water like some sort of sea demon. I grinned, filled with sudden exhilaration—this was the Mermaid in her element, an incarnate at the height of her power. As the wave crested, she flipped backward and away to return to the sea, the wave crashing into Vox Populi and pounding them to the floor.

The ladder was only feet away. "Gregory, Scarlet!" I yelled, indicating the overturned table. They quickly helped me drag it—and one other—in front of the ladder to create a temporary barricade.

Caden's light winked out right as we crammed into the shelter the tables created. He was gasping for breath, sweat running down his sheet-white face.

"Are you all right?" I asked, an edge of panic in my voice.

He winced. "I'm good," he managed, wiping his brow.

Gunshots cracked into our impromptu barricade, pelting us with splinters of wood. Not good. We were wedged between the dubious protection of the tables, the hull with the ladder, and the railing and open water.

"Captain," Iris reported, "we have a problem. They must've figured out our plan, because someone's guarding the top of the ladder now."

*Shit.* This was going from bad to worse. The tables wouldn't last long, but at least they provided some measure of cover. But our backs —and tops, for that matter—were exposed.

Scarlet looked up, her yellow eye peeking out from her bangs and making her look fiercer than usual in the relative darkness. "One person? I'll take them."

Gregory was reloading his guns. "I'll cover you."

Scarlet gauged the distance to the top of the ladder and crouched, as if she planned on taking the ladder in a single jump. She indicated to Gregory that she was ready. He listened to the rounds hitting the wooden table, waiting for something I couldn't determine. Then he nodded sharply and popped up over the lip of the barricade, returning fire. I heard swearing, but I barely noticed. My attention was on Scarlet.

Because at Gregory's nod, she *sprang*.

She rocketed upward, propelled by flames that burst from the soles of her feet. Even knowing she had more tricks in her arsenal, I watched in awe as she cleared the railing above, at least a ten-foot vertical leap. She tucked into a front somersault, then landed beyond my view. A fluorescent blue lit up the deck for a moment, accompanied by that high-pitched static sound.

A moment later, Scarlet was firing down at Vox Populi from above. The endless sound of bullets pulverizing our table-slash-barricade finally ceased.

"Got four advancing," Gregory said, ducking back down. "We need to get up there."

Rachelle released a growl and spun to look over the barricade. She pumped the shotgun and fired, repeating the action twice more in quick succession before slipping behind the table's once more. No sooner had she done so than a hail of return fire hammered into the wood.

"They're not advancing anymore," she said with smug satisfaction. I stared at her, and she huffed. "Don't look at me like that. I just scared 'em."

Iris appeared next to us. "Scarlet says the area at the top of the ladder is only big enough for a couple of people."

Gregory looked grim. "Get going, Emery. I'll keep them busy."

I shook my head. "It's too risky. You can't hold here."

"This is more protection than I hoped for, and I won't find a better choke point than a ladder." He met my gaze, and I swallowed. He wasn't in his element, precisely, but he was determined. I had to believe in the Watchman's resolve. "I'll hold them as long as possible, then jump into the water. It's as safe of an extraction point as we're going to get."

That would have to be enough.

"Rachelle," I said, "you're out. You've only got one life, and..." She set her shotgun on the deck.

Seeing my surprised expression, she rolled her eyes. "What? I know when you're right. I'll tell the Mermaid to expect the rest of you shortly." She crawled forward to give me a quick hug, then exchanged one with Caden, too. "Be careful." With that, she crouch-ran to the railing and gracefully dove over the side, disappearing into the waters of Puget Sound.

Iris still floated at eye level, but since I was squatting, her calves and feet disappeared into the deck. "Captain," she said, "Vox Populi are swarming this level. It's now or never."

"Caden, stay with Gregorius in case he needs healing. But don't risk yourself."

He was shaking his head. "I'm not letting you get yourself killed when I can protect you."

A gunshot sparked off the hull above us, and I flinched. I didn't have time to argue with him. And, if I was being honest with myself, I didn't want to let him out of my sights.

But looking at his oh-so-pale features, I realized something else, too. He couldn't protect me, not in his current shape.

I prodded him to climb. "I'm right behind you."

He started up immediately, feet slipping on the rungs in his haste.

Gunshots erupted, and my heart leapt into my throat, but it was Gregory, providing cover fire for Caden and me. Scarlet, too, rained gunfire from above, trying to keep the Vox Populi from advancing. I couldn't see if it worked or not, but in any case, the two of them couldn't hold back dozens for long.

As soon as Caden cleared the first few rungs, I scurried up the ladder after him. Rounds whizzed past me, sparks igniting against the ladder and hull.

*Shit, shit, shit.*

I tried to make myself a smaller target as I climbed. I still had my gun, but I didn't have the opportunity to fire it. I had to trust Gregory to cover me. Sure enough, he squeezed off a few more bullets from below, then swore as a storm of return fire bombarded his cover.

"Emery, come on!" Caden screamed over the noise. My body felt as tense as a taut wire, electricity coursing through me. Something stung my calf. A grazing shot? Or was adrenaline keeping my pain manageable? Either way, my leg still obeyed my urge to climb faster.

Above me, Scarlet leaned over the edge of the railing and, taking aim, squeezed the trigger. Curses and yelps followed her shots. She covered me as Vox Populi fired up at her. I was almost to the top, now, maybe eight steps to go. Then she cried out and disappeared back behind the railing.

*What happened?* Was she shot?

A bullet took me in the hand. Blood sprayed the right side of my face. Tiny bones cracked and splintered, and the pain was momentarily blinding. I howled, and the agony receded as adrenaline pumped through me. It didn't numb it—not by a freaking long shot —but it was something. I was almost to the top, but I couldn't use my right hand anymore. I stumbled upward, using my left hand to haul myself up rung by rung.

I barely made it. Caden rushed to me, pulling me over the lip of the ladder. With his touch, I felt energy flush through my body, my heart pumping liquid healing through my veins, my bones knitting back together, skin regrowing.

Nearby, Scarlet was gingerly prodding at her face. A bullet had apparently struck her just below her mechanical eye, ricocheting off the metal plate there. I could see the exposed steel and the dent where the bullet had met its mark. She seemed shaken but unharmed.

The surface where we were was not expansive; this area was not meant for people. It was part of the hull itself, stretching for a dozen feet or so before coming up against a wide bank of black windows.

The captain's quarters.

"Those windows are reinforced," Scarlet told me, "but I can get you in. The hull is slick, though. Are you two ready?"

"You going to walk across," I asked, "or are you just going to rocket-boost yourself there?"

She grinned at me, an honest smile that mocked the seriousness of our situation. Or celebrated our surviving it so far. "Why? Do you want a piggy-back ride?"

I snorted, a jagged, cracked-glass type of laugh. I wiped my mouth and looked at Caden. He inhaled deeply, helped me up, then gestured for her to lead.

Before following her, I looked down once at Gregorius, our lone defender. As I watched, I saw him pop up, fire off two rounds, then duck as a mob of men and women returned fire. He jumped up again, fired once, and a man in the crowd yelped. Gregory spun and aimed over the railing, firing at a man hunkered behind a chair, then ducked back down behind the bulwark as more shots riddled the space where his head had been.

He was only one man.

He *held*.

We scampered across the slick surface and to the tinted windows that loomed before us. Scarlet stepped up and pressing her palm to the glass.

"Might want to cover your ears," she advised.

A warbling sound fluted against my inner ear, and I clapped my hands against my skull. Even so, I could hear a resonant pitch, almost like an inverted whistle.

The bank of windows *rippled*. Then the pane shattered into thousands of glass fragments that rained down to the ground with a roar like a waterfall. For a moment, it even drowned out the gunfire below. Through the ragged hole, I glimpsed more of the wood-and-cream marvel that graced the yacht's interior design.

Scarlet stepped back, examining her handiwork. "I've got the Watchman's back," she said, almost shouting to be heard. "But we'll only be able to hold for a short time." She met my eyes, that yellow one boring into me, the lines changing and reshaping. "I'm talking minutes at most, Emery. Make it fast."

I understood. We exchanged salutes, and then she returned the way she came, leaving Caden and me to walk into the captain's quarters.

"It's just one guy," Iris said, appearing at my shoulder. "He's arguing with the boat. Something about overriding the lockdown sequence?" She shrugged, but I thought I knew what that meant: Unum was keeping the room clear for us.

"Keep an eye on the others. Everyone makes it out."

She nodded gravely, then vanished.

I stepped through the broken window, glass crunching beneath my shoes. Caden followed, his wariness mirroring mine.

The interior was as splendorous as I'd have expected, the rich tastes shown throughout epitomized here. Polished wood floors met cream-colored carpets; rich blue tapestries hung from the wooden panels on the walls. Banks of equipment spread like wings from the enormous metal-and-wood-wrought helm, a steering wheel with polished spokes radiating from its center. Cream sofas with blue pillows lined the room, window glass glittering among the plush cushions.

Griffin stood near the entrance to the room, opposite where we entered. He leveled a handgun at us, tracking our movements.

He didn't fire. He must've realized if he failed to bring us both down, he'd escalate the situation and lose his chance to escape.

"Disengage lockdown. Password: dum spiro spero." Behind him, thuds and an ominous crack sounded from the door. A Vox Populi crew was working to break it down. Minutes, indeed.

"Password not accepted," Unum's voice chirped over some over-head speaker. "Oh, hello, Emery Luple! And a pleasure to make your acquaintance at last, Caden Malek."

"Piece of shit," Griffin swore, but he'd paled.

I advanced on him, but not too quickly. I wasn't sure if Caden could stop another bullet at this point. "You know what I came for." Griffin held something under his arm, partially concealed by the bulk of his body.

"You're not content with saving the boy?" he demanded. "What else do you seek? Not the ship, surely? You can't fight us all."

I glimpsed it as he shifted. It was a crystal. No, not just that. It was a cane, tipped with a delicate orb that could have been made of spun glass. I couldn't make out the shaft of wood from my angle, but I could guess at its stylishness. *Oh, Artie*, I thought. *You always wanted to be something elegant.*

"I come for the incarnate," I said. "The Artifact."

Griffin's lip curled. "Damn. So you know." He shook his head in frustration. The noises coming from the door met the cracks of gunfire in the night behind me, spurring me on. I needed to wrap this up.

"Give me the Artifact," I said, raising my own gun, "and we will leave. You can keep your life."

He sneered. "No." In a smooth motion, he pointed the gun away from me.

At Caden.

I didn't even have time to cry out.

I don't know why I did what I did next. I'd say I acted on instinct, but that wouldn't be entirely true. I'd never done anything like this before, so how could it be instinct? But as a detached portion of myself evaluated the situation, I realized Caden couldn't protect himself and Griffin would squeeze that trigger before my bullet could take him. Understanding flashed through me, faster than thought, faster than a lightning strike. I thrust my pistol not toward Griffin but *to the side*. I fired at nearly the same instant as he did.

Twin thunder shook the cabin.

*Not in my story.*

This wasn't a tragedy.

*Not today.*

I couldn't see it, but I *swear* I did. The Protagonist's weapons of fate and coincidence intersected. My power of fate guiding his bullet toward Caden's heart. My power of coincidence guiding *my* bullet into his.

They met a foot from Caden's chest, a flash of metal driving into metal.

And two bullets missed the boy I loved.

Griffin gaped, too stunned to fire again. But as I strode forward, he snarled, "If Vox Populi can't have it, no one can!"

He smashed Artie into the bulkhead next to him. The fragile crystalline tip smashed first, exploding into tiny fragments that bounced off the wall and scattered across the floor.

"No!" I cried, rushing forward. "Artie!"

While I was distracted, Griffin tried to scramble around me. I caught him in the face with an almost careless whip of my pistol, my attention wholly focused on the shards of glass—the destroyed Artifact. The heavyset man's feet flew out from beneath him, and he crashed to the ground, groaning.

I fell to my knees before the crystal fragments, vision swimming. I ran my hands through the jagged slivers, scooping them up. They bit into my skin, but I didn't care. "Artie? Please, say something. Please. Are you there?"

The only response was more gunfire from below. I'd been so close. After centuries, we'd nearly reunited again.

More than that, I'd failed to save a friend.

I sat there, shoulders shaking, gunfire outside reminding me I didn't have time to grieve. I would, later. Right now, I needed to get Caden, Gregory, Scarlet, and Rachelle to safety. I had to focus on the ones I could still save.

But I felt like a piece of me lay on that cream-colored carpet, shattered into a thousand pieces. It reminded me of another failure, clothed in a sweater two sizes too large.

Artie. I would find him again. I vowed it. I'd mark the day 1,001 days from now, and I'd seek him out—I owed it to him, and to myself.

Oh, Artie.

"I am here," a voice said softly, a sense of awe in his words.

I snapped my head up. He was still alive? How? Could I repair him? I hadn't imagined that voice, had I?

No. But his voice hadn't originated inside my mind, as I expected. It...

It had come from the speaker. From Unum.

I stood, barely daring to breathe. "Artie?" I asked, uncertain.

"Hello, Emery."

It *was*. It was the Artifact, and it was the Artificial Intelligence.

How had I not known, not recognized? I laughed in wonder as I realized "Artie" was short for both.

A tear escaped, curving around my wide smile. "This entire time?" I asked.

"No. The memories returned just now. When I heard my name. But... I think a part of me always knew. When I met with you and Rachelle Grey in Asker's office. I felt like I could trust you, even though feelings defy my logic protocols." His voice held a note of wonder. "And, wouldn't you know? I dare say this may be the most sophisticated incarnation I've ever achieved."

"What the hell was this bauble, then?" I asked, gesturing to the splinters of crystal stinging my hands.

"A very expensive acquisition," Artie responded, sounding embarrassed. "And the crux of a clever ruse, I believe. It was used as payment to Vox Populi in exchange for services rendered. The agent who put me in touch with Vox Populi vouched for its authenticity. I remember, because when she handed it to them, she assured Hope they would 'be gaining the full powers of the Artifact.'" He paused. "Oh. Oh my. I see now. How duplicitous."

I paused, confused, tears sliding down my cheeks. "Someone *referred* you to Vox Populi?"

"Oh, most certainly. An incarnate who made my acquaintance shortly after I gained sentience. The same one who convinced me of my fatal flaw and devised the best way to safeguard against my vulnerability. I had deemed her an invaluable informant who worked most diligently to ensure I received the assistance I required. It wasn't until my conversation with you and Rachelle Grey that I came to understand I might have made an error in trusting her." Artie hesitated, his voice seeming to shrink. "As my experiences return, I fear you may be acquainted. Her name is Morrigan."

I felt a numbness creep over me, drying my eyes. I swiped at my cheeks, shoving it away. Right now I wanted to celebrate the fact that I had saved Caden and unexpectedly reunited with an old friend. "You and I have some catching up to do."

"Oh, I very much agree," Artie replied, cheery again. "But before this reunion is cut tragically short, may I recommend that you and the others withdraw to safety?"

Iris shimmered into view. "Captain! Gregorius has been shot, and Scarlet's being overrun."

It was too much. "Time to go. First mate, sound the retreat."

A splintering crack sounded, followed by timber and plastic fragments breaking free of the door leading into the captain's quarters. I backed away as an axe head chipped away at the material, widening the jagged gap.

My hands stung from the slivers of glass I'd brushed them through. I took Caden's in mine anyway, pulling him back toward the shattered windows. Our footsteps crunched as we crossed the threshold, and shots rang out from behind us, blending into the ceaseless gunfire outside.

At the top of the ladder, I was surprised to find both Scarlet and Gregorius. He'd somehow made the climb alive, though blood stained the left shoulder of his white dress shirt. Caden crouched down next to him, and even as he tried to heal him, Gregory lifted his good arm from his seated position and squeezed a few shots off toward the general direction of the deck below.

"Give me your gun," I told him, looking over the edge of the hull. A gangly man was climbing the ladder. Before I could snatch the weapon from Gregory, though, the Mermaid emerged from the wake on an eruption of water, grabbed the gangly man, and tore him free of the ladder on her descent. His cry was cut off by a splash.

Scarlet fired at Vox Populi on the lower level, keeping the enemies there scrambling for cover. I noticed they'd adopted our strategy and converted several dining room tables into bunkers.

My eyes were drawn to Iris, who was sowing chaos among the Vox Populi by running screaming across the deck, vanishing, and then reappearing elsewhere.

Caden backed away from his work, looking spent. Gregory pulled himself into a crouch, wincing as he rolled his shoulder. "Sorry," Caden said. "Best I could do."

Gregory put a heavy hand on Caden's shoulder. "I won't bleed out in the water. It's more than enough." He met my eyes, and we nodded. He stood and spun toward the edge of the ship, in the direction of the water. He pushed off, leaping through the night, his trench coat flapping behind him as it caught the wind. Before he hit the waves, I could *swear* I heard a whoop.

Two bullets ripped into the hull just below my face, and I ducked back down. "Scarlet!" I shouted. "You're next."

She grunted and stood, but instead of dashing toward the edge like Gregory had done, she tossed me a wild grin and then leapt directly from where she stood. Trailing blue fire, she launched herself through the air and over our heads in a perfect arc. She splashed into the water several yards out to sea.

"Show-off," I muttered.

"Just us, Em."

An alarm began blaring, and red lights flashed. "Attention!" Artie's voice pierced through the alarm, speakers pulsing with the volume of his voice. "All members of Vox Populi. New orders. You are to regroup in the rec room. This is not a drill. I repeat…"

Across the vessel, turmoil rippled through the Vox Populi. Some began to retreat; others ignored the announcement. Most just looked baffled, turning to their comrades in confusion.

Iris thrived in the chaos, darting through them and sowing her own discord. She shrieked, delighted, as two Vox Populi members chased after her.

"No," I said. "We're not alone, my love." I laced our fingers together. "You ready?"

He nodded.

Hand in hand, we jumped over the railing. We soared, the salty wind whipping our faces as the surface of the water rushed up to greet us.

We hit the freezing Puget Sound together. I held tight to his hand, keeping him from his natural instinct to resurface. He thrashed weakly, confused.

I couldn't see anything but dark bubbles and gradients of light—

vast murkiness below and a wide band of deep blue nearer the surface.

Caden stopped fighting me as the Mermaid caught and kissed him. After leaping into the ocean with my heart pounding, it wasn't easy to hold my breath. She found me as my lungs began to burn. After she kissed me, I inhaled eagerly, taking large gulps of... water? Best not to think about it.

She towed us along behind her for a few moments, then pulled us up to the surface a distance from the yacht. As we crested the waves, hands reached down and helped haul me out of the water. It was Rachelle, leaning over the side of one of those rubber rafts from the yacht's aft. I clambered aboard while Scarlet pulled Caden over the lip.

Everyone was there. Gregory sat at the stern with his back to the tube lining, massaging his shoulder. Even near exhaustion, the activity of the night had energized him, countering his usual air of weariness. He nodded once to me, then leaned backward, resting his head on the tubing and staring up at the starry sky.

Scarlet helped Caden settle into the raft before relaxing. I'd never seen her lounge before, but she did even that dangerously. She reminded me of a cat, ready to pounce at any moment, yet pleased at its most recent hunt.

Iris appeared on the lip of the raft, swinging her legs and tilting her head back and forth. "That was fun," she said. "Can we do it again?" Despite her excitement, she floated a fraction too high—maybe an inch above the lining—and the heels of her feet phased through the raft's side. I wondered if those were signs of her exhaustion.

Caden sat next to where I reclined on the floor of the raft, my back to a tubular seat. He leaned on me, his head resting on my shoulder. Rachelle plopped down on my other side, wringing out her hair. "That's enough excitement for me for one day," she muttered.

I reached up and put an arm around each of them, pulling them close.

I could see the superyacht hundreds of yards away, red lights still flashing across its sleek surface. The shrill alarm was a minor annoyance at this distance. I even heard the occasional gunshot as disorder among the Vox Populi continued.

Melusina climbed aboard the raft and sat primly on the bow, facing all of us. "Good thinking getting a raft, Rachelle," she said. "I don't think the swim back would have been easy on any of you." She looked around quizzically. "But where are the oars? And who's on rowing duty?"

A murmur of discontent arose, but I saw the spark of amusement in her eyes. "I'm kidding," Melusina said, holding her hands up to fend off the glares. "Hang on, Team Incarnate. I'll have you home in a jiffy."

She splashed back into the water, legs shimmering into a beautiful tail.

The first-ever meeting of Seattle's Incarnate Watch took place at E-Pluribus's headquarters in Bellevue, in Micah Asker's suite. It was a tribute; in some ways, his death had started all of this.

We had put last night behind us.

I'd made it home after dropping Rachelle and Caden off at their apartment. I even stayed while Caden showered. After his ordeal, I thought maybe he needed to feel safe again. I'd tucked him into bed and stayed with him until his breathing evened out and he slipped into sleep. When I'd arrived home, the most jarring part was Mom greeting me like it had just been another night out. I made excuses, washed up, and collapsed on top of my bed, not even bothering to peel back the sheets.

"So how's this thing going to work?" Scarlet asked. Though she addressed the room, she directed the question to where Caden and I stood. Well, he stood. I leaned back against one of those strange pillars. Trying to look casual, relaxed, despite how excited—and anxious—I was.

This was Caden's thing. I mean, it was our thing, but it was his dream. I wanted to support him.

That morning I'd contacted Gregory, and he'd put out the call to the incarnates of Seattle: the Guardian Angel wanted to make Seattle a place of safety for incarnates. To prove it, we'd even chased Vox Populi from the city. Artie said he'd set their superyacht on a course toward the Bering Sea. He had a bet going on whether or not Vox Populi would manage to reclaim control of their ship from him before they reached Alaskan waters.

To prepare for the meeting, Mikey had revealed himself to the media. Not as the Android, of course, but as Micah Asker. He made a statement about faking his own death and seeking protection following an attempt on his life—and his sorrow over the string of murders of his tech industry colleagues. He simultaneously announced he would be taking some personal time off in the wake of recent events. It would provide him the time he needed to learn everything about assuming Asker's identity.

Before that, though, his suite was the perfect place to hold a conference that could affect the fate of all incarnates—or, at the very least, the local ones. The impressive presidential suite lent weight and prestige to our cause, giving an inspiring first impression to those who knew nothing about us. It was a not-so-subtle statement about the resources behind Caden's proposition.

In the long term, Mikey assuming leadership of E-Pluribus would provide us with the means to find and reach incarnates around the world with our message, as well as the assets we'd need to equip the society we envisioned. To give it a fighting chance.

As I looked around at the people gathered in the room, I examined each in turn. The reasons they had responded to our call were, I suspected, different—and likely complicated. I tried to gauge their motivations anyway. For Gregory, it was personal. He'd failed to protect someone for whom he felt responsible: Jax, the Cyberpunk. Gregory stood before the bank of windows, bathed in the light of the setting sun, the field hat he wore casting his face in shadow. He was half here, observing the meeting, but also half out those windows: the lone sentinel, ever vigilant, watching over his city. It was more than Jax, I knew; he felt responsible for all the crime in Seattle. It was his job to keep the peace, to protect those who could not defend themselves.

Today, if Caden had his way, the Watchman would no longer stand quite so alone.

The Cyborg, the Android, and the Artifact were here to represent the victims of Vox Populi's recent strikes. Their attendance was a testament to the strength of working together. A message to the others that despite losses, they would not let fear send them back into hiding. They would stand up and add their voices to a coalition for change.

Scarlet, I could tell, cared little for the formalities of such meetings; you could see it in the way she lounged, arms crossed, on one of the couches in the middle of the room. Whether she endured it out of obligation to Caden and me or based on the understanding that such procedures preceded real change, I didn't know. She'd already informed me that she'd be moving on from Seattle as soon as possible. But the fact that she'd postponed her exit to be here was an endorsement of Caden's dream. I adored her for that.

Plus, Mikey followed her around like a younger brother. And the more incarnates to kick-start this dream, the better.

Artie joined us—virtually, of course—for the sake of old friendship. Now that I knew he was the Artifact, I suspected "the Artificial Intelligence" was simply an updated, contemporary *form* he assumed, much like I was "human." Though I hadn't had time to give it real thought, it didn't make sense that he was *the* Artificial Intelligence; after all, Mikey was a type of AI, too. Maybe they were both personas of the Artificial Intelligence archetype, like how Bloody Mary and the Headless Horseman were both ghostly.

Which brought my attention to Iris. The Ghost hovered above the heads of the others, sitting and rocking back and forth as if there were a physical swing installed in the ceiling. Seeing my attention shift to her, she gave me a little wave. Her presence surprised me. Not only did death often call her away, but she rarely kept her attention on any one thing. Perhaps she was growing up, even if her body didn't change.

She stuck her tongue out at me.

Melusina watched Iris swing back and forth from where she stood with her guest. I had hoped she would attend, after our teamwork last night, but I hadn't been certain; I hadn't even known if Gregory's message would get to her if she was out in the middle of Puget Sound. Seeing the determination on her face as she looked at Caden, though, it made sense; she'd been through a lot with us, including a fledgling abduction. While she could seek the security of the sea, I'd seen the longing on her face when she talked about companionship. What Caden promised was safety on land, too.

She'd brought a man with her. He was her senior by at least a generation, with Polynesian features and bright white hair. He kept it short, but it crept down the sides of his face until the two sides met in a smart, pointed beard beneath his chin. He was tall, filling out his sharp dress suit with wide shoulders and a hint of a rounded gut. She called him "Uncle Dagan," though I got the impression he wasn't biologically related to her. Incarnates were rarely actually related, though it could happen. When I'd asked her if he was the Merman, she'd giggled like I'd said something really funny. He'd frowned—he had an *incredible* frown, like a thunderhead on the horizon—and called himself the Triton.

I turned my attention to the remaining three incarnates in the room: a woman, a man, and a bird.

The woman was short and comfortably plump, with dark skin and hair dyed a shockingly vibrant red. She had an easy smile and stood slightly ahead of her companions, as if a little more eager to be here. She sported a floor-length fur coat made from an animal with a dark pelt, like a bear.

Her human companion—at least, they had arrived together and stayed near each other as the meeting began—was a man with Native American features, brown skin roughened by nature and lined with age. His hair was more black than gray, though it had its fair share of both, and was long, worn in a tail. Biker leathers completed his outfit, along with a necklace of some unknown beast's teeth.

My eyes drifted to the final incarnate, on the man's shoulder. She was the most fantastical of any in the room, even Iris, who was clearly transparent and disregarding the laws of gravity. This incarnate was a large bird, the size of an eagle if not larger, her primary coloring the charcoal hue of thunderheads. The dark shading on her face and breast flared to white at the tips of her wings and tail feathers. When she spread her wings—as she often did while readjusting her position—I could almost make out a *glow* from within her feathers. As though the flesh peeking through the dark plumage was incandescent.

The Protagonist and the Guardian Angel.

The Watchman.

The Artifact.

The Cyborg.

The Android.

The Ghost.

The Mermaid.

The Triton.

The Selkie.

The Kushtaka.

The Thunderbird.

And Rachelle.

Twelve incarnates—including Caden and me—stood, sat, lounged, or perched throughout the room. Twelve incarnates and one mortal. The turnout had surprised me. Oh, it wasn't the *number* that impressed; it was the fact that anyone outside of our immediate circle showed up at all.

The conversation in the room petered out, and the occupants turned their attention to us, various degrees of curiosity in their expressions. Caden glanced at me, so I nodded and smiled encouragingly. He cleared his throat. "It begins with the people in this room," he said. "As incarnates, we tend toward solitary lives. By now, you've all heard about the recent deaths of incarnates at the hands of Vox Populi. A tragedy. Not just because we lost four incarnates whose light brought innovation and creativity into the world. Not just because we lost four unique personalities that will not be reborn wholly intact. It's a tragedy because it was preventable.

"For millennia, the world has been a dangerous place and isolation a shield to keep incarnates safe. Preserving independent Sanctums, secluded Safe Havens, remote Territories... we've sequestered ourselves in an attempt to hide from the world. But in doing so, we hid from each other. We surrendered our sense of community—of connection—and, in the process, convinced ourselves we are safer apart.

"The world is still a dangerous place, even as it evolves. It becomes smaller by the day, cities creeping nearer to outlying lands, encroaching upon once-secret places of power or peace. As mortals expand in number, they bring with them urban legends, new and ancient. So, while the danger intensifies, so too does our culture." His natural—well, *super*natural—charisma radiated out from him, his earnestness pleading for the others in the room to listen to his words. To *think* about them.

"All of these developments lead to one conclusion," he continued. "For incarnates, the age of isolation has come to an end. In response to a changing world, I implore us to band together. To pool our resources. To care for one another. To collaborate for safety, and community, and a better future. A future we create alongside mortals, respecting them but not fearing them—because, together, we can create a Sanctum large enough to cover a city. Create a network of Safe Havens in every neighborhood. Make all of Seattle our Territory."

I could see the possibility rippling through the incarnates. Melusina's look of yearning, Dagan's contemplation. Iris had stilled her swinging and watched Caden raptly. I saw Rachelle's wistful smile mirrored on the Selkie's face.

It wasn't perfect. Scarlet and Gregory, for all their support, wore unchanging, stoic faces, and the man in the biker gear wore a similarly unreadable expression.

"We are greater than the sum of our parts," Caden said softly. "We can merge our individual strengths to cover our weaknesses. Imagine it: a place of safety. We could seek incarnates around the world as they're born or reincarnated and give them this gift. A place of peace, where they can contribute to a purpose greater than just existing for eternity. A place of community, where they can be who they truly are among others who understand—and welcome others to do the same.

"It begins with the people in this room. Incarnates are immortal, and we can build an immortal sanctuary. It begins with a neighborhood watch, an Incarnate Watch. But it doesn't end there. Today, an Incarnate Watch. Tomorrow, Seattle will be the first Sanctum City." He took a deep breath and exhaled, light shedding from him like hope made real. Like Light incarnate. "Who will dream this future with me?"

Silence laced with abiding, heavy emotion hung throughout the room.

As badly as I wished to pledge my support, to proclaim my approval, I knew that someone else had to speak first. I already stood by his side, my position evident. It wouldn't strengthen him to throw my voice into that silence. It needed to come from without.

I took in the faces arrayed before me, my heart accelerating as glances were exchanged. Dagan and Melusina. The Native American man leaned back and mouthed something to the Thunderbird on his shoulder. Even Scarlet glanced at Gregory, though the Watchman kept his silent vigil out the windows as the sun died.

Iris suddenly appeared before Caden, facing out toward the others. "I have a better question," she announced to the room, diminutive face grave. Then she let out an explosive breath and spread her hands wide. "Who *wouldn't* like this dream?" She levitated a few feet upward, rotating as she went, until she was eye level with Caden. She stuck out her little hand. "I don't sleep," she told him seriously, "but I will dream with you."

Caden took her hand and shook it solemnly, the two perfectly synchronizing the movement—I mean *perfectly*. If I didn't know better, I'd say he *actually* gripped her hand. "Thank you, Iris."

"Well," the Selkie said as she shrugged and stepped forward, sending her fur coat swaying, "count me in. I'm not about to be outdone by a wee lass." Despite her words, her accent was faintly southern, of all things.

From there, several others joined in: Gregory pledged his support, then Mikey. Dagan said he was moved by Caden's speech but far more impressed by the interest it inspired in others, and he vowed to contribute to the cause. Melusina cheered, blushing from the looks her exuberance drew until Rachelle repeated the cheer and grinned across the room at her.

"Although I believe it was implied," Artie said from the speakers in the room, startling some of the guests, "it would be an honor to serve such a worthy cause."

"What of you, my friends?" I finally spoke up, addressing the man and the bird on his shoulder.

To my surprise, the Thunderbird answered for them. "Your dream is beautiful, Guardian Angel," she piped in a high, feminine voice. "But we are not willing to commit just yet."

Caden hid his disappointment well, I thought. "Is there anything I can say to change your minds?" he asked.

"It is not words we require," she replied, "but deeds. Your glamour clouds the room, and we would make this decision with time and meditation."

The Guardian Angel bowed his head in respect. "I sincerely hope to convince you. I believe every incarnate deserves security and a sense of community. We would eagerly welcome your assistance in building this dream."

The Kushtaka—I had no idea what that was, but that was how he had introduced himself and I didn't want to offend him with my ignorance—finally broke into a smile. "If your deeds are half as successful as your words, we will talk again soon, young angel." His voice was deep and rough, like weathered stone.

They didn't leave, though, which I took as an encouraging sign. I pledged my support in order to smooth over the awkwardness of their rejection, and Scarlet said she'd support the cause but couldn't necessarily be a part of the Watch, since she was leaving Seattle.

Individual conversations broke out as people came forward to congratulate Caden and express their enthusiasm for his project. Details would be hammered out soon enough, and Caden suggested monthly meetings, scheduling the first for the following week.

Eventually, Scarlet and Mikey excused themselves. Watching them, I patted one of the pillars in the middle of the room. "I'll be right back, Artie."

His voice sounded in the Bluetooth earpiece I wore to speak with him privately. "You knew all along?" he demanded, surprise evident in his tone.

I grinned, looking at the dark pillars before following the Cyborg and the Android. "Yeah."

"If you knew where my mainframe was located when you first encountered me, then I was vulnerable to you from the very moment you confronted me." I didn't answer as he pondered this knowledge. "Yet you did not utilize this information as leverage. Did not intimidate or threaten me. You didn't know I was Artie. So... why?"

"Because if I abused that knowledge, I would have violated your trust," I said quietly. "And we couldn't have become friends."

"You risked much for friendship with me."

"That's how every meaningful connection starts," I said. "But friendship isn't about risk or vulnerability. It's about strength. You're better together. *Amicitia vera illuminat.*"

Artie's response was affectionate. "*Amicitia pulchra est,*" he replied.

"Emery," Scarlet said as I approached.

"Just came to see you off," I told her, smiling. "Though I'm bummed you have to go."

"We'll meet again."

"Before you go," I said, "may I ask you a question?" At her nod, I said, "Were you going to tell me the truth about Mikey?"

Her brows knit. "Which truth?"

"That he killed Asker."

Their reaction was immediate. Mikey backed up a step, eyes widening, mouth opening in shock. Scarlet, meanwhile, froze, watching me like a caged animal. I waved away their concern. "How?" Mikey blurted, then cringed. "I mean, what makes you think that?"

"I'm not going to turn you in," I assured them. "But some of the facts didn't line up. With Vox Populi attacking and Caden being abducted, it took me a little time to put everything together. I'd forgotten that Unum helped Vox Populi steal Asker's corpse from the coroner's office. I realized it must have been to keep the police from realizing his murder—the first murder—was different from the following three. Which led me to remember the most important clue: Dr. Yamamoto said that Asker was killed by someone with a prosthetic limb."

"And you figured out that you hadn't met a person with a missing arm," Mikey said in a small voice. "But you *had* met a person with an entirely prosthetic body."

I nodded. "And I remembered how terrified you were to enter E-Pluribus. At first, I thought you were just hesitant to return to the place where your creator was murdered. But then you agreed to use the space for the meeting today, and I wondered what had changed."

Mikey cringed. "And what did you conclude?"

"The only thing that changed was Unum. He wasn't your enemy anymore."

Mikey and Scarlet exchanged glances. Mikey was all nerves, but Scarlet just looked sad. "Mikey's systems were connected to the internet. Artie took control of Mikey that night, and he used him to murder Micah with his own creation."

I frowned. "Asker, as the Technopath, couldn't control Unum?"

Mikey was visibly upset, so Scarlet inclined her head, speaking softly. "We wondered the same. If Micah could control machines with his mind, how could he die from an android? As near as we can figure, instead of using his powers to control Mikey, he spent his dying breath sealing Mikey away from Artie's control. He placed Mikey on a self-sustained intranet, disconnecting him from the web."

Mikey spoke, his voice ragged with grief. "Even as I unwillingly strangled him, he was thinking not of his own life, but of mine. Instead of saving himself, he died protecting me. We confirmed with Artie earlier today: he can no longer take control of me."

"I'm sorry I misled you," Scarlet said softly. "I was protecting Mikey, of course."

I nodded my understanding. "You're only wrong about one thing," I said firmly. "It wasn't Artie who took control of Mikey. It was Unum. The Artificial Intelligence under the sway of Morrigan, scared and seeking drastic measures to keep itself safe." I looked them both in the eyes. "Unum is gone, now. Artie is a different person entirely."

"And he's very sorry," Artie added, speaking softly through a speaker in the hallway that had escaped my notice.

Mikey jumped at Artie's voice, then looked to Scarlet. She pursed her lips. Eventually, she said, "We accept your apology, Artie. But we need time and space. To grieve as well as to forgive." She nodded sharply, as though to herself. "We will return, though."

I walked them out of the building. Scarlet shook my hand, and Mikey enfolded me in a hug. They'd both be back; Mikey would return to take over daily operations of E-Pluribus. I was still sad to see their forms fade to silhouettes against the dusk.

"Thank you, Emery," Artie said in my ear. He didn't need to elaborate.

"It wasn't just for you, my friend." He didn't answer, and I wondered if he understood that it was for me, too.

## 34

*THE CAMBION INCARNATE*
*Name: ...*
*Height: ...*
*Weight: ...*
*Eye Color: ...*
*Hair: ...*
*Classification: ...*
*Bio: I don't want to talk about her.*

〜

"Take the next left," Mom said.

I flicked on my blinker. We were in my car, the back seat folded down to create a cargo space. Mom had asked me that morning if she could use my car to pick up some antique dresser she'd found from a seller online. Being the outstanding son I was, I volunteered not only my vehicle but also my services. Besides, Caden was working at the hospital.

Again.

Mom shifted in her seat, and I smothered a sigh. She was acting all squirmy. She got this way when she had something on her mind, when she was excited or anxious, and especially when she wanted to talk about something but didn't want to be the one to bring it up.

"Should we discuss the elephant in the car?" I asked brightly, suppressing the nervous flutter in my stomach.

"Elephant?" she asked innocently.

"Gregory. I know you think I don't care about your love life, but I *do* want you to be happy. I'm just worried that he isn't right for you."

I kept my eyes on the road ahead. I could still see her amusement in her glance. Or maybe I just felt it.

"Sweet pea, you don't have to worry so much. It isn't your job to make sure I'm happy." She paused. "Though... *why* isn't Mr. Tall, Dark, and Handsome right for me, again? Just while we're on the subject." She saw my knuckles flex on the steering wheel and added, "That you brought up. Without any prompting from me."

Yeah, except the whole squirming bit. "Because he leads a dangerous life," I said quietly.

"Ooh. Mysterious, handsome, *and* dangerous? Yuck. Women hate that."

"I'm serious," I said. "I don't mean that you'd be in danger. I mean you'd be constantly worried when he's on the job, afraid something would happen to him."

She was quiet, mulling over my words. "Take the next left."

I pulled into a complex of townhouses tucked a street or two away from the main avenue. We were in Renton, a city more kitty-corner to Seattle than next to it, in the part of town bordering the more affluent Newcastle zip code. The neighborhood was hilly—like just about everything in the greater Seattle area—and the townhomes were painted a subdued brownish-beige and were a good size to boot. Mom consulted her scrap of paper and directed me to a covered parking stall.

As I pulled in, she put her hand on my arm. "The risk of getting hurt scares me sometimes," she admitted. "And the older I get, the more comfortable I get, and the less I seek change. Why make changes when life is *fine*, right? But other times, I don't want to settle for 'fine.'"

I opened my mouth, but she shook her head, sending her dark hair swaying. She hadn't straightened it today, so it had its natural curl. "However, you're more important to me than a potential boyfriend. So, if you don't want me to see him, I won't. It'll just make for a very awkward start to our coffee date tomorrow."

I laughed. "And you probably thought the most awkward part of the date was going to be explaining that you don't drink coffee anymore."

She frowned, then opened her mouth. Then broke into a smile. "Does that mean I have your blessing?"

I nodded. "But if either of you asks me to call him 'Dad,' you'll never see me again."

She laughed and stepped out of the car. "Deal."

"I'm deadly serious about that." I exited the car and hit the lock on my remote, hearing it chirp. Mom texted the seller we had arrived and received a response that we should meet them at their front door.

The pathway leading to the townhouse was charming, lined with flowers and trimmed bushes that didn't obstruct the paved walk. Each unit had a fenced plot of yard space and a covered balcony on the second level. A friendly woman we passed by waved down to us. She was grilling meat, and the smell made my mouth water.

We made it to the front door of unit seventeen. I hoped the dresser wasn't too heavy. It wasn't a lengthy walk back to my Rogue, but I wasn't eager to maneuver a bulky piece of furniture by myself. Even with the muscles I'd been working on.

I knocked on the door, Mom standing beside me. She was squirmy again. She must have been more excited for her coffee date tomorrow than I'd realized. Good, I decided. I'd be supportive. This wasn't about me.

The door opened and...

"Hey, beamish boy."

*Wait, what?*

It was Caden. He took advantage of my stunned silence and grabbed me by the arm, pulling me in for a kiss.

"Hey, I have a boyfriend," I murmured against him, dazed. He laughed and squeezed me tight before withdrawing. I was staring, articulate words refusing to find their way into my brain, much less have any chance of making it to my mouth. Funny, I thought, how I could react in a blink to danger, but I stood there like a fool now. "What's going on?" I stammered, glancing at Mom. She wore a huge grin, and it began to dawn on me that I'd been set up.

"Surprise, sweet pea!"

Caden gestured grandly at the front step of the townhouse. "You know all those extra shifts I've been picking up at the hospital?" he asked. "Well, I was saving up. For a place." He looked down, then back up at me. "For us," he added shyly.

"No way." A disbelieving smile was widening my mouth, pulling at my cheeks.

"Caden came to me a few months ago," Mom said. "He wanted my help in picking out a place you would like."

Caden grabbed my hand, tugging. "Want to check it out?"

In answer, I pushed him into the hallway, but truthfully, I barely saw it. A small room to the left of the front door had caught my attention. It was my office.

No, I mean, it was *my office*. The very same one that had burned down in the Genie's attack. It was the same desk I'd bought; it even had the same damn flowerpot in the corner.

"What—" I gaped. "How?"

Mom had stepped back to give us some privacy, and Caden tugged me forward. Leaning close, he said in a low voice, "I hope you like it. With all the hundreds of times you've bought a home, over years and lifetimes, I wanted to try and do something that was *truly* a first for you."

I turned to him. For some reason, something was stinging my eyes. "Like it?" I let out a sound I couldn't describe and put my forehead against his. "I *love* it." I pulled back and said, "I'd love anywhere with you."

"It's just a starter home, really," he said. "We'll outgrow it in a few years. But for now, it's a place we get to define, together."

"I wouldn't have it any other way. But I hope you know we're never selling this place. I'll own it thirty incarnations from now, just try and stop me."

Mom walked in, glowing. "Seeing your face was worth all the hours spent negotiating with the insurance company on your arson claim." She ran her hand over the desk self-consciously. "We replaced everything from your office. It's not the same desk, obviously, but we tried to find a close match."

"It's beyond words, Mom. Thank you."

"She was amazing, Emery. She not only dealt with the insurance company, she also helped me find the place and even cosigned the loan."

"Oh, please. Caden, honey, this was all your doing. I was just so honored to be asked to help."

Caden shook his head. "She even bought us a new bed."

"As a housewarming gift," Mom said, blushing at Caden's compliments. "Besides, I had an ulterior motive. I wanted to keep your bed at home, Emery, so you always know you're welcome home and have a place to stay if you want."

I... I couldn't believe it. My smile had slackened into disbelieving wonder. And why was the room swimming like that? "You guys..." I turned to Caden, gesturing at the walls. "It's ours?"

He bobbed his head. "It's ours."

I stepped forward and enfolded him in a hug. "You're incredible."

"I'm sorry I've been working so much," he said in my ear. "I'll need to keep it up for a while, unfortunately, to afford the mortgage. But at least every night I'll come home to you."

A joyful hiccup bubbled out of me, and Caden tightened his embrace, then stepped back. "Shall we take the full tour?"

The townhome was perfect. It was longer than it was wide, with two floors. The kitchen, dining room, office, and an exit to a one-car garage were downstairs, while upstairs contained the bedroom, bathroom, and an open space we could use as anything. It wasn't really furnished yet, other than my office, and our dining room table was just a glorified patio set, but I loved every inch of it. Mom had even replaced my couch—the one I'd reincarnated on—with an updated model of a similar color.

Even seeing some of my things—*there* was my favorite blanket, folded neatly over the back of the couch!—I couldn't quite believe what was happening. Caden and me, living together? I poured all of my feelings into my hug, hoping it in some way conveyed the emotion I felt. Mom beamed. Caden blushed.

For the first time in a long time, everything felt *right.*

"Oh no," I said, suddenly. "Does Rachelle know?"

Caden scoffed. "Of *course* she knows."

"You think I could remember every detail of your office by myself?" Mom added.

"In fact," Caden said, "she's waiting for us to go meet her. Says she has a housewarming gift for us."

We spent a few more minutes admiring the townhouse before all exiting together. Caden closed the door behind us and held up the key. "So? Will you move in with me?"

I swiped the keys from him and locked up our new home—*our new home!* Mom gave us a moment, so I pulled Caden into a kiss on the front step. "I love you. You're perfect," I breathed.

"Really?" he asked, kissing me back. "Would you say I'm perfect enough for an immortal, badass monster hunter?"

"Wha—?" I spluttered. "When did—?"

His seafoam eyes sparkled above an impish grin. "You talk in your sleep, beamish boy."

*L*ess than an hour later, after dropping Mom off at her house, Caden and I strolled through Paradise Lake Cemetery. The graveyard was becoming as familiar to me as Mom's house, though there had been some changes: police tape overlapped the chain between the two poles at the entrance, and for the first time in four visits, no one was waiting for us on the large boulder to the left of the tape.

We found Rachelle and Matlas sitting on a bench near the first staircase. They were close together, watching something on Rachelle's phone. Matlas caught our movement first and waved to us, surreptitiously sliding a little farther from Rachelle on the stone seat.

"Busy morning?" Rachelle asked, spearing me with a too-knowing smile.

"I can't believe you didn't blow the secret," I said, grinning.

She gave an offended eye roll, but for the briefest moment, her smile faltered and she glanced away from Matlas.

Inwardly, I cursed my careless slip. She was clearly *exceptional* at keeping secrets.

I covered the awkward moment with a hug, then I stepped up to

Matlas and clapped him on the shoulder. "Good to see you're unharmed," I said.

"The cops got here seconds after you left." He shrugged. "Just glad I could help."

Rachelle bumped his shoulder with hers. "He's downplaying it a lot, Emery. His quick thinking saved our show."

Intrigued, I leaned in. Rachelle showed me several photos on her phone. "He snapped pictures of the holy relics Vox Populi brought in," she explained, swiping through the photos. "It'll be perfect for debunking the activities here as those of some outlandish cult."

She flicked past one too swiftly, and I stopped her. "That looked like a video," I said. The thumbnail had been of Matlas holding out a rose.

"It's nothing," Matlas said quickly.

She beamed. "It *is* a video," she remarked smugly.

"Is it something we can use for the show?" I asked, my attention swinging back and forth between them.

"Not exactly," Rachelle said coyly. Matlas looked like he was about to die of mortification, and I realized what was happening.

Caden rescued him. "Hey, I've heard a lot about you," he said, stepping in front of me and offering his hand. "I'm Caden."

"Matt," he said, relieved. "Everyone calls me Matlas."

"So," Rachelle said, "we can use the photos as footage for the show. Spin the story that some ridiculous cult had trespassed in order to perform a satanic rite or something. The cops were called, but not before some shenanigans ensued—all completely rationalized away, of course. Nothing supernatural to see here, folks."

I nodded, but I turned to Matlas. "We owe you an explanation," I said. "No, not an explanation. Answers. Truth."

Matlas, however, shook his head and held up his hand. "No way, man," he said. "I don't want you to tell me anything about the other night."

I blinked. "What? You must have seen some things that made you question..." I trailed off as he started waving his hand to keep me from continuing.

"Sure, I have a few theories brewing. There are clearly some things in this world that aren't completely what they seem. I do want answers. I want to get to the bottom of it. But I want to find the answers on my own, figure it out for myself." He hesitated, then grinned at Rachelle. "I do love a good mystery."

I stared at him, baffled, then turned to Rachelle to let her know it was okay if she wanted to tell him. She met my eyes with a devilish smile, then poked Matlas in the ribs. "And we already agreed that it's only fair if I stick around until he solves it for himself," she said. And I swear she *giggled*. "But I'm not going to give you any clues, sir. You have to figure it out all on your own."

I couldn't believe it. They were treating this like a game of Twenty Questions. But as he growled and said, "Call me 'sir' one more time, I dare you," I got it. Rachelle knew she had my permission to tell him about incarnates, now, so they wanted to make a game out of it.

Playing along was the *least* I could do to thank the both of them.

"That sounds like it will take up a lot of my assistant's time," I mused to Caden.

"*Not* your assistant," Rachelle interjected.

"Maybe we should help Matlas solve the mystery faster, so you can get your partner back," Caden suggested, catching on.

"We could go on a double date," I agreed. "Somewhere we could drop some clues about what's going on."

"That's a great idea," he said, turning an innocent look on the two of them. "Maybe we could go to the pier. Do some Mermaid watching?"

Matlas scoffed. "Yeah, right." He shook his head. "I'm not a sucker."

Rachelle, however, glared at us. "I hate you both." She jumped to her feet. "Come on, jerks, before I change my mind about your house-warming gift."

Astoundingly, the two of them led us back to the Thirteen Steps. "Any news on Hope?" I asked as we approached the Gates of Hell.

"Unfortunately, no. It appears she got out," Rachelle said.

Matlas chimed in. "There were only four arrests. So everyone else must've gotten away. Hope disappeared shortly after you did."

Well, that wasn't terribly surprising. The Thirteen Steps to Hell had done a number on her, but I knew she'd recover. I doubted she'd stay in Seattle, though. I held a weapon against her, now, and she couldn't fight against her very identity. Vox Populi would never accept an incarnate as their ruler, and we both knew it.

As we approached the Thirteen Steps, I saw the stone slab was in place, and no fog rolled in. The clearing was peaceful.

It took a few minutes, but Rachelle managed to coax the three puppies out of the undergrowth. Mittens and Beard came bounding out of the bushes, tails wagging, and began to play around our feet. Mask limped out a minute later. He appeared to still be injured, but his little tail wagged just as fiercely as his siblings', and he joined in their frolicking, though he was a bit wobbly.

"Three puppies for your new home," Rachelle said proudly. "I even made sure you got a place with a little yard for them."

I looked to Caden questioningly. He was on the ground, scratching Mittens behind the ears, when Mask came up from the side and started licking his cheek. He cooed at their attention.

I lifted Beard, and he licked my nose. "I think that's a yes," I said with a grin. The puppy began to wriggle, so I put him back down. I looked at Rachelle and Matlas, alarmed to see Matlas was looking past me with widening eyes. I followed his gaze.

Caden was glowing. With his head bowed, the light shimmered in his golden hair, hinting at a halo, then spilling outward to form the faintest hint of his translucent wings. He held Mask in his lap, attention fully upon the puppy.

The moment passed, the light shifted, and Caden was a simple boy again. Mask leapt out of his lap and pranced around the clearing, no longer favoring an injured leg. Caden looked up, smiling at us, but his grin faltered as he realized what he'd done. We all turned to look at Matlas.

To his credit, Matlas swallowed and said, weakly, "You should probably name them."

Mittens rolled over, and Caden rubbed her belly. "Yeah," he agreed. "Any ideas?"

I regarded them thoughtfully. "What do you think of the name Asker?"

"Oh! In tribute to Micah," Rachelle said. "That's really sweet, Emery." Beside her, Matlas nodded, though I noticed he was carefully avoiding looking at Caden.

"No, no," I said, shaking my head. "We'd name the girl one Asker, so when people come up to us and say, 'What's her name?' you can shrug and reply, 'Asker.'"

Caden gave me a flat look. "You're horrible. We're not doing that." He squinted. "I really liked the name Hope, but now it's ruined. What about something fierce, like Storm?"

"I like that," I agreed, considering each in turn. "So, which one? Should we give that name to Mittens, Mask, or Beard?"

There was a pause, then Caden laughed. "So you *already* named them." He stood and kissed the tip of my nose. "I love those names."

"Is it like a 'war between heaven and hell' kind of thing?" Matlas blurted suddenly, clearly rattled. Then he shook his head. "No, no, don't answer that."

"You afraid I'll vanish after you solve it, Atlas?" Rachelle asked with a smirk.

He gave a wan smile. "No, ma'am. I'm just not sure I could handle something that enormous."

She smacked him on the shoulder. "I swear, if you call me 'ma'am' one more time," she growled. Then she sniffed. "And no, it's not a 'war between heaven and hell' kind of thing."

His smile widened into something more genuine. "Good. I'd hate to think my new girlfriend was caught up in something dangerous."

Caden and I exchanged looks, but they didn't see us. Matlas was too busy watching Rachelle try—and fail—to hold back a grin, her cheeks coloring at being called his girlfriend. She melted into him, and he wrapped his arm around her shoulders.

Eventually, Caden and I scooped up the puppies, and we all left the graveyard behind us. It was time to introduce our new family to their brand-new home.

∾

*My name is Emery Luple, and I am the Protagonist incarnate. I live in Seattle, the first Sanctum City, the only city to have its own personal Guardian Angel. It is a place of peace. We welcome incarnates and mortals: those seeking community, protection, answers, or help.*
*This is not the end of our story.*

# ACKNOWLEDGMENTS

*THE ALPHA READERS INCARNATE*
*Name: James, Todd, Tonya, Michelle, and Tyler*
*Height: 6'1", 6' even, 5'4", 5'8", and 5'11"*
*Weight: ~20 cats, muscular, skinny, just right, and 77 kg (he likes the smaller number)*
*Eye Color: Brown, brown, blue, blue, and hazel-green*
*Hair: Light, on his chin, brown, dirty blonde ombre, and changes pretty much daily*
*Classification: Benign x5 (yes, even you, Todd)*
*Bio: I couldn't ask for a better group of Alpha Readers. Thank you for your patience, your feedback, and most of all, your encouragement. I'm so grateful to all of you.*

*The very first Alpha Reader is James, my husband, who suffers through every rough—and sometimes I mean* rough—*draft and who listens to me read each chapter aloud, often in voices and accents neither of us is proud of! Thank you for celebrating all my victories, from word count milestones to Emery triumphing over Vox Populi, and for your astute feedback that pushes my writing to the next level.*

*Todd, too, has read every chapter in just about every version. As a police officer and avid fantasy reader, he helps me bridge the gap between reality and fantasy to create compelling crime scenes and interactions between Emery and law enforcement. If anything is inaccurate, it is wholly on me, because despite Todd's best efforts, sometimes Emery ignores inconvenient things like forensics, crime scene protocols, and how Tasers really work. Far more importantly, thank you for believing in the world I've built and for the long hours spent theorizing what-ifs in Incarnate lore.*

*Mom, this time you get a whole section to yourself. Thank you so much for believing in my talent and for your enthusiastic support. Receiving your long texts about how proud you are of my accomplishments drives me onward to keep writing, to keep creating. You'll never know how amazing it is to have you in my corner, cheering me on. I love and appreciate you so much.*

*Speaking of cheerleaders, Michelle is one of the best. Having her read my earliest drafts is like giving your script to a superfan and getting to watch their reactions as they consume your newest work. Phenomenal at celebrating every inch of the story, from the funny moments to the shocking ones, she makes every scene rewarding. Thank you for just being you.*

*And last but never least, my brother, Tyler. As a creative artist and writer himself, he understands, appreciates, and respects the amount of work that goes into creating Emery's adventures. I can't thank him enough for investing not only time but emotion into my stories. Thank you for your support, but also for your questions, for making sure the "feel" of the book is authentic. You are a visionary. #Club20.*

I have poured my soul into this book, but I am blessed to have a lot of help along the way. In addition to the Alpha Readers, I want to thank another person who's poured so much of herself into my work: my editor, Alicia Z. Ramos. Thank you for dragging my book from the shadows and into the spotlight. I can't truly express how masterful you are at helping bring my words to life and giving them the space they need to breathe and grow. Your attention to detail, immense treasure of knowledge, and charming wit are an absolute delight to work with every time. At the end of the day, I'm so proud of my work, and I owe some of that to you.

A special thank-you to Jeff Brown for the gorgeous cover art. You have a gift for taking my rambling depiction of what I'm going for and transforming it into a compelling vision. They say a picture is worth 1,000 words, but you have the unenviable task of making your illustration worth an entire book of words—yet you somehow capture exactly that and more with your art. Thank you so much for lending your talent to the world of incarnates.

Thank you to my "proofers": Sunshine Dunning, Peter Brown, Nick Rood, Kevin Nolan, Linnea Mulvaney, Katie McDaniel, Shayda Abab, and Heather Conti. You caught the errors that slipped through the cracks, offered invaluable feedback both small and large, and provided inspiring reactions and thoughts on the overarching story. I love you all.

The technical pieces of my book wouldn't have come together without the combined efforts of the people above, but it also wouldn't have happened without the ongoing love and support I feel day in and day out because of my family. So a special thank-you to you, Dad, for reading my book and believing in me. And thank you to Susie, Teresa, Terry, Nancy, Pop, Ang, Steve, Maddie, Colleen, Cody, and Lucy. Your love keeps me going.

And thank *you*, Class, for reading my book and fueling my dreams. Authors don't always get to see or hear from fans, but your contribution to me on a personal level is staggering. It's everything. In return, I hope Emery's adventures make you laugh, cry, love, or feel. Just know, whoever and wherever you are, that you are loved. I can't wait to set out on the next adventure with you.

# ABOUT THE AUTHOR

Justin Schuelke

I'm a Washingtonian living in the greater Seattle area with my husband, James, and our cat, Vincent. I graduated from the University of Washington with a degree in—wait for it—English. When I am not writing, I enjoy games of all kinds: board games, roleplaying games, video games, computer games, phone games... you name it, I'll play it!

Learn more about me at my website: https://justinschuelke.com.

Please subscribe to my mailing list for exclusive content, limited promotions, and more!

www.ingramcontent.com/pod-product-compliance
Lightning Source LLC
Chambersburg PA
CBHW070839260626
47170CB00007B/2439